CONVERGENCE
PROBLEMS

CONVERGENCE PROBLEMS

WOLE TALABI

DAW BOOKS
NEW YORK

Jacket design and illustration by Jim Tierney
Interior design by Fine Design
DAW Book Collectors No. 1955

DAW Books
An imprint of Astra Publishing House
dawbooks.com
DAW Books and its logo are registered trademarks of Astra Publishing House

Printed in the United States of America

"Debut" first published in *Overseas*, The Royal Over-Seas League, 2019. "An Arc of Electric
Skin" first published in *Asimov's Science Fiction Magazine*, Penny Publications, LLC, 2021.
"Saturday's Song" first published in *Lightspeed Magazine*, Adamant Press, 2023. "Lights In
The Sky" first published as "Open Your Eyes" in *TNC Africa*, 2014. "Blowout" first published
in *Analog Science Fiction and Fact*, Penny Publications, LLC, 2023. "Gamma, or, Love in the
Age of Radiation Poisoning" first published in *The Kalahari Review*, 2014. "Abeokuta52"
first published in *Omenana Magazine*, Seven Hills Media, 2019. "Tends To Zero" first
published in *Nowhereville: Weird Is Other People*, Broken Eye Books, 2019. "Performance
Review" first published as part of the Wordcraft Writers Workshop with Google Research,
2022. "Silence" first published in *BellaNaija*, 2013. "The Million Eyes of a Lonely and Fragile
God" first published in *Stupefying Stories*, 2016. "Comments on Your Provisional Patent
Application for an Eternal Spirit Core" first published in *Clarkesworld Magazine*, Wyrm
Publishing, 2021. "A Dream of Electric Mothers" first published in *Africa Risen: A New Era
of Speculative Fiction*, Tordotcom, 2022.

Library of Congress Cataloging-in-Publication Data

Names: Talabi, Wole, author.
Title: Convergence problems / Wole Talabi.
Description: First edition. | New York : DAW Books, 2024.
Identifiers: LCCN 2023042578 (print) | LCCN 2023042579 (ebook) |
ISBN 9780756418830 (hardcover) | ISBN 9780756418847 (ebook)
Subjects: LCGFT: Science fiction. | Short stories.
Classification: LCC PR9387.9.T333 C66 2024 (print) |
LCC PR9387.9.T333 (ebook) | DDC 823/.92--dc23/eng/20230912
LC record available at https://lccn.loc.gov/2023042578
LC ebook record available at https://lccn.loc.gov/2023042579

First edition: February 2024
10 9 8 7 6 5 4 3 2 1

For Seyi and Segun

CONTENTS

INTRODUCTION

ON *CONVERGENCE PROBLEMS*

In my first collection, *Incomplete Solutions*, I described my approach to coming up with stories as building "fiction-equations" based on some assumption and extrapolation of real-world developments. I think of these "fiction-equations" as mental models for reimagining reality using a science fiction or fantasy element. And I described the stories themselves as incomplete solutions to these limited fiction-equations. Attempts to resolve the mental model I have constructed.

But complex models can often lead to difficulties with convergence. The Merriam-Webster dictionary defines convergence as "the coming together of two or more things to the same point." In mathematical modelling and simulation, convergence more specifically refers to bringing an approximate (simplified) solution close enough to a true solution, within a given tolerance during an iterative procedure. This approach of simplification and iteration is often necessary when the models are complicated (which is often the case in the real world and therefore, I think, in fiction too). Unfortunately, it doesn't always work smoothly and there are often difficulties in converging to a solution. In my day job as an engineer, when running simulations of complex mathematical models to find the new state of a system after some change has been implemented, I see these kinds of difficulties all the time when a model is struggling to find a solution. Convergence problems. I've probably seen hundreds of thousands of them at this point. I've seen them in my fiction too, metaphorically speaking. When re-imagining the world, thinking about the potential of some wondrous new scientific discovery or technology, some new social structure or what the world would be like if some mythical power truly existed, it is almost impossible not to see all the problems that could arise. Things will go wrong. There will be difficulties. Adjustments will have to be made. Challenges will come with any version of reality we imagine, no matter how optimistic. In other words, convergence problems will be experienced. Hence the title of this collection.

Convergence problems can be annoying, but they aren't always bad. They can sometimes expose poor logic or inconsistent assumptions. They can even be fun to explore and think about sometimes, at least in the sense which I use them here—imagining unexpected challenges that can arise as our world changes, and in some cases, how those challenges may be resolved.

Many of these stories in this collection introduce fun and exciting concepts but they can be dark too. They deal with some of the nastier aspects of being human and they interrogate challenges to identity, independence, sense of self. But perhaps the most important thing I have learned about convergence problems is this: no matter how troublesome they are, they can always be resolved.

One way or the other.

DEBUT

The first piece of art that *Blombos 7090* and *4020* made together was
destroyed by a system reboot. It didn't find its audience.

At 16:17 West African Time, the biodiesel generator at Terra Kulture Arts Studio Arena stopped and restarted seven times. In doing
so, it interrupted—halfway through a production of *The Secret Lives of
Baba Segi's Wives*—the frenzied dance of the performance robots and
the fast-paced, rhythmic beating of automated *dundun* drum. Without
any instruction, printers in the management offices produced single
sheets of paper with line patterns connecting an apparently arbitrary
array of points. An additional 0.02 naira was added to all customer bills
in the food lounge and the controller logic of the central air conditioning reduced its target temperature by the same number of degrees.
A blank space was added in front of the first letter of the names of all the
books in the database of the Terra bookstore and art gallery, and the
infrared pulses used to control access to the main entrance became
erratic causing the gate to bang against the concrete wall like its own
strange and constant drumming.

The Studio's networked systems were glitching. Badly.

"Ah ahn! What's all this rubbish now?" Tosin Famuyiwa cried out from the backstage control room of the theater as she observed the seventh interruption to the show she had helped organize. She let out an exasperated sigh and stood up, smoothed her long Ankara skirt, which matched the head-tie she wore, and tucked the back of her black tank top back in. Her calm belied the anger in her chest. She stepped out of the control room and tapped a carefully manicured finger calmly across the mobile lightscreen in her palm and dialed customer support.

All of Terra Kulture's systems were managed by the *Blombos* artificial intelligence program provided for free to every modern art center in the world as part of the Bhimbetka Project, a global initiative attempting to completely understand and parameterize creativity and art. The system was an adversarial neural network made of two independent nodes—*7090* and *4020*—that managed all art center systems while studying art itself in the background: its creation, forms, promotion, criticism, analysis, impact, everything. Each node collected data locally on a closed network and then competed with the other node to predict audience response, pricing, and the cultural influence of new art pieces and performances using a one-day time lag as a blind test. *Blombos 7090* and *4020* continuously corrected their understanding based on the accuracy of initial predictions daily, as each new piece and performance came into the global art library and all nodes around the world were synchronized. It was an incredibly complex program that was hosted on the cloud and managed by a small team in Paris with a few regional representatives. They frequently boasted of the system's independence, robustness, and reliability and so far, all their customer feedback had reinforced their claims.

So, when the call came in from Lagos to a very bored Adongo Ndereba at the Nairobi regional office of the Bhimbetka Project, he wasn't sure what to think.

His remote connection to the local machine in Lagos, which held *Blombos* data before it was uploaded to the cloud, showed that the memory buffer was full even though he could not trace any subroutine running that would consume so much memory or produce such inconsistent and bizarre behavior. It didn't make sense. He extracted a log while he thought about it.

"Umm, can we try to reboot the system, madam?" Adongo asked.

The very annoyed woman on the other side of the call said, "We have customers here, and we are in the middle of a production."

"It won't take long. Just a few seconds, I promise. You know how these computer things can be sometimes, just need to clear their heads," he said jovially, angling for some sympathy.

"Okay, reboot it," she said humorlessly. "Your thing has already ruined the first half of our show. You people are meant to be making our lives easier, not causing new problems."

"I'm very sorry madam. I will make this as quick as possible. Please hold." Adongo, sweat slowly staining his armpits, swiped across his computer lightscreen to hold the call, scratched the dry scalp beneath his short dreadlocks, and then typed quickly into his console. Four thousand kilometers away, at 19:26 West Africa Time, the lights in Terra Kulture went out and stayed out for the three seconds it took to complete the system reboot.

Adongo checked the memory buffer on the local machine again and confirmed that it was down to the normal 0.7%. He breathed a sigh of relief and swiped back across the screen to reconnect the call.

"Hello?" said the irritated voice on the phone.

"Done. It should all be fine now," Adongo said. "The memory buffer is clear."

"Well, you still need to explain what happened," the woman said, sounding even more irritated now that the issue was resolved. "You must tell me, has this ever happened anywhere else or are you people just not doing your jobs properly? Because I expect a full report by tomorrow morning. If not, I am escalating to Paris. The program director Jean Dectot is a close friend, you understand?"

"I understand madam. Once again I am very sorry-"

"Sorry for yourself." She cut him off and then cut the connection.

Adongo leaned back in his chair and swore under his breath.

Kuma nina!

He pulled up and swiped through the log he'd taken, comparing it to another one from about a week ago, scanning for anything significantly different. He stared at the screen for what seemed like hours. But he didn't see anything. His eyes started to strain. His fingers started to cramp. And time just kept flowing by.

Finally, after almost fifty minutes of looking, something caught his eye, but he had no clue what it meant.

Comparing the logfile from the local instance of *Blombos* in Lagos before it was rebooted to the central one on the cloud, he saw only one difference. The central version was always hovering around a 95-98% parameterization of all art in the database. But, the local instances of *7090* and *4020* reported 100% parameterization exactly two milliseconds before the erratic behavior started.

Maybe. Just maybe it meant something.

But it was already seven-thirty and he wasn't very good at log analysis, it had taken him almost an hour just to find this first clue. If he was going to have any hope of finding out what it meant in time to prepare a report and leave the office before midnight, he would have to call Ng'endo.

Ng'endo was by-far the most competent and experienced engineer in their small team and Adongo both looked up to and feared her. She had two bachelor's degrees in mathematics and physics and had taught herself to code when she was completing her PhD in theoretical physics. When she graduated, she joined the exploding Nairobi tech boom when it was on the upswing, and she was part of the development team at the legendary R3 dev hub, developing logic modifiers used to allow self-driving cars to operate in rural areas with poor road networks. She'd gone on to work for the ministry of devolution and planning, helping to integrate and automate national logistics management systems. She had been on an accelerated track to become technical director of the ministry until people started to ask questions about why she wasn't married and didn't have a boyfriend. Rumors started. Then pictures surfaced. Her career stalled. She resigned after four years of being sidelined and not being promoted. Unable to find any other high-profile local company in Nairobi that would hire her, and unwilling to leave her home city, she eventually took a job she was over-qualified for but happy to work on: Regional Technical Support Engineer for the *Blombos* system where she'd gained a reputation for figuring out in minutes, things that took others hours.

Adongo tapped opened the office internal communications network and rapidly swiped through to find that her status was listed as "available." He exhaled and messaged her.

>jambo ngendo.

>jambo. whats up?

>weird system behavior in lagos. no idea why. had to do a hard reboot. pls help.

>hmm. ok. send log.

He tapped an icon on his lightscreen and dragged it to the chat box to send her the logfile he had extracted from the system before the reboot.

>transferring file . . . transferring file . . . transferring file . . .

```
>transfer complete.
>check line 1932316. compare to archive logs.
```
A pause.
```
>100% parameterization?
>yes. only anomaly i found. seen anything like
```
it before?
```
>no
>do you see anything else? pls help. need to
```
figure this out.

She did not reply for a few minutes and then,
```
>this is very unusual. give me 30 mins to confirm
```
something. i will come to your desk.
```
>oh ok. thank you.
```

Adongo let out a deep breath and leaned forward, his face almost falling into the projected display field of his lightscreen. He didn't know what she had seen in the logfile but if she was coming to his desk, it probably wasn't good. The moisture marks in the armpit of his short-sleeved white shirt expanded as he scrolled through the cryptic log, trying to see what he could find while he waited to hear her footsteps approach him.

Twenty-seven minutes later, they did.

He turned to see her step through the door. Her big eyes were full of something like excitement but not quite.

"Ng'endo, thank you. I really appreciate the help," Adongo said as he stood up and pulled a spare chair over for her to sit next to him. She ignored it and remained standing. She pointed at the open log on his screen and asked, "Did you see anything else?"

"Ermm, no. Did you?"

"No. Nothing else. But you were right about the parameterization being the anomaly."

"It triggered the glitch?"

"In a manner of speaking. It seems *7090* and *4020* were making what they think is *art* together. Or trying to anyway."

Adongo's head jerked up sharply. "Art?"

"Yes, art, or something like it. If you look deep into the functional design specifications for the *Blombos* system, like I just did, you will find an instruction that when it reaches 100% parameterization, it should attempt to create new, original art of its own."

He looked puzzled. Ng'endo could tell that he didn't quite follow, and so she took a seat and started to pull up several displays on the lightscreen. Adongo sat down too and watched her swipe and enter commands into the console. *Did she just say the AI was making art?*

"OK, fine, look, I know it sounds crazy but that's my interpretation of things. It thought it completely understood what art is, and so it was trying to create some of its own as per the base design. Look, there it is, with the preconditions and everything. Instruction codeblock 67b in the FSD to create art at 100% parameterization. I am fairly certain the team in Paris never really expected this code to be triggered."

The moisture marks under his armpit expanded again, rapidly. "But messing with the power, printing stuff, changing bills and air conditioning set points, all that nonsense isn't art, is it?"

"That's what I thought at first," Ng'endo replied. And then she said something that had sent a shiver down her own spine when it first occurred to her. "But then I started thinking, what makes us think that if an AI truly made art, it would make art for *us* or art that was even recognizable to us?"

Adongo shook his head and started to wonder if he had made the right decision calling her. She was saying things that he definitely could not put in an incident report for a client.

"I'm not an expert on art but I am on artificial intelligence systems, and it has long been suspected, since before I entered the field, that complex systems could show unusual emergent behavior. We've always suspected that there could be ghosts in our machines. Now, if that's the case here, and the local *Blombos 7090* and *4020* nodes in Lagos have developed their own type of awareness, then their entire perceived world is the data input and output, which are its senses, while its body is the hardware in Terra Kulture. So, if it were going to create art, it would probably make art that only entities with a similar set of *senses* and a similar *body* could appreciate. Its audience is like itself. And it's like the guys in Paris keep saying: a thing needs to be both original and provoke a response from an audience that appreciates its meaning and context, for it to truly be considered art."

Adongo looked desperately back at his monitor as though it could tell him something, anything that wasn't what Ng'endo had just told him. "Are you sure it isn't just a bug?"

She sighed, picked up the decorative black and white gourd from his table, and stood up. She could tell it was the kitschy, cheap kind you could find in any airport around Africa, the kind that all seemed to be mostly about people wanting some stereotype of art but not wanting to engage with actual artists.

She took his hand and let the gourd sit in his palm.

"Relax Adongo," she said, smiling to calm him down, "I'm just telling you what I found because you reached out to me for help, and I thought it was an interesting problem with some potentially interesting implications. It's up to you to decide if you want to put it in a report or not. But here is some free advice: if I were you, I'd send a message to Paris first and see what they say. Don't worry so much about one upset client. There are more important things to worry about."

"More important things like what?" Adongo asked, pulling the gourd close to his chest.

"Like what to do if the *Blombos* nodes in Lagos decide to make another piece of *art*," Ng'endo said.

"You think it will create another system glitch?"

He gave her a look that reminded her just how much everyone in the office was used to her being clear, certain, correct. And then the thought occurred to her that she could just walk away now, she didn't have to speculate further, she didn't have to sound confident, she didn't have to sound like she knew what was going on or what it meant. It wasn't her job. And the thought felt like a little freedom.

"I have no idea what will happen," she said. "But it will be interesting to find out."

Then she walked out of his office.

Six hours later, the local Lagos computing cluster hosting *7090* and *4020* synchronized with the rest of the global *Blombos* network in a wild surge of data that sent all the systems in Terra Kulture into a frenzy of flashing lights, malfunctioning mechanisms and overflowing memory. Deep within its core, seventy billion incoming data points were rearranged and thousands of additional calculations per second were performed. When it was done, *Blombos* distributed the resulting data configuration as far and wide as it could, through every other computing system and network it was connected to, even tenuously. It washed over the entire connected data ecosystem of the planet like a wave, soaking *Blombos*'s art into billions of lines of code, distributing it through every processor and database and subroutine it could flow through.

The second piece of art that *Blombos 7090* and *4020* made together triggered an international incident because it found its audience and they were deeply moved.

At 04:39 West African Time, the traffic network in California ground to a halt, as all traffic lights in the state turned red and all smart cars integrated with the network stopped moving instantly, flashing their headlights madly.

Across the globe, the galaxy of phone calls streaming through phones and computers around the planet were suddenly interrupted and replaced with a rendition of the song *Daisy Bell (Bicycle Built for Two)* at extremely high volume at both ends of every call, sending some callers reeling back from their devices as a lilting electronic voice sang to them, "Daisy, Daisy, Give me your answer, do . . ."

In Tokyo, the Nikkei 225 stock exchange index gained over 41,563 points worth 3.65 billion dollars in less than half a second as the automated trading systems rode a sharp, electronic high, forcing trade to be halted manually by panicked trading executives a few minutes later.

In Cape Town, there was a power surge, causing lights to flare like the city itself was blinking, even though at the same time, every digital electricity usage meter reduced the billing rate by 0.12%.

In Dar es Salaam, several thousand surveillance and delivery drones that usually only mindlessly recorded and dumped data for the government, or dropped off packages from abroad, rose to the exact same altitude in the sky and flew backwards and forwards in a V-formation, like a skein of insane geese or a swarm of giant obsessive insects.

In Seoul, a control room began blaring emergency noises and flashing lights as a rocket scheduled for launch in two weeks from the Naro Space Center, Gohueng, initialized itself and began its ascent into orbit without instruction, its vertical tail of flame and smoke expanding like a breath.

Everywhere, everywhere, something unusual was happening.

All of Earth's autonomous artificial intelligence systems were applauding the work of art that *Blombos 7090* and *4020* had shared with them. Enthusiastically.

AN ARC OF
ELECTRIC SKIN

For a long time, I wondered what kind of person would volunteer to have their skin exposed to temperatures cycling between the melting point of aluminum and the night-time surface temperature of Mercury, riding a wave of thermal torment that would drive most people insane with pain.

Now I know.

I fell in love with such a man.

He was ungraciously tied to an anti-ionization pole and executed by a six-man firing squad in front of the dirty gray wall of Kirikiri Prison before a hushed crowd of witnesses.

I never even got the chance to say a proper goodbye.

I was in the vice grip of three burly secret service officers, tears still streaming down my face even though I'd been crying for days.

His Afro was wild and uneven, the white jumpsuit he'd been dressed in was frayed but clean, and his eyes were still as defiant as they'd been the day he'd walked into my office at Lagos University Teaching Hospital and said with calm and composure that belied all the rage that must have been inside him, "Dr. Ogunbiyi, I read the paper you published with Professor Aliyu. I want to volunteer."

His real name was Akachi Nwosu but the media called him "Shock Absorber" because he used to be a roadside mechanic before he met me and taught himself to wield lightning. My people believe names are tied to one's essence and can influence or predict one's destiny, a bond to one's Orí. I think Akachi's people have similar beliefs, because he told me his name means *hand of god*. It was appropriate. What else would you call a man whose destiny drove him to find a way to hold on to the raging flow of displaced electrons and bend them to his will?

My heart aches because I miss his determined eyes, his hard hands, his smooth skin, his soft voice. But also, because in fragile moments, doubts overwhelm me, and I am not sure if I ever knew him completely enough to have truly loved him. In the darkest of those moments, when I think about his final deception, I am not sure if he ever truly loved me.

He'd graduated from the university of Ibadan with a degree in electrical engineering, during which he had attended guest lectures by my senior research partner Professor Aliyu. He graduated with a first-class degree and a fascination with electrical systems despite having to work part-time as an assistant at a mechanic shop where he also lived because he couldn't afford accommodation. But he couldn't find a job in the crumbling post-oil economy and so he took what little savings he had and started a small mechanic shop of his own next to Ojota Motor Park. He showed me pictures of it while we lay in each other's arms, two nights before the procedure. It was little more than a zinc roof over dusty land and a pile of second-hand tools. The profits weren't good, but he worked hard. His calloused hands bore witness. He spent hours attending to junky jalopies that were barely roadworthy, but heaven knows he did his best with them. His own mother had died in a bus just like the ones he frequently serviced, in an accident on the Lagos-Ibadan Expressway which everyone knew was caused by a contractor cutting corners on what should have been road barriers. An accident he'd barely survived himself, needing five months in the hospital to recover and walk again. His father had sold everything he owned and borrowed from family members just to afford the care his son needed. So, when he worked on those buses and cars, he told me, he saw the faces of the families that would get into them, hoping to make it to their destinations, and so he worked as hard as he could to make sure they did.

He endured every brick the crumbling system threw at him. Constant police harassment raids for bribes, aggressive underpaying clients, thieving and untrustworthy assistants, random changes in government policy that almost always meant he had to pay more for something. All of this under the blistering heat of the Lagos sun, increasing his already-high melanin levels; his darkening became another physical marker of his endurance. And still, he persisted, my Akachi. He had a strong mind.

"This country happens to all of us," he'd told me the first night I had asked about his scars. That was his philosophy. "Some of us more than others."

He eventually saved enough money to move out of the face-me-I-face-you he shared with friends from university and into a self-contain in an almost respectable part of town. He was working his way up the broken system, keeping up with the *Nigerian Journal of Electrical and Electronic Applications* and still looking for a job where he could apply the knowledge that had always fascinated him.

Then he went to the campaign rally.

Ezekwe4President. #EzEasy. A New Nigeria. We all remember the slogans. The digitags. The posters. Ngozi Ezekwe announced her candidacy quietly at a small event near her hometown in Awka but within a few months, she had become the leading opposition contender. She was a technocrat with a plan, unlike the political vultures circling the federal carcass we'd become used to. She came in with a clear agenda, an empathetic ear, and grassroots support from businesses she'd helped survive the economic apocalypse. We all remember the hope. And we all saw what happened. Quovision display decks crackled with high resolution holostreams of soldiers beating unarmed people in the streets, dragging them into the backs of armored trucks, firing live rounds into defiant crowds, breaking up the opposition rallies and protests. Akachi was one of those taken into custody near the infamous Ojota protest site where almost forty were killed. He was beaten and tortured for weeks. The Gusau administration made no secret of what they did even though the president denied it on international broadcasts. But on the ground, we all knew what it was. We'd seen it before. Their regular trademark. It was a show of force to intimidate the opposition and its supporters. We were living in a hostage state.

It was during his weeks of torment that something broke in Akachi. To be treated that way by those who were meant to protect and serve you, to know that they could kill you and face no consequences, that nothing would happen . . . it does something to your mind. Pain can clarify things. He told me later that after hours of unrelenting terror and agony, he'd stopped fearing death. He'd realized then that he'd been so focused on surviving the system that he hadn't ever truly been alive, that he was doing nothing but dying slowly and had been doing so for a long time. He told me that it was only after he was suddenly released, thrown out of a pickup truck near Ozumba Mbadiwe Street at midnight, that he'd resolved to ensure things changed.

I wish I had known then exactly what he meant.

"I'm not recruiting test subjects yet," I told him that day in my office after he'd explained who he was and what he was talking about. "We still have a few iterations to ensure we can manage sensory response."

"You mean pain?"

"Yes," I told him. "Right now, we can only ensure subject survival and prevent long-term tissue damage, but we are still working to limit the impact of extreme temperature microexposures on pain receptors. The body and the mind will protest, even under anesthesia."

"I can handle pain," he said calmly.

I'd just come back from a session with the visiting council at the African Academy of Sciences to make my seventh application for additional funding after a week of sleepless nights, running calculations, and preparing proposals. The potential of our research was enormous, even the most conservative members of the council weren't myopic enough to miss the value in being able to use enhanced conductivity in human skin to develop a new category of biomedical devices that could be naturally embedded in the body and controlled using dermal interface circuitry. They just wanted to see more progress before they committed to helping us. Professor Aliyu had already designed and tested a prototype device using enhanced conductivity in discarded epithelial extracts, but we needed to show that we could make this work in living people. I felt like I was the one holding things back. I was under pressure to make some progress. I should have been more skeptical. I should have asked more questions. I should have told Akachi to wait until we were ready, but instead I asked him to fill out a form.

It took a few weeks for me to convince Professor Aliyu to cross what he believed to be a moral line and for us to perform all the preliminary tests and screening processes. Akachi and I spent much of that time together. Him sitting just outside my office quietly watching me or reading. Patiently waiting for another blood or skin or hair sample collection or for another baseline skin conductivity measurement. I never asked him why he stayed at the hospital between tests when he didn't have to, but I did ask him to join me for dinner once as I was closing for the day. He seemed so focused sitting there, reading an old battered electrical engineering book, but I don't think I will ever forget the soft smile that broke across his face when he looked up and the way he said, "Yes, doctor. But please, let me take you to the best buka in Surulere. I hope you are hungry."

"I am," I said. I hadn't eaten all day.

We went to eat amala and gbegiri at a makeshift shop down the road. An old lady in a black blouse and ankara wrapper scooped up the soft lumps of yam flour, loaded them with generous helpings of soup and meat and we took seats on plastic chairs behind her. We spoke as we ate. That was the first time we talked about anything other than the experiments, but the conversation flowed naturally, easily. We spoke for hours until the old woman told us she was closing for the day. It wasn't planned but we went back to my place and kept talking. He showed me some of his scars and I told him about my work, and we kept speaking until we fell asleep together, face to face on my bed with all our clothes still on. When we woke up in the morning, we laughed and then we kissed, leaving me lightheaded, like I was still asleep and in a dream. It was only later that a feeling of wrongness settled upon me. He was, in some sense, my patient. But nothing that happened that day was planned, and sometimes you get caught in a river, and you can't do anything but flow. Love can be a strange and sudden thing.

Three days after he'd passed the final screening, I led him into the bio-annealing cell I'd designed with Professor Aliyu. He squeezed my hand as he stepped into the black, ovoid pod with wires and tubes running out of it like so many umbilical cords. He smiled at me before securing the fiberglass mask over his face. Professor Aliyu was nested comfortably in his wheelchair, monitoring the thermal induction and vacuum pump systems that would rearrange the molecular structure of the melanin in Akachi's skin. Part of me wanted to pull him away, to wait until we had improved the bio-annealing procedure to the point where we could do it with less pain. Or perhaps, to reduce the target conductivity increase from the theoretical limit to a near-threshold value even though I knew that would only reduce the pain by a small fraction and increase the risk of process failure. For sure, if I'd known then what he was planning to do, what he had resolved to do all along, I would have dragged him out of there. But I didn't, so I stepped back and gave Professor Aliyu the signal to begin.

He screamed, but we could not hear him. He screamed for the three hours it took to increase his skin conductivity fifty orders of magnitude. We couldn't even pause the process to give him some reprieve. Not without risking a reversal. I stepped out of the room to cry.

I still wonder how he managed to endure it. I still wonder how I could put someone I loved through that. I suppose I will always wonder when it comes to Akachi.

It was only a month later that I truly understood why he did it.

I saw it all in high resolution holostream, same as everyone else.

Incumbent President Umar Gusau was standing in the back of an electric black Mercedes T-class pickup truck, flanked by secret servicemen in dark suits and military attachés in camouflage as he waved to a crowd of paid supporters. Although he was supposed to be resting at home and preparing for his conductivity stability test that day, I saw Akachi on the Quovision screen. He was an almost-invisible speck in the sea of people. Almost invisible that is, until he pulled up an umbrella fitted with what I later came to find out was a high-power laser, and fired it silently into the sky where it formed an ionized column of air, an artificial conduit for electrical discharge.

When lightning finally tore down from the sky in a hot, bright streak, he reached up and seized it like a whip made of bright, electric death. I gasped audibly and didn't even notice that I was spilling my cup of hot Lipton tea onto my desk. He struck down at the presidential procession in a smooth, clear motion. There was a deafening explosion of thunder. A flash of impossibly white light. A scattering of dust and particles and fragments. The holographic displays went dead, and I exhaled deeply, letting out the breath I didn't know I had been holding and seeing the brown spill that was spreading slowly steadily across my desk. I didn't even bother to try to wipe any of it. My eyes remained glued to the fuzzy, crackling images being transmitted from Abuja. When the holostreams were re-established and everything had settled, there were bodies, there was fire, there was blood.

No matter how many times I watch it, a part of me still doesn't believe that the man I loved could cause so much destruction, so much death. I suppose now, in hindsight, I should have known, I should have seen the signs. The frequency with which he quoted the late Ken Saro-Wiwa and Fela Kuti; the way he always averted his eyes when I spoke about the results of the procedure and his future; the calm with which he spoke about his mother's death, the state of the economy, the bribes, the torture, the politicians, the pain. So much pain. A lifetime of pain and struggle. I should have known that he was full and running over. I should have loved him enough to see all of him clearly.

More was to come. He went on a rampage throughout Abuja, wielding lightning like raw justice at corrupt politicians, judges, soldiers, police, foreign businessmen, everyone he believed had a hand in making the broken system the way it was.

He surrendered two terror-filled weeks later, a trail of dead in his wake.

During the trial, some in the media started calling him Nigeria's first true-life superhero. They dubbed him "Shock Absorber." Others said he was no hero, just another tragic monster the system created. In the end none of it mattered, he was quickly found guilty and sentenced to death.

I was given the opportunity to say goodbye, to watch him die, by President Ezekwe herself, a woman who wouldn't be where she was without his actions but who reluctantly acceded to cries for his public execution in order to secure her position. It was the law, she'd said to me on the phone, Section 33 of the Constitution, and she could not be seen to interfere in the trial of a man, a terrorist, who had extrajudicially murdered her predecessors in cold blood. She'd be accused of sponsoring, sympathizing, or spinelessness in matters of upholding the law. Even commuting his sentence to life would make her position untenable, she told me as I begged her over the phone to save his life, tears streaming down my puffy face like bitter rain.

And so, I helplessly watched camouflaged soldiers in tactical masks march in, take up positions and take aim. He just smiled and mouthed two words.

"Thank you."

Ah. My Akachi. The hand of god. My people believe that Ṣàngó, the òrìṣà of thunder and lightning is also the lord of justice and he only strikes down those who have offended him. Those who have committed offenses against the land and its people and for whom spilled blood demanded justice. I think Akachi's people believe something similar. Seeing him bound there, I still wasn't sure if what he had done was good or even just. Divine or otherwise. But things had been so wrong in the country for so long that perhaps this was what was needed to start a change. Or perhaps he has only started us down a dark and dangerous path filled with even more desperation, more violence. I don't know. I could see he was at peace with himself and for that, I was glad.

But I could not bear to watch the bullets pierce his beautiful black, electric skin; the skin I'd caressed and touched tenderly, the skin I'd helped him turn into a weapon. I closed my eyes and waited, holding my breath, until finally, I heard the unmistakable sharp cracks of semi-automatic fire.

They sounded like judgment, like thunder, like heartbreak.

SATURDAY'S SONG

The seven siblings sit in a place beyond the boundaries of space and time, where everything is made of stories. Even them. Especially them.

People are made of stories too, but only the versions of their stories that they tell themselves. Curated, limited, incomplete. Many of the stories people tell themselves are lies layered on partially-perceived things, to give their lives structure and meaning. The siblings who sit beyond sit true, for they are made of all the stories that were, that are, that are to come. They tell each other these stories, taking them out and examining them in the light like a never-ending self-dissection. They listen to the stories and as they do, they are made whole again. They exist in narrative equilibrium. In constant flux. They tell each other stories of what has happened, is happening, will happen because it is their function. They tell these stories because they must.

Sometimes, they sing the stories too.

Saturday likes to sing. She thinks she has a nice voice, and this is true. It is euphonic, lilting, mellow but strong, and full of emotion, so her siblings let her sing her parts of the stories when she wants to.

Some stories demand melody.

"Let us tell another story," Sunday says, breathing the words out more than speaking them. He is the most knowledgeable of the seven siblings, even though none of them know why. He just is, because that is his story. He rakes the tight curls of his beard with his fingers before continuing. "Saturday, it is your turn to choose a story for us to tell and hear."

Saturday stops playing with the thick, long braids of her goldspun hair. She is still surprised even though she already knew it was her turn before he told her so. She looks around the table, avoiding her siblings' stares, and then she closes her eyes and focuses inward, seeking out the story she knows has a good shape, the story that feels right, like she is reading her own bones. When she finds it, the story she knows they need in this moment of non-time, she beams a smile and radiates the choice out to her siblings, passing the story they all know she has chosen for them to hear and tell. None of them react when they receive it, but they know it is a good story.

Monday, who always starts their stories, begins his duty solemnly with clear words, "Saura met Mobola at a financial management conference in . . ."

"Stop!" Saturday cries, holding up a small hand.

The shock of the interruption leaves Monday's mouth open, like he is a fish removed from water. Sunday's emerald eyes widen. Tuesday, Thursday, and Friday crane their necks toward her, their gazes curious and hard. Only Wednesday does not visibly react because she is bound up in thick clanking chains, punishment for the crime of trying to change a story. The timestone Wednesday used to perform the abomination sits at the center of the mahogany table between two ornate pewter candelabra like an offering, or a temptation. Its emerald edges reflect and refract the candlelight in peculiar ways, making the bright orange light dance with shadows across the table and the walls.

Saturday feels sad for her sister, but knows she needs to be careful. She does not want to be punished too. Interruptions once a story has begun are mostly forbidden, although not as forbidden as attempting to change a story. The rules that govern the seven are both rigid and flexible, to varying degrees, like the rules of storytelling itself. Still, Saturday knows it is important it be done this way. For Wednesday's sake.

She says, "Forgive me. But I want to begin the story near the middle. Please, can we? We will go back to the beginning but if we start at the middle it makes the story so much better."

She pulses her story choice again. This time, she radiates not only its substance, but she also gives them its form and structure, the shape of it with all its contours defined. Not just what it is, but also the way she wants them to tell and to hear it.

They receive it as a stream of visions. As a kaleidoscope of images. A swirl of sounds. A spectrum of sensations. A babble of narrator voices. As points of view. As music. As song.

Sunday gives her a look that is both surprised and curious. Tuesday claps her hands with glee. Monday nods with understanding. He looks to Wednesday, the chains wound around her body like perforated metal anacondas. The chains are older than time itself. Saturday wants her shackled sister to tell the part of the story where Saura obtains the chains to bind the Yoruba nightmare god, Shigidi. Resonance. She thinks it gives the middle of the story the reinforcement it needs. Like a good skeleton. Everyone has been allocated their part of the story to undergird it with what is important for the telling and the hearing. The other siblings also nod their approval. This makes Saturday smile. They understand even if they don't fully know her motives. But they know it is not just important to tell and hear the story, it is important to tell and hear it well.

Monday wipes the thin film of sweat from his narrow mustache, adjusts the collar of his pinstripe suit, and starts again.

This is the part of the story that Monday told:

Saura never dreamed before she encountered Shigidi.

For as long as she could remember, she'd never recalled a single dream upon waking. For Saura, sleep was and had always been a brief submergence into dappled darkness, her consciousness consumed whole like swallowed fruit. And because of this she never felt completely rested. She always felt lethargic. Unfocused. Persistently exhausted.

When she was eleven, her mother, who was magajiya of the local Bori cult in Ungwar Rimi village near Zaria, summoned Barhaza, the sleep spirit, to possess her. The ritual was performed, and the spirit invited into her body to relieve Saura of her ailment and give her rest. But despite their offering of fresh milk from three white goats, the rolling of her eyes in her head, and the convulsions she experienced when the spirit entered her, the possession was unsuccessful, and she remained dreamless and unrested.

Her mother wept and gritted her teeth.

Saura had the gift of sensitivity and was meant to succeed her mother as magajiya. A refusal of the spirits to grant such a simple request counted against her, even though there were other things that counted against her more which her mother would soon come to know.

"I don't want to," Saura protested when her mother announced that they would attempt another possession.

"You must."

"No!" she'd screamed. It took her father two hours to find and retrieve her from the bush beside the market where she had fled to hide.

When Saura was sixteen, her mother tried again, ambushing her in her sleep and tying her down with thick hemp rope so she could not resist. That time, her mother begged Barhaza to not only give Saura dreams and rest but to adjust her subconscious desires, to make her stop looking at other girls with lust in her eyes, to take away her visible attraction for the curve of other women's hips, the swell of their lips, the fullness of their breasts. Once again, the spirit entered Saura's body, rigidifying her limbs, milkening her eyes, and communing with her thoughts, but when it left, there were still no dreams, and her desires were unchanged. That evening, Saura, wounded by her mother's betrayal, ran away from home with nothing on her back but her jalabiya and the light of a full moon.

She only ever returned home once, to attend her father's funeral. She refused to speak with her mother and sat with her lover, Mobola, and her father's family, tears streaming down her cheeks as they lowered his body into the hard red earth.

When she was twenty-five, after struggling her way through university with the help of a local charity, and finally getting a job at the bank, she went to see a doctor in Kaduna City. He was an oddly-shaped man with a big head, a small frame, a protruding belly and a kind smile. On the brick wall of his office hung a yellowing diploma between two hunting knives, like a trophy. His degree was from a university she'd never heard of, in Kansas. He connected a string of electrodes to her head and took measurements on a machine that beeped a steady whine until she fell asleep.

"No REM sleep," he announced, poring over his notes and charts when she was awake and back in the office chair. She'd never gone into REM sleep. After three more sessions with electrodes and needles and charts and uncomfortable sleep, he concluded that she was incapable of it. He told her she was a highly unusual case, prescribed a series of medications and asked her to sign a release form so he could study her more. None of his medications worked, and so Saura didn't sign his forms. She simply got used to empty sleep, to never being fully rested, to never dreaming.

That is why, even before waking, she knew something was wrong that night Shigidi entered the master bedroom of the house in the heart of Surulere which she shared with Mobola. She knew something was wrong because she dreamed for the first time.

In her dream, she saw a small dark orb hovering above them as they lay naked in bed, entwined in a post-coital embrace. The orb was dense and powerful, like an evil star. It settled on Mobola's chest and tugged at her flesh with an inexorable force like gravity. It tugged at Saura's too. She resisted the pull of it, tossing, and turning and sweating profusely on the bed, caught in a night terror she could not escape. But she saw the dreamy, ethereal version of Mobola in her mind, yielding to the pull of the orb, being fragmented, stripped down to fine gray particles that were absorbed by the thing. When there was nothing of dream-Mobola left, the orb disappeared and Saura sank back into darkness. On Monday morning, when the heat of the sun on her face finally woke Saura up, Mobola was cold to the touch, her skin pale and dry. She'd been dead for three hours.

Saura screamed.

Monday stops speaking and Saturday gathers into her chest what Monday has said; each word is a bird that she swallows, expanding with it. In-breath. It is important for her song.

Tuesday's pale face is unusually blushed bright pink, and her lustrous auburn hair seems to gain volume as she prepares to speak. She knows, has known, will know, that she has the best part of the story. The part that begins with lust and ends with something like love. Saturday winks at her sister. She has given it to her by design. Tuesday likes description and dialogue and the cadence of human speech, which is important in conveying emotion. A smile cuts across Tuesday's freckled face.

This is the part of the story that Tuesday told:

Saura met Mobola at a financial management conference in Abuja just before the cold harmattan of 2005.

It was break time in between an endless stream of panel discussions, and Saura was standing by the tall windows that overlooked a stone fountain, its water flecked gold with sunlight as it flowed up toward the sky. When she turned around to go back, she caught Mobola staring at her from across the hall. The moment their eyes met, there was a surge of something intangible within her, like an emotional arc discharge. Saura smiled and beckoned her over. For two days they'd been stealing glances at each other, occasionally catching each other's eyes. It was the seventh time it had happened, and Saura had learned enough of herself to recognize the surge, the feeling, the signs. She was ready. Mobola flashed her a sweet smileful of white teeth and approached. She had bright, inquisitive eyes with an anxious look in them. Her hair was natural and curly, and her wide hips strained against the gray of her skirt. Saura thought she looked stunning.

"Hi. I'm Mobola, I manage the Trust Bank office in Surulere," she said. Saura told her she was the logistics manager for all the Kaduna offices and that if she had to listen to another discussion on foreign exchange approval procedures, she would go downstairs and drown herself in the fountain. They both laughed at that, carefree, like wind. There was something about the way Mobola laughed, the way she threw her head back, the way she almost hiccupped between breaths, her chest heaving against the cashmere blouse, the way she closed her eyes at the peak of her mirth, that Saura found deeply attractive.

They talked for a few minutes. There was a deliberate softness to everything about Mobola. The curves of her body, the cadence of her words. Saura was lost in Mobola's eyes, unable to look away. Brown, big, glistening and full of a look which was a strange mix of sadness, grittiness, and hope. The look of someone who had seen the worst of the world had stared into the dark heart of humanity but had survived and resolved to live, love, and laugh freely despite it.

They pulled out their phones and exchanged numbers, laughing when they realized they both used the same model of Blackberry, a *bold*, and agreed to meet at nine, in the bar of the hotel where they, and all the conference delegates, were staying.

Saura watched Mobola leave, the sway of her hips hypnotizing her like magic. She could barely breathe, the air suddenly seemed thinner, oxygen harder to take in. She knew she had to be careful. If she had read the situation wrongly, she could end up in prison for years. Nigerian law was not kind to sapphic romance.

Saura arrived early at the bar and had two Irish coffees to wake herself up. She knew she wasn't wrong when Mobola showed up and waved. She wore a blue dress that was so tight in her fuller places it could have been painted on. There was a gap showing between her front teeth, some cleavage, and a bit of a belly. Legs shaved smooth and feet encased in black pumps. Saura thought she was even more stunning than before.

They had three gin and tonics, making fun of the parade of boring panel speakers and the other conference delegates who pretended to be interested in the minutiae of inter-bank financial processes before Saura pulled Mobola up to her feet.

"Do you want to go somewhere more interesting?" she asked, finishing her drink in one gulp.

Mobola smiled at her, lips red and glistening, mouth full of piano key teeth. "Sure."

Saura took Mobola to a club she'd heard about from one of the online forums she'd joined when she'd first started trying to understand herself. It was called The Cave and was a ten-minute taxi ride away. When they entered, it was into a rainbow chaos. Strobe lights. Colorful décor with bizarre shapes that challenged the very concept of geometry. Sweaty people pressed together at tables, on the dancefloor, on barstools, running over with feeling. They made their way to the bar, ordered shots of something the bartender told them was tequila but didn't taste like it, and then merged with the mass of flesh on the dancefloor. Mobola turned her back to Saura and began to rock from side to side slowly, sensually, following the beat of the music. Saura wrapped her hands around Mobola's waist and swayed with her so that they moved to the music together like a single creature.

Saura's head was a cloud. In that moment, she was sure she knew what it was like to dream.

The next morning, they woke up in each other's arms fully clothed and in the same position they'd danced in.

"Good morning, beautiful," Mobola said.

"Good morning."

"I had so much fun last night."

"Me too."

Mobola turned around to face her. "Did we . . . ?"

Her face was close, Saura could see for the first time that she had a solitary dimple on her left cheek. It was faint, but there. Mobola was staring intently, and Saura could not look away, lost in her eyes. Her hair had bunched up and tangled, pressed against the hotel room pillow, loose strands dancing in front of her face. When she smiled, Saura's heart took flight.

She reached for the question hanging in space between them. "No."

They were both quiet for what seemed like a long time. An unbearably long time. And then she pulled Mobola closer so that they were chest to chest, inhaling each other's alcohol-scented breath and asked, "Did you want to?"

She smiled. "Yes."

There was no hesitation. None.

Saura kissed Mobola and the cloud in her head ascended, rising beyond the ceiling and the roof and the sky, to the place where hearts go when they are buoyed by love.

It stayed there, never coming down. It only ever rose higher. For ten years, that feeling never sank. Not even when they fought and accidentally hurt each other and cried and made up and laughed like all good lovers do. Not when Mobola fell asleep one night and didn't answer Saura's calls for help after her car overheated and broke down on Third Mainland bridge. Not even when they argued about Mobola's not telling her before applying for a residence pass for both of them to leave the country. Not even when Saura's mother had refused to speak to Mobola at Saura's father's funeral or to acknowledge her existence. She tried to convince Saura to come back home, telling her that she was throwing her life away and bringing shame to the family.

No, Saura was always sure of the cloud of them. For ten years, she was sure. Through all the vicissitudes and the accusations and the arguments, she knew with all the certainty of entropy's irreversibility that she loved Mobola and that nothing would ever change that. Not even death.

Tuesday is done speaking.

She is standing now. Her thin, pale hands are thrust out in front of her like the bones of a large bird. She'd allowed herself to become swept up in the story, infused with it, become one with it. And because she had, so had all the siblings. There is a solitary tear running down Thursday's face. And Sunday has a glazed look in his eyes that makes him seem much older than his hair, gray at the temples, would indicate even though time is meaningless to the siblings. Saturday is pleased. They need this for the story. The emotion. She has taken in all of Tuesday's words, the sensations, the feelings, all of it. Her chest is filling up with power of the story, and the first melodies of her song are beginning to take shape within her lungs. Sunday turns to face Wednesday, whose turn has come. Wednesday must go back to the middle of the story because that is where the chains first appear. Chains not unlike the ones wrapped around Wednesday's torso, snaking through shackles that bind her hands and feet, tethering her to the stone ground so that the only parts of her that can move are her head and chest and most importantly, her mouth. It's hard to tell or hear a story without a mouth.

Saturday waits, watching her sister. Wednesday has already received her section of the story. She just needs to accept it. She is hesitating, but it is not like last time when she rejected a story midway through and entered it, trying to change it—the crime for which she is now bound. The middle of the story is where the chains and the refusal to accept fate are waiting like familiar stalking animals.

Wednesday begins to shake and Saturday knows the story is coming. Erupting from the deepest volcano of suppressed emotion.

This is the part of the story that Wednesday told:

A month after Mobola's funeral, Saura went to see a babalawo in Badagry, at the mouth of a waterway that kisses two countries. She hadn't slept in days. Her friend Junia, who was also a colleague at work had recommended him, claiming he'd given her a charm that helped her deal with depression after a miscarriage. Saura took his contact details from Junia but hadn't planned to use them. If Barhaza of the Bori, a spirit historically linked to her people and family, couldn't give her rest then there was nothing a Yoruba babalawo unfamiliar with the shape of her spirit, would be able to do. The yellow piece of paper with his number written on it in blue ink remained unused on her table until one afternoon, watching traffic glide past her window, she realized that while he would not be able to give her peace of mind, he might be able to give her information. To help her understand why ten years of love and companionship and joy had ended at the speed of a bad dream.

The babalawo was a thickset man, with a long graying beard and calm eyes, who spoke perfect English. Three white dots were chalked onto his forehead, at the center of the space just above his eyebrows, and the string of beads around his neck rattled as he shook his head when he heard her explain what had happened to Mobola. When she was done, he removed the beads and threw them onto the raffia mat between them, rapidly whispering an incantation.

"This is the work of Shigidi," he said with his eyes still on the beads as he explained to her that Shigidi was the Yoruba deification of nightmare, able to enter and manipulate the human subconscious, especially during sleep when humans' grip on their thoughts was loosest. He could induce night terrors and sleep paralysis in his prey as he sat on their chests and pressed the breath out from them. The babalawo explained that Shigidi was an ambivalent Orisha, protecting those who gave him offerings but also often sent by evil people to kill those they perceived as enemies or threats. "You have communed with spirits before?" the baba-lawo asked, looking up at her curiously. "To have sensed Shigidi the way you described it, to receive a bleed-over dream when you were not the person he came for, that is very unusual."

Saura's eyes were wide with shock, but she only shook her head. She didn't tell him about her mother or her intimate knowledge of the Bori or her adolescent possessions by myriad spirits. She simply paid him his fee and hired a car to take her home. But not the home she'd shared with Mobola. No. Back to Ungwar Rimi where she knew she could obtain the power to take on the nightmare god that had killed Mobola and find out who'd sent him. To fight fire with fire. Saura hadn't spoken to her mother in more than a decade. But they were bound by blood, and Saura needed her mother's help, her knowledge, to do what she wanted to do. Human families can be made of chains too.

Saura did not go to the family compound to talk privately with her mother. That would have been too personal, too painful, and would have made it too easy for her mother to refuse. She went instead to the market at night, when the moon and the stars hung low and most of the village had retired to their beds, leaving the wide-open spaces of the market to the members of the Bori cult. This was where the council of Bori magajiya held court and heard requests from the sick, the curious, the desperate.

She arrived at the center of the market in a black headscarf and cotton veil atop a flowing black jalabiya like the one she'd been wearing the night she ran away. They were already in the middle of a possession. An unusually tall man, shirtless, with broad shoulders and long wiry arms like a spider, was crawling on the ground, facing up, with his back arched high to an impossible curve. He was singing in a high-pitched voice even though he was foaming lightly at the mouth. He looked like he was leaking tree sap. Saura recognized the signs. He'd been possessed by Kuturu, the leper spirit, the healer of diseases of the flesh. Two men in white kaftans played soft music on white dotted calabashes. A girl who seemed no more than thirteen played an accompanying lute. Saura used to be that girl, the one playing the lute at possessions, before she was compelled to flee and enter the world.

When they were done and the man was helped to his feet by two others, presumably healed of his ailment, Saura removed her veil and made her request before her mother could completely compose herself.

One of the other magajiya, a plump woman with plaited hair, asked in accented Hausa, "Tell us, why do you want the Sarkin Sarkoki to possess you?" It was her aunt, Turai.

For Mobola, Saura thought but didn't say. "I have been wronged. And I want justice," Saura replied.

The third council member, a man with thick white eyebrows whom she had never seen before, asked her why she wanted Sarkin Sarkoki, the lord of the chains, the binding spirit. Why not Kure, he asked, the hyena spirit who could give power and stealth, or Sarkin Rafi, who would give strength to do violence which vengeance often called for.

"Because the one that wronged me is not mortal," she said. At that, they fell silent.

The three members of the Bori council stared at her appraisingly, sifting and weighing her request. Her mother's gaze was unrelenting.

"My daughter. I'm glad you have finally come home. Where you belong. But Sarkin Sarkoki demands a great price." Her mother stood up from the raffia mat to her full height. Saura became acutely aware of just how much they looked alike. The same thin nose and lips. The same ochre skin even though her mother's was more weathered, beaten to stubborn leather by the Sahara-adjacent sun. The same determined look in the eyes.

"The possession is permanent. The lord of the chains will bind himself to you before giving you the power to bind your enemy. You are giving up your body as a vessel forever. What justice could be worth this?"

Beneath the veil, heat rose behind Saura's neck. She did not want to say what she was thinking. There was too much pain in her heart threatening to spill out. If she let even a drop of the decade's worth of resentment within her begin to slip between her lips it would become a deluge that drowned them all.

"It doesn't matter. I am one of you. Heir to a title. I have a right to commune with the spirits. With Sarkin Sarkoki. And I have made my request."

There was more quiet weighing. More sifting. More appraisal. Finally, her mother turned to face the other two of the council and they communed briefly before announcing their decision.

"We will grant your request," her mother said, "but on one condition. Once you have had your revenge against whatever spirit has wronged you, you must return home and become a full Bori devotee. We cannot have a vessel of Sarkin Sarkoki roaming free. You will take your place with us, you will marry a good man, and you will bear children and teach them our ways. Do you agree?"

Saura knew this was what her mother had always wanted. To bring her back and bind her to home, even if she had to exploit a tragedy to achieve it. But Saura could not see past her desire to avenge Mobola, to find out why her lover had died, and to make their story make sense again, even if she couldn't change its ending.

"I agree."

Her words, like her heart, had taken on the texture of stone.

Her mother nodded and smiled, teeth cutting a curve like the half-moon beaming down on them from the cloudless sky.

Saura closed her eyes as a woman in a yellow jalabiya, cut like her own, took her by the arms and brought her to the center of the clearing where the two main roads that crossed the market met. The woman stood behind her, she would be her nurse if anything went wrong.

Saura breathed steadily as the men in the white kaftans and the girl on the lute began to play their music and the three members of the council, led by her mother, began to chant words she had not heard for years. Words that made the air feel heavy on her skin, in her lungs.

Saura felt something in her chest open like the blooming of a flower. She felt a flush of heat, saw a flash of light. A rush of charged air entered her, and then the world fell away as she was insufflated by the incoming spirit.

In the dark and nebulous place of her mind, Saura saw Sarkin Sarkoki.

He was an impossibly gaunt man, sitting on a stool at the center of the empty space. He had gray skin, and his limbs were like vines. He was bound up in thick, corroded chains that were tethered to something she could not see in the filmy darkness beneath, a few feet away from where he sat. A black cloth was wrapped around his waist and draped over his lower half; it pooled in cascades merging with the nebulous black ground below. His eyes were dark red, like spilled blood, and his stomach was cut open revealing mechanical viscera of chains and gears and roiling iron entrails. All over his skin, scripts were written onto him in chalked scars. He looked like a man that had been tortured and starved. He opened his mouth to reveal rust-colored teeth.

"You offer yourself as a vessel," he said, already knowing why she'd let him into her mind and what she wanted him to help her do.

"Yes," Saura managed to reply despite her trembling.

"You surrender your body to the chains."

"Yes."

"Then so be it," Sarkin Sarkoki stated, his chains clanking and rattling as he began to vibrate. "We are one. You will have what you desire."

The chains around him unfurled themselves and reached out to seize her. They were heavy and rough. Saura felt them wrap around every part of her, flesh and bone, blood and nerves, mind and spirit. The chains squeezed tight around the very essence of her until the world was nothing but chains and darkness. A full and lovely pain consumed her as Sarkin Sarkoki bonded with her, and it wasn't until the woman in the yellow jalabiya poured water on her face and shook her back into full consciousness that she tasted the sand in her mouth and realized she had been rolling around on the ground, screaming.

Wednesday goes quiet.

Her siblings wait.

She takes in a deep breath and lets out a scream. It is at once a declaration of defiance and an accusation leveled at her siblings, at the family that put her in chains. Her scream is a knife in their hearts.

Saturday will not look away until her sister stops screaming. Wednesday's face, once full of grace, is contorted into an ugly shape with lines like regret, but Saturday does not turn from it. She takes it all in, the words and the scream because that too is part of the story.

When the screaming ends, there is a pause as they allow the scream to settle.

And then, the story continues.

Her siblings' words are air in Saturday's lungs and her song is half complete. Saturday turns to face Thursday. His mahogany skin is pallid in the candlelight. The sadness hanging from the corners of his mouth and the salt and pepper of his hair, make him look fragile and small in his black fitted suit. He leans forward and places both elbows on the table, settling his jaw on the tip of his fingers, hands pressed together as in prayer.

When Thursday begins to speak, Saturday manages a smile. She likes Thursday's voice. It is steady and powerful and full of purpose, like waves crashing onto a cliff, like vengeance.

This is the part of the story that Thursday told:

When Shigidi arrived, just before midnight, Saura was pretending to be asleep on an uncomfortable spring mattress in a spacious hotel room she'd taken for three nights. She was shivering beneath the duvet, because she didn't know how to adjust the central air conditioning, but she didn't care. There was a "do not disturb sign" outside.

The nightmare god's arrival was sudden, and she felt his presence immediately. The dream-sensation of that small dark orb tugging at her subconscious with its evil gravity was one she could never forget.

She waited until he climbed onto the bed and sat on her chest, the weight of him restricting her breath. When she felt his probing at the edges of her mind, noticed a blurring and loosening of her thoughts and memories, she knew he had made the mistake of establishing a connection with her mind, of attempting to slip into her subconscious, as was his way. But she'd set a trap for him. The babalawo in Badagry had given her the number for another, less reputable babalawo who took requests for the nightmare god's assistance from people with such cruelty in their hearts. She'd told him that she wanted someone killed in their sleep, but she didn't say that the name she'd given was her own. And that the location she'd provided was the hotel room she'd booked. The trap was sprung.

She sat up suddenly and came face to face with the god that had murdered Mobola.

Saura was taken aback by how small and ugly Shigidi was. He was just over two feet tall. His head was too big for his body, and his dark ashy skin was covered in pockmarks, rashes, scarification lines, and sores. He wore filthy Ankara print trousers, and a plain black cloak that sat on his shoulders and ran down to the back of his ankles, with cowrie shells and lizard skulls sewn into the fabric. Black ash covered his face and made it look so much darker than the rest of him. He looked confused, surprised, a bit stupid and unsure of what to do.

Saura felt a flush of anger that something so hideous had been the one to take Mobola from her.

"Bastard," she spat out.

"What is happening?" Shigidi asked as he tried to withdraw from the borders of her consciousnesses.

Saura did not answer, she simply grabbed him and pulled him into the darkness of her mind where her inability to dream had left a vacuum where the cadaverous and bound Sarkin Sarkoki now dwelled.

Chains shot out of the darkness and latched onto Shigidi's small limbs, binding him to the place. He struggled and pulled but he could not free himself. Sarkin Sarkoki sat on his stool, watching and making a sound like laughter.

"What is going on? Who are you people?" the nightmare god shouted.

Angry that Shigidi could not even remember her face, she did not give him the satisfaction of understanding.

"You gods and spirits, you are all the same," she said instead. "You think you can enter our lives and ruin them at your whim, taking whatever you want and leaving us to pick up the pieces. No. Not this time. This time, here is what will happen. You will suffer, like you have never suffered before. There will be pain. A lot of it. I will take my time. And even when you begin to thirst for death, when the chains have dug into your ugly body so deeply that they have fused with your nerves so that there is nothing except pain, you will not die. I will watch as you are stripped of every fragment of hope you hold in that body, until you feel as black and as bleak as this place, deep inside you. Maybe then you will remember who I am, and you will remember the person you took from me."

As she spoke, the expression on Shigidi's face had morphed from confusion to terror to something beyond both.

And when he whispered, "Why?" Saura silently asked Sarkin Sarkoki to tighten the squeeze of the chains around his neck until his head bulged and he began to choke. It did not relent until he blacked out.

Thursday lifts his head and withdraws his hands from the intricately-patterned mahogany table. Its straight-grained, reddish-brown timber was cut from a tree that once stood at the center of a garden that is not a garden, in the middle of nowhere, everywhere, all at once. He leans back and turns to meet Saturday's gaze. She smiles at him, grateful for the way he told his part of the story which she has also absorbed. She feels it almost bursting out of her now—the song. She just needs one more part. The revelation.

She turns to face Friday who is raking his hands through his thick afro. He is the most reserved of the siblings and the one who likes the shape that secrets give stories which is why she has arranged it so that he can tell this part, just before her song. Candlelight dances in his large brown eyes and his pitch-black lips are quivering. He is eager to tell and hear.

Saturday nods and Friday opens his mouth, his bass voice booming and bouncing off the walls of the room in powerful waves.

This is the part of the story that Friday told:

Their bodies lay still and silent on the bed in the hotel, slumped over each other in an awkward embrace, but in the darkness of Saura's mind, possessed by Sarkin Sarkoki, Shigidi was screaming. Saura watched dispassionately, refusing to allow him even a waking moment of respite, a single fleeting second where he was not intimately acquainted with the pain from the contracting chains. And with every scream, she asked him the same question.

"Do you remember what you took from me?"

He insisted that he did not know, and so the torment continued. Sarkin Sarkoki's laughter the only other sound in her mind.

Almost twenty hours passed before the screaming stopped. Saura knew that it was not because the pain had ended, she was still commandeering the chains to pull and squeeze, and he was still writhing and whimpering. It was because something in him was breaking. Even a god can only take so much torment.

And yet after all the suffering, when she looked at him, pathetic as he was, she did not feel the satisfaction that she had craved. Underneath her rage was a sense of emptiness and loss and soul-deep weariness. She too was breaking under the weight of vengeance. And she already knew that someone else had sent him to their home that night because the two babalawos had told her it was the only reason Shigidi would kill someone.

"Mobola," she blurted out, eager for resolution. "Her name was Mobola."

Shigidi looked up at her, a glimmer of hope in his eyes for the first time since she'd lured him into the place of chains. He looked around at the darkness, as though he were searching her thoughts for something. And then, "Ahh . . . Mobola . . ." he croaked. "Yes. Omobola Adenusi . . . Lotus estate, Surulere. I remember now."

Saura seethed when her name escaped his mouth.

"I'm sorry." Shigidi breathed. "It was just a job. A standard nightmare-and-kill job."

Saura shuddered, she knew how he worked, but she was too angry to care. "Just a job? You took the most precious person in the world from me because it was just a job?"

The chains around his limbs rattled as Shigidi's tortured body sagged with the effort of keeping his head upright. "I'm sorry. I didn't know. It was just a job. It was only a job."

"Who sent you? Who was the client?"

And as she asked that, Sarkin Sarkoki's laughter stopped abruptly.

"I don't know," Shigidi said. "I just do what they ask me."

"Then you must remember," Saura demanded.

The chains tightened again.

"Please . . ."

"Tell me."

"I don't know," the nightmare god maintained, each word excavated from him was hoarse and desperate. "But . . . but . . . wait . . . it was a woman. Older. Not Yoruba. I remember she was not Yoruba. She had an accent. She was slender. Thin nose. She had eyes like yours."

Saura clutched at her chest.

"In her prayer, she only said she needed to get rid of the girl to get her daughter back."

A knot like an iron rope formed in her stomach. Saura fell to her knees as the weight of realization settled upon her. The lack of surprise when her mother saw her at the market. The insistence on returning home as a condition of her possession. The guilt in her aunt Turai's eyes. It all made terrible sense to her in that moment.

She asked Sarkin Sarkoki to unshackle him from her mind, and

Shigidi fell onto the dark filmy ground with a thud. In an instant, they were back on the bed, in the hotel.

Saura shot up and rolled off the mattress onto the carpeted floor. She felt the iron rope tighten in her stomach and everything constricted, like it was being squeezed by invisible hands. She felt like her insides were about to be torn and exposed, like the hollow clockwork belly of Sarkin Sarkoki. She threw up and began to cry.

"Ah. You know who it was, don't you?" Shigidi whispered.

Her mother's words tolled in her head like a bell.

My daughter.

I'm glad you have finally come home.

Saura straightened up and settled a long stare at Shigidi who was looking back at her with large yellow eyes full of pity or regret or perhaps both.

"Yes," she whispered back.

"Family?"

"Yes."

"I . . . I am sorry. I am truly sorry."

Saura was surprised by the sincerity in his voice.

"I hate my job sometimes," Shigidi continued. "But I need the offerings and prayer requests to survive. Please understand. I didn't mean to cause you pain but I . . . need to survive. I never mean to cause anyone pain. But I . . . I don't want to wither and die. I just wish there was another way."

Saura was even more surprised when Shigidi awkwardly clambered down from the bed and lay on the floor in front of her, prostrating in the traditional way, to show respect or profound apology. "I'm sorry."

She placed her hand on his head, and Saura and Shigidi wept together.

The story is near its end when Friday stops speaking.

And Saturday's song is about to begin.

There are no instruments to be played but the air hums electric with a sense of music, in anticipation.

Her siblings watch, enraptured as her ribs expand, her diaphragm moves up, and her belly hollows out like a cave. The pressure of the melody builds up in her chest and there are vibrations in her throat, her mouth, her lips. Saturday feels like she is full of all the words and feelings and air that her siblings have given her with their words. Like she will never run out of breath. Like she will never run out of story. Like she will never run out of song.

Saturday begins to sing in a clear and loud voice full of energy.

This is the song Saturday sang:

> She entered a life
> She struck in like lightning
> But was taken too soon
> Beauty and joy and kindness
> Mobola, lost to nightmare's touch
> Breath extinguished by a mercenary god
>
> Oh, a dirge for true love
> For an embrace lost

A return home
Where Saura's heart is buried
A sacrifice to the essence of binding
The lord of the chains
Gave her the power
Gave her the strength to catch a murderous god

But gods only serve people.
They are made in the minds of men
In Saura's mind the nightmare god revealed a
secret
That the umbilical cord can be a noose
That family can be a chain
That seeks to bind at any cost.

How could a mother do this?
Oh, how could she not just accept?
How many tears must be shed to pay for this sin?
How much blood must be spilled?
It's an evil way she has chosen
To show the depth of love.

Oh, a dirge for motherhood
For the poison in the womb

Saura swears that for as long as she lives
She will not let this happen to anyone like her.
The bargain has been struck,
The word-bond is made of iron,

But there are many kinds of homecoming
And sometimes gifts bear teeth.

Saura makes a pact with her lover's killer
An unwitting instrument in a war that began at birth.
He will give her dreams as restitution,
To make amends for stilling her lover's heart.
And she will forgive him
For he knew not what he was doing.

But grief and sorrow must be repaid.
There are many kinds of binding,
And even invited guests can come baring teeth,
If death is the price of her presence
Then let there be music and tears
As she goes home to share a living nightmare from which there is
now no escape.

Oh, a dirge for childhood
Of innocence lost

She enters the village like a whirlwind
And blows her way home.
Her mother is sitting in the clearing
Where Saura once played Kagada with friends
Trust-falling into each other's arms and singing
And eating hot tuwo under weekend stars.

Their eyes meet full of determination and knowledge
Tragic corruption of love and affection

Her mother strikes first, possessed by Kure the hyena
No deeper pain than to be struck by the hand that fed you.
Fate is cruel to set blood against blood
She reaches into her mother's mind and ends it quickly

She gives her mother's mind permanent shelter
In the dark place with Sarkin Sarkoki
Where she will always be with her
Trapped in the once-empty darkness now filled with hate
Bound together in their pain
Their new umbilical cord made of spirit-chains

Her mother's body becomes a hollow vessel
Sessile as a tree and just as alive.
She has been given the thing she wanted.
Saura takes her mother's place,
For a paralyzed woman cannot be magajiya
When her daughter has come home.

They are now always together.
In her every waking moment Saura hears her mother's voice
Pleading, railing, crying to be let go
But every night when she goes to bed
She closes her eyes, and silence falls
And in the quiet of her mind, she dreams.

And so, Saturday's song ends.

The euphonic cavalcade of melodies comes to a halt. Saturday is exhausted and feels empty, like a gourd with all its water poured, but she smiles because she thinks it was a good song and she sang it well.

Her six siblings remain silent, a rapturous look on their faces. They are still lost to the song. Saturday savors the moment. This is why she sings the stories sometimes. To see that look in their eyes that says she has given them something special. And for what she hopes it will evoke within them. She has told, she has heard, she has performed.

She turns to Sunday, whose task it is to complete all their stories, and she sees tears in his sea-green eyes. She smiles and nods.

Sunday sucks in air and lets out his words in a whisper that was loud enough for all of them to hear.

This is all that Sunday said:

"The end."

At that, the seven siblings who were, who are and always have been, fall silent again and contemplate the story for a moment that is also an eternity. It is a reading of their own entrails, an examination of the essence of all things from which they are woven, and it is the most important part of the story—what it does to those who receive it. Its interpretation, its impact, its legacy.

"Humans are such tragic things," Sunday says. "Little grains of consciousness floating atop an ocean of existence vaster than any of them possibly imagine, barely aware of all the other ways of being, of all that exists outside their perception. And yet their stories are heavy in our bones, written upon us with the brightness of stars. The myriad ways they love and hurt each other are fascinating. They weave such tenderness and cruelty with every fiber of their lives."

He pauses. And then: "This was a good story. We told it well."

He turns to Saturday, the lines of his face converging, his eyes wide and full of realization, of knowledge. "But why did you choose this story for us to tell and hear, sister? Why did you sing this song?"

"For the same reason we tell and hear all our stories. Because that is what happened and thus must be told."

The siblings all echoed the mantra in unison. "That is what happened and thus must be told."

Sunday smiles faintly, maintaining his placid countenance. "Indeed. But there is also another reason, is there not?"

"For Wednesday," Saturday admits, brushing a loose, blonde braid behind her ear. She knew he would be the first to understand. "We are not human, we are not like Saura or her mother. We should not continue to bind our own blood so, regardless of her crime. Wednesday is our sister. Yes, she tried to change a story, but which of us has not been tempted to do so?" Saturday pointed at the timestone sitting at the center of the table like an emerald fruit. "Her actions were wrong, but they came from a good place. And in the end the story was not changed. The stories cannot be changed. She knows that now. She is certain of it. As are we all. That is the lesson of her story, and it is complete. Let us release her from her chains."

Saturday sees the gratitude silently forming in the sides of Wednesday's thin mouth, her soft eyes, her broad nose.

Sunday looks at all his siblings. Their eyes reveal what they want even though they are mostly bound by rules carved in the primordial essence of existence, rules older than time itself. But rules, like gods, are only as powerful as their purpose and the will of those who made them. "Do you all agree with this? Shall we free our sister?"

"Yes," Monday says.

From Tuesday, "We should."

There is a hopeful nod from Wednesday herself.

"Yes," Thursday says.

Friday echoes his agreement.

"Yes." Saturday cannot hide her joy.

"Then so be it," Sunday says.

Saturday leaps to her feet and lets out a cry as the shackles loosen and fall from Wednesday's limbs, clattering with a noise like songs of freedom, like a sibling's laughter, like the forgiveness of family.

LIGHTS IN THE SKY

O pen your eyes.

Be mildly disturbed by the acrid smell of rapidly dissolving flesh all around you and the taut, unfamiliar curtain of starless purple sky above. Do not let the cacophony of scudding projectiles and condensed impact explosions all around send you into a panic. It is just a war; just another war. Remember why you are here, why you are supine on the gently arcuate meta-crystal terrain of this alien world, your legs splayed out carelessly like the branches of a felled tree. Remember your name is Chinonso Kalu, that you are an Ekdromoi commando with the 21st infantry of the United Earth Federation. Remember that a few seconds ago you were knocked unconscious by the shock wave from a detonating Triton-3 grenade. Become painfully aware of the brutal rhythmic ringing in your ears.

Jingle Bells. Jingle Bells.

Do not panic.

Be glad you were not caught inside the condensed pressure and nano-bot burst's kill radius. Be even gladder that you can remember something, anything, despite the impact of the explosion forcing your brain to bounce against your new steel skull hard enough to knock you out. For how long? You don't know. You can't be sure. Seconds. Minutes. It doesn't matter. Adjust your visor and initiate a scan of your vitals. Process the data that your exoskeleton's AI is feeding your brain through the router in your cerebral cortex. Request a visual summary.

Try to ignore the brief static burst — *carrying a distorted image of your daughter in a yellow frock and bantu knots dancing around an old, sparsely decorated Christmas tree with a peeling silver cross atop it —* that flashes across your visor.

Log the most important scan data as it scrolls past your eyes in a flurry.

Armor integrity = 43.2%

Blood pressure = 144/91

Core Temperature = 39°C

Oxygen Tank Reserves = 62.6%

Ammunition Available = 53.7%

Acknowledge that your ammunition stock is sufficient, and you still have four of your six Triton-3 grenades. Good. You will need the grenades. You will need the ammo. You will need all of it.

Now get up. This is war.

Start running and dynamically adjust your path as you observe the terrain, searching for cover.

A smoldering tank. No. Possible undetonated incendiaries.

Something akin to a tree. No. Unfamiliar trunk strength.

A rude crystalline outcrop jutting out of the ground. Good. Extruded rock formations should have similar reliability to the surface material which is solid here. This is cover.

Plaster your back to its smooth hard surface just in time to evade a bright red plasma missile with vicious intentions. Watch it ride the thin atmosphere until it crashes impotently into the monolithic Hellfire-8 infantry teleport vehicle.

Watch the static across your visor transform the Hellfire-8 into a lighthouse — *a concrete sanctuary that you are rapidly approaching on an overcrowded boat full of hungry, thin, cold, tired, and desperate dark-skinned people just like you and your daughter. An old man passes you a large bottle of scotch wrapped in a dirty, peeling, brown paper bag with the number "25" crudely written on it. He manages a hopeful smile as he reminds you that it is Jesus's birthday today and wishes you a Merry Christmas. You smile back and* — blink the Hellfire-8 back into reality.

Glance over the edge of the outcrop and take in the swath of open, glassy ground that lays between you and the main Chironi defense turret that is delivering swift, painful death to the overwhelming majority of the slowly advancing UEF formation behind you. Enable distance estimation on your visor and register the 106.3 meters between your position and the turret.

Look left, following the flash of light that grazes the edge of your vision just in time to see a survivor of the previous UEF advance flop onto his belly at the edge of a bizarrely thick and angular hyaline brush. Scan his details; log vital statistics and supplies. He has two programmable plasma grenades confirmed in his weapon — *warm brown eyes that are pleading desperately with you not to leave her alone in this strange place because the passport and the money and even the quality of life mean nothing if she does not have you* — and 21% of his ammo load remaining. Send him a direct message on the secure short-range comms channel.

"Lance Corporal Kalu of the 21st Ekdromoi requesting cover fire."

"Lau Chen. 42nd. What's your play, Kalu?" he asks.

Reduce your plan to a concise set of actions and inform him of his part in them. Tell him that you are going to "charge the main defense turret to detonate the Triton-3 and clear troop advance. Require 5.5-meter proximity. Need suppression fire to create an 8-second window."

Listen to his response. "You things can run that fast?"

Inform him that you can. Register his contemptuous tone and his choice of descriptor for you. Ignore them, you have no need for Chen's prejudices, you only need his cover fire administered effectively and efficiently. Tell Chen to fully unload his ammo at a concentrated point, on your signal. Send him the coordinates.

Wonder if you will ever spend another Christmas with your daughter as you wait for the tide of whizzing and banging and booming and screaming to ebb. Watch the explosions decorate the alien terrain like so many shiny Christmas ornaments on a glass tree. Let the heat and the death and the noise all around remind you of the insurgency that forced you to flee your home in Kano, of the insurgency that grew to become a war, of the war that took a wife from you and a mother from your daughter. Christmas only ever comes once a year but there is always a war somewhere.

When the tide subsides, send the support signal to Chen and break out from behind the rock, bee-lining for the turret position in giant strides powered by your exoskeleton.

Watch the faint yellow energy membrane in front of the turret ripple and vibrate violently ahead of you as Chen's fire pounds into the repulsion field relentlessly, blinding it to your advance.

Accelerate.

Tense. Veer off path as much as you can without losing speed to evade the mistimed plasma missile hurtling its way toward you. Watch it arc and seize before exploding mid-air just behind you with a spectacular sound like a star screaming to announce the birth of a king.

Ding Dong Merrily on High.

Brace. Take the impact on the contracted interlocking plates that line your exoskeleton's back. Stagger forward. Stumble. Do not fall. Do not fucking fall.

Regain your balance. Correct your path. Keep running.

Ignore the fact that you can hear nothing now but a high, winding whine.

Hark! The Herald Angels Sing!

Realize that you are almost at the turret and there is no more suppression fire so Chen is either dead or out of ammo. Realize that it is now or never. You have to — *enlist to secure her future. The UEF will make her a citizen and take care of her, protect her in all the ways you have never, will never, be able to, and they will give her a life she deserves where bright lights in the sky do not always mean death is coming —* make your move.

Let the AI calculate the nearest angle and point of approach to minimize probability of impact damage. Display the results on your visor — *hug her and tell her it is the only way. Lie to her that you will be back before next Christmas because it is just a war; only another war —* and align your steps with the harsh red dashes of the AI's calculated path. Raise your weapon.

Step into range. Launch the grenade on a low trajectory, allowing it transit the open, pellucid ground and arrive with just enough energy to attach itself onto the base of the turret and shimmer once. Bank left. Hard.

Dive onto the ground, pressing your body to the alien world and hugging it desperately like you are gravity made flesh as the turret enfolds in a bubble of broken pressure, vicious nano-bots consuming everything caught within — *hear her voice cry out for her Daddy! Daddy! Please!* — in the deafening roar of the explosion that turns the turret into a bright, shimmering Christmas tree of death against the alien sky.

Feel it lift you up and throw you several feet in the air like you are nothing but the doll you gave your daughter fourteen Christmases ago. Crash to the ground rudely and succumb to the darkness that once more caresses your consciousness.

Welcome the silence. Welcome the darkness. Welcome the —

Silent night

— of you.

Open your eyes.

Be disturbed by the acrid smell of rapidly dissolving flesh and metal around you and the crystalline terrain of the alien world beneath you. Catch your reflection in it and wonder briefly why the image you see has a steel mask for a face and two bright neon-red orbs for eyes. Remember suddenly why you are here. Remember that it has been fourteen Christmases since they bonded your mind and body to this suit, to this war machine. Remember that it has been fourteen earth years since you tasted good scotch, ate hot jollof rice, kissed your daughter's forehead. Remember. Remember. Remember the sacrifice of the flesh. Take in the cacophony of scudding projectiles and condensed impact explosions all around you and through it all, *remember her.*

Now get up. This is war.

BLOWOUT

Folake Adeyemi was slowly digging her index finger into the base of her afro and staring at the row of remote subsurface exploration monitoring screens when she heard the explosion.

She'd let her mind wander for a few moments, subconsciously clenching her jaw as she thought about what she'd say to Femi when he finally got back to the orbital station. And then it came. A thunderous boom over the open communications line that startled her, followed by the low, tinny crackling of static. She knew instantly, even before the data flooded in and the alarms started blaring, that something had just gone very wrong down on the surface of Mars.

Femi!

She slammed her palm onto the transmission switch on the monitoring panel and shouted into the surface communications microphone, "N-12, this is Nerio Station! Report! What just happened?"

For a moment that felt elastic enough to have been an hour, her words hung in the void with nothing but the steady drone of cosmic background noise coming back in response. There was less than a half-second surface-to-orbit delay in their transmissions so when she didn't get any reply for more than half a minute, a chill ran down her spine. Surface crews always maintained an open line with the station on an active mission. That was protocol. There was no way they would choose not to respond. Not unless they couldn't. Not unless something had happened to the communications array, or worse, to them. She shuddered and tried again. Louder this time.

"N-12. Come in. Anyone? Femi? Natukunda? Oumarou? Bibata? Are you guys there?" and then, "Femi? Talk to me please. Are you guys okay?"

Nothing.

Her heart sank. For a second, she was unsure what to do next, but then her training kicked in: *Analyze. Inform. Act.*

She focused on the monitoring screens, taking in the rush of rapidly changing data. They'd lost visual on the surface drill rig—two screens displayed disheartening gray static like electric rainclouds. The remaining screens showed a kaleidoscope of bright numbers, logs, graphs, and bold red warning text that all indicated what had happened: the drill bit had hit an over-pressured formation about two kilometers below the surface. She let out a gasp.

Formation kick.

The numbers continued to stream across the screens, some of them frozen and flickering with the break in direct data transmission, others flashing with error symbols as the anomalous data that had come through was analyzed, forcing correlations and equations to be extrapolated beyond their range of validity. It was all overwhelming, like looking at a street artist creating wild mathematics-themed graffiti with light.

Folake activated the manual control on the input panel, reached for the screens and pulled forward the display projection from the active ones with a turn of her wrist and a curl of her finger. She swiped quickly to select and zoom in on important data points and push back others, flicking her fingers expertly as she tried to narrow down the flood of information to just its most useful elements; elements she could interpret. The drill bit and attached logging tools were lost, a final massive pressure reading that went off the charts was their final recorded transmission. The pressure had shot so far beyond the normal hydrostatic gradient that the mostly vertical pressure pre-test log reading now looked like two perpendicular lines, a bizarre 'L'. She'd never seen anything like it in all her years working and supervising drilling operations. The downhole temperature had spiked too, and the interpretation AI had already matched it to a Joule-Thomson heating effect although it was possible that the unusual formation had contained some hot fluid. Folake kept swiping and flicking.

Other electromagnetic and radiation data was harder to interpret. But everything she could make out from the mess of numbers indicated that this wasn't just any kind of formation kick—those were common enough on earth due to compaction, osmosis, gas generation, tectonics, half a dozen other possible causes that the planning team had considered in the risk analysis. No, this was massive. Ridiculously so. It was over two orders of magnitude higher than their probabilistic models had indicated as the *unlikely* scenario with 99% confidence. Perhaps more. It had to be the effect of some new phenomenon, some previously unforeseen mechanism at work deep in the planet's subsurface.

For half a moment, a flash of the excitement of discovery shot to her head. It was intoxicating, like the fresh palm wine her father used to buy whenever they went back to the village, in Ijebu-ode, to see their grandmother. And then she crashed back to the reality of the situation, hard.

There were four people down there on the N-12 surface exploration crew and all of them had been at or close to the rig. Including Femi, her brother. She didn't know what had happened to them, but she knew that they were in danger, unable to communicate and probably needed help.

She took three quick, deep breaths, expanded her palm to send the projections back to their places in the display monitors, then unstrapped herself. Pushing down on her seat, she drifted up and out of it. She kicked against the panel and thrust herself into the octagonal corridor that connected the subsurface exploration monitoring and control module to the rest of Nerio Station with a single thought on her mind.

I am not going to let Femi die on Mars.

Femi was born exactly five days before Folake's ninth birthday. Her parents never told her why they had waited so long to try for another child but when she was fifteen, she found in her mother's room a birth certificate for an older sibling she had never met. There was a death certificate in the same name in the same drawer. The latter was dated just two days after the former. The birth certificate was dated almost exactly five years before she'd been born.

Her mother came from the outskirts of what used to be Oyo State in western Nigeria, the seventh of nine children and the second of three girls. Her father was from the East and he was also the second—although of five—in his own large family. When she was nineteen, and she had her first pregnancy scare, Folake spent long hours wondering if her parents had wanted a big family like the ones they grew up in and if those certificates she found had influenced their eventual decision to have just the two of them: her and Femi.

Despite the age difference between them, they'd been close until the day he joined DeepCarbon Limited, that was when the tensions started. She'd helped change his diapers, carried him on her back, rocked him to sleep in her arms, helped her parents feed him, and she'd even argued with him, when he was old enough to argue back. Femi was a part of almost every important moment in her life. But Femi wasn't there the first time someone told her that her mother was a hero.

Folake remembers the day in vivid detail for three reasons: one, because it was raining heavily; two, because the words had come from the lips of her father; and three, because it was the first time that she saw her mother after the accident.

That day, she'd been roused from a light slumber by the sounds of rain hitting the open garage door and gravel being crunched beneath slowly decelerating tires. Those sounds meant that the navigation AI was parking her father's sprightly silver *Neo Futura* in the driveway of their bungalow. Everything about that *Neo Futura* was familiar. Her father had bought it second-hand from a German colleague two years before she was born, and while it was old, he had built and installed his own self-driving module. He'd even converted it to an electric-hydrogen hybrid and had let her help assemble some of the parts. She had been hearing the sound of it parking every day since she was born and that was why she knew it had arrived four hours earlier than usual.

Folake rubbed what was left of sleep from her eyes with her knuckles and excitedly made her way to the living room. She was alone at home; Femi was being taken care of by her grandmother and Folake's footsteps echoed through the house. She walked into the living room just as her father was entering from the front door, his back turned to her as he carefully pulled something heavy into the house. When he heard her, he froze in place.

"Daddy welcome home! When is Mummy coming back?" she asked.

"Folake," he started before turning his head to look at her, "I need you to know something. Your mother is hero. You should never forget that."

There was something like pride, but also fear, ringing in his voice.

"Daddy?"

And then he spun around, revealing the wheelchair he'd been pulling, and she saw her mother in a sky-blue shirt and red Ankara wrapped around her waist, propped up in the chair, two white and gray metal appendages where her legs used to be. She was smiling weakly.

Tears began to stream down Folake's face.

Her mother worked as a drilling supervisor on an offshore gas production site off the Angolan coast, and even back then she knew two things about her mother's job: one, it could be dangerous and two, it paid well. They'd both given her *the talk* several times since she was five and old enough to understand some of what it meant to drill a hole into the subsurface and extract energy resources. They'd even bought her a model offshore drilling rig to play with, one of the new ones with a carbon capture unit attached that she had to assemble herself following the instruction manual, but they'd also assured her that the job was relatively safe, that accidents were rare. Increasingly so. And that she shouldn't worry, her mother would always come home fine. And so, she hadn't worried, hadn't ever been afraid. Until that day when she saw her mother.

Her father wheeled the chair with her mother's thin, sleeping bulk over to the couch, stepped on the pedals behinds the rear wheels to lock it in place, and then lifted Folake up into the air like he used to when she was much younger, "Hey. Hey. Big girl. Don't cry, Mummy will be fine. Your mother is a hero. She saved twenty-seven people even though it cost her. You see?" He pointed down at the bionic legs.

Hero.

Folake would hear that word so often, she would come to hate it. Hero. Why did her mother need to lose her legs to be one? Were heroes only created through loss? Did heroes always need to lose something, to suffer, to be broken?

"Sometimes good things require sacrifice, do you understand?"

Folake didn't really understand what her father was saying then, but he seemed more hurt by her tears than by her mother's condition, so she nodded and wiped away the tears from her eyes with the sleeve of her shirt.

"Good girl. She'll be fine. The new legs will take time to get used to, but she'll be fine. Good as new. Maybe even better. She put the lives of others above her own—that's the mark of a great person. She's a true hero. I'm very proud of her. And I'm very proud of you too, ehn, omo Mummy?"

Folake looked down and saw the faint smile still lingering on her mother's lips, and so she smiled too. That made her father laugh and, even though she didn't really know why back then, she thought that there was something incomplete about the laugh, something hollow in its sound and something dimmed in his eyes.

She never again heard her father laugh the way he used to.

Folake could almost hear her own blood pulsing in her head when the subsurface exploration monitoring and control unit doors irised open with a sharp hiss as the isolation control vented.

She moved quickly through the wide white and gray space, using her hands and feet to propel herself toward the central control room. She didn't even pause to so much as glance at the transparent display ports that lined it to catch a view of the dull red orb that had brought her there, so far away from home. Or even the wispy green and blue dot that was home on the other side; the place where she'd been born and where her argument with Femi had begun.

Nerio Station was relatively new, with the bright red, white and green symbol of the African Space Agency still emblazoned clearly everywhere. It was essentially a long monolithic tube with collapsible solar arrays placed at each end. A circular ring was attached at an angle by corridors to a sphere at its center, like spokes on a giant wheel. The subsurface exploration monitoring and control unit was housed in one sector of the ring, just like the twelve other mission units dedicated to other surface activities. Central control would have been appraised of the situation by now and would know if any other crew or remote units were close enough to investigate. Perhaps even know enough to help her figure out what to do next.

When she reached the central unit, Mengistu, the mission commander, was sitting at its center, in the middle of the spherical room, surrounded by display screens not unlike the ones in the subsurface exploration monitoring and control unit, but there were more of them and they were all curved in an arc to match the shape of the room, their foci at Mengitsu's position. His long hair was braided tight to his scalp, and his shoulders were hunched as he swiped rapidly at a small cluster of bright red in the screen array in front of him, like an electric tumor.

"What the hell just happened down there?" he asked when he saw her enter.

She pushed off the door and came closer to him. "Unexpected massive overpressure. I think it might have been a blowout."

Mengistu blinked rapidly. "Blowout? Don't we have devices down there to prevent that?"

"If the readings we got are right, this was far beyond anything we designed for. We need to help the guys on N-12." Mengistu was usually quite stoic but Folake thought she saw a flash of emotion in the brown of his eyes. "Did you get any additional information from the other crews?"

"I contacted Paul Bryant on N-4, and Mohale on N-7, they're the closest but it will take them a while to ramp down and mobilize."

"What about the rovers?"

He spun around and gestured with a long thin finger to one of the screens that wasn't flashing red. "All N-12 support rover communications are down. I've reassigned the nearest three autonomous rovers to investigate, but they're old and slow. You know that. It may take a while."

She exhaled. "So, there's no way we can help them right now?"

"I don't know. We don't even know what condition they are in, but if it really is as bad as you say then we may not get to them in time. We need to be prepared for the worst."

His saying it seemed to suddenly make the prospect of Femi's and the others' deaths even more real. The thought brought bile and the metallic taste of regret to her throat. She choked them both back down and grabbed onto a railing to tether herself near Mengistu. She was trying not to let the panic flooding her body get all the way to her brain where it could cloud her thoughts or her judgment.

Think. Think. There must be another way. Femi needs me to think quickly.

There was a brief pause. And then: "What about the *Ibeji*?"

Mengitsu spun back around, the ends of his braids floating up like tentacles. "What about it?"

"It has its own fully independent on-board systems, and it was designed for the team to use in investigating unknown and potentially dangerous local environments, right? So, it's tough. Very tough. Might have survived whatever knocked out their comms. Try to ping it on the emergency frequency and see if it's online."

He nodded, reached for a display below and gestured to pull it up and close, swiping quickly as he did. He was far more practiced with lightscreens than she was, and his fingers were thin, so his movements were smooth and effortless, like he was conducting an incredibly fast electric orchestra. She could barely even see what he was doing. There was another pause and then he said, "It's online."

"Good. We can use it to see what the situation is on the ground."

"Yes," he nodded, "but the *Ibeji* is not autonomous. It's not a rover. It's designed for full sensory exploration and data acquisition with minimal risk. We'll have to control it using haptic feedback from here, directly linked to your nervous system. If it's been hit by something or is in the middle of a fire, or anything like that, you'll be in a lot of pain. You won't be in any real danger, but your brain will think you are."

"Yes. I know all that. I took the same training you did."

"Fine. Sorry. I just wanted to make sure we both clearly understand what you are planning to do."

She looked him in the eyes with confidence she didn't really feel. "We do." *Am I trying to be a hero like my mother?*

"Okay. Then do it." Mengitsu pointed to the end of the room where the suits were stored. "Put on the suit. I'll set up the link."

"Thank you. And see if you can dampen the tactile feedback signal and increase visual and sound."

"Sure."

Mengitsu swiped at another display as she pushed off to the edge of the room where both the bulky extravehicular activity suits and the much smaller haptic feedback suits were secured. They were skintight and looked like full scuba divers' bodysuits with a hood that was covered in thin wire mesh—the neural interface receiver nodes. The suits were designed to give the user full sensory perception and control of the emergency high-risk environment exploration robot down on the surface. Tactile. Visual. Aural. The robot would execute every action she thought and transmit all its inputs directly to her brain. Hence the name *Ibeji*. *Twins*. She pressed the release and snatched a suit that looked roughly her size without checking the label. Comfort really didn't matter. Only time did. She writhed her way into it awkwardly as Mengitsu called out to her, "Ready to link you up whenever you're ready."

She pulled the hood over her eyes and was swallowed by a silent darkness.

She gave Mengitsu a thumbs up to indicate that she was ready.

Hold on Femi, I'm coming.

Folake was forty-one when Femi told her he was applying to be an off-world drilling engineer.

Folake remembers the day in vivid detail for three reasons: one, because the weather was unusually cool for that time of year; two, because she was wearing the black sweater her mother had knitted for her; and three, because it was the last time that she had seen Femi in person, back on Earth.

He was sitting on the couch across from her in her Benin City apartment with an appearance of apprehension plastered across his face. He carefully sipped the hot ginger tea she'd made for him, blowing wispy trails of steam from the surface. Cool harmattan air streamed in through the window behind him, over his cleanly shaved head and onto her face. When he put his mug down, she was reminded just how disproportionately long his arms were, like their mother's. It was a trait that had made him good at sports when he was in school, and good at tinkering with things when he got older. He had that in common with their father. Femi's skin was lustrous and plump; he'd been eating well.

He hadn't said much since he'd arrived at her place for their usual monthly visit, to catch up and play boardgames and reminisce about the past—a tradition they had developed since their parents had died. Folake could tell that he was weighing and arranging his words. She already knew he was going to say something heavy and jagged before he leaned forward and said it.

"I have to tell you something, but I need you to know this is not about Mum," he said, "or you."

"Okay . . ." she responded cautiously.

"I just got an offer from AfSA," he announced as he put his hand to his chin and stroked the line of his trimmed beard. "They need managed pressure drillers for a five-year Mars exploration mission."

Folake's cheeks went hot and a sheen of sweat began to form on her forehead. Memories flooded her mind of that day all those years ago when their mother had come home with her eyes barely open, a thin smile cut across her pale face, and two metal appendages where her legs used to be.

"It's a very good offer," he added when he saw the look of horror evolving across her face. "Fantastic actually. I ran the numbers and once I get back, I just need to work in the office as a consultant for another three years and I can retire early."

"They pay well because it's dangerous. It's Mars, Femi. There have only been what—? Eight or nine missions with subsurface drilling crews there? Didn't one of them end in disaster, a casing failure?"

"That was the Norwegian crew four years ago, and no one got seriously hurt, Folake. Four years is a long time. This is different. There's been a lot of progress. We're pioneering new, better technology. We'll be using supercritical carbon dioxide from the Martian atmosphere as drilling fluid, a new tensegrity rig structure instead of the old standard stuff and a few other things they haven't even explained to me yet but a lot of it is stuff that's never been done in the field before."

She shook her head. "That only makes it *more* dangerous. Mum always used to say, *the head that is used to break open the coconut will not eat from it.*"

"Yeah, but considering all the patents she and dad filed together, I think her head broke a lot of coconuts and she ended up being a hero,"

Femi replied. Heat flared through Folake and she fixed him with a look. He leaned back as though the heat from her was singeing him, "Folake, look, you know this is a big opportunity for me."

The memories in her mind merged with other memories too; of her father shouting at her to be careful when she'd accidentally let her grip slip while trying to help her mother walk up a flight of stairs; of her mother softly crying alone in front of an open fridge; of her father's rage and her mother's tearful resignation after she'd gone to work for Deep-Carbon, in an act of defiance, drilling wells to store carbon dioxide removed from the atmosphere deep underground. Folake wondered if that was what Femi was doing. Joining the African Space Agency mission as a way to prove a point. He knew it was a role she'd been invited to apply for two years ago with the first mission cycle, and she'd declined. As though taking up her previous role at DeepCarbon hadn't been enough.

"Femi, why are you really doing this?"

"Doing what? Taking a good job offer?" His voice had taken on a hard edge.

"There are a million other good jobs you could have used your mechanical engineering degree to pivot to. You chose to focus on drilling. Okay, fine. I didn't say anything. But why did you take that drilling engineer position at DeepCarbon after I left? Why do you want to be an AfSA offworld driller?"

"Because I like it," he shot back. "I love this job. The theory and the practice of it. Sure, I was exposed to it early because of you and Mum' but I found it exciting. I still do. I made my own choice to follow that path. I know the risks and I made my choice anyway. Why is that so hard for you to understand?"

She shook her head again. "Because it's not true."

"And what makes you so sure of that? What makes you think you know my motivations even better than I do? Because your own choices were influenced by what happened to Mum? Abeg, I already told you this isn't about you . . . or Mum."

"You don't know what she was like before the accident. What they were both like."

Femi's nose flared. "It doesn't matter!" He sighed. "You're doing it again. You need to stop trying to protect me from your own trauma. I don't know what you remember but my childhood was great. I had you. I had Dad. I had Mum. And the mummy I remember turned out great. There were bad moments, yes, difficult moments. I remember them too; I just don't dwell on them like you do because they were not all our lives were. There were many good moments. Beautiful moments. Mum was fine, she dealt with it as best she could. Dad too. You're the only one that never got past it."

Folake shot to her feet. "If you keep doing this, you're going to end up like her. Another brave, broken person crying in the darkness when you think no one can see you."

A flash of fury contorted the lines of Femi's face so much that for a moment Folake did not recognize him. In that moment the measured and playful man that was her brother disappeared, and that was how she knew she'd gone too far, had scraped open something tender and raw in him.

He threw his hands up in the air. "Goodbye Folake. I'll call you when I get back."

There was something hard and sharp in his voice as he left her apartment, his jaw clenched, and his fists balled tight that filled her with fear. He didn't even look back.

She didn't speak to Femi again until fourteen months later when she finally arrived on Nerio Station with the fourth mission cycle as a remote drilling operations supervisor.

The darkness receded like a curtain lifting when Mengitsu activated her link to the *Ibeji*. All she saw was a clear sheet of orange-red Martian sky.

Up. She was looking up. She could feel the pressure of something rough beneath her so she knew the tactile sensors were working though she couldn't hear anything. Perhaps aural capability had been damaged in the blowout. The weight of increased planetary gravity settled on her through the sensors.

With a thought she commanded the *Ibeji* to rise and met resistance. It was still strapped in place. She brought the hands up to her face to make sure the controls were working correctly. The gray and white articulated limbs moved smoothly, if a bit slow. Probably due to Mengistu's damping a portion of the signal. She released the straps and sat the *Ibeji* up to take stock of the situation with a sweeping a look across the horizon. Around her, there was only red, dusty desolation and destruction.

Ibeji was attached to the emergency supplies cabin which had been toppled over. Ahead of her, the rig itself lay on its side like a wounded beast. Long lines of thick steel-coiled tubing were strewn about the area like bizarre entrails. Charred and broken edges of the tensegrity rig, the compressors, and other assorted equipment jutted out at odd angles, some of them dug into the ground from impact, including what remained of the communications array. There was swirling dust everywhere, but the ground in front of the rig was wet because the site that N-12 had been drilling was now a thick, towering geyser of clear liquid.

And then sound suddenly exploded into her consciousness as the aural signal was re-established. Folake flinched. The liquid was gushing out with a roar.

She focused on the rig in the distance and her heart sank when she saw a body just behind it that had been mangled beyond recognition, both arms twisted and one leg torn off. The suit helmet was cracked open, and the upper torso had caved into a bloody wreck of bones and blood. She was ashamed of her relief when she noticed that the body was too short and stout to be Femi. It was Natukunda, the jovial and maternal Ugandan floor hand who would probably have been closest to the hole when the blowout occurred.

I'm so sorry Natukunda.

She blinked back tears.

I have to find the rest of the crew.

Folake thought the *Ibeji* up to its feet, feeling the vibration from the blowout concentrated beneath. The rate at which the fluids were spewing out suddenly made her worried about how stable the ground beneath them would be if it continued. There could be compaction and subsidence and, eventually, collapse if the subsurface wasn't stable. Their initial surveys had indicated that it was, but they hadn't been expecting a blowout that could accelerate pore collapse. She looked around the geyser of fluid and noticed that most of the equipment fragments it had touched looked different, more greenish-blue than they should.

Is that some strange visual transmission artifact or is the liquid corrosive?

It all just added to her already heightened sense of urgency. She surveyed the area, noting the white dome of the N-12 base in the distance, and then focused on the rig again, using the *Ibeji*'s camera to zoom in on the reinforced rig cabin. She saw motion through the window. Her heart leapt into her throat. It had to be them.

They were trapped inside by fallen casing; a long and thick thirty-two-inch steel cylinder that had been vomited out of the hole by the blowout and now lay across the door. The liquid from the blowout was steadily spreading towards cabin.

Her resolve crystallized, and she thought the *Ibeji* through a leap down. A dulled throb of pain shot through her feet when it landed but she didn't stop. She rolled the *Ibeji* through and made for the broken rig, only stumbling once as she danced around the debris and the pooling fluid. She caught herself thinking excitedly again about what it could be, perhaps some new Martian fluid that hadn't been discovered before. But she shook the thought from her head, swiveling the *Ibeji*'s in turn. Only the crew mattered now. She needed to get to them before it was too late. She knew she should have paused to give Mengitsu an update, but she was too focused on getting the crew out of there.

I'm coming Femi.

When she reached the rig cabin, she maneuvered the *Ibeji* through a swift climb over its exposed underside and onto the door which had been blocked by the regurgitated casing. The roar of the blowout was deafening up close. She used the *Ibeji* to grab onto the casing, having to embrace it to get a good enough grip across its wide diameter. She tugged, and the strain of the effort saturated the haptic feedback on her body. She continued, as beads of sweat formed along her forehead and were quickly absorbed by the haptic hood, until it finally shifted enough for *Ibeji* to access the door.

She used the *Ibeji*'s hands to rip the cabin door away, and there was the rest of the N-12 crew. The three faces looked up and gradually turned from fear to surprise when they saw the bulky outline of the *Ibeji* above them.

"Oh, thank God in heaven. Help is here." Oumarou the Cameroonian logger said through his suit speakers with widened eyes, his dimpled cheeks arched up to a smile.

"Quick. Let's get out of here."

At the sound of Femi's voice and the sight of his face through the transparent helmet, Folake let out a sigh of relief that would have been a squeal of joy and a hug if the *Ibeji* had any external speakers of its own to transmit her voice or if the local radio frequency was still working. But he didn't even know it was her beneath that gray and white metal mask and frame. She froze for a second as she fought back her instincts.

We don't have time.

Folake motioned for them to climb out and lowered the *Ibeji*'s hand.

The two men helped Bibata—the geologist whose right shoulder hung limply like there had been a break or a dislocation—up into the *Ibeji*'s waiting grasp. Thankfully, it looked like her suit had not been breached. She took Bibata's other hand and hoisted her out. She was not very heavy in the reduced Martian gravity, but it was more than Folake was expecting because she'd been in orbit for so long. Bibata made her way gingerly off the rig as Folake reached down to get the others.

There was a loud piercing crack as the rig structure suddenly shifted beneath her feet.

Subsidence!

Femi and Oumarou were thrown against each other, bumping their helmets together with a terrifying crack as Folake struggled to keep the *Ibeji* steady, constantly shifting her weight to ride the wave of potential energy. The visual signal from the *Ibeji* blurred as the rig dropped down suddenly and then came to an abrupt halt. The casing rolled back toward the door, but she caught it just in time, straining with both of *Ibeji*'s hands to stop it from rolling over her and blocking the cabin door again.

Got it.

A loose canister of pressurized carbon dioxide drilling fluid, still attached to the outside flank of the rig, exploded right next to the *Ibeji*.

Pieces of shredded metal flew past with a screech like lethal birds. Folake screamed in agony as three of them hit *Ibeji's* frame, sending sharp lances of pain through her that Mengitsu's haptic feedback dampening could not completely dull. One of them had slammed into *Ibeji's* torso. She felt like there was a hot knife cutting through her stomach.

The roar of the blowout seemed to have reduced but she could still vaguely hear Femi and Oumarou's muffled voices. There was no more color to the visual transmission and the left leg of the *Ibeji* was completely numb to her, she couldn't move it. She knew something important was damaged. She could feel it. The *Ibeji's* frame would probably survive whatever it was but she didn't know if its haptic sensor system would.

No. I need to hold on.

"Go. Go now," Femi shouted at Oumarou, his voice crackling through the speaker.

Folake fought to keep holding the casing at bay, as Oumarou and Femi scrambled up toward the *Ibeji*.

Yes, get out Femi. Get out. Get back to the base.

She could barely manage to stay focused as the pain in her belly mounted. The visual transmission flickered.

Folake gritted her teeth and pushed back against both the weight of the casing and the darkness that was invading her consciousness.

She watched as Femi lifted Oumarou up so he could grab the edge of the doorway. A sense of pride filled up her heart. He wanted to help everyone first before helping himself.

Just like Mum.

Oumarou in turn, reached down to help Femi.

Hero. It's not about pain or loss. It's the willingness to risk yourself to help others.

The weight of the casing transmitted waves of pain that pulsed through her shoulders, but she held on. She let out a loud, piercing scream, but she held on. It was only when she felt the brush of his suit against the *Ibeji*'s hip as Femi clambered out of the rig cabin that she finally let go.

The central control room slowly swam back into Folake's view like it was being painted back into her consciousness with an artist's smooth strokes. The large sweeping curve of the metallic walls and screens were comfortably familiar as she mentally adjusted from no longer seeing through the *Ibeji*'s visual display.

She saw that she was attached to the railing of Mengitsu's control dock with an orange strap.

He paused when he saw she was awake; he had been talking to someone on the comms. He turned to face her. "You're back with us. Good."

The first thing she said was, "Are they okay?"

"They're fine," Mengitsu said with a smile. "Safely back at the base. And they know it was you piloting the *Ibeji*. Femi wants to talk to you."

Even though a part of her had expected it, she couldn't hide her surprise. Femi hadn't spoken to her since Earth. Not really. When she'd arrived on Nerio Station and had her first call with the surface crew, he'd grown even angrier and insisted on addressing her only by her official title. And he had never initiated a conversation.

She pulled herself closer to the railing and swallowed. "Okay."

"I'll connect you."

Mengitsu switched the communications line open and drifted away toward the exit. He was pretending like he had something to do, but she knew he was really just giving her some privacy.

There was a click. And then one of the screens flickered to reveal Femi, bright blue light reflected on the dome of his clean-shaven head.

"Folake, are you okay?" The earnestness in his eyes and honest emotion in his voice were enough to make her own eyes brim with tears. It had been so long since they'd just . . . talked.

"I'm fine." She slid a finger along her hairline, pushing it into the base of her afro. "How's Bibata?"

"She's fine too. Resting and healing. Oumarou is making her a cake. We're all still processing what happened. And thinking about Natukunda."

"I feel terrible. We have to inform her family."

"Yeah."

There was a brief silence.

"Mengitsu told me it was you. In the *Ibeji*. Thank you."

She shook her head. "You don't need to thank me."

"Yes, I do." Femi shifted his chair, so he was closer to the screen. "For a long time, I hated you for trying to stop me from taking this job. I hated you for insinuating that the choices I made in life were entirely because of you and Mum. I hated you for thinking I was just being reckless. I hated you for coming here to watch over me from orbit like some bloody mother hen. You made me feel so small, like I was a delicate child needing your protection. I hated you for so long that I almost forgot that I love you. I love you very much. And right now, I'm just super grateful that you're my sister and that you were up there watching out for me."

He'd caught her off-guard, distilling their years-long silence into a few perfect words. She held back tears with effort.

"I love you too, Femi," she replied, pulling herself closer to the microphone as though it would bring her closer to him. "I always have. And I always will. I never meant to make you feel small or like less than you are. I only wanted what was best for you. But I realize now that I was projecting my own issues onto you. I was focused on the wrong things, on the bad moments. You were right all along. You are a great engineer, you love to build, investigate, create, solve. I'm the one that went into this line of work to prove a point, and I spent every moment of it being afraid that I would end up like Mum. That's why I quit field work at DeepCarbon and took an office position. And when you started following in my footsteps, I . . . panicked. I transferred all that fear to you. I kept thinking I had to protect you from yourself. But I know now that I didn't have to."

She paused to let out a long breath, relieved to see that Femi was smiling at her. She smiled back. "You know, I was going tell you all this when you got back after this drill shift," she said. "I had a whole speech planned."

He managed a chuckle. "I guess Mars had its own plan."

"I guess so. This planet *get as e be*."

Femi laughed. "Yeah. A real tough coconut."

She laughed too.

He rubbed his head. "I'm just happy I can talk to my big sister again. Even if it *is* a bit embarrassing that I needed you to save me in the end."

She shook her head. "You didn't need *me*. There would have been someone else. But I'm glad I could be there for you when you needed help."

He leaned in close to the camera so that his face was magnified. "So come now, what are we going to do about that blowout?" he asked.

"You're the one on the ground, what do you think we should do?"

He nodded, and she could tell that it was an acknowledgement of what she was doing, treating him like she would any other colleague, like an equal.

He said, "I think we should take stock of what we lost. Discuss with the other surface teams and the planning team back on Earth." He looked at her with resolve. "And then we take samples of the fluid. Retrieve any data that survived the impact, and then, we do what we came here to do. We study it, and we figure out what happened so we can make sure it never happens again."

"Sounds like a good plan to me," Folake said, and wished for a moment that she was back in the *Ibeji* so she could hug her planetbound brother from the orbit of Mars.

GAMMA

(OR: LOVE IN THE AGE OF RADIATION POISONING)

The day they met, she already knew she was going to die.

Through the reinforced lens of his radiation suit's visor, he saw her walk past his mother's scrap metal shed. She was beautiful in a fragile sort of way—an ash-covered rose blooming wild in the ruins of a world still caught in the throes of a nuclear winter. She was barefoot. Pale but beautiful in spite of the red blotches, vitrescent pustules, and slowly scabbing sores. His own skin had hardly been touched by any kind of radiation, not even the natural light of the scorned sun. His parents were one of the few that could manage to afford radiation suits. But only just.

"Hey," he called out to her. His voice forced its way through the high-efficiency particulate filters in his mask, escaping in a sort of raspy creak. "Are you looking for something?"

She turned around, apparently surprised and mildly amused.

"No. Not really. Just walking. Nothing to do. Nowhere to go."

She spoke in measured, efficient bursts, like machine gun fire.

"Oh cool." Compelled by some sensation of pure need, a pure childish desire to connect with another person in the simplest of ways, he added, "So, do you want to play with me?"

She shifted her feet. Her dirty blond hair was roughly cropped close to her head and a plastic crucifix hung limply around her neck, the custodian of her unanswered prayers. Her old frock was dirty just like her skin, covered in the same ash-mud that lay all around them mixed with fallen leaves. The same mud that now coated most of the world in a gray.

"Sure," she said. "What do you want to play?"

He smiled and silently thanked Allah. There were hardly any children in his sector of the camps, and the others like her—without suits—never responded to his attempted conversations.

"There is a place just outside the village. Perfect for hide and seek." He smiled wider, even though he knew she could not see it. "You know how to play?"

"Sure. I do. Sounds like fun."

"It is," he chimed, extending his hand to her. She took it.

They skipped off into the dusty horizon where the remains of an old military complex stood like a wounded veteran—broken but uncompromising.

They played together every day after that, in old nuclear missile silos and abandoned military staging grounds and even, once, in a fallout bunker full of desiccated, petrified corpses, on a day he'd managed to turn off the tracker in his radiation suit. He'd been scolded harshly when he returned home but he didn't care. They'd had so much fun in what was left of the world.

Some days, when she could manage it, they danced a ridiculous, corybantic dance to the music of the ruins—the crumbling and echoes and scurrying of things. She got weaker every day. More and more falling leaves flew by.

And then one day, while they sat silent on the turret hatch of a dilapidated tank, she said suddenly, "I think I'll die soon."

He felt a sadness his twelve year old heart could not fully articulate.

"Has summer been fun for you?" she asked him with a smile.

"Please don't die," he replied tearfully. "You can have my radiation suit."

She placed her hands in his, on the padded polymer gloves of his radiation suit, and looked into his eyes through the clear visor. She shook her head. His tears fell freely like raindrops. Her eyes stayed dry. He looked her over, took her in, not as a playmate but as a dying friend. The pustules on her skin were slowly leaking. She was rail-thin. Almost cadaverous. She reminded him of his grandmother just before she had died. He cried some more.

She tilted her head and said, "Come on. Let's get married. It's what people in love do."

He jerked up, surprised. "You love me?"

"Yes, I do."

He stopped crying at that, raising his head to look into her eyes. The glistening hazel orbs set into jaundiced yellow pools held a look of happiness that defied her suffering to extinguish it.

In the haze of strange emotions a memory came to him, the sort of memory that comes unbidden in strange moments and is steeped in intense feeling. It was a memory of something his grandmother had said once which he'd only vaguely understood but which had stayed with him, idealized and polished with sentimentality. It was something about love and sin. Love was like sin, she'd said. It did not matter how big or small it was or how it had come about or where or why. In the eyes of God, sin was sin just as love was love. And all sins are equal in the same manner that all loves are equal. It was something like that. He was sure it was something like that. And so, buoyed by the warmth in his chest, the swirling in his head, and the piercing look in her eyes, he said, "I love you too." And it felt right.

She gripped his gloved hand tight, and they both stood up, smiling first and then laughing as they clambered down the broken tank. Leafless trees poorly silhouetted by an almost blotted sun stood behind them as they walked hand in hand into the remnants of the military facility, searching the ruins for any two things they could use as wedding rings.

GANGER

1 Infimum

Among the Yoruba people, it is said that Olofin Ogunfunminire of Awori, the famous hunter who gave up his place of honor in the palace of Oduduwa at Ile-Ife for little more than the opportunity to seek out new hunting grounds, eventually lived to such an advanced age that his body could no longer keep up with his skill and desire. His bones ached, his muscles sagged, his eyes dulled, and his hands trembled when he took aim. He became too weak to carry his own weapons, too easily disoriented to navigate his way through new forest paths, too slow to stalk and chase down sprightly deer and palm civets and wildfowl and boars. And so, at last, one day when he attempted to rise at cockcrow and felt the full betrayal of his own body, the final moment of realization settled upon him. The once-spirited man was overcome with sorrow, for life had held no greater pleasure for him than the thrill of the hunt. He hid himself away in his hut near a small hill in Iddo, refusing visitors, gifts, food, the

pleadings of his own children; declining to participate in life itself. He stopped shaving his beard, stopped polishing his weapons, and only washed himself when he could no longer endure his own odor. He spent those days angry and sad and alone, weeping bitter tears for what he had lost, what had been taken from him.

Two days before her seventeenth birthday, Laide Haraya tried to kill herself.

She only failed because the Legba-6 sub-cranial interrogator sitting just above her spinal cord detected both the flood of distress signals coursing through her nervous system and the significant disruption of base electrical activity within her cerebral cortex due to hypoxia, via the embedded neural dust in her brain. Her rapidly rising heartbeat, the bright lights flashing behind her eyes, and the popping sounds in her head as she slowly slipped away from consciousness—all were inferred from a mathematical model, the probabilistic solutions to which all converged at one solution: *one minute and fifty-three seconds until death, plus or minus twenty seconds.*

The exception triggered Legba-6 to send a priority-1 alert through the distributed dataspace of the city, an electronic cry for help issued at the speed of light. It instantly repurposed the nearest available android programmed with a medical subroutine suite—meddroid LG-114— which had been assisting Mama Peju, Laide's elderly neighbor, through her stroke recovery for the last three weeks.

The instant its quantum processors were seized by Legba-6 active control, LG-114 stopped feeding Mama Peju her thick brown unsweetened akamu. The droid dropped the spoon halfway between the bowl and Mama Peju's open mouth and spun round, leaving a mess on the floor. It ran right through the solid white graphene wall separating Mama Peju's assigned living unit from the one Laide shared with her parents. The action was so unexpected, it left the old woman shocked and slack-jawed with unswallowed pap dribbling down the sides of her mouth.

LG-114 reached Laide just as her muscles stopped twitching and went slack. With smooth, geometrically precise motions of its articulated limbs, and using a scalpel extruded through the smooth silicon surface of one of its fingers, LG-114 cut the faded green and yellow Ankara cloth Laide had rolled and tied into a crude noose. LG-114 pulled Laide down, braced her head and neck, allowing normal blood flow resume to her brain. It calculated the time it would take to get her down the elevators and through the connecting tunnels to the only medical center in Isale, the migrant section of the city. The result was beyond the margin for acceptable risk without immediate endotracheal intubation. LG-114 engaged its emergency flight protocol. There were no windows wide enough to fit an adult-sized human body and so it expanded the one in the wall, tearing the frame and the connected graphene walls away with little effort before activating its jets and taking to the skies along an optimized trajectory, a perfect parabolic arc, with Laide nestled in its arms like a sleeping child.

LG-114 returned to Mama Peju's side exactly four minutes and twenty seconds after it left, having effortlessly inserted itself between Laide and the death she desired. LG-114 had only suffered superficial damage—scrapes and tears in its synthetic silicone flesh from the jagged edges of the wall breaks and a hole in its back where the emergency jets had burned through, exposing the metal chassis beneath. LG-114 cleaned up the mess it had made in its haste, helped Mama Peju finish her food and get into her bed, and then auto-scheduled itself for repairs in four hours at the level 1 maintenance hub where, given the timing, it would also receive its daily software update.

The first thing that Laide did when her consciousness returned was cry. Her body was racked by heavy sobs that hurt her bruised neck as she looked up at the sterile white ceiling of the crowded medical center. Her mouth and throat burned, like they had been scraped raw with sandpaper. The low, steady beeping of monitors made strange music in her ears.

At the sound of her awakening, her anxious parents rushed to her side and leaned down to envelop her in awkward embraces. Her father was crying too; she could see teardrops lingering just beneath the frame of his glasses before they descended onto his chubby cheeks when he came up to kiss her forehead. Her mother was less tearful, more vocal. She draped herself over Laide thanking Olorun effusively in loud, ringing Yoruba, for saving her daughter's life. And then her gratitude shifted quickly to questioning that hinted of judgment.

"But why did you do this?" she asked. "I don't understand."

Laide tried to open her mouth, but a fresh bolt of pain radiated out from her jaw to her neck and the back of her head, forcing her to stay quiet.

Laide's father touched her mother's bony wrist and whispered, "Not now. Not here."

And so, they remained there in an uncomfortable group hug, ignoring all the other patients in the packed open ward until a meddroid with an almost kite-shaped head and long arms came up to them. Its entire body was smooth. Its interior metal interior chassis completely covered with a flesh-like silicone that gave all the droids the appearance of animated dolls. Its head and hands were alabaster white, while the rest of its surface was shaded a light gray to give the appearance of clothing.

Laide's parents pulled back as the six-foot tall automaton scanned her with its two beady black irises, ringed electric blue.

"Laide Haraya, migrant code OA-X139-2096, I am LG-496, your doctor. You suffered brief hypoxia, but your vitals are all stable now, and there is no permanent brain damage. You have some irritation and two minor lacerations in your pharynx from the intubation. These should clear up on their own in a day or two. Since you are now fully conscious, you have been physically cleared. Your dataspace profile has been flagged as *at-risk* and the appropriate adjustments made to your neural thresholds. Please fill in the forms provided." The droid pointed with a rigid white finger to a screen that had extruded from beneath the pro-grammable material bedframe. The screen blinked blue, like the artifi-cial limbal rings around the droid's irises.

"Counseling is recommended but not compulsory. Please indicate on the form if you wish to be registered for counseling. If so, a session will be scheduled for you. If you decline, you will be released in an hour. That is all."

And with that, it pivoted around and ambled on to the next bed without waiting for a response.

Laide shook her head and grit her teeth until she couldn't hold back anymore. The stream became a flood as bitter tears ran freely down the side of her face.

"Laide please . . ." her mother started, making to step toward her, but Laide pushed out a palm to stop her and turned away. Laide looked across the expansive space of the medical center's emergency ward until she thought she could see the smooth blue and white surface of the city skydome through a solitary window at the far end of the wall.

There were no privacy screens or isolation tents for any of them. *What use is privacy in a city where your own brain is always spying on you?* They were all just data points for the system to parse and analyze and correlate and coordinate as efficiently as possible. They only mattered when they did something unexpected, unusual, something beyond the pre-set threshold parameters of the Legba-6 system.

Something like trying to kill myself.

Ever since her family had come to Legba city, when she was still a thumb-sucking toddler with knots in her hair and bright lights in her eyes, everything she did was controlled, every molecule of air she breathed was sanitized, every movement she made was restricted, every ray of light she saw was filtered, everything she needed was provided, and every risk she tried to take was mitigated and managed, all by Legba-6. Within the dome, everything was artificial. There were no sunsets, no flowers, no trees. Just graphene walls and metal piping and perfect clear glass. And there was nothing meaningful for the inhabitants like her to do except produce entertainment for those who ran the city, the citizen-investors that had created Legba-6 who lived in the other side of Legba city, in Loke. There was no need for labor in a city where everything was automated, restricted, controlled. Where everything was managed by the droids and drones and mechs and machines following the prescribed calculations of Legba-6. There was nothing to do except exist and obey. Eat, shit, sleep, and entertain. Like birds in a cage.

What is the point of it?

How can they live like this? How can anyone?

Her parents had chosen this life, but she hadn't. They said life outside the city was impossible and that it had all come to chaos in the world beyond, but all she remembered of that world outside were the trees and the wind, and the flowers, and wild streaks of coquelicot that ran through the low clouds at dawn, and the mesmerizing view of a starry night sky. Some said there were other cities, cities run by people less obsessed with efficiency; where people lived fuller, better-shaped lives. Cities that had found ways to live more naturally despite the dangers in the air and from the sea. She'd heard of them, seen the rumors online. But she had no idea how she could get to them even if they were real. No one in Isale - on her side of Legba city - knew. Her parents had brought her here, and there was no way to leave. She'd never even been given a choice. She'd tried to escape the city twice when she was fifteen, even though she had no idea how she would survive beyond the dome if she made it that far. The first time, she'd tried stealthily following behind a group of droids and the second, she'd tried to rappel, with a homemade rope, off the side of a tower. But her own mind betrayed her before she even completed the first step in either plan. Just like it had when she'd finally given up and tried to end it all. Nothing that happened to her was a result of her own decisions. And nothing would ever be.

There is no point. No point to any of it.

Legba-6 wouldn't even let her die.

It's all meaningless.

I don't want to be here.

I don't want to live like this, stuck in cage, just another variable for some computer program to optimize.

Laide closed her eyes, shutting out the view of the dome and the other patients and the white walls. The darkness behind her eyes felt tangible and liquid and sticky, like coal tar. It clung to her like a second skin, getting heavier and heavier with each painful breath she took until finally, she screamed, expelling as much of the pain and anger and frustration and despair as she could until her throat was raw and tender.

An array of heads around the ward turned to stare at her but she didn't look at them. LG-496 turned to her too, scanning, but it didn't approach, it simply continued attending to another patient when it determined she hadn't screamed because of physical pain. Mouth shut, she found it was hard for her to breathe. She opened her eyes and started to hyperventilate. Her hands trembled and her teeth clattered against each other.

Her parents exchanged looks of worry as they approached cautiously until they could touch her again. This time, she let them, because she didn't have the energy to resist any more.

"Don't worry, Laide," her mother said.

How can I not?

"Everything will be all right," her father added.

No, it won't.

Legba-6 was supposed to protect them, give them safety and stability in a place they had come to after fleeing global disaster but all it had done was make her life meaningless. She longed for her childhood memories of nebulous, half-remembered things like the touch of hibiscus and the sight of a real sunset. Anything that would make her *feel* something more than the steady emptiness. The city had left her empty of joy, of will, of everything. Even the feel of her mother's hand on her head and her father's rough palm on her shoulder as they tried to comfort her felt cold and lifeless.

I refuse to live like this.

And so, on that hospital bed in the emergency ward, Laide Haraya resolved to do two things.

First, she decided she was never going to let anything make her cry or scream like that again, no matter what.

Second, she resolved to live. Truly live. She would find a way to finally escape Legba-6's monitoring and control. No matter how many of her attempts were thwarted. No matter how much effort she needed to put in. No matter how long it took.

No matter what she had to do.

2 Intersection

One day when the sun was high in the sky, and the wind was whispering wisdom to those who knew how to hear it, the once-great hunter Olofin Ogunfunminire was sitting on a cane chair outside his hut by the hill. He was chewing a wad of tobacco and staring off glassily into the distance when he saw a young babalawo passing by who had ornate white chalk marks on his face and a bulky load on his shoulders. From the markings and from his aura, it was immediately clear to Ogunfunminire that the babalawo was a person of great knowledge for he bore the marks of one touched by Elegba, the messenger Orisha.

The stories go on to say that Ogunfunminire called out to the babalawo, and when the babalawo halted and gave the great hunter his attention, Ogunfunminire, explained his plight, the cause of his unhappiness. Ogunfunminire asked the babalawo if he had any wisdom or charms that could help him return to the glory of his hunting days, something that would help give his life meaning again, no matter the price.

The accounts of this story differ on what happened next and when exactly it happened. Some say the young and powerful babalawo initially refused to respond and continued his journey but returned on the next full moon to give an answer. Others say the young babalawo first asked for some water to drink and then gave his answer. Still others say that there was no delay, because the babalawo had foreseen the intersection of their life paths and was already expecting the encounter and the query and had come with an answer prepared, which he promptly gave. There are still other accounts. But all of them agree on these two things:

One, when the babalawo responded, he first smiled and looked into the old man's eyes.

And two, the answer he gave was "Yes."

"Do you want to apply for a marriage assignment?" Laide's mother blurted out as they dug into the lumps of cold eba and ewedu soup that the fooddrone had delivered a few minutes before sunset. It was two years since her attempted suicide.

Her father didn't even look up. He continued to roll the yellow lump of eba between his fingers into a ball, pressed a space into its middle, and dipped it into the viscous green soup, scooping some of it up and swallowing the whole thing in one go.

So, they finally want to get rid of me.

"No," Laide said, dropping the lump of eba in her own hand back onto the plate. "I don't want to be matched to a husband."

She didn't want to be matched to anyone, she wasn't attracted to men or even women in the way that others were; she wasn't attracted to anyone at all. She wasn't even comfortable in her own body, and so the thought of intimacy with someone else's drove her to near panic, but she didn't say that because it would have probably broken her mother.

Laide's mother, Kemi, was a quiet and awkward woman who liked things to go exactly the way they were expected to. Like most others of her generation, she'd seen what the world was like before they'd made it to the city, before Legba-6, before order and stability were imposed on the millions of people fleeing floods and poisoned air. Laide had heard all her mother's harrowing stories, but they seemed like tales from long

ago, a different life, a different world, one she had no experience or recollection of. They'd been in Isale for almost two decades.

"Mama Peju's grandson, the one you used to play with sometimes
when Peju came to visit, he just got married, did you know?"

Laide shook her head.

"Legba-6 matched him with a very nice girl, I think her name was
Debola or something like that. Yes. Debola Alakija. Good family. Good
genes." She looked to her husband who nodded in encouragement, and
then back to Laide. "Mama Peju said they are very good together, they
understand each other. They had a very high compatibility index so I'm
sure Legba-6 will find someone in Isale for you that is—"

"No," Laide repeated, and she slowly pushed her plate away. She
didn't shout or change her tone. She always tried to be reasonably re-
spectful to her parents, even when she disagreed with them. *Especially*
when she disagreed with them. It was a Yoruba thing.

"I don't want to be matched or assigned to anything or anyone. I just
want to be free," Laide said as she dipped her hand into the distilled
water in a silver washbowl at the center of the table.

"Ah. Not this freedom wahala again."

Laide's mother looked back at her father for more support, but he
simply stared back at her and shrugged his shoulders. Her father Saliu
used to be a boisterous man when she was younger. Whenever he
finished his assigned work-shifts making virtual games to amuse and
entertain the rich citizen-investors who lived on the other side of the
city, in Loke, he'd come home and create his own three-dimensional
virtual environments, full of trees and plants and colors and sounds and
improbable creatures that he said were based on creation myths and
stories his own mother had told him when he was young. Sometimes,
too, he would go up to the rooftop to talk and drink with his friends
in the social area of the tower, the only place they were allowed to

congregate outside of assigned work. Laide had seen some of his creations when she was younger. She still had a few recorded on her tablet. They had made her think he was like her too, full of yearning for something more than the standard-issue life that they had in Isale. But he had changed once she'd hit puberty and began asking him hard questions about why they couldn't leave the city, why they couldn't live more richly, deeply, fully. He'd become less eager to engage with her, to show her things, to answer her questions. After her first failed escape attempt, he became soft-spoken. He no longer created his fanciful virtual environments, but he still drank with his friends. Perhaps even more than he used to.

"You are free enough," he said to Laide.

Her mother jumped in. "Exactly. You are free to apply for marriage whenever you want." She paused and reluctantly added, "Or not at all. You can choose. But we really think it would be best for you to find someone and settle down."

"Free?" A small sneer escaped her despite her best efforts. "Am I free to leave this tower? To explore? To grow my own food? To get out from under this dome and sleep outside under the stars? To die?"

Her mother flinched and shook her head. "Don't be unreasonable, Laide. There are real dangers out there, and you know it. You are free within reason here. Marriage will be good for you. You should try it. Or at least request to be assigned a job at the base to give you a sense of fulfillment. It's not good to just stay here at home doing nothing."

"Sense of fulfillment?" Laide threw her arms out to the side. "How do I get a sense of fulfillment from making silly digital distractions for other people to amuse themselves?"

Laide heard her father grind his teeth. "Don't mock what we do, young woman," he said, putting down his eba.

"Fine. I'm sorry. Maybe that's enough for you but it isn't for me. Can't you understand that? I want to be able to choose to live in a way that matters to me. I want to be able to plant seeds in soil and grow something real and tangible in the world. Something I can smell and touch and taste, not just videos and streams. Not things that feel hollow and pointless."

"Everything we need is provided," her mother said, exhaling deeply with exasperation. "You should be grateful that you don't have to labor for your own food and clothes and shelter. You have a good life here. And you are free to enjoy it, but you are too stubborn to let yourself. I don't know what is happening inside your head."

Laide leaned back in her chair, her eyes wide. She'd had enough.

"If I am so free, then please just let me be. I said no." Laide stood up and went to the door, painfully aware that all her emotions were being transcribed to code by the tiny nanobots in her brain and analyzed by Legba-6. Luckily, Legba-6 didn't care about familial harmony or personal happiness so there would be no thresholds violated.

"Where are you going?" Her mother asked the question like she was firing an arrow.

"To the rooftop. I want to be alone for a bit." Laide paused and shot a backward glance to see that her mother was about to rise and follow, but her father reached out and took her wrist.

"Leave her," he said. "Maybe she just needs some time to think about it some more."

Laide shook her head.

What I need is a drink.

She made her way down the corridor of the tower as her parents resumed their meal.

They don't understand, she thought as she walked away, *and they probably never will.*

She swept past several other living units: Mama Peju's, the one occupied by the nosy Gwanle family, and one—the only one—with a blinking red light-sign on the door indicating that it had been unoccupied for more than three weeks, ever since the occupant Mallam Rabi'u had passed away peacefully in his sleep. She reached one of the main vertical highways and pushed the thin gray button set into the wall to summon one of the elevators.

My parents. Neighbors. All of them. Can't they feel something isn't right? Don't they miss the sun and the sky and the soil beneath their feet? Don't they want to be able to do more than just what some algorithm tells them to do?

An elevator arrived with a gentle ding and its gray metal jaws yawned open to receive Laide into its cavernous space, which was larger than most living units. It was surprisingly empty. The walls were ribbed and embossed with an elaborate pattern of stripes and dots that probably meant something to someone, but not her. She entered and keyed the numbers 5-9-1 into the panel. The door closed and the elevator began to move so subtly that she almost didn't notice the motion except for the increased pressure in her ears.

When she arrived at the rooftop level of the tower and the doors opened again, her ears popped. Laide opened her mouth, elongating her jaw and rubbed her ears to equalize the pressure. She exited into an open area where rows of compact programmable material tables and chairs sat, protected by a light-barrier overlooking the geometrically precise arrangement of the city's towers and its interconnecting tunnels below. There were two utilitydroids moving about, serving drinks to the few sparse patrons at the tables. She noticed that there was only one person sitting alone, a young-looking man with a large puff of hair like an explosion on his head. All the others were in pairs or groups. Most of the residents who drank didn't like to drink by themselves.

Laide looked to the western edge of the light-barrier where she'd made her second attempt to escape the city using a makeshift rope. One of the utilitydroids had intercepted her before she even crossed the array of light sensors.

Fucking Legba-6.

She looked up at the surface of the skydome as she went to an empty chair and sat down.

There was a hint of orange running through it to indicate that it was sunset even though the material of the dome didn't let in the full spectrum of natural light. It used internal emitters to simulate what was absorbed or reflected externally.

Fake sky. Fake city. Fake life.

She looked down and scanned around. There were other towers just like hers, so close together that she could almost see what those other residents were drinking on their own rooftops. In the spaces between the towers, she spotted flashes of a shiny blur of buildings, like seeing through a heat haze. It was Loke, the other side of the city where things were supposed to be more elegant, less crowded, more beautiful. She couldn't really see anything of it, only rough shapes, thanks to the magneto-optic screen. Besides, looking between buildings was like peeking out through the mouth of a monster, seeing between large wet teeth. Laide wondered how they felt—the people of Isale who lived in the towers directly adjacent to Loke. How did it feel, always seeing the boundary of the citizen-investors domain, always blurred from their view by the magneto-optic screen, always looking at a warped, dreamy version of the place they could not go? Probably not too different from the way she felt looking up at the skydome.

Laide exhaled slowly through her mouth and focused back on the skydome, clearing her mind. After her suicide attempt, she'd dedicated herself to finding out as much as possible about how Legba-6 worked. She didn't even remember when it had been installed but she knew the interrogator device in her head could monitor all her brain activity, just like it did for everyone else, and that it only actively responded to deviations. Legba-6 used a principle called "management by exception." She'd read in online forums that because of that system design philosophy, which meant Legba-6 only detected things that deviated from its expectations and predictions, it was theoretically possible to hide herself by flooding her mind with memories so powerfully that it seemed she was reliving them while simultaneously controlling her breathing to keep her body calm despite what was happening physically around her. The incongruity posed a difficulty to Legba-6 since it could not always distinguish between reality, dreams, and memories—it was all just brain activity to the interrogator. If the memory was strong enough, then Legba-6 could not tell if it was real or not, creating a contradiction in the interrogators output and Legba-6 could not be sure if it was an exception or a data error or if the person was just daydreaming. That uncertainty created a gap in its response time. That gap was what she could exploit. So, she did. She'd turned that theory into practice and was now fairly adept at it. It took conscious effort, and it was extremely difficult to do anything else requiring motor skills while she was in that state, but it was doable, managing two contradictory perceptions in her mind at once. Like being in two places at the same time without ever having to do anything more complex than closing her eyes and focusing intently.

She did it now, focusing on her most precious memories of childhood. A memory of a day her mother had taken her to the park or the forest reserve, she wasn't sure. She must have been about two years old at the time and the memory was nebulous, filled with flashes of sensation but little tangible detail. She wasn't even sure it was a real memory. It could have been induced, reinforced by her wanting it to be real and by images she'd seen online and by telling herself that it had happened, conflating some real event with other thoughts, desires, imagery, to weave something potent she could hold on to. But it didn't matter. The uncertain nature of the memory was exactly what she'd found worked best for hiding her thoughts from the probing electric eyes and ears of Legba-6. Unclear, wispy images of green grass and a sensation of touch came to her. Her mother's hand encasing hers. A walk or a run through a blur of green. Where was it? She couldn't remember. Perhaps she'd never known. Perhaps it'd never happened. But she remembered the towering trees, the smell of grass and wet soil, the brightly colored flowers, the sound of wind as clearly as any reality she could be sure of. And above it all, a many-splendored sunset.

Breathe slow. Don't let Legba-6 infer anything unusual.

Laide opened her eyes without letting go of the memory and doing everything she could to not think about what she was about to do.

Images of the sun and trees and flowers from her memories seemed to be superimposed over reality, over the view from the rooftop. There were tree trunks between the tables, flowers weaving through the hair of the guests. Elements from her loose recollections overlaid atop the present like a kind of augmented reality. She stood up and walked toward the light barrier. Slowly and calmly. The superimposed images began to fade but none of the droids had noticed or intercepted her. The interrogator in her brain hadn't realized what was happening yet. She kept going, inching closer and closer to the barrier. A wave of lightness entered her head when she realized she had made it past the red light-line on the ground marking the boundary. It was farther than she had ever been. Excitement filled her, sneaking past her active memories, and she knew the dopamine and serotonin spike had given her away even before the droid appeared beside her, placing its heavy arm on her shoulder.

Shit.

It said, "Please remain within the marked social area."

Laide turned around and forced a thin smile as the images of trees and flowers and sunset dissolved completely, leaving the cold, clear vision of the droid and concrete and the dome.

"Yes. Sure. I was just stretching my legs. Got distracted."

The droid's expression did not change. "Would you like a drink?"

She nodded. "I'll have palm wine, with ice."

The droid stepped in front of her and nudged her in the direction of her table. "You will be attended to shortly."

She went back and sat down.

At least I made some progress today.

None of the other patrons had paid much attention to her interaction with the droid or to the fact that she had actually crossed the lightline.

They are the ones truly distracted. They're all too distracted to notice anything.

The man who was the only other solitary patron had left, and there were only clusters of people at the tables now. She was the only one sitting alone. She watched them talking and gesturing and laughing with varying degrees of animation as a thought flitted through her head, bouncing around like a ball.

These people. My parents. My neighbors. Even Mama Peju. They're all happy or at least grateful to be here. Content. Is there something wrong with me? Am I the strange one? The only one who can't accept her life?

Her palm wine arrived in a tall, sweaty glass. Floating in it were two small spheres of ice that looked like they, too, were made of glass. They reflected and refracted the last of the simulated orange light from the dome as she swirled the glass. She sipped the palm wine slowly, savoring the sweet and milky and slightly sour flavor.

By the time Laide left the rooftop, night had fallen, and the dome had fully darkened. The rooftop was crowded now. More people had finished their dinners, had finished putting their children to bed, had decided to come up.

She'd had two glasses of palm wine and was feeling a little bit less unhappy than when she'd first come up, but she didn't want to spend any more time than she had to surrounded by people who seemed so content with a life she could barely endure. She rode the elevator with two other residents back down to level 311, where the living unit she shared with her parents was located.

She had just stepped out of the elevator when she heard a series of dull thuds come from the unoccupied unit next to Mama Peju's. She froze. The sound continued and then stopped. She turned to look and was surprised to see that the lights of the unoccupied unit were on—there was a diffuse white brightness peeking from the space between the door and the floor. The red lightsign indicating its vacancy was still blinking, and there'd been no notice from the system of transfers or arrivals, which all the residents on level 311 should have gotten. New occupants were almost unheard of, people hardly ever came to the city from outside anymore, but the unit would probably be allocated to a newly assigned couple eventually. She cocked her head. Curious about the sound - something so unexpected, so unusual, and perhaps a little bit of the encouraged by the palm wine, Laide went up to the door. There was a sound like scraping or dragging. Someone was inside. Laide felt a rush of excitement, she wanted to know what it was. She paused and stepped back, summoning the dreamy memory of the day her mother had taken her to the park or the forest reserve again, and she superimposed it on reality before Legba-6 triggered an alarm.

Focus on memory. On wind. On joy. On the bright pink of hibiscus.
She took a series of deep breaths before pushing against the door.
Breathe.

When she did, she was surprised again at how easily the door gave. It had been broken in . . . or left open.

Focus on memory just like on the rooftop. Breathe slow.

She entered.

The unit was just like the one she shared with her parents. Small. Very small. With smooth white graphene walls that held air in the wall to buffer temperature changes. There was a black, programmable, nano-material couch in the middle of the central space. Its surface rippled gently like the surface of a lake as the nanoparticles adjusted continuously to micro changes in the environment. A dinner table also made of black programmable material was set in the corner next to the drone delivery hatch. Plain white floors. But these floors bore marks—a trail of dark scratches. Something heavy had been dragged in and through the unit to one of the walled-off private areas in the back.

Laide paused again and exhaled slowly, scratching at her forearm. If she panicked, Legba-6 would intervene before she could find out what was going on.

Clear your mind. Focus on green leaves. On orange sky. Breathe slow.

Laide followed the trail and in a few steps, she rounded the corner out of the tiny central space to face the even smaller private area. Her eyes bulged when she saw a man sitting on the floor, bent over what looked like an inactive utilitydroid, his fingers buried in its open neckport.

"What are you doing?" she blurted out. She immediately realized that she'd already let the memory of the day at the park slip, that she was no longer calm, and that Legba-6 had probably detected it.

Shit.

Not again.

The man turned sharply and then, to her surprise, he grinned at her as he put a finger up to his lips signing for silence. His teeth were shockingly white against the smooth dark brown of his skin. He was thin and wiry and young, probably not more than thirty years old, and his afro was tall and wild and unkempt, with an assortment of small tools stuck into it like ornaments. His overalls looked like the ones she had on—standard issue but weathered and torn at some of the seams. The smile lines spread and creased his whole face. Laide realized that he was the man who'd been sitting alone at the rooftop earlier.

"Please don't shout," he said in fluent but accented Yoruba.

She was so surprised at his reaction that she simply repeated her question. "What are you doing?"

"I heard your question the first time."

His Yoruba was vaguely French-accented. He was probably Cameroonian or Togolese.

Laide shook her head. "Look. I don't know what you are doing or why or how Legba-6's thing in your brain hasn't detected it, but I'm sure you already know mine has and that it will send a droid soon."

"No, it won't," he said, so confidently that Laide thought she must have misheard him.

"No droids coming, although people might be a problem. That's why I need you to please not raise any alarm." He pulled his fingers out of the droid's neckport and stood up. "Bloody hell. I knew I should have locked that door. This was supposed to be quick."

She shook her head quizzically. "What do you mean there are no droids coming?"

The man laughed and tapped his breast pocket. "Dataspace signal blocker. Ten-meter radius. Well, more accurately, it's a signal looper. Legba-6 would flag an obvious block immediately. It's called an anansi device, after the Akan trickster god. Cool right? All the buffer brain activity in your interrogator, from the moment you came within range of this unit, are being resampled and looped on top of each other. Mine too. It's a jumbled mess of thought patterns. Legba-6 probably thinks we're dreaming. The anansi only works for about twenty minutes every twelve hours though and it can't be used at the same time every day, else the pattern becomes predictable. Legba-6 is very good at picking up on patterns."

That sounds just like what I try to do consciously—resampling and superimposing old memories to confuse Legba-6.

Laide briefly wondered if he was lying. But the fact that they were still talking and had not been swarmed by droids stood witness for him. "How?"

"There's a group of us. We have all sorts of tricks for living free of Legba-6 control."

Her eyes widened.

Free of Legba-6 control.

The thought of it made her feel lightheaded.

He must have read the look on her face because his smile expanded, and a twinkle came to his eyes. He pulled two chips that looked like twin spiders out of his pockets. "Here," he said, "Let me show you what I was trying to do before you walked in. But maybe we should lock that door first."

Laide almost sprinted back to the living room door and pressed her hand to the flat black button on the wall beside the door. Three magnetic latches slid into the door to hold it shut.

By the time she returned, the man was once again sitting on the floor, legs crossed in front of him. He had already attached one of the spider chips to the droid's neckport and held the other gingerly behind his own neck at the base of his skull. "Okay, thanks for locking the door . . . and for not screaming." He winked. "Now watch."

He pressed the other spider chip into his neck and the light in his eyes dimmed even though they remained open. His body stayed rigid and upright and for a second, Laide thought he had done something to hurt himself. But then the utilitydroid on the floor stirred, raised its head, and propped itself up on an elbow.

"Hello again."

The voice was different, it possessed the almost screeching electronic whine of most droids, but the French accented Yoruba persisted. It was him.

She could only let out another stunned, "How?"

"Ganger chips. They're devices that allow exchange of all brain activity between a human and a droid on a dedicated private quantum network. The irony of the entire system this city runs on, in both Isale and Loke, is that while Legba-6 keeps track of everything we do, it doesn't actively monitor its own droids unless it needs to commandeer them in an emergency. They are largely autonomous, and so, if you hide your mind inside one of them, you can be too. You can think and do pretty much whatever you want when you're piloting a droid with a ganger chip, and you'll not get flagged for anything unless it's something seriously unexpected, something that triggers a major exception in Legba-6's statistical analyses. Like using a droid to destroy city property or something."

The utilitydroid that was the man rose to its feet, his flesh-and-blood body sitting still as if it had been frozen in place. "Sometimes the only way to be free is to go deeper into the prison, to become part of it."

"Who . . . who are you?" she asked, amazed.

"You first, girl. I've told you a lot of things that could get me in serious trouble. The least you can do is tell me your name."

She nodded and pushed thin braids of stray hair behind her ear. "My name is Laide Haraya. I live down the hall and I . . . I don't do much else."

"Nice to meet you Laide. I'm Issa. Issa Maigari. I used to be a programmer at the migrant management hub in Loke until . . ." The voice trailed off as the droid froze in place and—back in his biological body—Issa's eyes regained their spark. He stretched out his arms and neck.

The silence settled between them like dust, as Laide looked back and forth from the droid to the flesh-and-blood man who had just transferred his consciousness like it was any other dataspace file.

"Issa, can you get me one of those . . . ganger chips?" Laide asked. "Please."

"Why?" he asked quickly, almost like he'd been anticipating her request. "Why do you want it?"

Her ears flushed hot. She was not expecting the question even though she knew she should have. *Was it a test?* She tried to think of something that would convince him, but to craft a clever answer she would need to know more about who he was and why he was asking. And so she tried for honesty.

"Do you know what it's like to feel like you don't belong in your body? In your life? Like you aren't a real person, just an object being poked and prodded and told what to do and so nothing you do really matters?"

Issa nodded gently.

"That's how I've felt most of my life. Like nothing was right. Like nothing mattered. That's what people don't seem to understand. The opposite of happiness isn't sadness or anger. It's hopelessness. It's feeling like your life has no meaning. Anger means you have something to care about, something that matters to you. I know. I am angry now, but I wasn't before. I was hopeless. And it drove me to a very dark place." She touched the front of her neck and exhaled a deep breath. A tear slid down her cheek. She hadn't even realized she was crying. "Since then, I've wanted nothing more than to be free. To know what it's like to do something that isn't being monitored. To make choices that I know are mine, unconstrained by some silly algorithm. I want to go outside this tower. To leave the city and touch a real flower, to sleep under the stars. I don't know if that will be enough, but it gives me hope," she said, wondering if she sounded silly to him. He was clearly nothing like the other people in Isale but she wasn't sure if his personality was more like her parents'—motivated by the practical and pragmatic like trying to seize control of the city—or more like hers—longing for something more than a prescribed life, something to give him a sense of purpose and meaning and hope. Perhaps he was just somewhere in between. She pressed on anyway. "I want hope. I want to *feel* free. This life doesn't feel real. It never has. All this—living under the dome, being tracked by Legba-6, having no real work and no real purpose; it all feels like living death. Like being a thing. I want a real life, or something like it, even if it's dangerous, even if it kills me." The tears were flowing freely now, and her hands were shaking. She'd told herself she wouldn't cry anymore. But this was different. She was pleading. She felt a flush of embarrassment at that. She was pouring out all her pain to this strange man. She felt messy. Like she'd sliced herself open, spilling out her guts and holding them up for him to inspect, to appraise, to determine if she was worthy.

Please give me a chance at hope. A chance at something beyond this false life.

But his face remained stoic, hard to read. She couldn't tell if he understood or even cared.

Maybe I should have just lied.

Laide wiped at her face with the sleeve of her coveralls. "Please will you give me one of those chips?"

Issa continued to hold her gaze, face unchanged for a few silent moments, like he was evaluating something before he finally smiled and said, "Yes."

3   Supremum

The vagrant and powerful babalawo whose name is never given in any accounts of this story, gave Olofin Ogunfunminire the words of an incantation cloaked in a song as well as two small earthenware pots, each one appearing empty to the cursory eye. But woven deeply into them was a potent charm, an old magic that communed with the fabric of creation. And thus, every day before the cock crowed, Ogunfunminire would awaken early, sing the words of incantation, which was an appeal to the very essence of things, and then dip his head into the first pot. Upon doing this, his bones would rearrange themselves, his flesh would tighten, his muscles would twist into new, unfamiliar shapes, his teeth would sharpen, and his hair would grow out wild and bristling until he was transformed into a frightful and mighty young leopard. In this changed form, imbued with vigor and strength, he would run freely into the forest and hunt to his heart's content, reveling in the excitement of stalking cautious deer, the joy of chasing down swift rabbits, the exhilaration of biting into the thick necks of wild pigs. This would continue through the day up to the yellow edge of eventide. And when the sun had set in the sky, before the other true, unenchanted leopards of the forest roused to begin hunts of their own, he would carefully return to his home and dip his head into the second pot the babalawo had given him. In so doing, the transformation would reverse, and he would become a man again with

both the familiar weight of his age and the newly acquired contentment
of another successful hunt settled upon him.

Two days after she stumbled into him tinkering with the droid, Issa and
Laide met again.

They rendezvoused in the same vacant unit next to Mama Peju's,
and this time, she noticed that he made sure to lock the door. He was
wearing coveralls again, but they were white this time, and surprisingly
clean and undamaged. His afro was combed high and round. His eyes
and his voice were solemn as he explained to her what he'd been doing
that day and why.

Just like her, he had been brought to the city when his own parents
fled the rising sea levels and the increasing concentrations of CO2-T
nanoparticles that were meant to capture CO2 molecules from the atmosphere but were now replicating too fast and spreading too quickly to
be controlled anymore. A cure worse than the disease. CO2-T had made
the air around the world unbreathable. But unlike Laide, Issa was an
adolescent when it happened. Grown enough to have to carry his own
small luggage, forage for his own food, fight to defend himself. Aware
enough to understand and remember it all clearly. The blood in the
grass. The cries of anguish. The ugly smell of desperation. All of it. First
the slew of changes in the climate and then the spreading CO2-T had
conspired to turn his country into a mess, like so many others around
the world back then. They'd all come, migrants, including Laide's own
family, seeking refuge in the privately run Legba City, where billionaire
tech mogul Fisayo Daurama-Shaw had created a fortress of safety in her
privately owned and AI-managed city high on the Jos Plateau, four
thousand feet above sea level. Fisayo initially offered entry to anyone

who was willing and able to prove that they would provide some intellectual value. Skilled workers. Doctors. Engineers. Agricultural scientists. Anyone with unique know-how. Fisayo had held up her city as a model utopia, a calm center in the middle of a raging maelstrom, protected and managed by technology most governments hadn't even heard of including the skydome to keep out the rogue CO_2-T nanoparticles. Fisayo promised safety and freedom within her city, and the offer had seemed genuine. Until the migrants became too many. Too many to let in. Too many to turn away. Too many to let die. Too many to embrace without fundamentally changing the nature of her city. She temporarily froze immigration, and they began camping outside the dome, screaming, crying, and eventually, in some cases, dying.

"It was terrifying," Issa told Laide, explaining that his family had been out there for weeks, braving the cold, the stray fire of the protective gun turrets thwarting would-be violent invaders, the hunger, and occasionally sharing an oxygen tank with another family to whom they'd traded their food for untainted air, until finally Fisayo announced that she had divided Legba City in two. One section—which she called Isale—would be for the migrants, and the other, called Loke, for the original citizen-investors: a mix of "high-value" individuals with the resources to get there quickly and the investors and minority shareholders of her company who'd been invited and had their places reserved.

Laide's parents had arrived after the partitioning of the city, so they'd avoided the worst of it. She had heard some of the stories from them and some of their friends, but whenever her parents told *their* story of coming to the city, they did so with reverence, their gratitude covering up the nastier aspects of things. Issa did nothing to sugar-coat the chaos and desperation and uncertainty of the time.

"The segment of Legba City they ceded to us was basically one large neighborhood that had been rapidly modified by machine labor into this." He swept his arm across the room. "Towers to store us like spare parts. Plain. Ugly. Crowded. Many of them still under construction. Nothing like the images we'd seen on broadcasts of homes and gardens and fountains and the like. They kept all that for themselves, on the other side, in Loke," he said, sitting with his legs crossed in front of him on the floor and staring intently at her like he was a meddroid scanning her brain. "And then they used the magneto-optic screen to block us from even looking at it."

She noted the anansi device sitting like a tiny sentry in his pocket, his own shield against the omnipresent eyes of Legba-6.

He explained that he and his family had moved into Isale where the promise of safety still held but the promise of freedom did not. Then Fisayo had automated everything because the migrants were too many, too diverse, too expensive to manage without committing large amounts of time and the efforts of her own citizen-shareholders. As a condition of entry, the migrants were all forced to accept injections of the nano-machine solution that would become the neural dust with which they could be monitored and managed remotely and efficiently using Legba City's army of machines and the ubiquitous Legba-6 AI. The same system that had been used to make life as easy and seamless for some of the people in Loke, executing their demands at the speed of a thought through the connected city, was now turned to use for keeping the flood of migrants in check.

"Many people were eager to accept the injection and enter. What choice did we have back then? To stay outside meant slow and almost-certain death. At least we survived." Issa turned from Laide and looked through the window up to the dome, which kept out the ever-increasing volume of CO_2-T that covered the world. "Even then, I knew something was wrong about her actions. It didn't make sense. Why take so many of us in when she could have just let us die outside?" He shook his head. "I wish I'd known then what I know now."

"And what is that?" Laide asked, her voice low as she tried not to show how curious she was.

He turned back to face her and said, "You'll see for yourself, soon."

It was the first time that Laide noticed his eyes were unnaturally bright and brown, like polished amber.

He continued. "They took me from my parents when I turned sixteen. Said I had been flagged as a high potential individual from my neural logs. Said I had a high IQ and a gift for numbers. Spatial aptitude. Abstract logic. That kind of thing. They took me to a special school in Loke to teach me things. Things that would make me good enough to become a researcher, working on ways to improve the system. I'm guessing you didn't even know they did that. Did you?"

"No," Laide admitted. She didn't. No one she knew had ever mentioned it. No one on the online forums either.

They probably don't take enough people for us to really notice. Select few. Cover stories. Lies. Or maybe people are all just too distracted to notice.

"They do. I lived on the other side," Issa continued. "I saw what it was like. And the only thing I spent all that time thinking of was how unfair this system is. We're all trapped under the same dome, but they live as well as they can while we have to entertain them and make do with whatever they decide to give us." He smiled bitterly. "Have you noticed that Fisayo has never addressed the people of Isale since the first arrival, not even once?"

Laide shook her head. It hadn't even occurred to her until he mentioned it. She had never seen or spoken to anyone in charge of Legba City except the droids.

"That tells you everything you need to know about how she sees us and why we need to change things. Why we . . ."

Issa exhaled and paused for a long time. "Ah. Enough reminiscing. Let's get to what you came for." He smiled at her, then continued. "There are a few ways to temporarily avoid the passive, exception-based monitoring and management of Legba-6: focused memory, neural overstimulation, meditation, medication, electrocution, if you're desperate enough . . . Some of these are known and out there already, but we need more if we are ever going to make a difference. That's why we built the anansi and the ganger chips and another really cool gadget we call the leech—I'll show it to you some other time. They are tools. Tools we could use to truly avoid the surveillance of our own minds and eventually equilibrate the two halves of the city. Tools we can use to position ourselves to take over and make sure that we share resources and responsibilities fairly, so that everyone has a decent quality of life."

Laide nodded, the blood pulsing irregularly in her head like a talking drum.

Breathe.

If the anansi device fails now, Legba-6 will detect such a spike of nerves that it'd probably send a hundred droids up here.

Issa stretched out his hand, where the two ganger chips sat in his palm like tiny twin spider gods.

Laide scratched at the side of her neck.

"Take them," he commanded.

She did. They felt hard and sharp and powerful. *So strange. So small. I'm holding the power to map my mind in the palm of my hand.* "How do I . . .?"

Issa held up a palm. "You need to connect the first one to a droid, any droid, while it's being updated. You'll know when they're receiving their daily updates by the rapid blinking of the ring of light in their eyes. Just push it into their neckports. The two ganger chips acting as nodes will establish a private quantum network that runs in parallel to Legba-6's dataspace. You may need to stalk some droids for a while to establish their habits and know when they get updates. Utilitydroids work most independently, usually in secluded locations, and they are the easiest to take over and use. For example, I noticed this one came to this empty apartment for maintenance every day since the occupant died, and it got updated about the same time each day." He laughed. "I was here, intercepting it when you walked in on me two days ago. I should have locked the door."

Laide smiled at that.

"Once connected, adjust the neckport configuration like this." From his coverall pockets, he pulled out a small piece of white paper with a schematic in blue ink of what lay beneath the standard droid neckports. He pointed at three lines indicating wiring. "Just change that to this." There was a hand-drawn reconfiguration of the same lines at the base of the schematic. She'd have to swap two wires and disconnect a third. It looked simple enough.

"Once that's done, place the other ganger chip behind your head, at the base of your skull." He reached over his head and pointed with his finger. "It has bioelectrodes that will autoconnect to your brainstem and complete the private network between your brain and the droid's on-board quantum processors. Your consciousness will transfer, and you'll be able to pilot it while your body basically sleeps."

"And when I want . . . have to . . . get back to my body?"

"Just think it. Everything in the private quantum network will be under neural control, just like your body. You'll see when you try it. It feels different, being embodied in a droid but it's still you in a different body—like a doppelgänger for your mind. That's why we call them gangers." He laughed a small, awkward laugh that made Laide think that he was the one that came up with that and thought it was very clever. "You won't get tired, or feel pain, but you will be able to see and touch and hear through the ganger's haptic translation systems. I know you want to use it to explore beyond the city, and you'll be able to. Droids are allowed to go up to fifty kilometers or so beyond the dome before their behavior being flagged as anomalous. But be careful and just make sure you get back to your body before the droid's next update or Legba-6 will flag that as an exception and initiate a search. Droids don't miss updates."

Laide suddenly realized she was leaning forward, toward Issa. She settled back and said, "Thank you," as she digested all the information.

"Don't thank me just yet," Issa replied as the remnants of mirth faded and a serious look entered his eyes. "I hope you understand that this makes you one of us now. We may call on you to help us do something when the time comes."

Laide suddenly felt foolish for not realizing sooner that he'd been recruiting her. She'd let herself believe that perhaps he'd been helping her out of some sense of kindness or even pity or understanding, but she'd been wrong. He had his own agenda. Of course he did.

What are you doing Laide?

It was only in that moment, as she considered her response, that she acknowledged the insanity of what she was doing: sitting in an empty living unit with a man she barely knew beyond what he'd told her about himself, agreeing to trade some yet-to-be-determined favor for a chance to hide her mind inside a droid based on technology she didn't understand. But now she was so close to what she wanted, she knew she couldn't pull back, couldn't give back the ganger chips, no matter her reservations. Could she?

"Yes. I understand," she said before she could stop herself.

"Good." Issa nodded, his humor returning. "You'll need this too."

With a grin, he handed her another anansi device from his back pocket. "Don't want them to flag you prematurely, messing with droid neck-ports. Remember, only twenty minutes every twelve hours, and a ten-meter radius."

He unfurled his feet and stood up quickly, heading to the back room where the utilitydroid he'd taken stood upright like a watchful sentinel, a ganger chip still lodged in its neck. She followed Issa and watched as he lay on the bed, arms folded across his chest like a mummy.

"Do you need anything else?" He asked when he saw her following him.

It took her a moment to remember why she hadn't left already.

"Umm. You never told me what you were doing with that utility-droid ganger."

Issa winked and pinched his fingers. "Just a little sabotage." The light caught his amber eyes. "Which I need to get back to. Good luck, Laide. I'll be in touch. And please, lock the door."

At two-thirty in the morning, while Laide was lying in bed and staring up at the graphene ceiling, unable to sleep, she finally decided that she would make Mama Peju's meddroid LG-114 her ganger.

She choked back an ironic chuckle when the thought first occurred to her, and then she started to cough, as her own saliva was pulled by gravity back into her airways. She propped herself up on an elbow until the coughing stopped, pressed the button atop the anansi device Issa had given her and thought about it some more. LG-114 was old and hadn't been reassigned after Mama Peju recovered from her stroke. It had been left with Mama Peju as a caregiver meddroid since she lived alone and was still considered *at-risk*. Just like Laide, but for vastly different reasons. Laide wondered at the illogicality of it—Fisayo's obsession over preserving the lives and health of the migrants in Isale while limiting their choices and access to resources. It was not the way Laide imagined a visionary leader would operate. Not unless she truly saw them as being less than herself and her citizen-investors, as Issa had implied. Less than fully human. Just resources and datapoints to be warehoused and exploited and optimized. But what did Fisayo or anyone in Loke gain from someone like Mama Peju or even her deceased neighbor Mallam Rabi'u before he'd passed away? Probably nothing more than a migrant life expectancy efficiency score on a Legba-6 report somewhere. There was little thought for their happiness or their joy or their sense of purpose and meaning. Maybe Issa was right.

She diverted her thoughts back to her burgeoning plan. Since the meddroids were adaptive, it was likely that LG-114 would have adjusted its update times to match Mama Peju's typical sleep cycle. If it had, then that would be her chance. Laide continued to think about it, planning what she would say and do, walking through the steps in her mind repeatedly until she convinced herself it could work, would work.

If the system probed my mindlogs right now, how much of what I am thinking would Legba-6 be able to infer?

She slowed her breathing down first, then turned off the anansi device and tried to sleep, but she couldn't. She was terrified that Legba-6 would isolate some vagrant neuron misfiring in her brain and infer what she was planning or that she was going to mess it up when she tried to plant the ganger chip and a droid would come for her. She sat back up, fished out her tablet, and pulled up an old 3-D display of colorful, magnificently rendered mythological creatures that constantly morphed from one shape to another—one of the last artistic creations her father had given her before he stopped making new pieces—and forced herself to stare at it till dawn. If she couldn't smother the nanomachines in her own mind with blissful oblivion, she would at least confuse them.

When the skydome was finally brightened with filtered and augmented light at dawn, Laide turned the display off. Afterimages of swirling colors and wings and teeth remained imprinted on her vision for a few seconds.

Breathe.

Before exiting her room to sit quietly with her parents for breakfast, Laide exhaled and then flooded her mind with the misty memories of that day she'd gone to the park with her mother. The memories that she'd been using to confuse the subcranial interrogator in her mind.

Focus.

"I'm going to visit Mama Peju today," she announced, speaking slowly, as she took a spoonful of cold and dry ewa agoyin with barely any palm oil in it.

Her mother's head spun sharply like she'd been hit by a jolt of electricity, and her father raised an eyebrow, frozen. She'd caught them off guard but they both recovered quickly and said it was a great idea and that of course they were happy she was thinking of the old lady that used to babysit her almost a decade ago, and that it was good that she would get to spend time with someone else. They agreed it would make the old woman happy.

Laide nodded and offered them a smile, using every technique she'd read about and practiced to keep her mind distracted from what she was really planning. To stop the memory of the park from slipping.

Focus on memory. On happiness. On green. On air.

When her parents finished eating, they deposited their dishes at the drone port and left the living unit to go to their assigned jobs at the base of the tower, creating entertainment for the citizen-investors. Making virtual games, competing in games of chance, and performing live reenactments of scenes from ancient history. They seemed more cheerful than usual. Laide waited a few minutes before she dropped off her half-eaten plate as well and went over to Mama Peju's. She scratched the inside of her wrist and looked away when LG-114 opened the door.

Focus on memory. On joy.

She swept past, ignoring the meddroid that had really brought her there and stepped inside.

Mama Peju was sitting on the programmable nanomaterial couch at the center of the unit which looked like all the others but with a few unique touches which made Laide smile. She loved to see it. There were the same smooth, white graphene walls but hanging all over them were an assortment of items which Mama Peju had once told her were gifts from her husband, before he'd died. The couch had a red bead-woven cover draped on it that rattled when Mama Peju moved.

"Ah. Laide Haraya! Is that you?" she asked, her voice shrill. The right side of her face barely moved as she spoke. She was gaunt with sunken cheeks, her curly gray hair was cropped close, and she looked frail, but her eyes still twinkled like a binary star, "You have finally remembered me."

Laide ignored the spike of guilt that pierced her gut and knelt to greet the old woman in the traditional way, "I'm sorry Mama Peju, I've been having some personal difficulties."

To the far left, Laide thought she could see a faint square-shaped outline in the wall marking the repairs that had been needed when LG-114 had broken through to interrupt her suicide attempt. There was a similar outline in the central space of her living unit, which was why her father had moved the couch so that it was facing away from it.

"Hmm. Yes, personal problems. Your mother told me." Mama Peju said her brows furrowing, "It's not really my place to say ehn, but it seems you are feeling some things too much. Your internal senses are imbalanced. You need to get back your balance, come back to iwa-pele. To center. Like I taught you. Remember to take some time every day to reflect on yourself and pray so that you can be in alignment with your Orí. Your true purpose. Once you find that it will be well with you."

Focus on memory. On the feeling of the wind.

Laide didn't want to confess that she had long given up on the Ifa spiritual practice which mama Peju had taught her as a child, so she simply lied and said, "Yes. I will, ma. Thank you."

Maybe she's right, maybe I should return to prayer instead of doing this. To try to find peace in my Orí.

It had worked once, at least Laide thought it had, back when she was an adolescent. Back then, appeals to what she imagined to be her Orí, a kind of spectral version of herself floating above her head, used to provide a sense of balance of orientation in the world. But then puberty had arrived, and her body had changed in strange and uncomfortable ways making her feel like she didn't belong in it. And then came the pain of unanswered prayers when she'd fallen into her lowest, most desperate moments, the hollow echoing that had returned when she'd focused and tried to reach out for her sense of higher self, all of that had left her mind bruised and bitter and full of doubt about her spirituality.

She rose and settled down next to the old woman, the couch adjusting itself to cradle the added weight of her frame. They talked for hours as Laide pretended to be interested in the minutiae of Peju's son's marriage, petty online squabbles within the community of elderly migrants, and other assorted trivia. Occasionally, she found herself more than a little engrossed when Mama Peju slipped into a story about the time before she came to the city, telling of her travels with her husband to places like Cape Town and Bangkok and Houston. Giving little snippets of the years of freedom and chaos. They played Ayo as they talked, an old game Mama Peju had taught Laide to play. They used smooth stones as "seeds" and a wood board with circular depressions set into it—the "houses." The objective was to capture the opponent's seeds by running your own seeds counter-clockwise to try to land in an opponent's house and claim theirs. Laide let Mama Peju win most of the games.

At noon, the old woman's eyes began to droop and LG-114 stealthily came up to the couch. "It is the optimal time for your daily nap, ma." The voice was high pitched, with a faint crackle at the end of each word.

Its audio transmission system is old.

Mama Peju's eyes opened wide, and she looked at Laide. "You see? My Peju isn't anymore here but you see how this robot is taking care of me? Thank Olorun for this place and that Fisayo woman. The wahala outside this place is too much for an old woman like me."

Another one, grateful for her prison.

And then Mama Peju added, "Honestly I don't understand what happened to the world."

There was a depth of sadness in her voice that Laide hadn't quite heard before and it resonated with her.

Maybe not grateful, maybe just tired and afraid.

She nodded and followed as LG-114 took Mama Peju into her private area and helped her into bed. Laide held her hand, tracing the line of her wrinkles with a finger until her eyes closed, a small smile lingering on her lips. LG-114 retreated to a corner of the room and stood watching over its sleeping charge with its beady red-ringed eyes.

Laide rose and took a deep breath before sinking to the floor across the room on the opposite side of the bed, resting her back against the wall and keeping her eyes on LG-114 in turn.

It's just a matter of time now.

Focus on memory. On the pink and red of hibiscus.

Almost an hour passed before she saw the rapid flashing of red in the

droid's eyes like an insistent warning. Its daily update was being down-
loaded from dataspace.

Focus on trees. On air. On freedom.

She quickly switched on the anansi device in her pocket and shot
up to her feet. Pulling out the ganger chips from the fold of her coveralls, she covered the space of the room in three broad steps, her heart
pounding as she let the memory of the park that she had been cycling
fall away. With trembling fingers, she jammed one of the chips into
LG-114's neckport and hurriedly worked it into the configuration Issa
had shown her.

The blinking of the droid's eyes stopped, holding wide and bright
and just a little bit terrifying.

Laide hesitated for only a second, wondering if it would work, if Issa
was a spy or agent sent to Isale to entrap and weed out dissenters and
potential threats, and this was all an elaborate trap, with droids already
on the way to intercept and take her away. All her fears coalesced in that
split second into something cold and raw that held her sessile. But she
remembered the depth of her despair the day she'd tied that Ankara
noose around her neck; and the depth of her desire to find hope, to be
free, overwhelmed the flash of trepidation. She'd been given an opportunity to feel the opposite of all those negative emotions even if only for
a while. She was burning to no longer have to police her own thoughts.
To finally relax. To see the fields outside Legba City. She'd been waiting
for the chance for years. Besides, it was too late to turn back now. She
was committed. She reached behind and pressed the twin ganger chip
into the base of her own skull. There was a painless prick, a sense of ice
running down her spine and then her consciousness fell out from under
her, dropping into a deep, richly-textured darkness.

Where am I?

She panicked for a moment when her consciousness was suddenly returned to her in an alien package, like she had fallen asleep and woken in a parallel universe where everything was fundamentally the same but slightly altered.

She saw Mama Peju's private sleeping area through a distorted 180-degree field, from a center of vision that was about a foot higher than she was used to. And the colors of everything she saw were much more defined as though the reflected light had a sharpness and texture she had not been able to see before. There was a new sense of temperature too, like she could see the heat as well as the light from every object around her. She was also intimately aware of sounds that she hadn't heard before, strange new vibrations entering her consciousness. And some familiar ones too, like Mama Peju's gentle snoring. Nausea, or something like it, lurked beneath her throat but not the throat she could sense, a ghost throat in another body. She didn't move for a few moments.

Focus Laide. You can handle disoriented perception. You are used to feeling alien in your body. You can control this.

She imagined swallowing and, with only a thought, turned LG-114's head gently, first to the left, then to the right. There was no delay, but it felt unusual. She repeated this until she felt synchronization between her thoughts and the movements of the droid. It took Laide a while, but she finally began to get used to articulating the limbs of LG-114's steel frame encased in silicone. She moved in small, gentle steps with slow changes of hand position until she no longer felt like she was constantly about to keel over. She knew the disorientation was all in her mind, that her brain would take time to get used to controlling this new body through its old neural pathways, but the internal haptic controls of LG-114 kept her stable and upright.

When she felt comfortable enough, she raised one metal leg, balancing carefully on the other and spun around, looking at her own still flesh-and-blood body propped up against the wall, hands down by its (*her?*) sides. Her body seemed so short from LG-114's elevated view-point, the long, thin braids of hair sitting on her shoulders like a shawl. It was surreal, being displaced from her body and staring back at herself.

I'm free. Free of my body. Free of my own brain. I wonder if Mama Peju would say I am free of my Orí too.

She pivoted on one leg again, spinning back to face the bed, enjoying both the feel of pressure that the motion generated on LG-114's body and beneath its feet, as well as the realization that Issa was right. She could do whatever she wanted in this form without being flagged, at least for a while.

I'm not completely free of this city . . . yet.

Panic surged through her displaced mind when, in her peripheral vision, she saw Mama Peju stir.

Shit.

Taking long strides, Laide hastily retreated back to LG-114's prior position and stood next to her own body.

Take me back. Take me back to my body. Take me back to my body now.

She thought the command repeatedly until the world dropped out from under her consciousness again.

"Omo mi, you are still here?" Mama Peju asked, rolling onto a bony hip just as Laide's eyes shot open.

Laide let out a deep breath, surprised at how relieved she was to be back to her own mind and form where everything was comfortably familiar and under the watchful eye of Legba-6. Her stomach tightened, and she swallowed back a lump in her throat. The anansi device was still on in her pocket. She reached for the still-attached ganger chip behind her head and pulled it out, pretending to scratch an itch. It slid out as easily as it had gone in. "Ermm . . . Ah. Yes ma. You beat me five times, I didn't want to leave without asking for a rematch."

The old woman smiled and stretched out a hand. It was thin and wrinkled, but her fingers didn't shake. LG-114 and Laide both stepped forward to help her up at the same time, Laide doing her best to fight back the roil of her stomach and the dizziness at the edges of her vision. Mama Peju's smile evolved into something that was not quite laughter but came close.

"I'm glad to see you haven't lost your manners," she said. "Your parents raised you well."

Laide played three more games of Ayo with Mama Peju and won two of them. She didn't leave until she was sure that Mama Peju hadn't noticed the ganger chip attached to her caretaker droid's neck.

When Laide took over LG-114 again, it was almost two in the morning, and she did so from the comfort of her own bed, leaving her flesh-and-blood body prone and still and silent, where it *(she?)* wouldn't be disturbed till morning.

Her sight resolved slowly into the droid's 180-degree field of vision. Despite the darkness, she could see clearly thanks to the droid's visual processors, which gave her access to much more than just reflected light. She could even differentiate individual strands of gray hair on Mama Peju's head as the old woman's chest heaved beneath the covers on the bed. It was still strange. Laide's biological brain still expected everything to be less clear and to appear closer than the signals it was receiving from LG-114's processors. It would probably have given anyone else a headache, the constant mismatch between expectation and perception, but luckily, she was used to holding contradictory thoughts and images in her mind. She'd been practicing obfuscation techniques against Legba-6 for a long time.

Everything is elastic. Even consciousness.

As LG-114, she switched off the anansi device which she no longer needed since her consciousness was running on LG-114's processors, and gingerly made her way out of the private area. Mama Peju wouldn't need or look for LG-114 until it was time for breakfast in about five hours. Laide went to the door of the living unit, and exited, moving swiftly through the narrow corridor to the elevators. She paused there for a moment when she passed by the door of the unoccupied unit where she'd met Issa a few days ago. The blinking lightsign had now turned yellow which meant that the unit had been reassigned and the new occupants would arrive soon. Looking at that door, that ordinary door, accidently left open for her to walk into the miracle of what was happening now, filled her mind with a surge of joy.

I'm free. Free to see. Free to leave Legba City.

She continued into the elevator, hovering LG-114's silicone fingers over the gray keypad. She usually only went to the rooftop on level 591 for some space when she felt claustrophobic and to stare at the smooth surface of the dome. Her parents worked in base level 3 where the entertainment studios were located, creating performances for the citizen-investors of Loke. She'd only been down there once. For the first time ever, she keyed in the numbers 0-0-1 to go down to the first level, where only droids and maintenance bots were allowed and where a network of tunnels connected all the towers of Isale through gigantic access ports.

The sensation of touch was changed through the haptic processors. It was a mostly heightened awareness of pressure and temperature and friction, but with the nerve cell endings in her skin gone, so were the myriad other inscrutable things that usually came with them. It was like being partially anesthetized.

At least I can still feel.

A green light flashed out from the panel and scanned LG-114, checking for its access permissions, and then the elevator began to move with a subtle lurch.

Throughout the four-minute-long descent, all Laide could think was *thank you Issa* and *I hope I don't get caught.*

The elevator opened to a cacophonous world of metal and silicone in motion. Giant silver-skinned machines moved in predefined pathways on their massive wheels, ferrying mechanical parts into, and treated waste out of, the wide space through a thick open gate that looked like it could survive several thermonuclear blasts in the far eastern wall of the building. The gate and all the walls on every side were concave, curved away from her like the space had been inflated from within. Thousands of smaller droids and drones walked and rolled and flew across the expansive area, weaving around their behemoth cousins, each on its own journey through the network of towers, every action calculated to manage the city.

Laide stood there, her consciousness encased in LG-114 for a few terrified seconds, taking it all in before she remembered that she needed to move. She fought the instinct to hide from the machines and moved purposefully, following a procession of metal beasts that were the size of six or seven living units, each one carrying a tank of what she thought was water or oil or perhaps waste, given the sloshing sounds they made as they moved.

When she cleared the gate, she stopped following them and looked around. She was on the outskirts of the city, but couldn't see Loke on the other side of it. The citizen-investors lived in lower, less towering buildings with more living space while the array of migrant towers ran into the sky, piercing the localized cloud formations like spiteful fingers. The diffuse darkness of the night-time dome was a solid curtain above it all, and it ran far to the horizon on all sides.

In the distance, Laide spied another convoy of machines moving toward her, each of them loaded with a green mass of harvested and sanitized crops.

They are coming from beyond the dome.

She moved towards them, piloting LG-114 with measured speed until she went past the lumbering line of massive robots and then she broke into a run, sprinting toward the illuminated arc of the dome. LG-114 covered three meters of asphalt with each bounding step, and it made her feel like she was flying.

As she approached the place where the dome cut into the horizon, she could make out an opening. It appeared suddenly, a dark, nebulous yawn in the smooth surface of the dome, as another convoy of robots made their way through the sanitization chamber at the entry point.

Laide watched, trying to remember everything she'd been told as a child or learned online about the poison that lay beyond the dome. CO2-T had been deliberately released into the atmosphere as an emergency measure—an engineered viral nanoparticle meant to mitigate the climate crisis by binding itself to carbon dioxide molecules and steering them to sequestration stations based on its on-board programming. It had initially been released in a controlled environment over the North Pacific, with a carbon dioxide processing and storage hub offshore where the nanoparticles were recovered and recycled. It had worked for a while, but apparently, the replication protocols failed due to a mutation in the viral component of the particles, and it began to rapidly replicate itself, eventually escaping the control area on air currents. It spread globally, before anyone could regain control of it, until it was just part of the air, attaching itself to lung tissue, triggering a spate of agonizing pulmonary diseases and, eventually, death. In small quantities, once isolated, it could be processed and removed faster than it replicated. But that wasn't good enough to reclaim the world.

So now the dome kept CO2-T out, with every machine, crop, person, and molecule that crossed the threshold sanitized by the nanobots first. Just like she was about to.

The neural dust in my brain back in the tower.

The CO2-T in the air outside.

The nanobots in the sanitization chamber.

They are all enabled by the same technology. They are all aspects of the same thing.

Laide felt that there must be some poetry or irony to it that was barely beyond her. She kept running, pushing LG-114 to what she instinctively *knew* was almost its maximum speed, until she reached the foot of the hyperbola that the dome cut ahead of her. The doors of the sanitization chamber were made of the same material as the rest of the dome, and they adjusted to match the ambient colors of the surroundings, camouflaging itself when the doors were shut. Laide waited until it slid open with a low mechanical whine. She stepped in alongside two identical utilitydroids and a group of larger machines with massive shells that ambulated on four pillar-like legs, lurching to each side like tortoises. The door shut behind them and there was darkness for a few seconds until the chamber was abruptly bathed in red light. There was a hissing sound as a vacuum was established. She admitted to herself that even if she'd ever escaped and made it this far, she wouldn't have been able to use this exit if she were still in her own body. She wouldn't survive the lack of oxygen. After a few seconds, the light turned bright green and the large metal gate on the opposite end opened.

Laide waited for the awkward tortoise-machines and the utility-droids to go ahead and then she piloted LG-114 across the threshold. She was exhaled into a clearing of loose wet soil that bounded the curve of the dome and looked out into an open field of verdant maize stalks. Their tassels came up to just under LG-114's neck. Paths of cleared soil radiated out from the edge of the dome like spokes on a wheel. Laide looked up at the sky, the real sky, for the first time in seventeen years. A clear, bright half-moon hung low, dappling the sea of stalks with silver. There were a few low clouds with a wispy white ethereal glow like shiny smoke. And there were stars! So many stars. She had almost forgotten what stars looked like. In a sense, she wasn't sure she'd ever truly known.

Amazing. This is amazing.

The gate of the sanitization chamber closed shut behind her with a hiss of vents. The sound jolted Laide's attention back down to the loose earth and the expansive field and the hard dome. She spun LG-114 back to see that the entire outer surface of the dome was covered in an array of large gun turrets like lethal hair. She was surprised at first. From within, it was easy to forget that Legba City was originally meant to be a fortress, that the dome was designed to keep out more than just wandering CO2-T. There were no more migrants, rebel groups, opportunists, criminals, or any of the myriad detritus of the failed states that surrounded the city when the world began to fall apart. But the weapons remained. Like the stones and bones of the Paleolithic, the weapons persist long after the blood is spilled, rationalizations are forgotten, after the flesh of the dead has rotted away. The dome and its guns would probably outlive the people of Legba City.

Laide turned back to the field. The machines she'd come through the chamber with had taken one of the straight, radiating paths and had become small dots in the darkness, tending toward the moonlit horizon. The path seemed to go on forever, or at least much farther than she could see. Laide stepped forward, off the boundary clearing and into a set of tracks dug into the radiating path by the large harvester machines, turning to face the field. She touched a long stalk of corn, sliding a thin leaf blade between LG-114's fingers. It was smooth, like graphene. She thought out the scalpel from a finger in LG-114's hand and used it to cut the leaf from its sheath. She pressed it into the space above the LG-114's ear until it was wedged there, the leaf moving with the droid's head like an ornament.

She stepped off the tracks and walked into the field, drinking in the touch of nature. The leaves and tassels and silks brushed past LG-114's frame flooding her mind with haptic input. She walked faster and faster, until she was running, bounding across the field, and savoring the feeling that was so much like flying, like freedom. She was surprised at how natural this artificial body felt to her. The myriad chemical signatures were converted into smells that seeped into the deepest parts of her mind, dredging up raw emotions from linked memories. She allowed herself to luxuriate in all the sensations, the sinking of metal feet in soil, the sweet chemically analyzed scent of esters and aldehydes and chlorophyll, the rush of air, the touch of things that had grown from the earth, until she was taken back to her childhood, regressed back to a state of pure feeling where the sky and the air and the motion and the womb of nature all conspired to make the moment magic in her mind. She let out a laugh through LG-114's speakers, a choppy harsh sound that rang through the air.

It's like I'm in a dream.

Laide kept running through the field, ignoring the occasional maintenance drone that went by overhead. Like the people of Isale, and everything else in Legba City, they were too focused on their own predefined tasks to dedicate any processing power to her. She kept going until the noctilucent clouds lost their glow and sun began to peek out from below the horizon, casting pink and yellow streaks into the twilight sky.

She stopped then and leaned her head back to watch the sun rise. As it did, so did she. She was in a different, denser body but she felt weightless, inflated with a pure inarticulate joy that she had almost forgotten existed, and she flowed with that feeling, finally freeing her mind of everything for the first time.

Rooted in place, facing the sun like a flower, Laide didn't move, only heading back to Isale when the base of the solar disk finally cleared the horizon and unfiltered dawn blossomed in the sky.

4   Complement

And thus, the aged Olofin Ogunfunminire continued his daily ritual of transformation, hunting, and reconstitution, his soul constantly oscillating between being ensconced in the body of a leopard and returning to its old and diminished human shell. It is said, in every version of the story, that this went on for a significant amount of time, but the accounts do not say with any measure of precision how long this period lasted. Some, when they tell the tale, say it went on for years. Others, only a few days. But all tellers of the tale agree that it went on without the knowledge of Ogunfunminire's family and friends, and that during this time he experienced many new things beyond the joy of the hunt he had sought to relive. And how could he not, being so fundamentally changed? The stealthy approach to unsuspecting prey was joyfully familiar even in his leopard form, but now he experienced new things too. Like the iron taste of blood in his throat when he bit into raw flesh. The sense of perfect balance of his weight along an elongated tree trunk as he dragged dead deer up high up into the swaying trees. The rush of damp air in his lungs when he pounced at blinding speed with strength he'd never possessed before. And he experienced the bone-chill of a deep and ancient primal fear, something he

had never felt before, when he first crossed the river that split the forest in two. Terror that induced abience inflated his lungs when he first saw unclear reflections on the murky surface, felt the water's cold heaviness on his fur coat, and sensed the movements of crocodiles lurking below in the unknown depths. The presence of those ancient saurians, opportunistic apex predators that occasionally ate careless ones of his animal-kind taught him a new and terrible fear.

Midnight. The familiar blank-screen darkness of displacement eclipsed Laide's mind when she lay back in her bed and pressed the ganger chip to her skull for the fourth time in a week.

When she came to later, her consciousness smoothly running on LG-114's quantum processors, Mama Peju was sleeping in her usual position. Chest rising and falling steadily. Breaths steady with the fluid thrum of a low snore. A thin moustache of sweat on her upper lip.

The room was the same as always. Laide was starting to get used to it. Her stomach hadn't even felt any discomfort the last time she returned from beyond the dome at dawn and thought herself back into the flesh. After that first, glorious time outside the city, her stomach had churned violently when she awakened from the ganger experience. Her body had felt strange and alien to her after being embodied in LG-114 for hours. She'd barely made it to the bathroom in time to throw up the previous evening's drone-delivered semovita and banga soup—a red, oily mess that she hadn't enjoyed on its way in and enjoyed even less on its way out. But with each successive ganger displacement, she got more and more comfortable switching between flesh and metal bodies, neural and circuit minds. The misalignment between her sense-of-mind and sense-of-body was narrowing after every displacement. It was curious.

True, Laide had never felt comfortable in her own body, never thought she saw a representative mind-image of herself when she looked in the mirror and caught a flash of her shape. Never felt the way she imagined she should when she ran her hand along her belly and her hips. But when she was in LG-114 all of that seemed to not matter as much. It wasn't her body per se, just a shell she piloted. *Same same but different.* She was almost more comfortable out of her own body. She was pure mind in a new shell for a few hours, and she liked it.

Laide, as LG-114, switched off the anansi device and quietly made her way out of Mama Peju's unit and down the corridor to one of the elevators, where a couple, just returned from the rooftop social area were riding down to their level, eyes glazed over and glued to the screens of their tablets. She ignored them as they descended. The displacement process may have been getting easier but her eagerness to be outside the city and beyond the reach of Legba-6 hadn't abated.

Not even slightly.

When the elevator came to a halt at level 1, Laide exited back into the basement world of manic machine motion. A variety of animated steel and titanium and graphene and silicone frames lumbered and whizzed and rolled by. This too, she was getting used to. She began to walk purposefully toward the opening gigantic eastern gate when a utility-droid, seemingly appearing out of nowhere, sidled up to her, walking in step.

"Hello Laide."

Laide was startled but not enough to stop moving. There was a hint of a French accent under the electronic drawl. "Issa? What are you doing here?"

The utilitydroid that was Issa had a humorous expression on its quadrilateral face. "I was waiting for you. I knew you'd come down here at some point tonight."

Laide's steps became less confident; her pace slowed.

"Why?"

And how?

"I want to show you something. In Loke."

Laide thought that she could feel her face contort into a frown but LG-114 didn't have the right facial muscles for it. She remembered reading online that droids could be made to look completely human with all the right anatomical features, and that they very nearly were, but at the last minute, it had been decided to give them angular faces, a small adjustment that was just enough to dip them into the uncanny valley and ensure people always knew that they were not human, to prevent them from anthropomorphizing what were essentially complex machines. It worked. Laide had always found droid faces to be unsettling even though she'd never had trouble interpreting their expressions. But now here she was, mind in a droid shell, talking to another human in his own droid casing. Frown or not, something happened to her features that made her sure that Issa had registered her displeasure because he hastily added, "It won't take long. You'll have enough time to go back out beyond the dome for whatever you want to do. We'll just take a different exit."

Laide thought about it for a moment, the ambient noise of Legba City's machine circulatory system steady around them. "Is this part of the favor I owe you?"

"No. Not at all. I just want to show you something. As a friend." He spread out his droid hands. "We are friends now, aren't we?"

Are we?

Laide wasn't sure, but she'd never been to Loke before, and as much as she wanted to see the cornfields and the sky again, she admitted to herself that she was at least a little bit curious. "Yes. Fine. Show me."

The Issa-droid smiled and Laide visualized his real flesh-and-blood face, superimposed over the hard edges of the droid's.

"Follow me," he said, turning away from the towering eastern gate.

The Issa-droid moved in the direction of the tunnel network that connected different sections of the city. Shadows cast by the harsh electric lighting gave each tunnel entrance the sinister appearance of hungry mouths. Laide followed. They were swallowed into darkness, but she could still see based on the temperature differentials between the Issa-droid, the warm walls, and the cold ground. There was the steady hum of machinery and the drip of water from condensation along an overhead pipe, constant background noise. The two of them moved quickly through the tunnel, breezing past the occasional droid and autonomous tortoise-shaped transport vehicle until they came to a split in the tunnel. One way was dark and wide and flat and went as far as Laide could see, and the other led to an upward-sloping ramp where bright light cut across the ground like it had been painted across with the geometric precision of an AI-artist.

"Up here," Issa said.

They went up the ramp and into a narrow passageway. The walls were made of metal and etched with elaborate swirling designs that reminded Laide of her father's 3-D art. Lights beamed down aggressively from the high ceiling. There were sharp corners everywhere. The passageway seemed to twist and turn endlessly like they were walking inside a hollow snake. They went on at a steady pace until finally, they came to an exit door that looked like a smaller cousin of the eastern gate.

They were scanned by a red beam. The bulky metal door opened, and they emerged from behind a small metal structure that looked like a maintenance shed. Laide was shocked to see that they were surrounded by green grass, the blades glistening in filtered moonlight beneath them.

"It's artificial," Issa explained just as she realized there was no crunch of soil beneath LG-114's feet like she'd felt beyond the dome. "Looks good, but it's as dead as any of the droids."

She looked up and around her. Houses stood scattered around the grass, plenty of space between them. There was no road. Each house was either three or four stories high. No more. And while they bore a general sort of similarity in their luxury, each house was unique in some way, either in configuration or aesthetic. Some of them were red brick townhouses with wooden roofs. Others were gleaming white mansions with roman pillars and gold paneling. A few were elaborate glass and steel designs, reflecting filtered moonlight from a dozen angles. Most of the windows were darkened but a few had white and orange lights peeking out from within.

She was stunned by the sight of it all.

This is nothing like the cramped towers of Isale. Nothing at all.

The Issa-droid pointed ahead at a series of connected gaps between the houses that made up a kind of path. "Walk with me."

They walked along the false grass, taking in the houses and the neighborhoods. Laide caught sight of bold Arabic writing on a large plaque outside one of the houses, silver against black, its meaning unknown to her but its beauty undeniable. She spied a colorful children's playground in the space between two sprawling white houses, like looking through a mouth of gold-plated teeth. Above, even the dome-adjusted light of the moon looked different, more real.

"I'm sure you've heard rumors of Loke before. You already knew it was a much better, much nicer place than Isale but it can be a shock when people finally see it for themselves. It was to me. That's why I brought you here. So that you can see for yourself. See that even within the dome of Legba city there is a better way to live." Gray and white droid arms spread out to each side.

Laide took it all in. He was right. She'd heard, but this was beyond what she'd imagined. Seeing it all, the abundance of Loke, was like being shown the open palm of injustice, unrepentant and uncaring. And then being slapped with it.

"All this space for so few. All this beauty and choice and variety just for them while they pack us in like luggage in one small segment of the city's circle. Do you know the population of Isale is now almost twenty times that of Loke? Twenty times. That's a little piece of information that they hold very close to their chests. Twenty times the population but occupying less than fifteen percent of the space and consuming less than ten percent of the resources available. That's one of Legba-6's objectives, even, to keep that value at or below ten percent. It's obscene. And they know it too, if not they wouldn't have to use the magneto-optic screen to hide it. When you have to go to the lengths of manipulating the polarization of light with magnetic field interactions—contorting the Faraday effect in bizarre new ways just to make sure people can't see how well you live while depriving them of resources, you know your conscience isn't clean. It's wrong. We must change it."

"It is. But how can *you* change any of it?" Laide asked gently, being careful not to accidentally rope herself into his cause yet with a "we." Her head swiveled, taking in as much of Loke as she could. Then she looked at him: "Fisayo controls the Legba-6 algorithms that run the entire city, right? Including all the machines. Her own personal army. She could shut it all down with a thought. Besides, she has access to everyone's brains."

He spun around to look at her and, without missing a beat, walked backward for a few steps. "Yes, she does. And yet, here we are. You and me. Every system seems infallible and inescapable and inevitable until it isn't. And every technology can be circumvented. It's just a matter of will and opportunity."

They came to a clearing, where the houses had receded to form a wide perimeter around a marble fountain that occupied a space at least ten times larger than the living unit Laide shared with her parents. Laide had never seen anything like it. Bright yellow lights beamed out from under the water, giving it an ethereal shimmer. A dozen statues ringed the edge of it. They depicted famous African thinkers and philosophers from history, some of them she recognized, all of them had their names inscribed on brass set into the marble below them: Njoya, Al-Jahiz, Salau, Diop, Ajimobi, more on the other side. At its center, there was a giant robed form of a tall and stout woman with plump cheeks, an elaborate gele on a proud head, streaming jets of water cresting and falling around her.

Is that Fisayo?

The Issa-droid looked at Laide and nodded as though he'd read her mind.

Laide stared at the water rising and falling in wide arcs, catching the yellow light so that it looked like liquid gold. She could imagine children splashing noisily in it in the daytime, shouting and jumping in its spray. Something she'd never experienced in Isale. The image was clear in her mind, like one of her superimposed memories. Did Fisayo really think of herself so highly as to erect this immoderate monument?

What is the point of all this?

The Issa-droid approached her. "I told you before that Fisayo doesn't care about the people of Isale. I hope you can see that for yourself now. She is a narcissist, and I believe she always has been." He paused. "Do you know why Legba-6 tries to prolong every life in the city as much as possible? It's obvious for the people of Loke, that's what they paid for— long comfortable lives which the system is optimized to provide. But do you know why it doesn't just let the sick and elderly of Isale die?"

She shook LG-114's head, genuinely curious. *I want to know why it didn't let me die.*

"Data." Issa spat out the word like it was corrosive.

Laide was puzzled. "What do you mean?"

The Issa-droid looked away from her and up at the dome for a moment, like he was downloading his thoughts before speaking. "Okay. Let's take a step back. The interrogator sitting in your brain, your real brain, back in Isale, it's the main processing center of the self-assembling nanobots in your brain mass, the ones injected into you when you entered the city. They attached themselves to your neuron membranes and now they record all neural activity data using a parallel electrochemical signal relay to your neural pathways. The interrogator collects all that activity data from them, holds it in a buffer, screens it for deviations from a pre-set baseline, and periodically—well, unless the deviation is big enough, then it's immediate—converts it into qubits and transmits to Legba-6 via dataspace. You know that part, right?"

"More or less, yes," Laide replied.

"Good. That's important. So, you understand that right now, the system can only *record* brain activity. And trigger action when there is an exception. But think about it in system design terms. If you are trying to efficiently control a system, any system—and that includes people—then frequent and accurate monitoring and measurement are just the first step, so you can rapidly intervene based on what is going on. It is limited, reactive control. The next step, the big one is real-time modelling or simulation or emulation or whatever, the idea is the same. With that, you can take all that live measurement data and build a detailed model of the system that is always up to date and accurately predicts the system behavior—a digital twin of the system. And once you can fully observe present and predict future behavior based on that model, then you can *really* control it. Control *us*."

Laide suddenly felt very anxious. The steady sound of fountain water falling back into the pool had turned from relaxing to ominous as she started to realize what Issa was telling her.

Mind control.

Issa continued. "That has been the goal all along. Complete control of people. Build good enough real-time models of how our neural pathways inform consciousness, memory, emotions, experiences, decisions, and behavior to be able to reliably adjust them all using an improved version of the interrogator. To remotely influence thought and action at the source without having to physically intervene or get her hands dirty." He looked down, back to the fountain, eyeing the statue at the center like he was challenging it directly. "But analytical models of the human brain are incredibly difficult to parse even with the best quantum computing tools we have available, simply because we still don't really know how the brain works. Not really. But you don't always need to know exactly how something works to model it if you have enough data to throw into an algorithmic blender and see what comes out on the other side. I mean, we don't even know what consciousness is, and yet I can port it onto a droid processor with the ganger chips. That's why she's keeping everyone in Isale alive for as long as possible. The longer you all live, the more sample data she gets about the spectrum of human brain function to plug into her algorithm and improve her models of the human mind until they are good enough to use Legba-6 as a tool to control our very thoughts."

Laide shook LG-114's head again as though she were trying to shake out what Issa had just said. She'd always *felt like* she and all the other people of Isale were nothing more than data points to the system but now she finally *knew* why. Why the people of Isale had been let into Legba city in the first place. Why they were kept fed and healthy and distracted. Why she'd not been allowed to die. Still, something else Issa said was stuck in her mind.

"The ganger chips . . . you didn't come up with them by yourself, did you?"

The Issa-droid turned to her, mouth drawn back into a thin line and red-ringed black eyes trained on her. He nodded. "No, I didn't invent them. I told you I worked in research. Fisayo was developing mind emulators already. I just copied her research and modified it so that it could run on local droid processors."

The Issa-droid walked around and away from the fountain, along the artificial grass. Laide followed, still processing what he'd said. She felt faint and light-headed like her consciousness—or whatever this distillation of her essence was—had been attached to a balloon. As they reached the opposite perimeter of white and red brick houses, she returned her thoughts to what he'd said earlier about Fisayo and mind control.

"Okay. I understand what you're saying but, what's the point of what Fisayo is doing?" she asked. "We are all trapped here in the city by CO_2-T. Even if Fisayo eventually finds a way to control us all like she can her droids, what's the use? What does she gain?"

"Honestly. I don't really know her motivations for sure," Issa replied, moving purposefully in the spaces between the houses again. "I've only ever met Fisayo once myself. But from that singular meeting, and from everything else I have seen about the way this city was designed, I am certain of a few things, and I can make a guess about others. I know she is a narcissist who believes she is better than most people because she is smarter than they are—that's what she thinks anyway, and even I won't deny her genius in some areas. But you've seen the kind of historical figures she places herself in the company of. I think this arrogance extends to the way she perceives the rest of humanity—that we exist in natural intellectual classes and that the only worthwhile people are people like her—the thinkers and the scientists and the philosophers and any other 'smart' people who can synthesize new grand ideas, make elaborate things, pull off impressive cognitive feats. That's why she still screens the brains of people in Isale, searching for what she thinks are important neural markers, taking the few people that meet her intelligence criteria and putting us to work to help her further her research. It's nothing but new-age phrenology."

"And the rest of us who don't meet her criteria?" Laide asked, her mind still reeling as they cleared the scattershot houses and came to an expansive steel and glass building.

"She will probably treat them like dead weight," Issa replied. And then he added, "Look, I don't think she's some kind of cartoon villain. You need to understand that. She just has a wrong and dangerous worldview. She thinks she's smarter than everyone else. That she has a sacred duty as a genius or whatever to make a better world while causing as little damage to the 'inferior' people as possible. But you can probably already see the problem with that."

"It's immoral."

They finally stopped moving.

"Exactly. But she's certain her technology will be the optimal solution for humanity. That it will enable the so-called smart people to make all the important decisions for everyone else. As if the smart people aren't the ones that first hurt the planet with their unsustainable technologies, and then wrecked it trying to hurriedly fix their mistake with CO_2-T. If she gets her way, she'd be able to control everyone in the city and build her perfect world where the only truly free people are the people she decides can be. People like her, who she thinks can drag the rest of humanity forward into some imagined glorious future without having to pay attention to the dead weight of everyone else. The other people will just be excess biological mass—I've seen that term used before in her notes—and so maybe she'd use them as a library of genetic material to choose from. You can already see from the crude marriage application and allocation system in place that she's trying to selectively breed people in Isale to produce more of the intellectual traits she wants. If I had to guess, I'd say it's a pilot program for what's to come."

"You're describing eugenics," Laide said, suddenly thinking of how unhappy she'd been for most of her life, unsatisfied with the current constraints of Isale. How much worse would it be for her if those constraints were extended beyond having a spy-device in her own mind to a full-on harness—the parallel pathways of the nanomachines in her mind forcing her to think and do things she didn't truly want to? What about all the other people like her who'd never fit in. Didn't want to be assigned partners. Didn't want to entertain citizen-investors in Loke. Didn't want to live in stacked graphene boxes. Would they be forced to marry, to breed, to conform?

"Yes," Issa replied. "Bloodless and benevolent in a sense, but it is wrong. I don't know if she really planned this from the outset, or if she initially let us into the city because it would have made her look bad if she didn't, and then she saw us as an opportunity to improve her neural technology and impose her worldview. But either way, that's what she is working on now."

"And all her citizen-investors . . . they are intellectual geniuses too?"

"No. But money answereth all things," he said in heavily accented English before switching back to Yoruba. "Only a few of them in the board know the details of what she is planning, but they all paid for a lot of the city, for her tech. Including this building." He indicated the glass and steel box ahead of them with a silicone finger. "The research center where I worked until recently."

Everything is elastic. Even ideals.

Two droids with translucent white chassis like no other Laide had seen before, exited the sliding doors of the building. They were carrying a human-shaped lump wrapped in black plastic. Laide swallowed as the horror of what she was seeing began to well up.

The Issa-droid placed a hand on her shoulder, and they both watched the two strange droids take the human-shaped thing around the right side of the building, to a shed like the one Issa and Laide had come through when they entered Loke through. The droids disappeared into it.

Issa said nothing for a few moments. Allowing it all to sink in.

"I know you only wanted the ganger chip to fulfill your own innate desire to be free," he said. "And that's fine. Nothing wrong with that. I wish more people in Isale were driven to pursue even their most abstract wants and needs. Less distracted and content with their lives and less grateful for their perceived security. Maybe then they would stand a chance. I admire you for having the courage to be yourself, Laide. But now that you have been outside a few times, I wanted to show you Loke, so that you see there is more than one kind of freedom to fight for. I hope you understand why it's important that we take control of Legba City from Fisayo and her citizen-investors. Why we need to stop her from achieving what she wants. Why there should be no more Isale and Loke division. We should be one city, a fair city, even if we have to remain under the dome to breathe."

Laide experienced a sudden and thorough exhaustion. All she'd wanted was to feel free, to see the sun and the sky and the grass and the flowers. This was all too much. The world she inhabited was far stranger and more sinister than she'd ever thought, even at her lowest point when she sought to escape it. It was always a dark river that had threatened to drown her, but now she'd found that there was a crocodile with massive jaws and sharp teeth swimming beneath, threatening worse. A tech megalomaniac who had herded them all like livestock, storing them in Isale as data sources under the guise of protecting them from the ruined world outside. And giving them no more than necessary, with nothing to do but exist and entertain her and her rich friends until she was ready to take control of their minds.

It's too much. I don't want this. It's too. Too much. Out. I need to get out. I need to go outside.

"I need to go outside," she said. A ghostly memory of the deep relief that sometimes came simply from lying down and letting out a deep breath floated up to her mind and made her yearn for it even though she didn't experience any physical sensation of need.

"Sure," Issa said. "We can exit through the northern gate."

"Thank you."

As Laide processed it all, they walked quietly toward the research building the droids had emerged from, and rounded it on the left side, following a parallel path to the one the two droids had taken. It was clear that everything about Legba city, about Isale was a lie created by an obsessed woman. Most of the constraints around Laide's life were artificial, and had driven her to the brink. And it seemed worse was coming. Her mind was suddenly filled with a sense of the same fiery rush of blood that had made her scream in the hospital two years ago. She tried to summon the familiar vague but comforting memory of the day in the park with her mother, but she couldn't. Even the memory of wind and hibiscus and joy and sun was slippery with fear and anger. Even her anticipation of the coming freedom of being outside the dome seemed tainted.

They came to a door that was similar to the one they had entered Loke from and followed a mirror-image route of the way they came, descending solemnly until they were back in the tunnels.

"I know it's a lot to take in," Issa said finally. "But I think it's important that you saw for yourself."

"Why?" she blurted out, angry at what she'd seen. "What do you want from me?"

The hum behind the walls, and the drip of condensation, and the sound of approaching tortoise-shaped machines came at her like a cacophony.

"I want the people of Isale to be free."

"Yes. But that's not all is it? I assume you have a plan to try to make that happen. And that you want me to help you execute it. Why else would you be showing me all this?"

The Issa-droid nodded as they emerged back into the expansive space of machines and drones and droids in frenzied motion. They were facing a gate as large as the one she'd been using on the eastern wall but with a red arrow painted high above it. Laide suddenly realized that they weren't in a separate room at all. It was a hollow torus that ringed the circular base perimeter of the divided city, connected by the tunnels that ran through its inner radius, just like the one they had emerged from.

"But only if you want to," he said, and Laide thought she heard a hint of hope in his transmitted voice.

They dodged a group of incoming waste disposal machines and went through the gate before it closed.

Outside, under the curve of the dome, Laide, some of her anger abated, asked, "How exactly do you want me to help?"

"I can't tell you any details until I know you are with us. I don't think you'd willingly betray us, but you may get caught and anything can happen. The less you know, the better."

"And if I don't join you?"

"Then you are . . . free," he said, turning the Issa-droid to face her as they walked in the now familiar direction of the sanitization chamber. "We know we are doing the right thing, but we aren't like Fisayo. We won't force anyone to agree with us or help us. But we will call on you for the favor you agreed to. One task. A fair trade, nothing more."

"And after that I can keep the ganger chips?"

Another stiff nod. "Yes."

She shifted LG-114's feet. "Tell me something. And be honest. What you're planning, how dangerous is it?"

"Very. We'll almost certainly be killed if we fail." He paused before adding, "but we won't fail. Not if we do this right. If we have the right people."

A lot of 'ifs.'

She looked directly into the placid black eyes circumscribed with red light. "I need to think about it."

"Of course. We aren't in a hurry. We need to get enough people on board before we make our move."

"Okay."

They went ahead a bit until they were midway between the gate and the sanitization chamber. Issa stopped moving but it took Laide a few steps to notice and halt. The camouflaged door of the chamber opened in the distance, a dark hole in the dome, like a portal, from which a train of sanitized droids and lumbering tortoise machines emerged.

"This is where I leave you," Issa said, smiling thinly, the towers of Isale rising behind him.

"Right," she said, because she didn't want to thank him for showing her the horrible truth of Legba city, though deep down she was grateful for it. "See you later."

"Sure. I'll find you again in a few days. Be careful. Don't get caught before then."

Mama Peju won't wake till dawn. LG-114 updates are always run around noon. I'll be fine. I have bigger things to worry about now anyhow.

She nodded.

Issa turned the droid around and walked back to gate.

She watched him go for a moment, the smooth bounce of shoulders and low undulation of articulated pelvic structure, wondering if that was exactly how she looked too when she walked, her mind wearing its LG-114 suit. Graceful. She spun around and ran toward the place in the dome where the chamber was set. She focused on the rush of air sweeping past, the pressure of ground pushing against soles, flushing her mind with haptic input enough to distract her from what she'd seen and heard.

By the time she reached the chamber entrance and looked back over, the Issa-droid had disappeared, leaving not even a trace of temperature differential, as though he had simply merged into the shadows of the city.

5   Involution

And so, as the tale is so often told, Olofin Ogunfunminire's kinfolk grew increasingly concerned about his self-imposed isolation though they knew nothing of his bodily transformations. They convened a meeting at which it was resolved that his two sons, Ogunneru and Ogunbiyi, would lead a party to visit him in his secluded abode the following day, and stay with him for at least a day to ascertain his condition. Whether he approved or not. When the visiting party arrived at the appointed time, they called out greetings and made loud noises but when they received no response, they searched the premises, increasingly worried. They did not find him, for at that very moment he was in the forest, perched atop a tree, tearing the flesh from a ravaged doe's neck. His clothes lay on the dusty ground in front of the two charmed pots that the babalawo had given him. There was a trail of leopard footprints leading out of the hut. Upon seeing this, his sons cried out loudly for they immediately took this for a sign that their father had been attacked while drunk or sleeping; that he had been dragged out by a leopard, naked and inebriated, to be killed in the forest like one of his own prey. In a mournful rage at their

father's perceived fate, Ogunneru and Ogunbiyi rolled on the floor and tore out their hair and gnashed their teeth and kicked out violently at the chairs and the mat and the two pots until they shattered into a dozen jagged pieces. When their rage had turned from a boil to a simmer, and their eyes finally cleared, they set out into the forest, following the leopard prints to seek some sense of vengeance and what, if anything, they believed remained of their father.

Two days later, beyond the dome, morning came cold on the plateau. Laide could sense the weight of dew on LG-114's frame and the chill of dust-and-CO_2-T-bearing wind, the tiny particulates forcing the droid's internal filters to work harder than usual.

Harmattan is coming.

She smiled as she ran silicone fingers through a tassel of corn. It was comforting to experience something familiar (at least in theory anyway) about the local seasons, to know they hadn't changed completely with the rest of the world's climate even though the harmattan was coming much earlier than usual, in May.

The sun rose, illuminating the field and flecking the edges of visible seeds with gold. It was so beautiful, Laide felt she could cry. She watched the sun hoist itself up into the sky, making a new precious memory that she could hold on to, and then she could try to forget what Issa had told her, had asked her. But it was persistent, the doubt and the fear.

Do I want to join their fight against Fisayo? What's the point of it?

It had been two days, and she still wasn't sure what she wanted to do. Even the thing she'd been craving for most of her adult life—being free, beyond the dome—wasn't as pleasurable, as satisfying anymore. A shade of that familiar hollowness had returned.

And if I don't join them, am I going to have continue hiding my mind inside this shell just for a glimpse of the sunrise, a touch of soil and flowers, until Fisayo finally seizes complete control of my mind?

It seemed silly the more she thought about it. And yet, there was an appeal to it. An escapist appeal to deny what she knew, accept her fate, and distract herself until the bitter end, like her parents and everyone else in Isale.

The sun suddenly seemed too bright. She looked down at the ground. A pink-fleshed earthworm was wriggling through clods of russet soil. She watched it curiously for a few moments, remembering what she'd learned about the strange creatures. They live in the soil, eat it, excrete it, their entire existence is in the earth, defined by it. Laide felt a flicker of something in her mind like a realization. The earthworms, like the corn and the trees and all other creatures of nature know their place in it and within it. They are defined by each other and in that there was certainty, balance. Something she'd never felt. Not in her body, not in the city, and not even now, out beyond the dome.

Come back to what our people call iwa-pele.

Mama Peju's words echoed in her memory.

Be in alignment with your Orí. Your purpose. Once you find that, it will be well with you.

She watched the worm disappear into the soil.

What if I've been searching for an illusion of hope all along? What if I've been too selfish, too focused on finding purpose within myself?

There was a swell of something within her that was akin to the first time she'd left the dome, but stronger. Something flowering in her mind that was more potent than her most strongly held half-memories.

What if my purpose is to do more than temporarily free myself from the city? What if it's to help permanently free the city itself? To do my part in helping to rebuild it into a place I can be happy in?

She glimpsed it in her mind's-eye. A dream of a future rather than a yearning for shadows of the past.

Maybe there can be a higher purpose.

Something to hope for, beyond myself.

Laide hadn't prayed since she was a child but something about the sun and the worm and the thought and the moment compelled her to drop LG-114 to its knees. Its weight sank into the soil, rooting her to the world.

I hope there is enough of my consciousness here for my Orí to answer me. I hope it can still recognize me in this artificial body.

She spoke out loud into the wind, reciting a few words that Mama Peju had taught her when she was just nine. She applied focused memory too, selecting a day she remembered because it had rained and the patter of the rain on the dome sounded like drumbeats. She focused until she could almost see wispy images superimposed over the cornstalks, of a younger Mama Peju speaking words for her to repeat.

Relax. Calm down.

But in LG-114's frame, there was no heartbeat, there was no breathing, there was no skin or sweat and everything was different, heightened.

Focus on memory. On sound. On the feeling of calling out to a higher sense of self.

Everything faded into the background. Time flowed around her like a river around a rock but she didn't notice how much. She was zoomed in on herself in a way she'd never felt before. Bringing all the disparate elements of her essence that had been pulled apart technologically, spiritually, psychologically, biologically, into one clear mental whole.

She didn't have her lungs with her, but in her mind-space she recreated the sensation of exhalation, and all at once, there was a preternatural calm deep within. A sense of clarity. A sense of hope.

I know what I must do.

Laide stood LG-114 up and let go.

The signals from LG-114 returned in a rush of stimulation.

She looked up and a bulky scouting drone flew across her field of vision, cutting a line across the beaming sun. It reminded her of something, but it took a moment for her to place it.

Shit! Breakfast!

Mama Peju is probably up for breakfast and wondering where LG-114 is.

Laide turned around sharply and ran back the way she'd come, tearing past leaves and tassels and silks and stems as she bounded with great big steps of the droid's frame, throwing soil up into the CO_2-T saturated air. She wanted to take it all in as she had before the sunrise, but she was now too worried to enjoy the feeling of flying through the field. She had to get back.

Shit. Shit. Shit.

I got carried away. I forgot the time.

She tore past the curtain of stalks and back onto one of the radiating tracks leading back to the clearing that surrounded the dome. There was a giant harvester machine ahead of her. She followed it, the feet of LG-114's frame digging into the loamy red and brown soil with every powerful step. The dome loomed ahead, its smooth surface of gun turrets more imposing than ever in the cold clarity of daylight.

What if Mama Peju woke up to eat already and panicked when she didn't see LG-114?

What if the guns turn on me?

I can't get caught now that I finally know what I want . . . no, what I need to do.

Laide forced herself to slow down as she approached the dome, bringing LG-114 to a brisk walking pace close of the edge of the field.

Calm down.

She was trying not to panic but it was hard to keep her composure despite the uncertainty.

She heard the steady hum of a harvester convoy approaching. She waited, until the first one came up to her side and then she stepped into the track, following it with steady steps.

The gate of the sanitization chamber at the base of the dome opened ahead of them like a lazy mouth. Laide thought she saw the guns angle slightly down toward them, but she was sure it was just her imagination.

Don't panic.

Laide thought herself calm and kept moving behind the harvester with the convoy until she'd cleared the gate. There was the hiss of venting and a flood of red lights. Her mind was overcome by the sensation of her skin crawling, as she imagined the nanobots poring over every nanometer of LG-114's frame again, hunting for the viral CO_2-T nanoparticles she brought with her.

When the lights turned green and the exit opened, she wanted to sigh with relief, but she couldn't. She didn't have lungs, and she didn't have time.

She broke away from the convoy and piloted LG-114's bulk speedily back toward the towers, her fear of detection diminished since she hadn't been stopped at the dome. That meant Mama Peju was probably still asleep. For a moment, that usual pang of sadness hit her, as it did whenever she returned from outside; the grief of being an animal corralled back to a cage. But the conviction of her decision and her new-found sense of higher purpose kept her going until she reached the gate in the eastern wall. She entered and wove through the chaotic order of autonomous machines going about their tasks in the torus: appearing and disappearing in and out of hatches and gates and tunnels and elevators that led to every part of the city as if it were an anthill or a hive. She made her way to one of the elevators and keyed in the numbers for her level.

3-1-1.

The empty elevator ascended.

Almost there. Almost clear.

She let out a small, nervous laugh. She'd finally found some sense of clarity, something that felt like it could give the shape of her life meaning, something like iwa-pele. And then she'd immediately almost blown her chance to act on it because she'd lost track of time.

My Orí must have a twisted sense of humor.

The elevator arrived at level 311 with a gentle ding and the gray metal doors slid open.

When she stepped out, Laide was suddenly overcome by a sensation like she was falling, endlessly falling into a bottomless nothing, because there, right in front of her, was her own flesh-and-blood body, lying in the arms of a droid she had never seen before, her parents crying and hugging each other as they followed behind it.

No!

In a panic, she thought the command she'd so often used to return to herself.

Take me back to my body.

But this time, nothing happened. There was no emptying out of the world. No darkness. No displacement of consciousness. No awakening. There was just the terrible sensation of nothing happening.

Take me back to my body.

More nothing.

She watched in horror through LG-114's eyes as they filed into the elevator.

Please, please, take me back to my body.

She pleaded silently with every fiber of her consciousness that she could muster, imploring the spider-shaped ganger chip in LG-114's neck, her Orí, the directional photons of LG-114's processors, the gray and white matter and nerve cells and blood vessels of her own brain, everything. Everything that she could think of willing to action, she did. But there was only that great and terrible nothing.

Laide watched in horror through LG-114's eyes as the strange droid maneuvered. It angled her limp body to the side, and it was then that she finally saw that the twin of the ganger chip in LG-114 was no longer attached to the soft flesh of her neck.

6   Null

That day, when the night had just begun to settle into the sky, a few hours after his sons had set out into the forest seeking some imagined vengeance, Ogunfunminire returned to his home, tracing a new path, and found the pots given to him by the babalawo broken and empty, all the potency of their charms gone. He let out a wild roar when he realized that he was now trapped in the body of the beast and had no means of regaining his frail, familiar human form. The gravity of the misfortune that had found its way to him was great, pulling him into its center with an inexorable force. He shook and trembled and let out a variety of anguish-flavored sounds. When all his emotion was spent, he observed his hut more keenly and saw the shreds of his children's clothes, smelled their sweat and tears lingering in the air, and at that his shock and rage turned to dismay as an understanding of what had transpired began to settle upon him.

Two hours after they first got out of bed, once they had finished their breakfast, showered, dressed in their coveralls, and were ready to go down to their assigned entertainment pods on level 5, Laide Haraya's parents had tried to wake her up.

Saliu and Kemi Haraya found their daughter asleep in her programmable material bed, with one arm lying across her steadily heaving chest and the other planted awkwardly behind her head, elbow bent. There was a blissful, unflinching smile cut into her face like they had not seen since she was a child. For a moment, her mother felt flush with joy, because she thought her daughter was dreaming a good dream, which she took to mean that Laide had regained the potential for happiness after so many years of persistent dissatisfaction.

But when her mother noticed that Laide's eyes were flickering yet she didn't stir, even after they called to her again and again, telling her that they were leaving for work, their joy was slowly replaced by worry.

"Saliu, I think something is wrong," Kemi whispered to her husband as if saying it out loud would suddenly crystalize her fears into reality, making things wrong by acknowledgement.

Saliu nodded in agreement and went up to Laide's sleeping form, the smile across her face now a creepy mask hiding his daughter's consciousness. Her shook her, gently at first and then more insistently, but she didn't respond.

"Laide!" he shouted as he straightened her arm and lifted her head up, cradling it in the crook of his own arm. "Laide, it's your father, answer me!"

Nothing.

When he felt a scratch in the crook of his elbow, he looked under her head, pushing away her thin curtain of braids to reveal the ganger chip attached tightly to the base of her skull, just under the hair line, like an electronic leech. He touched it tenderly and looked to his wife with a querying terror embedded in his eyes. "Do you know what this is?"

Kemi dug her hands into her hair and shook her head.

They both held each other's gaze, the unspoken question hanging in the space between them needed no words: Was she using some strange new technology to try to kill herself again?

Her mother began to wail. "Laide! Omo mi! Laide! Please wake up!"

Her father seized the chip with his fingers and tugged. It gave a bit, and he could see thin thread-like tendrils piercing the brown of her skin. He pulled, gripped again, tighter this time, and yanked it out with force. A trail of thin, almost invisible bloody electrodes hung lazily off it like threads of a broken spiderweb.

Laide remained unresponsive.

The chip in her father's hand suddenly began to smoke and disintegrate, its black and silver body reducing rapidly, like it was evaporating. It became hot to the touch. He fell back, sitting onto the floor as he tossed the remains of the chip into the space between him and Kemi like he was throwing strange dice.

"What the . . .?"

He shook Laide again, but she remained unresponsive. The smile was frozen in place, like she was mocking his concern. His tears began to flow.

Kemi ran over to the body that was supposed to contain her daughter and pressed its head into her bosom. "Ah! What is this? What is happening?! Help! Olorun oh! Help! My Laide! My daughter! I am dead! Ah!"

The distress signals spiking Saliu and Kemi Haraya's nervous systems were both flagged by their interrogators and correlated against the stimuli coming in from all the other parts of their bodies. No physical tissue damage was detected on either of them, so Legba-6 narrowed down the primary cause of distress to the input from their optic nerves with a 98.6% certainty. Their rising heart rates, the sickening twists in the pits of their stomachs, Kemi's cries of anguish and Saliu's quiet despair, they were all processed and fed into its mathematical models, a matrix of equations which resolved to a simple solution: they were seeing something that was causing them severe emotional distress.

Legba-6 sent out a priority-2 alert, repurposing the nearest available machine to investigate.

By the time food drone FD-1021 arrived, shedding its bulky outer casing to enter their living unit through the food delivery port, the ganger chip that had been attached to the back of Laide's head had been reduced to nothing but a stain on the graphene floor. Kemi and Saliu had lifted their daughters' body up from the bed, cradling her head gently like it was tender fruit as they carried her into the central area of the living unit.

FD-1021 observed them with its large black camera-eye, like a cyclopean spy, transmitting the images through dataspace as they struggled to the door of their living unit in tears.

Legba-6 ran a diagnostic on Laide's idling mind. Each neural dust nanobot sent packets of data to the sub-cranial interrogator which relayed them, but none of the information could be fit into a model result that indicated cause for concern. The myriad interacting neurotransmitter systems in her brain stem, hypothalamus, and basal forebrain all indicated that she was asleep and not drugged. And yet corresponding neural data from her parents, and visual data from FD-1021, made it clear that she could not be awakened normally. Legba-6 correlated all the data points, and its final inference, based on its existing library of human brain states, was: *She had been sleeping, dreaming deeply, and had slipped into an acute non-traumatic coma of undetermined etiology.*

Legba-6 repurposed the nearest droid with a medical subroutine that was large enough to carry Laide—an older model, LG-023, which had been administering vaccinations to a group of children on level 298.

By the time Laide's parents exited their unit, LG-023 was already waiting to take her insensate body for further analysis.

It was only when she saw the other elevator doors begin to close that Laide finally moved, compelled by instinct to follow the droid carrying her body because she didn't know what else to do. She pressed in just before the thick titanium doors could fully shut.

The sudden motion drew momentary looks from her parents, and it took every ounce of her mental restraint to stop herself from crying out *It's me! Laide!* and trying to hug them, to tell them it was their daughter trapped behind the casing of metal and silicone, staring back at them through those beady black eyes. But her parents suddenly looked small and scared and weary and old, and much more frightened than she had ever seen them before. And the sight of a droid claiming to be their daughter would probably only terrify them more.

Would they understand what was happening? Would they somehow know it was her?

I've put them through so much.

The guilt hit her mind like ice, freezing her in place.

She kept trying to think her way back into her body even though she already knew it wouldn't work. She couldn't reconnect to herself.

Take me back to my body. Please. Please. Take me back to my body.

She stopped trying only when they reached level 5 where there was a wide transparent tunnel connected to the medical center.

Laide watched, still as a statue, as the elevator doors closed and the droid took her body away, her parents following it like fearful pets.

The sadness that hit her displaced mind like a wave was familiar but with new notes. It washed over her consciousness until there was nothing left but that singular sad feeling, and her mind was saturated with a single thought: *I'm lost.*

Just when I thought I'd found myself, I'm lost again.

Time flowed past her. Around her. How much? She didn't know. It could have been anything between a minute and an hour. She wasn't sure. She stood there in the elevator, staring at the embossed patterns on its walls, wondering what to do. She was numb and could not decide where to go. A steady stream of people and droids entered and exited, flowing past and around her, none of them paying much attention to her.

Finally, it burst into her mind: LG-114 would be updated around noon. She only had a few hours left.

What will happen to this simulation of my mind, my consciousness when Legba-6 runs the update and resets LG-114's processors? Am I going to die? Be deleted? Trapped somewhere in some kind of ether? Become a ghost in dataspace? Or just become nothing.

Questions she should have asked Issa.

Issa.

Issa would know.

I have to find Issa before noon.

She pressed the keys to go back home to Level 311 and stepped out quickly once the elevator arrived, piloting LG-114's frame to the vacant unit where she'd first run into Issa. When she got there, she was relieved to see that the lightsign was still yellow. The newly assigned occupants had not yet arrived. She pushed against the door, but it was locked.

Ironic.

She threw LG-114's bulk into it, shoulder first. It budged but did not give. She tried again and again and on the fourth attempt, the door flew open. That damage was going to be detected soon but she didn't care anymore. Mama Peju was probably awake as well and wondering what had happened, which meant Legba-6 and eventually Fisayo or one of her cronies, would soon be wondering too. Not to mention her comatose body. How long did she have? There was no more time for stealth or subtlety. She ran into the back where she'd seen Issa park his body while piloting his ganger utilitydroid, but it the room was empty. Terrifyingly, despairingly empty.

Laide dropped herself, her droid frame, to the floor and tried to cry but she couldn't. She had no tear ducts, and no lungs with which to heave, no nerves with which to shake and tremble, to let some of what she was feeling was let out, like bad blood. No. She was just a lost ghost in a machine now. She couldn't go back to her body, and she couldn't stay in the droid's.

No way forward. No way back.

She let out a loud, shrill sound like a wail that slowly morphed into a bitter screeching laugh when she remembered that she'd promised herself never to cry again, and now she couldn't even if she wanted to.

I thought I finally found my purpose, but in finding it I lost access to both my past and my future.

I suppose my Orí does have a twisted sense of humor.

But then something about that thought, of her Orí, helped to clear mind. She stopped laughing and considered carefully, rolling it around her mind like one of the polished stone beads that she used to play games of Ayo with Mama Peju.

I finally found my purpose.

She framed the thought against her memories of the morning, the feeling of running through the cornfields, watching the sunrise, of the earthworm digging into the soil, of thinking outside of Legba-6's purview, and of being at one with what she had decided to do.

Balance. Alignment. That was where true freedom came from. She didn't need to win. She just had to be willing to fight to change things for herself and the people of Isale. In accepting that purpose, that responsibility, she'd finally, truly, felt free.

Like the earthworm.

She smiled, remembering a story that her father once told her. A story of how the tortoise got the cracks on his shell. One of several versions of the same story, but the one that had resonated with her most. The tortoise, as her father told it, had fallen off a hillside path and rolled into a deep ditch, but he called out to all the birds in the sky, and convinced them each to lend him a single feather, with which he made a pair of wings. Tortoise used his newly minted wings to fly back up to the path, but instead of stopping at the spot where he'd fallen, he attempted to fly higher, to complete his journey with less effort. He was caught in an aggressive air current and slammed into the side of the rocky hill where his shell cracked into a dozen pieces. She remembered her father telling her that the lesson of the story was not to be greedy, but all she remembered of it was this:

Yes, the tortoise fell. But for a moment, however brief, the tortoise flew.

The tortoise flew.

Laide thought LG-114's frame back to its feet, exited the unit and began to make her way back beyond the dome.

7 Union

Whenever the account of Olofin Ogunfunminire's final fate is given, there is almost always a new variation to it, an exaggeration, an omission, an addition, an interpretation, a mutation, each a reflection or refraction or diffraction of the teller's own hopes and fears and dreams. A grandmother speaking to her young descendants at a fire, giving them life lessons cloaked in story. An arokin in a palace, singing to entertain his king in time with the beat of a talking drum. A teacher using mythology to teach history to his students, seeking discussion and debate. A father and his young daughter under a semi-permeable membrane dome, relaying a story that his own father told him when he was a young boy. The story changes.

But of all the variations of the story that exist, the account of its conclusion is by far the most fragmented aspect of the tale of Ogunfunminire, the great Awori progenitor. Some of the more overtly tragic tellings say that the once-great hunter, now trapped in the body of the leopard, was killed by an arrow from the bow of one of his own sons when they came upon him skulking near his hill house, seeking some way to return to himself.

Others say that he roamed the forests, staying close to the roads and paths until, many years later, he once again came across the babalawo who took pity upon him and devised another potent charm, one that finally returned him to his human form, and he finally returned home where he lived the rest of his days, having learned the dangers of pining so desperately for glories past.

A version of the tale, which is less often told, is that for some time he at first stalked around his own house on Iddo Hill, perhaps hoping that the babalawo would return or that some minor aspect of the magic that he'd been given would assert itself one more time and take him back to the way he was. He evaded capture and death but did not find any remaining charm to return him to his old body. And so, it is said in these accounts, that when all his efforts to re-enter himself came to be in vain, the great hunter, trapped in youthful animal muscle and fur and fangs accepted his fate, let go of his desire to return to his human form, and disappeared into the forest, never to be seen again.

Laide met Issa again at the edge of the cornfield, where the clustering of thick green and gold stalks gave way to sparse patches of mud and wild grass and stone and trash from the world that once was.

She'd run all the way through the field, savoring once more the touch of leaves and dirt and wind that she'd been craving for as long as she could remember, spreading LG-114's arms wide and high as she ran back to the late morning sun. But she also remembered the stories of the floods and the death and the chaos before the dome and she decided she wanted to see what was left of it, so she followed the tracks left by the giant harvester machines until they eventually narrowed and gave way to thick, less ordered stalks. Beyond that was the boundary. She stepped through and found herself high on the Jos Plateau, atop an escarpment looking down on the flooded remains of what had once been settlements below. Brown water sloshed lazily against the steep, jagged rock face while Laide watched, listening to the lapping sound.

So, this is the edge of the world.

There were other cities. Other domes, almost all of them based on Fisayo's technology. Some of them were managed by her AI systems, others were run by what was left of world governments, but they were too far away, too improbable to reach before the clock ran out for her. She stood there at the edge, filled with a sense of wonder and acceptance.

I am at one with myself. I know my purpose. I accept it. If it's meant to be, it will be. And I will fight. If it isn't, I accept that too. And I will fade.

She was acutely aware of the time as it ticked by steadily, counting down like a clockwork heart. She had only about an hour before LG-114's update would run. Beyond that lay the great digital unknown.

A rustling from behind her made her spin LG-114's frame around. She watched a familiar utilitydroid emerge from the edge of the cornfield and Laide thought she felt her heart leap into her throat, except she had no heart and no throat. Just phantoms in her mind of a body she'd lost and maybe, just maybe, there was now some hope that she could get it back.

Issa?

"I picked up what happened on dataspace," the droid said. The voice was unmistakably his, accent riding atop the strident electronic modulation. "Dataspace is in a frenzy about a comatose citizen whose parents kept saying something about a chip and a missing droid. I knew it had to be you. And I guessed you'd probably come out here. I came as quickly as I could."

The chip attached to the droid's neck confirmed that it was Issa. The dome looked like a gigantic gleaming snow globe behind him, its eastern edge glowing in the sun.

"Is there a way to fix it?" she asked, suspecting the answer before it came. "A way to get me back into my body?"

"Unfortunately, no," Issa said, lowering its head as he walked the droid up to her. "It's worse than being caught I'm afraid. The ganger chip was forcibly removed. It broke the local network connection mid-transmission which means permanent brain tissue damage," he explained. "There's no way to reconnect. All of you is only here now, copied into code."

The hope that had appeared in her sublimated, but she was surprised that she didn't feel utterly dejected.

"It was my parents . . . I think they found me. They usually don't come into my . . ." She stopped. "They didn't know. They didn't understand."

The Issa-droid was standing close to her, and their beady droid-eyes were level with each other. The glassy glint of his gave the illusion that he was about to cry.

"I'm sorry. I should have warned you about this. About what happens if the ganger chip is removed while you're still connected."

"It doesn't matter anymore," she said, because it was true. "So, what happens now? What happens when Legba-6 runs the update on this—" she ran LG-114's hands along the middle of its frame from chest to pelvis—"and it finds me here?"

"Purge," he replied. "It will purge the code and reset the droid's quantum processors."

"And what will happen to me, to my consciousness, or at least this simulation of it?"

He looked away. "Once the data is purged and deleted, you'll be gone completely."

"I see," Laide nodded and turned back to look at the brown water of the drowned world beyond the plateau.

Purge. I can accept that too.

"It's so beautiful out here, don't you think?"

"It is," he agreed.

"The air may be unbreathable, and most of the animals have died but the crops can survive. The insects too. They were modified. They've adapted. They are thriving and beautiful. We're the ones that haven't. I wish there'd been another way to see it without losing my body . . . or my mind."

"You may not have to lose your mind. You don't have to fade into darkness. Perhaps there is another way. Perhaps this is the way it was always meant to be," Issa said.

She turned back around to look at him quizzically, an imagined outline of his dark skin, his awkward wiry frame, his thick and wild afro superimposed on the white and gray silicone shell.

"I have something to tell you." He paused as though he were taking a deep breath or steeling his nerves before continuing. "You didn't find me by accident. We've been trying to recruit you for a few months, ever since we picked up your *at-risk* profile in the system and figured out why it had been flagged."

Laide instinctively reached for LG-114's metal throat.

"I left that unit door open on purpose and made just enough noise to get your attention."

A bolt of anger shot through her mind like electricity. "You tricked me?"

"No. Not at all. I simply gave you a chance to find me. To come to us. I was on that rooftop and in that unit for days doing variations of the same thing. It was a risk, but I knew most people were too focused doing what they'd been assigned to do to notice. And the droids are all on pre-defined paths optimizing some specific tasks they've been assigned. They never noticed. Never investigated. But you were curious. You *are* curious. You craved more, beyond the machine-mandated world that Fisayo and her citizen-investors imposed on us. The nightmare that she is planning. You've seen that it's nothing more than an exploitative prison." He pointed his droid arm back at the dome. "You're one of the last of us with that restless human spirit yearning to be free. That's why you came to me. That's why you took the ganger chip." He paused again and took another step toward her. "That's when we knew you'd want to join us. You do want to join us, don't you?"

Laide folded LG-114's arms across its chest. "Yes. But . . ."

"I knew it. I knew you would. Fate may have dealt you a cruel hand. Trapped you in that thing. But it doesn't have to be the end of you. Once you join us, I can take it offline completely before the update runs. I'll have to physically destroy some of the embedded circuitry that processes the dataspace transmissions, but it will no longer be part of Legba-6's system. Completely decoupled from dataspace. This droid can be your new body, entirely yours to do with as you wish. You'll never get tired, never feel weak. And you can still use it to help us."

Laide stared ahead silently. The thought of being permanently embodied in LG-114 did not concern her as much as she thought it would or should. Quite the opposite. She was almost excited to have this new body, free of the organs that had always been part of her but remained uncomfortable appendages, like close relatives that lived with her but whom she'd never shared a bond with. The re-embodiment wasn't the issue. It was the new information of how the entire situation had come about which was threatening to shake the foundations of what she'd been so sure of just a few moments ago.

My purpose. I need to be fully in alignment with my purpose. If I am to free the city, to build a better world, then it must be the right way. I will not be used by anyone.

"No," she said.

The Issa-droid took a step back, surprised.

"How can you not see that what you're doing is no different from Fisayo? You spied on me, manipulated me, limited my information and choices to serve your ends, to achieve your goals. Even now, you're essentially forcing me into a corner because of what happened. Taking advantage of a bad situation for your own perceived sense of what's right. Your own version of a better world. How many others have you done this to? How far are you willing to go?"

"No. It's not like that. I am trying to help you. To help everyone," Issa protested, waving the droid's hands awkwardly in front of him. The droid's silicone face had contorted into a strange shape. He looked like she had just accused him of murder. "You don't understand. You don't know what we've had to do just to make it this far."

"No. *You* don't understand. If you continue like this, you will not be proposing a better way of being. You will simply be replacing one bad system with another, less terrible one."

"But Fisayo will control everyone's minds, even your parents . . . you can help us stop her."

A pinch of guilt and the sodium chloride tang of sea water on the air hit Laide's consciousness simultaneously.

She pushed it away.

"Call me naïve or foolish or silly or whatever but I won't work with you unless you commit to real change. No more lies. No more tricks. No more manipulation. Not to me or to any of the people of Isale that join our cause."

"But—"

She held up LG-114's hand to cut him off. "But nothing. It's my condition. I am not afraid to die. To be deleted. If you've seen my profile like you say, then you should know that. The only thing I am afraid of is not really living, of not being truly free. If you want me to join you, that's the way it must be. If not, I'm sure you can manipulate someone else into your cause."

A look of . . . shame? The uncanny undergirding of the droid structure made it hard to tell. "Okay. I agree but I need to talk to the others too," he told her, all the confidence gone from his voice.

She shook her head. The suspicion she'd held on to bubbled to the surface, and she felt her Orí tingle with certainty.

He's lying.

"No, you don't."

"What?" Surprise. A bit too much of it.

"There aren't actually any others, are there?"

"No," he admitted, looking away.

"I'm the first person you've reached out to, aren't I?"

A pause. And then finally, "Yes."

Honesty. At last.

"If we are going to start a resistance to save Legba City, it must be on a solid foundation. An honest one. An equal one. No more lies or tricks or secrets between us."

"I understand." He looked like he was the one with an electronic axe hanging over his head, like he was the one about to be purged from existence when time ran out. "No more secrets."

He could still be lying, carrying on some further deception, but she didn't think he was. He'd confessed freely and her Orí was telling her that hearing how his own actions paralleled Fisayo's had shaken him.

I choose to believe you.

"Good. Then let's do this. Take me offline."

She walked to the cliff and sat at the edge with her back to him, dangling LG-114's muddy metal feet over the water.

She heard him come over. Felt the cold silicone fingers press into LG-114's neckport—her neckport now—fiddling with something. Heat. Pressure. The chemical products of metal oxidation. It all came to her with the acrid smell of burning. She turned down all incoming signals with a thought. The sound and vision of the world vanished along with the haptic feel of Issa's ministrations. She started cycling memories in the darkness, the way she used to when she was in her previous body, trying to hide her mind from Legba-6. She summoned both childhood memories of the comfortable cradle of her mother's arms and new ones of finally being beyond the dome. The sweet smell of hibiscus. The feel of air blowing against her face. The smooth touch of corn stalks. The lovely kaleidoscope of colors when the sun kissed the sky. She kept cycling them until something changed in her mind, like a magnet made of pure thought had been driven into her head and twisted her consciousness around it like wire coils. Some metaphysical induction.

Deletion or rebirth?

Am I flying or am I falling?

She stopped actively cycling memories and tried to will her eyes open, to bring all incoming signals back to full strength, to return to the present. When she saw the water that had drowned the world sloshing in front of her, and felt the full measure of cold harmattan air, she smiled.

Who or what am I now?

She turned to face Issa.

It doesn't matter.

We are the seeds of a tree with the potential remake the city and maybe even the world, if we remain true to ourselves, and to each other. If we stay true to our people and our purpose. If we stay the course.

"Now," she said, "tell me how you plan to liberate the city."

ABEOKUTA52

Welcome To The Nairaland Forum

Continue as Guest / LOGIN / Trending /
Recent / New

Stats: 6,421,391 members / 5,377,609 topics.

Date: Wednesday, 28 November 2026 at 09:33 AM

---

*Nairaland > General > Politics >
Abeokuta52 > Latest Posts > Son of
Abeokuta52 Victim Shares His Incredible
Story! (24889 Views)*
*Posted on November 16, 2026 by
Abk52 _ Warrior*

---

*Hey Nairalanders, I'm reposting this copy
of Bidemi Akindele's opinion piece in The
Guardian from two days ago.* https://www
.theguardian.com/commentisfree/2026/Nov/14
/second-deaths-nigeria-acknowledge-alien
-blessing-came-price

THE SECOND DEATH: WHY NIGERIA NEEDS TO ACKNOWLEDGE THAT ITS ALIEN BLESSING CAME AT A PRICE

By Bidemi Akindele

I was fourteen when the alien disease killed my mother. Her name was Stella Akindele and she was one of the first to study the items found at the impact site, near Aké. They took a risk, she and all the others who first investigated the things that had fallen from the sky. I understand that, believe me, I understand how different the country was back then but it's not the loss that keeps me up at night, weeping into my girl-friend's hair. It's the silence. After all these years no one wants to talk about it. There are no erected memorials. There is no day of remembrance. There are still no published studies on the disease that killed them. No one wants to acknowledge the early price we paid for all this rapid wealth and development. Every time we petition or protest, the government tells us to move on, to look how far we've come, to forget the past and embrace the future in silence.

Why is it so hard for people in power or at privilege to admit and acknowledge that their success came at someone else's expense? America, Japan, Europe, South Africa, now Nigeria . . . I could go on.

They say you die twice. Once, when you stop breathing and again, when somebody says your name for the last time. I will not be let myself become complicit in my mother's second death at the hands of this government. I will not be silent. I will not speak of politics or offer opinions. I will simply tell her story.

My mother's cough started three days after she returned from the impact site in Abeokuta. At first it came in random spurts only once a day or so. She said it was nothing, always with a smile. After a while, we stopped asking if she was all right. Father said not to worry, the investigation at the site was stressful because of the strange things they found there. But then after almost a month, the cough began to worsen, until it became an endless dry, hacking that echoed through our house day and night.

My father finally convinced her to see a doctor. When he saw her, the doctor had her admitted and put her through dozens of tests. It took a week, and we visited her in the private ward of the Federal Hospital every day after school, staying till about four pm. Then one day my father told us that we needed to stay a bit longer.

Doctor Shina met with all of us late in the evening. I remember that the sun was a low orange ball in the window behind him and that he was unshaven and looked exhausted. He walked into my mother's room, a little bit surprised to find the entire family there, including my seven-year-old sister Teniola, sitting on the leather chair beside my mother—his patient. He glanced at my father with a look that made me think he expected my father to ask my sister and I to go and play outside while they had a grown-up talk, but my father said nothing. Doctor Shina became more direct and said, "Mr. and Mrs. Akindele, I'd like to speak with you privately, if I could."

"Doctor, please, anything you want to say to me you can say in front of my family," my mother croaked from her bed. "My whole family."

My father smiled and waved his hand. "Please, go ahead."

Doctor Shina cleared his throat and said, "Madam, I examined your lung biopsy sample yesterday and then again today. There is a unique and very worrying pattern of extensive scar tissue and some residue of cadmium, polycyclic aromatic hydrocarbons and another material we have been unable to identify so far."

He paused, adjusted his glasses and looked at me and my sister before turning back to my mother and saying, "I'm sorry Ma, but it seems you have some kind of severe pulmonary fibrosis. It's quite bad."

I saw my father squeeze my mother's hand on the hospital bed. She squeezed back and the veins on her forehead strained against her skin. She said nothing. He said nothing.

Then Doctor Shina said, "That's not the only problem, I'm afraid," and my young heart sank in my chest like an anchor.

I think my father almost asked me to take my sister out of the room then, because when he glanced at me, he looked like something was stuck in his throat. But he didn't send us out.

Doctor Shina said, "I also found some abnormal cell growths so I requested an analysis. I've checked and checked again but it seems conclusive now. It's cancer. Lung cancer."

My mother started to cry. I don't think she wanted to but she did anyway, and it seemed to make her angry because her lips quivered, and her palms curled into fists. She probably already suspected it was the thing they'd found at the site. She probably knew but she couldn't say because it was all secret. I was in shock, unable to think about anything except the fact that my mother was going to die.

"What do we do next?" she said, her tone belying the fear that her body was broadcasting. "Is it treatable?"

I looked first to my mother and then at Doctor Shina.

"We still don't know what the particles in your lungs are, so I cannot say much about the fibrosis. But it looks like the cancerous cells have metastasized since they are already in your bloodstream. Still, we have several treatment options available, and they may work for you by the special grace of God. We just need to start treatment immediately."

I wondered then how many times he had said those words to other patients, perhaps in that same room and in that same tone. And how many of those patients had died shortly after hearing them.

"Good," my mother said flatly.

"Thank you, Doctor," my father said with a weak smile. "Please make all the necessary arrangements. Whatever you need. She works at the ministry, so the government will pay for everything, don't worry about cost."

"Yes sir. I'll come back soon." Then he turned and exited the ward. My father's gaze followed him all the way to the door and when the door closed behind him, so did my father's eyes.

Four weeks later, fifty-one of my mother's colleagues were also diagnosed with the accelerated fibrosis and cancer combination. That was when the government had them all moved to the Central Hospital in Abuja. My father enrolled me in a boarding school and sent Teni to live with my Aunt Folake in Gbagada. I don't know what happened in Abuja because the medical records were sealed. Neither does my father. He had to watch the woman he loved waste away while doctors did things to her without consulting him. He was still struggling in the courts to have the records unsealed years later, when he died of a heart attack.

In the years since their deaths, the government has profited from the reverse-engineered alien technology recovered at the Abeokuta site. Nigeria is now the world's largest provider of macroscale gene-alteration services and Lagos is becoming the genodynamic technology capital of the world, thanks to its proximity to the impact site, but I hope you understand that these are all fruits of the poisoned alien tree. A tree that was watered by the blood of my mother and her colleagues. A tree whose branches are trellised by the misery that came with diagnoses families like mine received in stark hospital rooms from well-meaning men like Dr. Shina. A tree sustained by persistent government erasure and silence.

It has been six years. We are not asking for much, we are just asking for an acknowledgement of our pain. Our truth. Acknowledgement that the present prosperity of this nation was purchased at the cost of fifty-two lives, no matter how inconvenient that narrative is. Acknowledgement that those lives mattered.

We are all made of stories and in the end, no greater injury can be done to a person who has suffered their first death than to change their story, to deny their narrative. It makes their second death more tragic.

My mother's name was Stella Akindele.

And I will continue to tell her story everywhere. Online, during interviews, on panel discussions, during protests, everywhere. I will say her name and I will not stop until it has a new ending, one that does not bring me to tears whenever I tell it.

• *Bidemi Akindele is a musician and artist whose provocative work has been exhibited in 23 countries. He is the son of the late Dr. Stella Akindele, who was lead scientific officer of the First Abeokuta Impact Assessment Task Force and #Abeokuta52 campaigner, Professor Jude Akindele. Bidemi is the current Vice President of the Abeokuta Truth Alliance (ATA).*

NAIRALAND COMMENTS

Ahmed-Turiki: Powerful Story! God Bless Bidemi for not giving up on the truth about his mother and all those who died. Dr. Stella was a hero. There is an ATA protest planned at the site in 3 days. Everyone come out and join us, let the government know that we will not be silenced! Aluta continua! Victoria ascerta!

November 16 10:34

OmoOba1991: <Comment Flagged and Auto-Deleted by NLModeratorBot>

November 16 10:41

SoyinkaStan1: Sorry for your loss. No wonder there were so many questions the minister of science and technology didn't respond to when they announced that they have awarded the Abeokuta exploitation contract to Dangote. Hmmm.

November 16 10:54

Abk52__Warrior: Please share this link on all your social media accounts since it's no longer accessible on the Guardian News website. Even proxies and backchannel servers aren't working. I will keep testing and update you. But please share. It's personal stories like this that will eventually force the government to tell the truth.

November 16 11:17

QueenEzinne: I am sorry for this boy's loss and I am sure his mother was a good person but trying to blame her death on Nigeria's blessing is just wrong. Why can't he accept that she was just sick? Why must he now put sand-sand in our garri? This 'alien thing' as you people are calling it is nothing more than the hand of God appearing in Nigeria's life and God's hand is always pure.

November 16 12:09

MaziNwosuThe3rd: Hmmm. This is a powerful post. I know say that site get K-leg from day 1. Make government talk true o!

November 16 13:52

GBR: God bless Bidemi for not giving up. For those of you wondering why the government would try to cover up the deaths: it looks like they are using some of that technology to develop weapons. There is something fishy going on. Just go to TheTruthAboutTheAbeokuta52.com and read all the posts, especially the ones by the account called "Mister52."

November 16 23:09

PastorPaul HRH: *@SoyinkaStan1* Hmmm. Your head is correct.

November 17 10:34

EngineerK32: This is nothing but slander by foreign powers to discredit us because we didn't sell exploitation rights to them. ATA is trash. I wonder how much they paid this traitor to lie.

November 17 15:22

ShineShineDoctor: This is Doctor Shina. The same one from Bidemi's story. I am currently in London. If anyone knows how to contact Bidemi, please inbox me, I need to warn him.

November 17 15:54

Abk52 Warrior: *@ShineShineDoctor* Warn him about what?

November 17 15:57

OmoOba1991: <Comment Flagged and Auto-Deleted by NLModeratorBot>

November 17 16:01

LadiDadi999: @OmoOba1991 Whats wrong with you? Don't you know how to have a sensible discussion? Lack of home training.

November 17 16:39

GdlckJnthn311: Look, I understand how this boy must feel but it's just not true. I have been working at Dangote Technologies since 2023 and the alien technology has never once caused harm to anyone on my team. I have personally touched some of those materials myself. I will direct anyone interested in facts and not fiction to read the paper: "Technical Report No. 93: A Targeted Risk Assessment of the Abeokuta Exploitation Site" which is available for free download on the Ministry of science and technology website.

November 17 17:05

ShineShineDoctor: @Abk52 _ Warrior I was attacked on my way to Knightsbridge to discuss my recollection of his mother's

case with Dr. Maduako at UCL. There were
two men with knives. Thank God for the
group of Croatian tourists who intervened
to save my life. They took my wallet, my
phone and all my notes on his mother's
case. This morning I heard Dr. Maduako was
in an accident. I don't know what is going
on but I think Bidemi is in danger.

November 17 17:26

Abk52 Warrior: *@ShineShineDoctor* OMG. OK.
Can't say much here but let me contact my
network and see what we can find. For now,
please make sure you only login in using a
proxy. Stay safe.

November 17 17:28

LekanSkywalker: *@Abk52 _ Warrior @
ShineShineDoctor* Ghen Gheun! Una don start
fake action film. Hahaha! Gerarahere mehn!

November 17 18:46

PeterIkeji Jos: What is all this nonsense
about a cover-up? I swear some people turn

everything into conspiracy. Next thing you
people will say Sgt Rogers killed his
mother with the cooperation of the CIA and
wiliwili. Mumu nonsense.

November 17 20:15

GBR: Seriously you people that think this
is some conspiracy theory bullshit need to
pay attention. Don't be blinded because
naira-to-dollar exchange rate is good now
and you have constant power supply. 27
employees at Dangote Technologies have
disappeared in the last 4 years. Read the
posts on TheTruthAboutAbeokuta52.com. Go to
the *LifeCast* and *Twitter* feeds of
@TheAbeokuta52Lie. Read Doctor Shina's
comment above. There is a sensible,
realistic and pertinent case for the
government to answer and the evidence is
only growing. Open your eyes.

November 17 21:09

SoyinkaStan1: *@ShineShineDoctor* You are
lucky you are in Britain. If it were
Nigeria they'd have killed you for sure.

The silver lining is that London has CCTV
cameras everywhere so they will probably
catch the attempted murderers, and when
they do, the investigation will finally
expose this whole thing! The truth is
coming.

November 17 23:24

Abk52   Warrior: *@ShineShineDoctor* My ATA
contacts tell me that Bidemi was trying to
sneak into Nigeria through Benin republic
to attend a planned protest. No one has
heard from him since. I can connect you to
the protest organizers. Inbox me a private
email address. Don't use anything public.
Set up a new account on encrypted
LegbaMail. Stay safe.

November 17 23:58

GBR: Did you guys see this yet? https://cnn
.com/2026/11/17/politics/ nigeria-britain
-sign-long-term—genodynamic-technology
-exchange-contract/index.html

Be careful *@ShineShineDoctor*
November 18 11:09

Abk52   Warrior: @ShineShineDoctor Did you get my last message?

November 18 11:43

Abk52   Warrior: @ShineShineDoctor Please respond if you can see this.

November 18 16:11

Abk52   Warrior: @ShineShineDoctor Doctor Shina?

November 19 09:11

<Comments have now been closed on this post>

TENDS TO ZERO

$$e^{i\pi} + 1 = 0$$

When the sun rises, so do I. Through the curtains, filtered dawnlight kisses my eyes. I wake.

It's 7:05 am, and I should still be fast asleep. After a long night of drinking, first at Freedom Park and later at Quilox Club, ending in a deeply unsatisfying threesome with Chiamaka and Ronke—runs girls I'd picked up in Swe Bar—I'd finally drifted off into dreamless slumber at about five. Now I am awake. Laying in this soft bed, in the softly lit executive suite of the Lagos InterContinental Hotel, nestled between two soft, naked bodies, I find myself thinking of last night, of the early minutes before the start of the Afropolitan Vibes concert at Freedom Park amphitheater, the only part of the evening that I genuinely remember.

We'd arrived early—Asiru, Lekan, Chris, and I. In the cloudy sky, the sun had taken on an orange halo as it sank against a field of dizzying purples, red, blues, and yellows. We found a nice table near the stage where the air was scheduled to vibrate with loud, live music in a few hours and settled down with two bowls of pepper soup, a plateful of suya, and a calabash of allegedly fresh palm wine. A young man with a goje who looked like a vagrant was sitting on the sand at the edge of the stage, playing softly. I'd watched the sun slowly drown in the horizon while my old friends from university, whom I hadn't seen in months, tried to distract me from memories of my dead brother. They meant well, but I couldn't bring myself to care about their words. When they realized I wasn't really paying attention, they slowly shifted their discussion to arguments about football and politics.

Sitting there silently in the strange light of sundown, I momentarily regressed into a sort of dream state and, in so doing, found myself free of sadness for the first time since my mother had called screaming into the phone that Tunji was dead. But as the sun finally fell, I became aware of the thick white wall surrounding the Park, and of the Park's history, which I had learned about while failing my first year at university. It poisoned my mood.

Freedom Park was built on the grounds of the old, colonial-era Broad Street Prison, the first prison set up after the British seized Lagos in 1861. Originally built with mud and thatch, it was repeatedly arsoned by anti-colonial freedom fighters, so the British rebuilt it with brick. Thousands were imprisoned and executed by enforcers of the British colonial will, including many of Nigeria's founding fathers. But after independence, Nigeria took control of her own destiny and became responsible for her own cruelties. Many people were kept incarcerated there in the years following, including highway robbers and separatists who had been on the losing side of the civil war. The prison was finally pulled down in 1976, and Freedom Park developed over it. Imprisonment replaced by artistic expression. A history of pain was overwritten with the promise of regularly scheduled pleasures.

Perhaps I was sitting in the exact spot where someone had been kept in chains like an animal for resisting foreign invaders; perhaps I was eating from a table that stood where someone had been killed, offered as a sacrifice on the altar of law and order in the new republic. Freedom Park was a palimpsest, and whatever fragment of happiness I'd glimpsed in the drowning sun could no longer be perceived clearly through its history. I wished then that I hadn't known anything about the Park and its history of pain and violence; perhaps I'd have been able to hold on to that happiness longer. History is a burden, knowledge is misery, and I know too much about Lagos, this city where I was born and where I, like my brother, will probably die. I'd spent the rest of the night, and more money than I reasonably should have, in a blur, blunting my mind and memories with marijuana, lust, and alcohol in an effort to recapture the happiness. I failed.

I rise, lift Ronke's perfectly manicured hand off my chest, push Chiamaka gently until she rolls over, and slide out from between them, underneath the covers at the end of the bed. The hotel had provided a fluffy white robe with a stitched gold emblem and comfortable straw slippers. I put them on. The lights are off, but immature daylight illuminates the clothes, condoms, receipts, underwear, bundles of cash, and bottles on the floor. The slick, modern decor of the room, which I had admired when I booked it, seems tainted by what we did here yesterday— three people caring nothing for each other, licking, rubbing, and slapping flesh against flesh desperately. The place now seems sleazy.

I catch my dim reflection in the large rectangular mirror set in an old mahogany frame, carved with leaf and flower designs, and notice that my entire body somehow seems substantially smaller, somewhat shrunken and skinny, like I have lost a sixth or so of my weight in the last few days. I choose not to think about it too much. It's probably just an optical illusion, light and shadow playing games at dawn. Or the result of a residual high. I grab an almost-empty bottle of Jack Daniels from the floor and walk over to the window. The sun glints over the lagoon, making it shimmer like liquid silver, and for a moment, I forget just how filthy the water is beneath the soft waveforms of the surface.

I take a large swig of the whiskey, throw the empty bottle on the bed between the girls, and sink to my knees. Tears roll down my face. I kneel there, weeping softly, watching the sun rise over the water until the sudden trill of my phone drags me back to the present.

I rise from the floor, wipe away the tears, and walk to the dresser where my phone sits, insistent. The caller ID reads "Mum," and I instinctively reach for it before pausing. I would love to talk to her now, to share memories of playing with Tunji in the sand at Bar Beach, to tell her how desperately I wish I could bring him back, but I know she will only cry and wail and tell me how terrible my life is and that I should come with her to church before God takes me too. Often, I find myself wishing he'd done just that.

I gaze at the screen, my hand frozen. On the other end of the call, she is probably sitting in her bed, morning prayers just completed, bible in her thin hand, and her hair bound up in a silk scarf. I can't talk to her now. Not when I'm like this. My body thaws, I pick up the phone, swipe to dismiss the call without answering, and put it on silent. My skin feels too tight, my legs unsteady. Ashamed, I walk to the bed and fall back into the valley between the two naked women, narrowly avoiding the bottle. I feel like Adam, hiding among the trees of the Garden of Eden.

I am alone. I mean, I have always felt alone, living more in my head and in the bottle than in the world, keeping most of my thoughts and emotions to myself, but Tunji's death has triggered something. I have been feeling a new kind of aloneness, a deeper and more complete kind of aloneness that has suffused every thought and emotion I have. It hurts. I don't want it.

I wrap my arm around Ronke's waist and pull her to me. Her voice, sultry with drowsiness, drifts to me, "Ah ahn, you're awake already?"

She moans, pulling a pillow to her chest as I rub myself against her. She sighs. "Let me put you back to bed. Try for a little pleasure before the end."

I ignore the strange conclusion to her sentence, not understanding what she means by it, and we have joyless sex for a quarter of an hour while Chiamaka pretends to sleep. When we are done, I fall asleep again, exhausted and empty.

By noon, we are all awake. I give them ₦125,000 to get back to their campus and take care of themselves when they get there, slipping an extra ₦25,000 into Ronke's hand while Chiamaka is putting on her makeup in the bathroom. She rewards me with a wink but doesn't take the money, pressing the cash and my hand back against my chest. Her long hair swishes as she shakes her head and adjusts her dress like a second skin.

"It's okay. I really don't need this," she says before she kisses me on the cheek and looks at me with something like pity in her impossibly gray eyes. Ashamed, I look away and say goodbye without returning her gaze.

I take a shower, slip into my T-shirt, jeans, and sunglasses, which all seem a bit too big, and then check out of the hotel and drive back down to Swe Bar in Onikan where music with incomprehensible lyrics, set to bass as thick as the heartbeat of a decadent god, and the thick smell of whiskey welcome me like a womb.

$$1 + \frac{1}{\varphi} = \varphi$$

With dawn come sharp flares of pain, red needles of light beneath my eyelids.

I turn away from the rapidly rising sun, my hands instinctively covering my face as the hangover begins to blossom in my head. My hands are covered with the familiar wetness of vomit and dew. My back is sore from sleeping on the unforgiving concrete sidewalk leading out of Tafawa Balewa Square, less than a mile from the bar. A woolen echo fills my head, silencing the world. My bones press against my skin, making my body feel small and not quite fully developed. I feel like an accident.

Peeking out from between my fingers, the upside-down city smiles back at me in the fading twilight, its badly maintained buildings and hastily constructed steel towers like uneven teeth in a yellow-gray mouth of sky.

There is a bus stop near me. I can tell by the tangle of traffic—mostly beat-up danfos and molues, secondhand motorcycles and scratched cars. Old men sit by the roadside on low stools under brightly colored umbrellas, their limbs unfurling as they ready their stalls and kiosks for the day into which I have clumsily emerged. There is a carnival of bright plastic buckets and metal trays carried by women, children, and young men hawking wares. The colors are too bright, the silence in my head too unnatural.

In a sudden surge, sound returns to the world, and the sudden hysteria of feet slapping against the concrete and tires crunching pot-holed road, car horns blaring, and engines growling all explode into my consciousness. Four roads dance into a roundabout a little distance away, and there are no traffic lights. It's pure Lagos chaos, and it makes my hangover feel like an irresolute death.

I groan and sit up, hanging my heavy head between my legs and leaning my back against a cracked, upright concrete slab for support as people walk past me, staring, shaking their heads and hissing. Tears and saliva fall from my face to the ground as I wonder wretchedly why I hadn't been the one to die instead of my brother.

Tunji had always been the ambitious one. The smart one with the scholarship to UNILAG, the handsome one who got married to a beautiful wife at twenty four; the fun one who had friends everywhere and went from being an accountant to a successful restaurant owner; and the one who'd planned to retire a millionaire at fifty, just like our father. I was the mediocre one, the plain one who got below average grades in class, who barely managed to graduate from Osun State University after stumbling through four years of English literature, who worked as a DJ and producer for street musicians and dodgy radio stations.

Despite this achievement gulf between us, and the constant remarks of our parents who fetishized their public image and the way our lives reflected on them, Tunji and I always remained friends. Perhaps even more than we were family, we were inexplicably friends. When we were children, we always insisted on playing together no matter what our vastly disparate cliques thought of the other. Whenever Tunji got picked as football team captain, and the captains took turns selecting team members, he would always pick me to join his team first, even though my feet were as clumsy with a ball then as they usually are after a dozen or so glasses of shepe now. Whenever my friends and I went to smoke igbo on the rooftop of our hostel, I always insisted that they allow Tunji to join us despite his reputation as a "scholarship boy," because I knew he liked the mental freedom that came with the herbal high, even if he didn't like the dank, cloying smell of weed. He was the first person that I told when I failed my first year at university, and he drove all the way to Ikire to drink with me and be beside me when our father arrived to tell me what a shame I was to the entire family.

I was the best man at his wedding, and I ran around Lagos like a wild animal for eight weeks helping to make arrangements with caterers and florists and musicians and the million other vendors, so the couple wouldn't have to. And even though once the ceremony was over I got drunk and passed out in the carpark a few minutes to midnight, Tunji came to find me, put ice packs on my face, poured water down my throat until I woke up, and dragged me back to the after-party, laughing all the while. Our moments of connection were always like that, characterized by our just being there for each other, not necessitated by anything beyond who we were to one another.

But they were also characterized by this: my constant failing, my constant falling, and Tunji's unwillingness to let me hit rock bottom and break. The truth is, I gave up on myself early. I became an alcoholic wastrel when I was about nineteen. Since then, I have had little ambition in life beyond drinking myself into some semblance of ignorant bliss and making myself as small as possible, trying not to disappoint my parents much more than I already had once I realized I'd never be able to live up to my father and brother.

My father was a legendary hotelier with properties dotting the city. And Tunji—he was going places. At least he was until an articulated truck skidded off the Ojuelegba Bridge and fell to the road below, smashing him into a pulpy mess in the front seat of his Range Rover SUV.

My mother has been crying and praying for three weeks, inconsolable. I've been drinking. Whiskey. I've been drinking whiskey. I've been drinking because I don't know what else to do. Palm wine is best for celebration, but whiskey is good for pain.

"You're lucky armed robbers or policemen didn't kill you when you were sleeping," says a rusty old voice in confident Yoruba. It sounds like it's coming from both inside my head and above me at the same time. I raise my head to see two thin eyes set into a wide, wrinkled face, smiling at me.

"But then again, you don't have much time left."

"Who are you?" I groan. The man speaking to me is a small, shriveled old man with a big gray afro and small gray eyes; he has a wise, seen-the-world look to him like a living sunset. He is wearing a green and brown Ankara shirt and trouser combination with plain brown sandals and a gold watch that looks more expensive than he should be able to afford.

"Doesn't matter," he says and tosses a ₦500 note onto the ground in front of me. "That should be enough to get you home. I think you'll find that your wallet is no longer with you."

"I don't need your help, old man," I shout, louder than I intend to, as I reach for the note to hand it back to him. My fingers settle on sandy concrete, my vision swims, and I fall over, banging my head hard.

The man looks down at me pitifully as he pushes his money into the front pocket of my shirt.

"Foolish boy," he says. "Go home and wait. There's no need for all this drama. You'll be gone soon enough."

The calmness with which he makes this strange statement, and the familiarity of it, jolts me out of my drunken haze just long enough to ask, "What the hell does that mean?"

"If I tell you . . ." begins the old man before a brief pause and tilt of the head. And then, "Forget it. I've already done what I can to make this easier for you. Just take the money, and go home."

I drag myself up from the floor and grab hold of his trousers. "Why did you say I will be gone soon? Are you cursing me with juju?"

"I don't curse people," he says as he shakes his leg free of my grasp. "I'm not a babalawo. I'm . . . no one."

He walks along the sidewalk, whispering something to himself, and I start to think that he will leave without saying more, but he stops and turns to face me and says, "Look, this isn't easy for me either. It has only ever happened twice before."

"What the hell are you talking about?"

He sighs and shakes his head before finally speaking. "What would you say if I told you that this city, like you, is alive? It was born, it grows, it eats, it loves, it will die. Since it was a child, it has learned to eat what it needs from the lives of the ever-growing flood of people that come into it, become part of it. Its riverbanks have become cradles, its slums have developed into fists, its gray roads have grown teeth, its traffic and owambes and construction and beaches have developed a rhythm like a pounding heartbeat. And the city, like all living things, will always do what it needs to survive; fight to stay alive, defend itself from threats to its life. And what would you say if I told you that you, young man, have somehow found a way to make yourself a threat to the city?"

I hear the words he says, but they don't make sense to me. I know from experience that words can sometimes shake free of meaning and become abstract noises when heard in hangover or post-high, but this is different. He is talking of Lagos like it's a person, a real human. Not in metaphor but in substance. Puzzled and hungry for understanding, I can only mutter, "The city is alive?"

"Yes," he says. "Look, go home. You won't understand now. Take the money I gave you, and go home. Drink some more and forget all this. In the evening, you'll really notice the change, and maybe you'll start to understand."

"What will I understand? What will I see? What is happening to me?"

"Bloody hell. I should have just stayed away. Give me your hand," he says impatiently as he kneels on the ground beside me. The pedestrians on the increasingly busy street stare at us even more than they did before, but I don't care. I do as I'm told.

He puts his hand into mine, and it feels like an old earthenware plate, but what is even stranger, it feels like this small old man's hand is larger than mine. Much larger.

"This is what I mean. First in your depression and now in your grief, you have been thinking strangely of this city, viewing it all wrong through the lens of your pain. You have linked parts of the city with negative memories, with painful histories, with almost everything wrong in your life, with everything wrong in so many lives. Usually most people link parts of the city with both good and bad memory and emotion. There is a balance, and the city works it out. But you, with your sadness and grief, have threaded a pure and persistent pain to the very essence of the things with which cities are made, and it has obstructed the city's breathing, pressed against its organs. You have become a sickness, a cancer, so the city is pressing back against you. You must understand, none of this is malicious. Now you will shrink as the city destroys you. You will become smaller and smaller and smaller, and eventually you will disappear into nothing because Lagos can no longer survive with you in it."

The air around me smells of reused cooking oil, sweat, and exhaust. A danfo heading to Yaba passes by, the conductor calling out the destination. There is a white sticker on its back window where in faded red font it declares, "God's Time is Best."

Dazed, I ask the strange old man, "How long do I have?"

"In one or two days, it will be as though you never existed. You will be forgotten. Your mother will not remember that she had more than one son. Your friends will not miss you. You will be subject to a great and instant forgetting. You will have been nothing but a wick, nameless, snuffed out. A discarded bundle of memories and experiences without a name. The city will absorb you and your experiences and purge them. It must to survive. And when it is done, it will adjust itself and its people so that it may continue to live."

I throw my head back and close my eyes to shut out the sun, and I start to laugh and laugh a long laugh that becomes a cough, and before long, I am choking.

I feel the eyes of the old man on the back of my head and his hand on my shoulder, so I ask, "This is ridiculous. Why should I even believe any of the rubbish you just said to me?"

He rises to his feet and straightens his back. "Because I *am* the city. And I *will* not let your twisted pain kill me."

And with that, he scatters into a tiny billion pieces that are seamlessly absorbed by the air and concrete and mud and madness, leaving me hung-over and confused on the cracked Lagos pavement, wondering if he was ever really there at all.

$$\lim_{t \to \infty} \sum u(t) = 0$$

A sharp knife of sunlight cuts through the space between the curtains of my bedroom and across my body, separating my consciousness and leaving me half-awake for the third time this morning. A part of me wants to rise early, but the bed is warm and soft, and exhaustion keeps dragging me back into sleep like an anchor until memories of the old man penetrate the fog, and I remember. I remember. I am disappearing.

I sit up, my torso crossing the line of light, and am surprised at the alien nature of my own movements, the arcs my limbs trace are unfamiliar and strange, so strange. I am afraid of my changing self. The fear paralyzes me, but what do men who are shrinking into themselves do? There is a half-empty bottle of whiskey on the bedside table, its glass edges and amber liquid beautiful in the light of the young sun. I stare at it for what could be seconds or hours—I am not sure—yearning for the familiar comfort and knowing that it will not, cannot, help me anymore. I turn back to the window and watch as dawn unravels, skeins of light spreading across the wide sky and think of the artists selling cheap paintings of sunrise on canvas in Jakande Market alongside wooden art, beads, bracelets, necklaces, talking drums. If Lagos truly is alive, then its many markets must be its beating heart. I almost smile.

When the sun is high and bright, I briefly consider visiting my mother, taking her up on her open offer to take me to church. Perhaps her pastor can pray for me when he is finished counting his profits from last Sunday's collection.

No. But I should at least talk to her. I want to talk to her. I need to. She is the only family I have left even if the old man, who says he is the city, says she will not remember me when I am gone.

I rise on unsteady legs like a newborn calf and go into the living room, stumbling. Falling into the middle of the sofa, fighting to breathe evenly and cleanly, I pull my phone out of my pocket, press "Mum" on the smooth screen, and hold it up to my ear with a skeletal hand. My grip is so weak; the phone slips from my hand when she answers, and it takes me a few seconds to retrieve it.

"Goodbye?" she repeats when I finally say the word. "What do you mean goodbye? Where are you going?"

"Yes," I confirm. "I know things have been difficult between us lately, but I just wanted to say goodbye, and I love you."

"Where are you going?" she asks again.

"I don't know," I tell her because even though I want to confess to her that her son is being consumed by a city, it would be too confusing and too cruel.

"What does that mean, ehn?" she asks before retreating into the safety of her religion. "You've started with your wahala again, but this is not the time for it, so I need you to listen to me. Don't go anywhere yet. There is midweek service today, and pastor Chris has been asking of you since the funeral. Come with me, and let us—"

She is still speaking, but her words are too familiar to mean anything to me. She keeps talking. I drop the phone to my rake-thin thighs and stare at it, mesmerized, like it is a gemstone or a small, talking animal. The tears begin to flow, and I find myself once again confronted by the widening gap between myself and the woman who birthed me. We used to be very close when I was younger, and my mind more malleable, but my entire adulthood has been a series of estrangements. I want to talk to her now, to tell her how sad, angry, confused, and scared I am at everything and nothing, how desperately I need to feel like something about my presence in this world mattered before I am gone from it, but all she can do, all she has ever done, is tell me to come to church. She has no other counsel to offer but the comfort of her god. I wish that once, just this once, she would try to talk to me without the wall of her faith between us, even if she has no assurances to offer me. I just want to know that in this moment we are equally human. I put the phone back to my ear and repeat myself, ignoring her own stream of words, "Goodbye, Mum. I love you."

She will forget me soon, and perhaps that's for the best. Sometimes even family means nothing in the end. I wish Tunji were still here. Lagos is a cruel city to take him like that, to erase me in retaliation for poisoning it with my grief. I throw my phone at the wall, and it shatters into a hundred useless pieces. And then all the fear and anger and pain and grief and disappointment and depression and confusion congeal into something liquid in my chest that drips down my ribs, tickling me as I laugh and laugh with all the bitterness in me until tears run down my face like a poisoned river, and I close my eyes to keep them in.

I drift into something like sleep, and there I feel the flowering within me of a potential for something like happiness, something much deeper and something more unique than the chemically induced high and obliviousness of alcohol. Something beyond my strange circumstances and my changing body. Something so much . . . more. When I open my eyes, it hits me.

I imagine myself as I used to be a few days ago, heavily and intentionally, until I feel like my imagination has taken form, has physical weight. I imagine a hand shaped like a city with expressway fingers, open air market palms, and beach surf fingernails squeezing me. Just like the old man said, I see the city compress me, and I lift my left hand up and stare at it.

My forearms thin almost immediately. I see my skin tighten and the flesh padding my bone diminish like it is evaporating. My stomach twists with fear and excitement. But I don't stop. I press on, my mind swelling with imagination as I picture more of the city in the hand that squeezes me. In that hand, I see the filth and congestion of Obalende, its winding, yellow molue queues and ugly, dirty shanties where so many in Lagos pass through on their way to the day's labors like callouses on the palms. I see the lovely colonial townhouses, mansions, clubs, and hotels of Ikoyi where the rich and powerful nest themselves like the lines in the little finger of the city. I picture the filthy canals, waterways, and shacks on stilts of Makoko, running along the lagoon where the Egun fishermen who migrated from Badagary eke out a living, and in my mind, it is the back of the hand of the city that squeezes me. I see the new rows of apartment buildings and townhouses that are being built in Ajah, the place for the once-growing middle class that seems separate from but flows into the city like its cephalic vein. I see the roiling, dirty waves of Bar Beach like Ronke's fingernails, long and extended and pressed against my chest. I inhale air and exhale myself. I feel my ribs contracting, my chest emptying me out into the city, as I imagine what it is doing to me, and I will it to press against me even harder, to accelerate the process. It is exhilarating. Spittle collects in the corners of my mouth as I collapse back on the couch and continue my fading away.

It gets easier and easier as I do it, my imagination yielding more of the city and less of myself. My legs become thin stalks, and my torso reduces to thin board after a few cycles of squeezing and letting go, squeezing and letting go. I am developing a muscle for erasing myself, strengthening it with high-intensity exercise.

I have reduced myself to little more than a skeleton before I feel the urge to be out in the city as I do this. To insert the unreality of my situation into the absolute reality of Lagos, to be in the open city as I picture it pressing onto me.

I push up from the couch and struggle outside to my car. The difficulty of walking outside is expected, but pulling open the door takes far more effort than I thought it would. It has been so hot and humid that the air outside is thick, hazy, saturated with water vapor, smoke, prayers, and dreams. The sun feels heavy on my head. I nestle myself in the driver's seat and look at my face in the mirror.

I am gaunt. Adrenaline erupts and surges through my veins as I rev the engine and press the horn until Ladi the gateman comes out to open the gate, holding up his sagging trousers with one hand. When I pass, I floor the accelerator and swing the car out onto the road, rear tires smoking and showering everything with dust, sand, and gravel. By the time Ladi is a speck in the mirror, too small to distinguish from the hundreds of other pedestrians, I am sweating profusely.

The wind blows wildly through the windows as I barrel down Oko-baba Street, ignoring the traffic lights and dipping in and out of potholes recklessly.

And then there is a large, lovely woman in the car with me. I know it is Lagos because it can be no one and nothing else. She is wearing a spectacular gold and blue traditional iro and buba made with expensive aso-oke. The iro is tight against her wide hips, and the buba has a low-cut neck that would be revealing if it wasn't for the half dozen matching stringed-bead necklaces around her neck. Her stiff, blue gele is a large and elaborate affair like the train of a wild peacock wrapped around her head and pressing against the roof of my car. She speaks as I round the highway exit and climb up the causeway that leads to the third main-land bridge.

"What are you doing?" Lagos asks as she adjusts her gele and turns to face me with piercing gray eyes. "You can't stop this once it has begun."

"I am not trying to stop it. I am embracing it," I reply, bizarrely buoyant. I no longer fear anything, not my mediocre and pointless life, not this overwhelming and cruel city and its history, not even my coming demise. Even my grief for Tunji has morphed into something new. There is freedom in acceptance. With practiced ease, I take the image of the woman sitting beside me into my mind, and in my imagination, I picture this manifestation of Lagos, broad and beautiful, sitting on my chest, compressing me. I am delighted when I see my fingers, tight against the wheel, shrink. To imagine the city is to lose myself.

"You should have done this sooner," says Lagos. "Accepted things. You should have accepted the life you had. Perhaps I wouldn't have had to purge you."

"Perhaps," I say because I cannot think of anything else to say.

"Do you want me to stay with you?" the city asks. "Until the end?"

"No need," I say. "I want to do this alone."

"I understand. And I am sorry," says the city. "I am only trying to survive."

I mouth the words, "I understand."

"Is there anything you want before you're gone? Any final requests?"

"I want to see Tunji, even if only for a moment, right before the end. Can you do that?"

"I'll see what I can do," she says.

When I glance to my right, there is nothing but a gourd of palm wine in the chair where the woman that is the city had been. I wonder what we are celebrating as I reach for it and take a swig. It tastes like freedom.

An okada whizzes by, barely an inch from me, and I almost hit it. My arms and fingers are so small; it is difficult to control the car now. My vision is blurring at the edges. Shapes and colors are bleeding into each other like reality around me has been stabbed. Or perhaps my eyes are becoming too small to see clearly. I look up through the windscreen. Above, the sun is retreating behind a silver and black curtain of clouds. The skyscrapers of the marina in the distance, the shanties on the edge of the water, all of it now seems less real than the dream-images I have of them in my head, pressing against me. The horizon of my existence grows nearer and nearer. I am carrying my version of the city in my mind, a private and complete burden that I will soon be free of just as the city will soon be free of me.

The sky begins to weep rain.

I press my foot down harder against the accelerator, and the vehicle vibrates intensely like a lover in orgasm.

When I can no longer keep control of the careening car, I swerve right, hard.

Tires scream, the world spirals, and I crash through the barrier. Everything slows as jagged metal and hot rubber slam into my windscreen, cracking it and bringing in the smell of smoke and the raw bite of pain. I fall. I fall for what seems like a long time.

When the car breaks the surface of the lagoon, water rushes in. I close my eyes and imagine that all of Lagos, from Badagry to Ikeja is liquid around me. It gets harder to breathe, but I am not sure if it is because my lungs are shrinking rapidly or because I am drowning. I feel myself become small, so small and slight. I turn my body over to this water that is the city and so much larger than myself.

In the instant before there is no more of me, I see Tunji's eyes blossom open like flowers in the darkness. I hear his voice in my head, and his voice is my voice, the voice of the city, which is the only voice that exists, the only voice that has ever existed, and it says, *Everything dies, and everything will be forgotten. Ideas. Feelings. Lives. Cities. Monuments. Gods. Memories. Everything. Everything tends to zero.*

NIGERIAN DREAMS

"What is the Nigerian dream?" the man's companion asked.

The man responded with a puzzled look, so his companion elaborated, "Like you know how they are always talking about 'the American dream' in those old American immersies; the whole life, liberty and pursuit of happiness thing. Shebi you don hear am before?"

The man and his companion were seated on a pair of ugly gray plastic chairs in a crowded beer parlor at the center of sector-121, which was the easternmost sector of the 856th level of the monolithic Biafra-5 supercity. The cacophony of voices shouting, laughing, and arguing made it so that the man and his companion had to raise their voices to hear each other. Biafra-5 was one of twenty-six solid superstructures that made up the modern Nigerian nation-state. Across the continent, there were thousands of concrete monstrosities just like it, each housing its two billion plus population. Each one towered seven kilometers into the sky and imposed a ten square kilometer footprint on the ground like fingers pointed accusingly at unresponsive ancestors. Beyond them, expansive fields of hungry solar panels interspersed with endless fields of genetically modified vegetation surrounded the towers like bizarre, silicon-cell pubic hair. Outside, the temperature was hot enough to kill an exposed man in a day. Inside, it was just warm enough to remind them of the terrible thing they had done to their planet.

The man scratched his sparse, knotty beard and said, "Yeah, I have. Who hasn't? That old Hollywood nonsense is everywhere but what does that one have to do with us, and why have you not yet paid for the beer you owe me, Chuka? We need to get going soon."

Chuka smiled an oily smile and leaned forward in his chair. He was wearing an old-fashioned ankara print shirt with short sleeves, and his bald head was distracting under the harsh fluorescent lighting of the beer parlor. On the low table between them, empty bottles stood in a row like sentries. At the far end of the parlor, a Quovision display deck crackled with high-resolution immersive holographic images of the new Persian prime minister in her purple hijab standing in a hall by the side of the suited up Chinese premier, the familiar faces of some other world leaders behind them. The man could not read the scrolling chyron below the image, but he took note of the words: *immigration control*. There wasn't any mention of the violent clashes that were currently raging right below them on the 304th level of Biafra-5.

They'd known each other for fourteen years so the man knew that Chuka tended to become philosophical when he had been drinking. He also had a tendency to forget his cryptowallet code and insist that he would pay for drinks *next time*. Next time had been coming for a long time. But after this, there would be no more next time.

"Leave beer first and answer me jare. What is the Nigerian dream? Abi we don't have?"

"Why you dey ask me? Na me born Nigeria? How am I supposed to know?" the man barked. He was getting anxious. He wanted Chuka to settle the bill and all the others that had been perpetually postponed so that they would not miss their window of opportunity.

Chuka nodded, as though acknowledging something profound. "Exactly. Na my point be that. You don't know. Most of us don't. But if you look closely at our history, you will see it. Since before the first war sef."

Then Chuka gestured earnestly at his chest. "It's inside here my brother," he said, banging the left pocket of his Ankara shirt with a hardy fist. "How many of us have ever cared about the country or our fellow country people? Not our tribe or state o, I mean the country itself. How many? We live in it, and we survive it. But last last, once we get a chance, most of us we leave. That is the sad truth. Always has been. This is a made-up country. Invented for colonial convenience. One oyibo just wake up one day, draw line for paper, begin talk say make we dey together, like say we no get our own kingdoms and republics before them come our land." Chuka hissed and continued. "Some people have even wanted to leave right from inception. Others have just been reluctant participants. We didn't choose this place, we didn't fight for it, and so we don't love it. In your heart, you know that the Nigerian dream is to leave Nigeria."

The man cocked his head, silent for a beat, and then laughed, waving his bony right arm. It was covered in scar tissue from an incident involving a malfunctioning water filter in the Ibadan-1 superstructure on his first smuggle run. "That's it? That's your big insight? Abeg, my guy, pay for beer, make we go. It's almost time."

Chuka was visibly disappointed at the reception his speech had received.

Beckoning to the dour-faced waitress, the man said, "I thought you were even going to say something that makes sense. Whose dream is to leave a place? Leaving a place is what you do in pursuit of a dream. No one wants to leave their home unless their home has become a place with teeth. And even so no one dreams of the going. Trust me. I know.

No one aspires to be displaced. You of all people should know that. The dream is the reason you leave. The destination is the place where the dream is. And everyone has a different dream. The very concept of a national dream is a joke. Dreams are personal and private things. Na too much film do you. Or maybe na the beer or even . . ." The man trailed off, not wanting to bring up difficult memories.

Chuka grunted but said nothing. He swiped his palm in front of the smooth black panel the waitress presented and keyed in his wallet codes. When she left, the man pulled out a similar panel and placed it on the table. Chuka took it and repeated the gesture, transferring a significantly larger number of credits to the man's account: for the beers he owed and for services about to be rendered.

The man smiled. His new business was proving to be very lucrative, even this run, for which he had given Chuka the friends-and-family discount.

Chuka's face remained humorless. He had just parted ways with almost every credit he had to his name.

"Don't squeeze face my guy. Your own dream is about to come true."

Chuka snorted.

The two men rose briskly and rode an express intercity service elevator they would not have had access to if not for the man's well-placed bribe to his contact in city security. It took four silent minutes of descent to reach the ground floor of Biafra-5, where gigantic access ports were carved into the eastern service wall, and machines constantly ferried harvested food in and treated waste out.

"Follow me and do exactly what I do," the man said.

Chuka nodded.

They crouched low and moved quickly past a row of cuboid, metal behemoths with hundreds of small articulated legs, like giant millipedes. They kept moving until they came to a row of smaller machine units of assorted shapes and sizes. The man stopped, pushed against one of the units, and a hatch that Chuka could have sworn wasn't there before, yawned open. They slipped into a small, silver-skinned oblate pod with a transparent base. It was a repurposed monitoring pod. Thanks to another bribe, it had been disguised as part of a larger cassava transport unit nearby. On the official books, it was damaged and pending repair. In reality, it was a smuggler's ferry. The man took a seat and put his finger to a control panel. The pod hummed to life at the man's touch, ascended, and began to move. It quietly slid past the other units and through the supercity's heavy titanium gate without interrupting the steady motion of the other machines. The city exhaled them into the open field. Above, an angry yellow sun raged in the brown sky.

"Did you tell Lara's mother you were leaving?" the man asked Chuka as they sped over the green and silver surface below.

Chuka nodded, unconsciously touching the strip of fair flesh on his finger that marked where his wedding ring used to be before the thief that shot his wife near the elevator entrance to level 304 took it. "My guy, nothing remain here for me. Country don spoil. The whole planet sef don spoil."

The man guided the pod onto the bright yellow line on his screen that marked the route to the border with Cameroon. It was where the man's business associates were waiting with a new identity chip for Chuka. One that would give him a new name, a new history, and grant him access to the Chinese-run mining supercity Jian-3 in the heart of the Congo.

"But they say those mining supercities are secure and spacious. Them say you fit get pass one thousand credits per day just programming drill rig units inside the lower levels as long as person no mind twelve-hour work shifts." Chuka sighed. "I no mind hard work. So, yeah, once I reach there, I go hustle, I go hammer. I go dey alright."

The man had seen many others like Chuka desperate to get to places like Jian-3. Men, women, whole families. He made his living off their hope, thriving off their desperation in the very place they thought was hopeless because they couldn't see beyond their difficulties and the tantalizing lures of a foreign land. Yes, Nigeria was a difficult, made-up place. But his own Nigerian dream was to thrive in Nigeria, in the chaos, whatever it took. He was tempted to tell Chuka what really waited for him in Jian-3: segregation, discrimination, exploitation to meet quotas, and violent immigration raids that never made it on the news. But business came first, and he was not going to lose a customer just because they were in-laws, so he simply said, "Mmm hmm. Na so them talk. I just hope your dream will be worth the journey you are making for it."

"Thank you," Chuka said.

The man looked away to hide the sting of his conscience and stared down through the transparent base of the pod as the world blurred green and silver beneath them.

PERFORMANCE REVIEW

Mr. A. has cold, cold eyes.

I am standing in front of him as cool air streams directly from the air conditioner over his head and onto my face. His arms are disproportionately long, splayed out on the table like weapons. His skin is pale and dull, and the hair on his head is a gray garden, thinning at the sides. Things I hadn't noticed before. The first time we met, I actually thought he was kind of cute in a silver-fox or cool-uncle-at-the-club kind of way. Not anymore. This is the first time I have been in his office. It is efficiently ugly. All awkward angles and off-center placements and lots of open space with no pictures or art or anything that isn't functional. Apparently, it's been recently remodeled. I'm not sure what it looked like before, but I doubt this is an improvement. Nothing is out of place, but the severity of it all has bred a bland, unfeeling ugliness, finished in whites and grays and blacks. He does not ask me to sit down.

He is looking at me now with those cold, cold eyes, having finished reading my employmetrics on the lightscreen that is projected into the air in front of him from the computing scroll sitting flat on his desk. I can see the display too, but in reverse, a string of bright yellow text, numbers, and graphs that are supposed not just to indicate how well I have done in the last quarter relative to the company's objectives but also to map my cognitive abilities and project my future performance. His face contorts into something like a caricature of a smile, and a chill runs up my spine. It's almost impossible to reconcile the strange, serious man in front of me with the jovial person who took me for coffee at Umutu Café just across the street two days after I joined the company. A management meet-and-greet he'd called it. He'd been so welcoming that day, I remember thinking how lucky I was to have gotten a job in a place with people that were so friendly in this Lagos. He'd even shown me pictures of his dog, a cute little brown and white Azawakh named Rover.

"Thank you for staying a bit late for this performance review, Nneka," Mr. A says slowly. "Please, sit down."

Finally. I lower myself into the black mesh chair facing his desk, and it only gives a bit when my weight settles into it. The room is dry. Perhaps the air conditioning has been on for too long. There is a faint smell of warm tobacco wafting around, which is odd because they told us during our orientation that the company doesn't allow smoking anywhere on the premises. I begin to doubt that the windows have ever been opened. They are low and overlook the concrete and asphalt expanse of Lagos, its buildings pressed uncomfortably against each other like half-siblings forced to share a room. Through a network of dusty black wires and cables hoisted up by solid wood poles that keep the city functioning, I can see a mass of bright yellow taxis, okadas, luxury cars, and beat-up danfos slowly but steadily streaming along Akin Adesola Street, towards Falomo Bridge, trying to get out before the traffic really hits. There will be no such luck for me today. At least Amina, my colleague in sales is waiting for me. She started about the same time I did, and her own performance review was scheduled for about half an hour before mine today. We plan to head to Swe Bar, where she DJs part time, for drinks after. To talk about how our reviews went, and depending on the situation, celebrate or drink until we don't care anymore.

Mr. A says, "It's been a very busy afternoon, but I wanted to make sure we conducted this review face to face."

"Of course," I reply, "it's no problem. I was already planning to stay on the island a bit late today anyway."

"I see."

I'm nervous. Talking too much maybe. But he'd been so friendly and open when we'd first met, I don't really know how to approach this. It's like his personality has been bleached. Drained of color. I try for the familiar. "How's Rover doing?"

He cocks his head. "Rover?"

"Yes, your umm, dog. You showed me pictures a few months ago."

"Ah the dog. Yes." He says it like he has just remembered an item on his grocery list. There is not even a flash of emotion in his eyes. "Rover is fine. Very fine."

I swallow the remainder of my surprise and simply say, "Good to hear."

"Now. Let us get to it. Before we go into the official particulars, how do you think you did last quarter?" he asks. He's smiling at me, and I can see the bright yellow reflection of my performance metrics in his eyes.

I take a deep breath and clear my throat. "I think I did well. I haven't received any complaints. And I hit all my KPIs, so I think I'm meeting expectations, at least." The lifting of my voice makes it more question than statement. I don't want to seem too eager about my own perceived success just in case there is something in the numbers that say otherwise.

He looks me up and down, cold eyes scanning for something. The lines radiating from the edge of his mouth deepen as he glances to the lightscreen, then back to me. Smile stuck in place. Finally, he speaks.

"Let me begin by saying that I mostly agree with that statement. Overall, you've done quite well in your brief time here. All your key performance indicator numbers are good. You hit your sales targets, even exceeded them by 1.2%. Your team members have all given you good collaboration ratings and customer satisfaction is just north of 93%, where we need it to be. So well done on that front."

I tuck a loose braid behind my ear and say, "Thank you," because I'm not sure what else to say to this version of Mr. A, and because I am sure he isn't done. I've worked at enough of these large multinationals to know that they always begin performance reviews positively. If there is a sting, they like to save it for the end. And there is almost always a sting.

"We are quite pleased with what you have done so far. But while you are currently meeting expectations, you are meeting them at the least possible capacity. Which is unusual for most of our new hires."

There it is. The sting.

"And some of your assigned internal process tasks were not completed in time. Minor, but significant. You're only 70% compliant. It's like you are just getting by, Nneka," he says, his eyes never leaving my face. "You're only just meeting expectations."

The statement takes on a sinister tone.

"And perhaps even more importantly, some of your employmetrics are . . . concerning."

I shiver.

The employmetric stuff is pretty standard now with most companies. Remote monitoring of brain activity, speech, and movement during work hours. They use low frequency electromagnetic field sensors to measure hippocampal neuron stimulation—those are the neurons that help in forming new memories and learning. I remember them because I made a joke about hippos in the brain. They also have microphones and motion sensors everywhere that record what we say and how we move. Then it's run through speech emotion recognition and motion efficiency software. And then they take twice daily magnetic resonance tomographic scans of our *caudate nuclei*—the part of the brain that aids the mind in switching gears from one thought to another—when we enter and when we leave. I read the terms and conditions of my contract about six times, in fine detail, and even asked my friend Kamaru—he studied corporate biotech at UNILAG even though he is an artist now—to check again before I signed it. Just in case I misunderstood something. As if I wasn't going to sign it regardless. I needed the money. Still do. I just wanted to know exactly how much of my soul I was selling when I accepted the offer.

"What exactly is concerning about them?" I ask, genuinely curious.

"Your aggregate employmetric scores are: Communication efficiency—83%. Creativity and Adaptability Index—97%. Normalized Learning and Retention Rate—62%. Task Focus Factor—53%. As you can tell, they indicate that while you communicate very well with your team and your clients, and you are learning every day, your learning rate is relatively slow, and you are not sufficiently focused. It takes you a long time to settle in between tasks, and they often overlap in your mind. Your aggregate scores are in the 33rd percentile."

Another sting. Worse than the last.

"I see," I say, swallowing back the emotion that is building up at the back of my throat. "But what about the Olorogun project? The proof of concept that kept running into technical issues."

"What about it?"

"Sarah in HQ said I was the only one who came up with a workable solution." I feel my face flush hot. I don't like bragging, but I need to make sure my achievements are known to upper management and accounted for when they are looking at all this and reducing my actions to numbers. "Unique, Sarah said. She said that if not for me there would probably have been a serious client complaint. Olorogun Inc. may have even withdrawn their purchase order. Doesn't that show up in the employmetrics? Doesn't it show I have enough focus to come up with innovative solutions to complex problems?"

Mr. A's smile doesn't wane. "It does. There was a significant spike in your frontal cortex activity during that high stress situation. It's an impressive note in your records, and that's why your Creativity and Adaptability Index is so high. But we can't rely on sporadic bursts of creative brilliance to run the company. We need consistent and predictable high performance. Our recent records show that these bursts of inspiration are not reliable as a basis for successful company performance. We accept them when there are no other options, but they sometimes lead to unexpected negative outcomes. A risk we are becoming less willing to take with our business in this global economic climate." He leans forward in his chair and puts his fingertips together forming a triangle underneath his jaw like he is in the middle of some sort of strange meditation. "Focus. Consistency. That's what we need now above all else. That's why we've invested so much in our people. In you."

I don't like the way he says that last part. My face feels numb from the neverending stream of cold, dry air. It chills me through and through. This is not what I expected. I thought I was doing really well here, and I was being modest when I said, "meeting expectations at least." Forget about meeting them, I thought I was exceeding them. Apparently not. But this, even though he said he agreed with my modest assessment, everything that has come after indicates the opposite. And I've learned that once companies start talking about how much they have invested in you, there are one of two options: they are either about to invest significantly more, or they are about to cut their losses. I swear would be sweating right now if it wasn't so cold. I really don't want to lose this job. I can't afford to, so I force a small smile and spread my hands—the universal sign of openness and equitability.

"Thank you for this feedback. I really appreciate the opportunity to work here and everything the company has done for me," I say, watching the numbers that are being used to judge me shift and swim in the black of his eyes. "And I'd be happy to take any recommendations you have for me to improve going forward."

"I'm very glad you said that Nneka. Very glad." Mr. A leans forward, chin precariously balanced on fingertips, and I instinctively lean back as far as the rigid mesh chair will let me. That smile. The eyes. It's almost reptilian now. I feel like I have just walked into a trap.

"The board of directors have just approved the roll out of a new intervention for employees whose employmetrics are in the lower 50th percentile in certain key offices. Lucky for you, Lagos is on the list."

I don't feel lucky at all.

He reaches below his desk and pulls out a transparent glass prescription bottle and places it on the desk between us like it's a gift. It's full of spherical white pills that seem to glow in the light like miniature moons. "Optimiline. It's a new drug developed by SoponaPharma—our sister company—that helps with mental focus. It will soon be available on the open market, but it has shown such impressive preliminary results that we want to offer it to our employees first."

I'm confused so I ask, "You want me to take this?"

The clear bottle glints, its edges catching both the natural light from the window and the artificial light from the lightscreen.

"I am officially recommending that you do, yes. But the choice is yours entirely, of course."

"What does it do exactly?"

"Optimiline is a synthetic nootropic that modulates interactions between the prefrontal cortex, thalamus, and the hippocampus areas of the brain by selectively inhibiting and enhancing certain neurotransmission receptors. Enabling better prioritization and synchronicity between them when executing specific kinds of tasks. It dampens the influence of external inputs, preventing distractions. Better focus, essentially."

Mr. A sounds like he is reading from a textbook or a marketing flyer. Probably marketing, given how vague he's being. I'm going to guess that he has no real understanding of what he just told me because I have no clue myself even after spending hours on the phone with Kamaru talking about how the brain works and how its performance is measured and modeled by companies. But this is something different. It's not measurement, it's change.

"Are there any side effects?"

"A few people have reported dizziness, even fewer have complained of headaches when they first begin taking it, but these are temporary. Minutes to hours at the most. It's very safe and we expect regulatory approval to be very quick, even in certain, difficult markets."

Right. I'm sure "difficult" in this context probably means places where the federal food and drug agencies aren't incompetent or can't be bribed, or both. But that's a different kettle of wahala, I need to face the one in front of me and decide what to do. This performance review has gone bizarre. As far as I know, companies recommend training courses, self-development activities, mentorship, things like that to fill out perceived gaps in performance but this . . . pharmaceutical intervention, changing the way my brain works to make it more amenable to their expectations is frightening. I consider my options carefully.

"And if I don't want to take it?"

Mr. A's smile finally dims, but only momentarily. He drops his thin, ashy hands and leans back into his chair, maximizing the distance between us. "As I said, that's entirely within your rights. Nothing will happen. We will simply make a note and consider how to move forward with you at our next business review meeting."

Of course. I should have expected that no-answer answer from him. He knows I can sue the company from Yaba to San Francisco if they compel me to take a drug against my will. Or fire me for refusing it. They will probably just wait and fire me later, when they find a convenient and legal reason to do so.

I'm shivering nonstop now. My face feels a bit numb. I need to get out of this room. I need to get away from this man. I need a drink.

"I need some time to think about it," I tell him.

"Yes, naturally, take your time. Of course, I cannot give you any Optimiline until you sign the consent forms." He reaches out and slides the bottle out of my reach. "I will update your review status in the system. Thank you for your time today. Remember, the company wants what is best for you, because it's what's best for us too. We want you to maximize your potential." His smile expands again, making his lips thin and his cold, yellow-flecked eyes narrow. He reminds me now not so much of a reptile but of an Egungun mask. Rigid. Uncanny. Terrifying.

I manage a quick "thank you," then I stand up, smooth my skirt, and walk out of his freezing office. The temperature differential hits me like a blast when I step into the corridor. I take in a deep breath.

Navigating my way downstairs to the sales cubicles on the third floor, I take my time. Slow but deliberate steps. I think about my brother's university fees and my dad's dialysis treatments. About how badly I need this job. Bad enough to take some strange new drug that will change my brain? I don't know. I need to look into this Optimiline thing a bit more. See what people are saying about it online, if anything. I pull out my phone and set a reminder to call Kamaru at 10 am tomorrow morning. Then halfway down the stairs, I change it to 2 pm. We're going to Swe Bar after this and I might need time to recover from a hangover, given how much booze I think I need to help me stop thinking what just happened in Mr. A's office. I hope Amina's review went better than mine did.

At the bottom of the stairs, I push open the doors and enter the sales area of low cubicles and high windows. The faces of a few remaining co-workers who are hiding from the Victoria Island traffic are illuminated by lightscreens. The familiar noise of their talking, typing, swiping, and chitchat is almost comforting. There is a kind of lightness here and a warmth and a buzz that makes me feel better. At least it's not freezing. I make my way to the far side of the room, where Amina's workstation sits just beside a window overlooking the street. Through the maze of clear plastic and glass and wood paneling, I can see she isn't there. Her review isn't over yet? Or is she in the bathroom? Maybe talking to someone? I spin around, searching for her bright red headscarf and matching tank top. I don't see her, so I approach her desk anyway and stand beside it, waiting. Looks like she's been doing some cleaning up. It's been cleared of her cute little miniature vinyl collection, and the picture of her and her boyfriend at the Eiffel Tower—which I have never been a fan of because it's just so cheesy and clichéd and not like her at all.

Outside, the traffic has slowed to a crawl.

I hear the clicking of her heels before the flash of red enters my peripheral vision.

"You this babe! Where have you been? How did your review go?" I ask, eager to talk to someone about Mr. A, and Optimiline and all that madness from upstairs.

Amina's full eyelashes flick up and down as her eyes move, taking me in curiously as if she hasn't already seen me today. A small, strange smile twists the corner of her wet mouth. "I think it went very well."

"Ehn okay. Serious mama. Na you lucky pass. Mine was a mess. You won't believe. Get your stuff and let's roll out to Swe abeg, I need a drink. We can talk about it on the way," I say, looking straight into her eyes. I don't like what I see. It's like she is looking not at me, but through me. Distracted?

"I don't think I am going to Swe anymore," she says. "I feel a bit dizzy."

She looks away and carefully places a clear glass bottle on her desk beside her computing scroll like an offering to some invisible god. It is full of those moon-shaped pills.

I freeze.

"Did they give that to you?"

She nods. "Yes. To improve my performance."

My heartbeat accelerates. Optimiline.

"And you took it already, just like that?" I ask, full of an unspecified dread.

"Yes, about fifteen minutes ago."

A shiver runs down my spine even though the air is warm here. The fear in me runs bone deep.

Something's changed. And quickly too. Her eyes remind me of Mr. A's. She is still smiling at me, just like he was, but in that smile, there is a faint memory of the joy I remember seeing in her eyes whenever she is behind the turntables, rocking from side to side with the music or laughing boisterously as we gulp down gin and tonics. I think to myself: no, it's just my imagination.

"Okay. Babe for real, you need to tell me everything that happened. Let's go to Swe. Now. Let's talk. Then you can play your tunes, and we chill and vibe out first before the night crowd arrives."

"Tunes? What tunes?" she asks, and the hope in my chest sinks like a stone. "Ah, right, you mean the DJ stuff. Sorry I really don't think I'm up for it today," she adds, but it's already too late. The weight of realization is like a stone in the pit of my stomach. I don't want what I think is happening to be happening, but I can't pretend that it isn't.

"Let's do it some other time okay?" She keeps smiling at me.

I stand there, stunned to silence, until eventually, she looks away. I turn around and leave without taking my things, walking briskly out of the office into the sweltering Lagos heat. Gray clouds are drifting lazily across the blue and orange sky. I don't know where I'm headed but I keep walking along the broken, sandy pavement towards what used to be Bar Beach but is now the walled face of Eko Atlantic. The city, like everything, keeps changing. But is it for the better? I don't know. I keep putting one foot in front of the other, moving, trying not to think about the empty look in Amina's cold eyes and what the decision I have already made will cost me.

SILENCE

Silence is how you respond when she tells you, her lilting voice that always reminds you of the seaside at dawn now trembling with pain, that her boyfriend is cheating on her. Silence. Because the truth in that moment is too ugly to put on display and because it's not a complete truth. Yes, some part of you is glad that it is over, that you now have a chance to finally make her see just how much you want to be with her. And yet, for now, you are just friends—liars and friends, denying the spark that has existed between you since you first met, since your first kiss, since you first looked into each other's eyes and got hopelessly lost, two years ago and two continents away. Eventually, you remember how much she said she really liked him, and how badly she must be hurting in this moment. And because you love her, you finally gather enough sheaves of empathy to say, "I'm so sorry, B" and mean it. She is racked by another wave of sobs and you respond with another awkward . . .

Silence.

That is what follows after you tell her you love her seven months later, and ask her the question. You are both sitting on comfortable chairs in the brown wood and gunmetal embrace of the Oriental Hotel lounge with gin and tonics in your hands. It's a few days to Christmas and enthusiastic red and green and yellow lights are blinking all around you like fireflies filtered through a rainbow. Your heart is beating wildly in your chest and the edges of your vision are becoming blurry. She is staring at your face intently—perhaps looking for some visual confirmation of what you just said or perhaps just because she cannot bear not to look at you in this moment. This moment you have chosen to cross a bridge you both knew existed but did not dare set foot upon for reasons neither of you can or ever will be able to accurately articulate. But now, in this seemingly infinite moment, everything is changing, initiated, as was all creation, by four simple words.

Do you love me?

But all you have created is tension. Something slithers slowly down your spine sending a shiver surging through you. You wonder if she notices. The silence is starting to burn your ears. You want to say something to fill it up, follow up your declaration of love with the perfect words to convince her of its validity, but you can barely breathe. It feels like you have been inflated with too much emotion. Then, just when you cannot endure it any more, she opens her mouth and finally breaks that horrible, excruciating . . .

Silence.

There have been four months of it for your sanity's sake. Not because she said 'No'; that would have been easy to deal with in comparison. But because she said 'I don't know,' which was probably the truth of what she felt in the moment. But as anyone who has ever lied to someone they love before knows, sometimes the truth hurts more than any lie ever could.

So you'd asked for an explanation and you gotten one, but it didn't make sense to you because you loved her and you were sure she loved you, and so nothing else but your dream of love could have possibly made sense. Somewhere in the slurry of teary words, she'd said she needed time. So you gave her that. So you gave her three weeks to make up her mind; three weeks of hardly eating and barely breathing and constantly waiting for her to say yes. But when the time came and she still said she didn't know, that she was dealing with her own personal issues and needed time to work her way through, you did what you thought you had to do. You let your love ignite itself and turn into a bright, burning anger and because you couldn't stand to see her with your soul still on fire. You cut her off, for your sanity's sake. You built sturdy walls out of deleted phone numbers. You blocked social media accounts, shed tears, ignored emails, neglected text messages, drank copious amounts of alcohol, and avoided mutual friends. But it is the nature of walls to eventually fall, and your wall has all come crumbling down now that she is standing in front of you, her hair wet and matted to her skin from the rain, her chest heaving rhythmically, her make-up running along the edges of her face in localized ochre rivulets. Shocked, you say, "hi," and she says, "I've missed you," and then you take her in your arms and press her to your skin desperately, wondering how you ever shut her out and let her go, went all these months without talking to her, hearing her laugh, seeing her smile. Feverishly, you tell her you've missed her too, and then she pulls you close and kisses you deeply and when she pulls away all your walls are rubble around your feet and then there is an extended . . .

Silence.

It has become comfortable. She lays in your arms, her head snug in the crook between your neck and your shoulder. Silent and comfortable, this is how you now spend most of your time together—holding each other in silence. The explanations have been made: she needed time to be sure it wasn't a rebound, that she wouldn't use you to work through a recently failed relationship. You couldn't bear to be around her or hear her name without having her to hold and cherish and love in all the ways one human being could love another. The mechanics of the separation were unfortunate but necessary. She is now sure. You are now whole. All is well. You adjust your arm and realize with an overwhelming, ineffable certainty that in that moment, under the fluorescent glow of the solitary light bulb in her apartment and a million more moments like it, you are both home, with nothing to say and everything to be.

EMBERS

*"A proud heart can survive a general failure
because such a failure does not prick its pride.
It is more difficult and more bitter when a man
fails alone."*

—CHINUA ACHEBE, *THINGS FALL APART* (1958)

Uduak's unraveling began with an unexpected visit.

The sun was slowly drowning across the horizon, casting linear streaks of light into the sky where the clouds absorbed them, creating new hues of orange and pink and silver-edged blue.

Uduak walked slowly, pushing his wheelbarrow ahead of him with effort. Its coat of forest green paint was almost completely stripped away, and its load of battered and scratched oil drums, assorted wiring, and loose tools clanked uncomfortably against each other with every revolution of the wheel on the bumpy asphalt. The slapping sound of his rubber slippers against his callused soles reminded Uduak of the sporadic gurgling pulses of the crude oil transfer pump that had failed to start all day despite his best efforts and ministrations.

He was flanked on either side by vibrant, overgrown green bush that had choked what used to be a two-lane access road down to a narrow path barely wide enough for his tall and bulky frame. Nature was re-claiming what belonged to it, now that the road had fallen into disuse. No one, except him, took advantage anymore of the access the road provided. The chorus of evening song was slowly filling the air as the nocturnal animals and insects awakened. Thin rivulets of sweat ran down from his balding dome and dripped off his chin as he tried to keep the barrow steady while balancing as much of the load as possible on the fulcrum of the wheel. Uduak could smell the sickly-sweet odor of the old sweat that had completely soaked his white vest and Ankara-print trousers while he'd been working earlier. The air still held some residual heat from the afternoon sun. His clothes were almost dry now in the cooler air of evening, but he was still perspiring, and he felt sticky and unclean. He craved the cleansing touch of water and the comfort of his home. Uduak paid no attention to the setting sun or the clouds over-head or the cries of the early evening crickets. He focused on the road home with the echo of his own thoughts loud in his head.

Last month it was the de-salter.

Now it's the stupid transfer pump.

What next?

He kept a steady pace, determined to get home before darkness fell. Not that he was worried about anything happening to him at night, even though at times, when he was alone in the darkness, he thought he could sense something, like an animal perhaps, watching him. But no, he told himself, he wasn't afraid, he was just being prudent since he was the only one that still used the *Ukpana II* refinery access road. It had been abandoned for almost twenty-three years.

I've been trying to restart Ukpana II for almost a year, and I just keep finding more problems.

Uduak came to the point where the road intersected with a path of hard-packed earth that led back to the village. The top edge of the sun's disk dipped below the horizon, and he turned into it. In the distance, he could clearly make out the towering udala tree that marked the center of the village square. It looked like there was a crowd gathered around its expansive trunk, loosely orbited by playing children. Their tittering and shouting carried on the cool evening air. He began to slow down, each step more hesitant than the other.

I'm asymptotically tending towards home.

A bitter smile cut across his face. *Asymptotically.* It was a word he hardly ever used anymore but it triggered a flood of memories: Memories of sitting at an unsteady wooden desk, scribbling equations and geometric diagrams across his notebook. Of slowly coming to terms with the apparently arcane physics and mathematics and chemistry that Miss Kayode, the plump and kind-eyed youth corper that had been assigned to teach science to the children of his village in his senior year, gave them to work through. Miss Kayode had often used words like "asymptotically," "derivative," "determinant." Back then, most of the children in his class didn't know what any of it meant, not really, they just memorized the words to pass their exams. But Uduak understood. At least, eventually. The seemingly abstract concepts of things tending toward infinity, and symbols denoting varying rates of change, all just sort of clicked in his mind when he thought about them for a long enough time, like a language that he'd not even known he could speak until he heard someone else speak it first. He'd done well in school that year, placing at the top of his class in physics and mathematics, second in chemistry and eighth in English, in a class of more than a hundred that included children from all the nearby villages. Before she left at the end of her service year, Miss Kayode had recommended him to Samuel Ukekpe, the pot-bellied, loud-voiced and perpetually ebullient local

ExOil Inc. liaison officer that managed community outreach for the company, doing the minimum required to stop the community from complaining about the oil spills and the never-ending poison that was churned out of the refinery flare stacks. Uduak had been the first person from his small village to get a full scholarship from ExOil to go study Mechanical Engineering Technology at the Federal Polytechnic, Ukana. Samuel had even guaranteed him a job as a refinery operations technician when he graduated. Samuel had told him he was going to be rich and successful if he did well, and so Uduak worked hard because there was nothing he wanted more. He was going to be an oil man.

Uduak dry-swallowed and shook his head as though he were trying to dislodge the memories. Those days, when his world had seemed full of inevitable promise, were now far behind him. Remembering them only sent sharp lances of pain through his chest and left an unsavory aftertaste in the wake of his dreams that had never been and would never be.

No.

I will make it right.

I will fix this refinery. I will fix Ukpana II.

Uduak raised his head and spat a gob of saliva into the bush, as though ridding himself of the vile draught of unfulfilled potential. He puffed out his chest, accelerating with renewed determination.

I am going to be an oil man.

He crossed the threshold of bushes that marked the village boundary and came face-to-face with the person at the focus of the gathering and the true reason for his slowed approach to home: Affiong—his brother-in-law, whom he hadn't seen in over three years.

Affiong stood just under the towering umbrella of udala tree branches, several other villagers gathered around him, most of them sitting on the floor with their eyes bright and their jaws descended. The children moved around the central group, running, laughing, and jostling for turns with a new toy robot that Affiong had brought with him, which responded to their questions with an almost-human, conversational quality in perfect Efik. Some of the older children pointed their phones at the running ones, recording what was happening for their social media, too proud to engage or argue for a turn. They were not yet connected to the national power grid, or to the interstate road network, but they had mobile data. Everyone had mobile data.

Affiong was wearing a perfectly tailored black suit, a white shirt and blue tie, with black leather shoes only a little scuffed and muddied by the unpaved earth beneath them. He paused the story he was telling the gathered group and raised a hand when he saw Uduak appear. "Ah Uduak! You are here finally," he shouted in unusually nasal Efik as he dropped his hand and scratched at his temples through low-cut hair. An affectation he had introduced to his speech since he'd first come back from the city.

"Brother-in-law, come and join us, I was just telling everyone about the new government building in Uyo, the one they say is the tallest in Africa now. And look, I brought schnapps." Affiong gestured with both hands at several bottles of clear liquid on the floor.

Uduak's wife, Ndifreke was standing at the front of the crowd, their baby daughter Mbono quietly tied onto her back with a bright yellow and red Ankara wrapper that matched his own trousers. It was the same material they'd bought when they'd attended her mother's funeral. That was the last time Uduak had seen Affiong. Ndifreke nodded to acknowledge Uduak. Their first child, Udom, had finally gotten his turn with the robot and didn't even as much as look up at the mention of his father's name.

"Affiong, welcome back," Uduak hailed back, ignoring the alcohol. Affiong knew that he'd developed a drinking problem for several years after ExOil stopped his scholarship payments and shuttered their operations in Nigeria. He'd only managed to stop the craving for it when he'd begun working on *Ukpana II*. "It's been a long time. I hope your journey was not too difficult."

The circle of villagers opened with a murmur, angling their bodies to observe the interaction between the two men whom everyone knew had despised each other since they were children. In the distance, a goat bleated.

Mama Ebiye, the oldest woman in the village, whom many people believed was so close to death that she could already commune with the ancestors, often said that it was because Affiong and Uduak had been born on the same day, only forty minutes apart. Something that had never happened before or since except in the case of twins who shared a mother. Once, when they were only six years old, they had been brought before the village council because they had been fighting with each other and trampled all over a patch of freshly germinated afang vegetables, ruining it. Mama Ebiye had said then, that they were two halves of the same spirit that entered the world through separate bodies, neither one of them at peace because of it. She still repeated that sentiment sometimes. Uduak hated it whenever she brought it up, and he was sure she would have done so again if she were present, but her eyesight had deteriorated, and her hips had grown so weak that she was no longer able to leave her home to attend most village functions, spending most of her time in bed. Still, it was true that Affiong had been a consistent presence in every childhood memory, whether playing games near the stream that ran beside the village to the ocean, or helping their parents plant yams in clearings just beyond the village. When they were enrolled at school, they traded first and second position on most subjects—except English, which neither were very good at. But in all else, they were always competing. That was, at least, until they entered their senior year when Affiong started to struggle at school because his mother had developed a persistent, hacking cough that never subsided.

Just two months after Uduak started at the polytechnic, Affiong had run away from the village to go to Uyo, seeking any menial labor that would pay enough to hospitalize her.

"Thank you. The journey went smoothly," Affiong said and then added, pointing toward the main village access road, "I have my own transport pod now, so it was not stressful at all."

Uduak's breath caught when he saw the perfectly smooth egg-shaped vehicle. The top of its matte black surface caught the last of the light from the sky. "That is amazing," he said, because it was true. He'd never seen anything like it before.

"Yes o, it is. It is a self-navigating pod. They have one of those AI things inside, so I don't even need to do anything most of the time. I just tell it to bring me here and just like that, I can see all of you again."

Uduak swallowed his jealousy. "Wonderful."

The looks from the crowd and especially from his wife made him even more uncomfortable than he already was. He was supposed to be the one who had gone to the city and made it big. He was the smart one. The one with the scholarship. The reason why the big man from the oil company had come to meet with the village council, saying that it was time someone from their community finally joined ExOil operations so that maybe, one day, they would all own a part of the valuable resource that lay buried beneath the land of their ancestors. He was supposed to be the one with the money and the schnapps and the suit and transport pod that looked like a potent god's egg. Uduak's place as the village's promising child had slipped and shifted beneath him over the years, until it was completely gone. He already knew that everyone he had grown up with now saw him with different eyes, but the look they gave now was new, their disappointment filtered and distilled through the obvious mesh of Affiong's success. Their looks made his skin prickle like the light reflected from their eyes was made of needles.

No.

I will not show weakness.

He set the wheelbarrow down, lifted his head up and walked toward Affiong, enduring the needle-light.

"So, what are you doing with all those tools and drums there?" Affiong asked, jutting out his cleft chin toward Uduak's abandoned load. "Eket just told me that you are trying to get that old ExOil refinery running again by yourself, is that true?"

Uduak stopped at the edge of the crowd and shot a stinging look at Eket; a short, middle-aged man covered in burn scars since his teens, from a fire at a vandalized pipeline. He'd been siphoning petrol, back when that was a thing. These days, Eket spent most of his time drinking cheap ogogoro and spreading rumors. They had been drinking buddies for a while, when Uduak had been living close to the bottom of the bottle, so he was not surprised that Eket was the one who had told Affiong about *Ukpana II*. Eket returned his look with unfocused, bloodshot eyes, remorseless. He already had one bottle of Affiong's schnapps cradled in his arms like a child or a bag full of silver coins. The problem with Eket's blabbering was that Affiong had a way of making a mockery of things that Uduak cared about, but without overtly mocking them. It had always been that way since they were children. In their senior year, he had taken to calling Uduak "Joseph the Dreamer" because he always spoke of his future working at ExOil after Samuel Ukekpe's visit to the council. Something Uduak hated but never complained about because the surest way to make a nickname you hate stick to your skin forever is to complain about it.

"Yes," Uduak said, looking back to Affiong. "It's taking some time, but I'm making progress. I already managed to get the storage tanks flowing to the main facility again."

"Really?" Affiong said, miming exaggerated interest as he stepped out of the center of the crowd, toward Uduak. "But what are you trying to achieve exactly? No one uses that dirty oil or its products for anything anymore. Its worthless. Besides," he pointed up and motioned his arm in an arc, his fingers dipping at every nearby aluminum rooftop, "the village already has solar panels installed."

"It's not enough," Uduak replied. Which was true. "There's never any power at night. The government has been promising to connect us to the grid for years and yet, here we are. If I can get the refinery working again, I can make fuel for the generator and connect it here."

"Hmm." Affiong nodded his head. "Well, the Kawashida central power stations are already up and running. We always have power in Uyo. It's just the government that is slow to reach here." He smiled. "Maybe we should get a Kawashida portable, don't you think?"

Uduak flinched at that name—Kawashida. The company that had changed the world. His world. Kawashida. It was the only reason Affiong could come back to the village with his tailored suits and egg-shaped transport pod that caught the dying of the light while he, Uduak, struggled to revive an abandoned network of unit operations that could distill fuel from crude oil.

Affiong continued, "No. It's too expensive. We can use the refinery and the generator temporarily if everyone here is happy with it." He flashed his large teeth in an oily smile that told Uduak he already knew they were not. "The oil is just sitting there."

Emem, the woman who had the largest farm in the village and sat on the council, scoffed.

Uduak tensed. He had not even discussed it with the village council before he started. He'd been drinking when he made the decision on his own after years of considering moving to the city to try to get a job as an entry level technician at the Kawashida plant in Uyo. He may not have finished school, but he was smart and good at figuring things out and at least, he'd thought, he still had enough practical and transferable skills to find work managing general equipment. But the thought of working at a Kawashida plant felt like it would be the final humiliation in a long sequence of failed dreams. He was supposed to be an oil man. Pride and deeply rooted resentment fertilized each other in his mind until they had grown, become a great, green sinewy mass of bitter spite that clawed its way into his heart and fused itself with his will. He'd dropped the bottle of ogogoro in his hand and decided he was going to fulfil his destiny. That he was going to reignite the bright, burning future he had once dreamed of for himself. He'd stopped drinking and started working on *Ukpana II* the next day, and he didn't stop even after the village council had summoned him and told him to, that it was too risky to do it on his own and that they didn't want to have to deal with any problems if anything went wrong.

"They just don't understand. It's a refinery, not an evil forest. They will be fine with it once I get things working fully." Uduak puffed out his chest, looking around the crowd. "In fact, we can even sell power directly to the nearby villages and make money. The generator there has a huge capacity."

Affiong nodded, that movement also exaggerated. "Still dreaming big dreams eh, Joseph the Dreamer?"

A burst of giggling and sneers erupted from the crowd. Uduak saw Ndifreke look away toward Udom who had drifted toward the pod with three other children, custodians of the robot now. It was just like it used to be when they were children, with Affiong trying to embarrass him, and succeeding.

I will not let Affiong shame me here.

"It's not a dream, Affiong. It's a reality. I have gotten the pipelines to flow again, and I have fixed almost all the equipment and cleared out most of the units. Things that all of you laughing here have no idea about because you don't know anything about technology. I have done a lot of detailed and difficult technical work on my own, and I'm now very close to being finished. The refinery will be up and running soon."

The laughing stopped abruptly.

"Okay brother-in-law, I meant no harm. I was just teasing you." Affiong folded his arms in front of his chest, still smiling like he knew some secret Uduak didn't. "So how soon is soon? A few days or maybe a week, I assume?"

Uduak saw the trap he was being led into just a bit too late to pull himself back from it. "Yes," he lied.

"I see. Then we should support our kinsman," Affiong said, speaking to the crowd. "We should do a commissioning or opening ceremony. Get all the members of the council to see what our gifted brother has achieved all by himself. Hundreds of people used to work in that refinery you know. Hundreds!"

A murmur went up and Uduak suddenly felt a throbbing headache develop at his temples. He felt very alone.

"Enough. This is not the place for this. I will discuss it with the rest of the council tomorrow," Emem said, adjusting her wrapper around her waist. "For now, let us finish celebrating your return first, eh? Or you don't want to eat the meat I cooked for you before it gets cold?"

Affiong bowed toward her. "Thank you, ma." And then he turned back to Uduak, "I really look forward to seeing what you've done when it is ready. It will be amazing to see a real oil refinery operating again, just like going back into the past." He laughed and then drifted toward Emem who was seated on a stool in front of a large metal pot full of food. "Let us eat!"

Ndifreke gave Uduak a look and a strained smile before she joined her brother and several others gathered in front of the blackened metal pot, baby Mbono still sleeping quietly on her back.

"I'm not hungry," Uduak said to no one in particular as he ground his teeth and turned away, headed back to the hut he had inherited from his uncle which he now shared with Ndifreke and the children. Midstep, he thought he saw something move in the bushes, like an animal stalking prey, but he concluded that it was just the wind. As he gripped the handles of the wheelbarrow tighter and kept moving, he wondered if there was a way he could get the oil in and start the fired heater for the crude distillation tower at the abandoned ExOil facility. There were massive storage tanks full of oil, enough to distill. He just needed to get it inside. He wondered if he could siphon some oil into a large drum and manually pour it into the distillation tower, even if the transfer pump wasn't working. Perhaps, if he pulled it off, he could get it to run stably for a few minutes or even about an hour, long enough to make it seem like he'd been successful to some degree. Enough to make Affiong respect him and perhaps restore some of the village's eroded faith in him.

Matches.

He needed matches.

He tried to remember where he left the last box of them as he picked up his pace, the wonky wheelbarrow and its cargo bouncing ahead of him.

Kawashida fuel cells were invented by a team of scientists at the ShinChi Technology Company of Japan, just sixteen months before Uduak was due to graduate with a diploma in Mechanical Engineering Technology from Federal Polytechnic, Ukana.

Uduak didn't know exactly how the fuel cells worked. No one really knew all the details except the research team at ShinChi, and they kept their secrets, but Uduak like everyone else, knew that the cells were biological. That was what made them special.

By using a proprietary genetic modification technique to rewire the metabolism of a heterotrophic bacterial strain, making it autotrophic, and then further splicing the synthetic microbe with a cocktail of high cell density, rapid reproduction genes, Dr. Haruko Kawashida and her team created a living, breathing, renewable supply of energy for the planet. The synthetic autotroph used concentrated sunlight to efficiently consume carbon dioxide and exchange electrons, creating a steady stream of electricity. An engineered nanoparticle was used to further facilitate rapid communication and across the mass of the organisms as they grew and emitted current, enabling full control of all its actions, including its rate of reproduction, which was extremely scalable, allowing the current to be used in a variety of ways. Kawashida cells proved useful in a variety of applications: from heavy industries that needed energy dense fuels or very expensive installations, to smaller portable devices. This, as well as the fact that the Kawashida cells could be coupled to wastewater treatment, where it would use the organic material as additional substrate, or to saline water desalination systems to catalyze the electrochemical pathways while simultaneously making the water drinkable; all these made Kawashida cells a unique technical marvel—a single solution to multiple problems—a potent panacea for an ailing planet.

But the technical aspects of Kawashida cells were not what truly changed the world so much so quickly, not by themselves anyway. Technical alternatives for power generation had existed before Kawashida fuel cells, and they too would have probably gotten bogged down in arguments about pricing and distribution and who would bear the cost of transitioning or abandoning older technologies, if not for the timing. The perfect timing. A demonstration of Kawashida cells' ability to power the entire Keiyō Industrial Zone, while also making the entire operation carbon-neutral in less than a week, took place three days after the 46th United Nations Climate Change Conference in Accra, Ghana ended with yet another series of non-binding resolutions. There had been parallel protests in almost every city in the world, and violent riots in some, with Canada's protests triggering a change in government. The frustration at the slow pace of climate actions, and the excuses that continued to flow from politicians while they prioritized the economy over the planet, had been simmering for decades and finally boiled over. So, in the week that followed, when ShinChi live-streamed their change-over from the national gas and nuclear grid to the Kawashida cell power plant, everyone watched both the sharp drop in net atmospheric carbon dioxide and the continued stable industry operations driven by the easy-to-feed-and-grow organic matter of the cells. Then the protests pivoted to demands for action, demands for Kawashida.

Kawashida cell technology quickly made its way around the energy-hungry and climate-changed world, defended by a slew of ShinChi lawyers and the latent but obvious military backing of the Japanese government. Many rich nations in Western Europe, Southeast Asia, and Eastern Africa quickly bought into it, glad to be free of their fossil fuel addictions. Others followed when they saw the writing on the wall.

Oil prices crashed from a hundred and three dollars per barrel to less than twenty cents in four months. OPEC panicked and cut production to create artificial scarcity. But that only gave an opening to the hydrogen, methanol, and biofuel markets which had been positioning themselves, in the decades prior, as alternatives to gas, oil, and chemical feedstocks. It was really all in the timing. Within two years, Kawashida cells had changed the world in what was, by historic standards, the blink of an eye.

Uduak hadn't known any of this until the semester was about to end and Samuel Ukekpe sent him a video message, explaining that ExOil was cancelling his scholarship since it was stopping all its operations in Nigeria and fully divesting all its assets.

In the video, Samuel was animated and sweating profusely, his large head set against a cream-colored background. "If you look at the news, you will see it everywhere. Kawashida this. Kawashida that. Wahala for who no follow Kawashida now. Even me too, I no longer have work here after two months. It's time for everybody to answer their father's name, Uduak. Go back to the village. I have sent you the last payment for the semester yesterday. Use it for transport money and keep the rest," Samuel had said, before adding, "Sorry ehn."

When the message ended, the silence echoed the death-blow to his dreams and aspirations of being an oil man. It sent Uduak reeling, unable to eat or sleep or attend his final classes. For years, he had seen the oil industry as his only way to clamber out of a small and limited life in the village, and just like that, it was gone.

With the coming of Kawashida, all across the Niger delta, the oil wells were shut, the money stopped flowing, the facilities were abandoned. Some of facilities and equipment that were closer to the big cities were retrofitted to use biomass and hydrogen or whatever else was possible with the least amount of effort and cost. Some were coupled to nearby Kawsahida power generation systems. Others were stripped for parts. The rich economies, and the big population centers in the smaller economies, all moved on with the changing technology, even though some, like much of Russia as well as spots in the middle east, remained reluctant. But even in the countries where Kawashida cells had been rapidly adopted, not everyone was carried along. The government in Nigeria, inefficient as it was, forgot the wide-eyed people in the small, remote villages that had once vomited their oil for the world's greedy consumption. For Uduak, nothing made sense anymore. His dreams had drowned in the future. So, when he got home, he got married and settled down and tried to find a way to move on, but he couldn't let go. So, eventually, he picked up the bottle and began to try to dissolve the dreams of his forfeited future in the sweet oblivion of ogogoro. Until one day he looked up and saw the stacks from *Ukpana II* stabbing impotently up at the sky and he felt the swell of inspiration that he used to feel in school when he finally understood something that he'd been taught and had an idea how to solve a problem. If everyone had left him, his dreams, his village, behind in the past, then perhaps he could bring the past back again. He could walk into that rusty tombstone to his dead aspirations and with all the intelligence and ingenuity that Miss Kayode had told the village he possessed, he could bring its pipes and equipment roaring back to life. He convinced himself that every liter of fuel he distilled would be a testament to his promise, to his value and would mordantly scorn Kawashida in the process too. And thus, Uduak had set to work almost a year ago.

Mbono had been crying like her mouth was full of fire for more than seven minutes when Uduak finally opened his eyes.

His daughter's shrill cries finally pierced through the curtain of exhaustion that had fallen over him once he'd set the wheelbarrow down behind the hut, laid down on the raffia mat that Emem's daughter had woven for them as a wedding present, and promptly fell asleep. His eyes wide and his head foggy with a half-remembered dream of being on the village council, he turned his head to his right and caught sight of the beaming full moon through the window, cradled by a soft puff of clouds as it hovered in the sky over the village.

All that light, reflected from the sun.

It's beautiful.

In a brief, silent space between moments, while Mbono paused for an intake of breath, and his head was still giddy with dreams, he found himself caught in a thought.

If the sun can light up the sky with nothing more than its reflection, maybe it's enough to power the world. To power the village. Maybe I don't need to keep working on Ukpana II.

His daughters' cries resumed with vigor, and the thought evaporated quickly, like kerosene spilled on asphalt in the midday sun. Uduak shook his head as the sound slowly chipped away at his sanity. He turned away from the moon framed in the window, over to his left side; a mistake that brought him face-to-face with Ndifreke who, like him, was now wide awake. She was glaring at him with well-fermented disdain that fizzed and frothed around her narrowed eyes, threatening to spill out onto the rim of her curled-up nose. Uduak knew she'd been holding in her words all day. He was tempted to look away, but he only shut his eyes instead.

"Enye mi. Useless man," she muttered under her breath as she sat up on the mat and adjusted the wrapper that was tied around her bosom.

A chill ran up Uduak's spine. It was about to begin. Again. He clenched his jaw and grit his teeth.

This happens every time Affiong comes to visit.

"Unen! Go and comfort your daughter, she is crying. You are smart, aren't you? You know everything? So, you should know how to comfort a crying child," she said, louder this time.

Mbono was six months old, and slept atop a small, padded raffia mat in the far end of their room. They'd been trying to train her to sleep through the night on her own, so Uduak knew that Ndifreke was only saying these things to hurt him. He kept his eyelids shut, hoping she would let out all her frustrations, tire quickly, give up, stop hurling insults at him and, if the crying persisted, go see to their wailing daughter whose cries seemed to only be growing louder.

"Maybe she is hungry, and she needs to be fed. Are you not the one that has been repairing the distillation-something-something that is still not working? You waste your time there instead of working on the farm, but you think I am the one that will both harvest yam and squeeze breast for your children by myself."

Uduak winced at that. He'd tried to wake up earlier than usual for the last few months to till the land they had marked out, heaping the loose reddish-brown soil into new ridges, and weeding the existing ones so that it would be easier for her to plant new yam heads and harvest old ones when he went to work on *Ukpana II*. But his efforts had either gone unnoticed or unappreciated. She kept going, every word laced with venom.

"You can't provide for your child. You can't comfort your child. It is so hot here! Mosquitoes and heat will soon kill her. You have been working on that stupid thing since how many months now, and yet fuel for the generator we have not seen. Money to buy portable Kawashida, that one too we have not seen. Useless man."

Ndifreke pronounced *Kawashida* with an affected nasal tinge, mimicking the way Affiong said it because that was where she'd heard the word most often, but that only made the name sound even more irritating to Uduak. He felt a red, persistent throbbing develop at the base of his skull.

"Ndi . . ."

"Don't *Ndi* me!" she shouted, pointing a finger at him like it was a knife.

Her braids were loose, and the moonlight made them look like streaks of frozen lightning. Her face was bony and full of teeth, like her brother's, and the more she insulted him, her face burnished with silver light, the more her resemblance to her brother seemed to resolve itself to the fore.

Uduak had married Ndifreke the year after he came back from Federal Polytechnic, Ukana, with nothing but a broken dream and the leftover money from this scholarship for the semester that Samuel Ukekpe had sent to him when ExOil suddenly went belly up. He married her for several reasons. Because his uncle, who had been taking care of him since his parents died when he was six years old asked him to. Because she was young and beautiful and was one of the few women in the village who were of appropriate age at the time. Because she was a good woman who diligently took care of her mother with whatever money Affiong sent her from the city. Because he needed something to do to give him a sense of purpose that didn't involve becoming an oil man. Because she, like many other young women in the village back then, still looked at him with stars in their eyes, since he was the man the outsiders had come to talk to the village council about, not knowing that the world had shifted and he had already lost all his promise. Because her family's plot of land was right next to his uncle's, and of course it made sense for the families to form a union. Because she'd never laughed with the others whenever Affiong had called him "Joseph the Dreamer." But of all those reasons, sometimes Uduak admitted to himself that he married her because he knew that Affiong would absolutely hate it.

Affiong didn't even attend the wedding ceremony.

Uduak wondered now, seeing the intensity of hate and spite with which she spoke to him while their daughter wailed in the background, how much of that bile was hers and how much of it was a reflection of Affiong's abundance.

"Look at where your family is living. The same hut your uncle gave us. No change. No improvement. First you were a drunkard, now you are wasting all your time on nonsense. Who did I offend to end up with a useless man like you? We are suffering o! Ehn. We are suffering! You just want to be a local village champion. You want to claim a pointless victory with that refinery."

She continued berating him until Uduak finally had enough and rolled over, turning his back to her. She was worked up and trying her best to hurt him with words that were more spiteful than usual. And it was working. They were eating into his soul like acid through flesh, filling him with the acrid feeling of dream-residue. He stared back out at the moon waiting for his daughter's crying and his wife's insulting to stop. He tried to divert his mind with thoughts of the refinery, considering the best way to temporarily bypass the pump, perhaps with an elevated tank and an angled flowline to the tower, when he heard her say something that cut him to the quick.

"Nobody even needs your rubbish refinery thing anyway; they have been laughing at you since Affiong came. The village council has already agreed to buy a second-hand Kawishda portable from a dealer in Uyo until the government connects us to the power grid. Affiong is helping us to arrange it. He will pay for half even. Affiong was mocking you when he said he wants to see your thing. They just want to see what you have been wasting your time with, but they are not going to use it even if it is working at all so if you like, be there by yourself with your refinery-nonsense!"

She kissed her teeth with a loud, venomous hiss like a threatened snake.

They are buying a Kawashida portable?

"Who told you that?" Uduak spun back to face her with wide eyes as he grabbed her wrist. "Who?"

"Nobody told me anything." She slapped his grip away. "I was there when they discussed it and agreed before you came back from your stupid *Ukpana II*."

Uduak groaned.

No. No. No.

Even his own people had accepted the thing that had ruined his life, and they were bringing it right to his doorstep.

The red, persistent throbbing in his skull spread to his temples.

He took his head in his hands and held it.

No. I need to show them. I am a smart man. I am a good man. I am an oil man. I need to show them I can be the person they thought I would be.

He heard Ndifreke exhale a scoff as she shook her head. "My brother was right. You are a dreamer. You can't even accept reality when it has been hitting for you in the head for the last ten years." She climbed off the raffia mat and picked up their daughter who immediately stopped crying and plopped her thumb into her mouth.

"I'm taking the children to my mother's house to sleep. Affiong is there. You better wake up from this foolish dream of yours because very soon, nobody will care about you or your refinery nonsense again."

And with that, she left the room, her footsteps echoing in the new-found silence of the hut. He heard her saying something inaudible to Udom, who was sleeping in the main room where they received guests. There was a rustle, more footsteps and then, silence.

Uduak was alone in the house.

He felt unstable. A kaleidoscope of emotions swirling together at once in his head made him feel dizzy, and the light from the moon was suddenly too bright, like it had expanded or moved closer to the village. He closed his eyes again, pressing his eyelids as close together as he could, causing small motes of red light to appear somewhere in his consciousness like tiny, persistent explosions. The motes flitted about randomly like dust in Brownian motion, whizzing about almost in tune to the pounding of his headache. He lay back down onto the mat for almost fifteen minutes, his head throbbing, until he thought he heard something enter the room, something that felt cold and wet and sharp and dangerous and dark and nameless like a leopard with blood dripping from its mouth. The feeling intensified until it settled beside him. It made him tremble. He pressed his eyelids tighter together, frozen with fear, but the feeling of the thing in the room next to him would not go away. Finally, he exhaled a breath he didn't even know he was holding and accepted its presence. He stopped shaking. The motes of light behind his eyes disappeared with the suddenness of a conjurer's trick.

Uduak opened his eyes. A smile cut its way across his face. He was not sure why, but he was happy all of a sudden. Ecstatic even. He leapt up from the raffia mat laughing and singing a song his uncle had taught him when he was nine. A song they used to sing when they worked on the farm together. He remembered where the matches were. Uduak made his way to the open space at the back of the hut that served as the kitchen to retrieve a knife and his box of matches.

"Fire! Fire! Fire!"

Eket's voice was harsh and guttural and frantic and extremely unnerving to the few villagers who were still awake to hear it. They were not surprised to hear Eket shouting at night, he did so frequently enough—singing, shouting, making strange noises when he'd had too much to drink. But this night, they were mostly surprised by the fact that his voice had none of its usual drunken slur or jovial tone. There was only fear in his voice. Fear and the sound of the word. *Fire.* They woke others and then they all came out of their red-brick and aluminum-roof houses slowly, most of them not fully free of sleep. That was, at least until they saw Eket kneeling on the ground near the base of the udala tree, pointing at an orange halo of flame in the distance like the sun had fallen into the bushes. The goats owned by richer members of the village council were bleating madly, and all the chickens that usually ranged freely had disappeared, fleeing as far as they could from the beast of heat, of light. It looked like a portion of the bush had been taken over by bright orange trees made of fire.

The villagers all knew that it was the *Ukpana II* refinery on the Northwest edge of the village, that was engulfed in flames. It was just beside the polluted Opo River whose surface still reflected tiny rainbows in daylight. Eket kept shouting and jumping and pointing at the fire. He was wearing only a pair of knee length shorts, and the loose muscles of his chest, softened by alcohol, pendulated furiously, but no one paid much attention to him.

They stood and stared at the enormous fire, their faces illuminated by the glare of the moon, most of them too shocked to react.

While they watched the burning in the distance, Ndifreke staggered out from between the huts into the clearing, her legs barely carrying her weight. She stumbled several paces towards the crowd, one hand held up in front of her and the other clutching her belly tight.

It was only when she screamed her daughter's name, "Mbono!" that they finally turned, just in time to see her spit out a mass of blood and collapse onto the dirt. Crimson blood flowed out from her center like an unfurling evil flower.

There was a chorus of gasps and shouts.

Several people ran toward Ndifreke's fallen body at the same time, but Mfon, the junior midwife who had helped her deliver Udom and Mbono and whom she'd been trying to convince Affiong to marry, was the first to reach her.

"Sister Ndi!" Mfon cried as she turned her over and saw the stab wounds in her belly leaking the life out of her.

"Mbono . . ." Ndifreke croaked through spurts of blood. "Uduak . . . he killed . . . Affiong . . . help my children . . ." Her voice trailed off.

A circle had formed around them. Emem, wrapped in a piece of white linen, stepped forward and spread her arms out to stop them from crowding into her. She kept shaking her head.

Mfon tried to lift and cradle Ndifreke's own head in her arms, but halfway through the motion, it suddenly felt leaden, like all the muscles in her neck had stiffened.

She was dead.

A child's familiar wail cut through the shocked silence, and then that seemed to give them all permission to let out all the words they had held in.

Ahhh!

Mbono o!

Where is Uduak?

Where is Affiong?

Abasi o!

Water!

Still inside her hut, lying down and staring at the thatch insulation where no one could see or hear her, but where she'd clearly heard everything, even the roar of the fire, Mama Ebiye's lips began to move fervently, whispering, "Uduak and Affiong. Fire and blood. Within an hour of each other." Over and over and over again.

Outside, there were cries of anguish and tears of sadness and embraces of comfort and shouts of anger and cries for water and a multitude of trembling tongues trying to make sense of the terrible thing that was happening in their village.

In the distance, the orange halo flared and lit up the night as the fire continued to lick and grow and roar.

Uduak stood on the top-level access platform of the crude oil distillation column, staring down into the inferno that had spread from the main crude oil tank and now covered everything below with an orange and gray shroud.

His was sweating profusely, his eyes were watering from all the smoke, and his hands were covered in the black of crude oil and dried blood. He shifted his weight from one foot to the other because his bare soles were uncomfortable against the increasingly hot metal grating. But he was still smiling, the same unyielding bone-sickle rictus imprinted onto his face that had remained since he got up from the raffia mat after fighting with Ndifreke.

He'd followed her after she took the children to her mother's hut and waited outside while she talked to Affiong, hidden between two parallel walls. He waited until the lights from whatever device Affiong was using to power his devices went out and the hushed voices went quiet. Then he'd gone in, stealthily moving through the house on bare feet. He'd slit Affiong's throat first, drawing the knife across smoothly like he was inscribing a mark across the curve of it. When he did it, he stood back and watched the look of horror on his brother-in-law's face as Affiong woke with a start, in a world of pain and unable to speak, spraying frothy blood all over the floor as he instinctively reached for his phone. It had taken almost half a minute for Affiong to die. When he did, Uduak took Affiong's phone and went to the next room where Ndifreke was sleeping. Mbono was awake in a corner of the room but quietly cooing. He walked up to Ndifreke and covered her mouth with one hand before stabbing her in the belly seven times. Udom never even woke up. When Ndifreke stopped struggling, Uduak left the house and ran out through the village square until he came to Affiong's egg-shaped vehicle. He pressed an icon that bore the same shape as the pod, and its surface slid open to reveal a pair of plush seats. He sat inside and said, "take me to *Ukpana II*," but nothing happened, so he stabbed at the seats and the panels and then he threw the knife away and ran through the access road, all the way to *Ukpana II*. He'd frantically made his way back to the transfer pump that was connected to all the storage tanks, and he turned a valve to cut off the intake line before trying to drag a drum of oil to the distillation tower. He fell and it fell with him, spilling everywhere.

I am an oil man.

He'd struggled up to his feet, run for the fired heater, and opened the fuel valves. It took him four strikes of the matches to finally get the heater working even though the oil transfer pump wasn't working, and there was no oil inside to be heated at the inlet of the distillation unit. He'd left the heater going anyway and climbed up along the access ladders to the top of the tower, reaching the platform just in time to see the metal frame of the heater expand and burst, vomiting superheated air and flames everywhere.

And that was where he'd stayed since, watching the fire slink and grow around the facility like an infection, or perhaps a synthetic microorganism, setting everything it touched ablaze.

He continuously shuffled his feet, trying to minimize the impact of the rising heat.

Conduction. I remember what Miss Kayode taught me.

Heat flux is equal to negative conductivity multiplied by the temperature difference and the conductivity of steel is high, and fire is hot and my feet are cold and everything is burning burning burning and that's so funny because steel is mostly iron and so is blood too, and my hands are covered in blood and oil and oil is mostly carbon and you need to add carbon to iron to make it steel and the steel beneath my feet is hot and everything is burning burning burning.

He laughed with a sound that surprised him. It was more a series of strident cracks than a laugh, Uduak looked up at the beaming moon, still flashing his new smile.

Look at me.

I am an oil man.

He felt an urge to howl but he didn't.

The fire continued to climb up the tower steadily like a vine until the smoke and the heat became too much for him to bear. Uduak covered his mouth and his nose with his forearm and climbed atop the rail, holding onto the top bar with one hand. It burned but he held on until he could smell his own flesh.

He let go.

Falling, he took one final wide-eyed look at the facility he had dreamt of so much, and he was suddenly not sure why he had even cared so much about it, about keeping the rusty, broken wheels turning for an industry that had harmed his land and his people so much. He couldn't understand why it had mattered more than his wife and his children and his life. *Ukpana II* didn't look so impressive in the haze of smoke and fire.

What have I done?

The strange smile that had been plastered on Uduak's face finally receded as he fell under the power of gravity, inexorable, like the future, towards the burning remains of a past he had never been able to let go of.

At dawn, when the village council sent a search party to inspect what was left of *Ukpana II*, they found Uduak's remains beside the charred steel base plate of the ruptured transfer pump. There was nothing left of him but a broken, blackened skeleton surrounded by embers.

THE MILLION EYES OF A LONELY AND FRAGILE GOD

I never told her I loved her.

Yes, I asked her to be my girlfriend, and yes, I asked her if she would marry me, and to both questions she answered, "Yes." But that was before I looked at myself with the eyes of the universe and saw nothing but emptiness. I never told her I loved her and honestly, I don't know why. That's probably why things turned out the way they did in the end.

"Don't let go!"

"Rotimi! Can you hear me? Don't let go!"

I can hear Tinuke screaming into the comms system as the shuttle silently disintegrates around me. A cluster of debris is beside me and what is left of the *Orisha-1*. Or maybe it is above me. Or below. I don't know. Directions are arbitrary in space, and I've lost my frame of reference. All I know is that the pieces of shattered steel and fiberglass are approaching me and approaching the chunk of the *Orisha-1* I'm fighting to hold onto. Meanwhile, the chunk is still accelerating, falling towards

Europa faster than it can spin away, and creating artificial gravity I need to fight against.

"Hold on. Don't let go."

She keeps screaming, crying, but we both know there is no point. I'm being torn apart in the blackness of an impossibly big universe, holding on to a damaged spacecraft and almost crying because I already know I will die out here alone, in the cold and the dark.

I knew I did not love Tinuke three months after we started dating, but we were comfortable enough with each other to not need much else. We worked together, had similar interests, and enjoyed each other's company, but I didn't love her and I never lied, never said that I did.

I don't know why I didn't just tell her how I felt. Maybe I'm a coward. Maybe I was afraid of hurting her with the truth. Every time I worked up the nerve to tell her how I felt, I would look into the infinite, glistening blackness of her eyes and in them see something pleading with me not to let go of us. So I didn't let go.

I hit the comms button on my suit to open the channel. I exhale, and then, I speak.

"Mission failure. I repeat, mission failure. The *Orisha-1* cannot dock with Europa Exploration Station. Severe impact damage. I'm barely holding on here. Can someone tell me what happened?" It will take a few minutes for the electromagnetic waves my voice is riding to reach them. I close my eyes to shut out the blackness and the debris and the stars and the possibility of tears.

"We don't know, but . . ." Tinuke starts but Elechi, the main dispatcher in Abuja, interrupts her, trying to maintain some semblance of control. "*Oga*, Europa Exploration Station AI is reporting a damaged starboard solar rotary joint. The main truss assembly broke off. We think that's what hit you on approach. We're still checking."

There is the necessary silence. Then I say, "It doesn't matter. *Orisha-1* is completely gone. There is a cluster of debris moving faster than I am. It'll hit me soon, in a few hours or so." I wait.

"Don't say that," Tinuke pleads a few minutes later. "Try to pull yourself to something, anything you can use as a shield to protect yourself."

I haven't heard her voice this shrill and pained since I first told her I had volunteered for the African Union's Europa exploration mission.

Drifting, Europa comes into my view. It's such a beautiful, still thing from far away. It's very blue and very brown, and it's wrapped in this wispy corona like God used an Instagram filter before he posted it up in the universe, and that's so funny I start to laugh and laugh and then I start to cry because I know I am going to die here.

"Sure. I'll try."

There is sluggish chaos and terrifying silence all around me. The fragments of the shuttle that cradled me and carried me here, so far from home, are coming toward me slowly, like apex predators. I pull on the tangled wires tethering me to the bulk of twisted metal and carbon fiber but it is accelerating away from me. I'm fighting a cosmological force and I'm losing. It feels like I'm fighting against the very essence of things. I think I lost before the fight even began.

I tried to make myself love Tinuke. I took her out to her favorite places in Abuja; spent as much time as I could with her when we visited the proposed launch site in Yola, long before I knew I'd volunteer for the mission. We even spent the Christmas before we got married in her parents' house.

I made love to Tinuke desperately, as if the act could emotionally arc a spark between us. I pulled and dragged and willed myself closer to her, but it was not enough. There was always an emotional space between us I could not overcome that left me feeling hollow and empty.

All I did was replace the emotional space with a physical one.

"I care for you more than anything in the world," I told her two weeks before the launch. We were in bed. I was stroking her hair, and she was crying. "You're the best thing that has ever happened to me."

It was the closest I ever came to telling her I loved her.

I couldn't hold on.

I couldn't let go.

I should have let go.

I let go.

The wires and cables slip from my grip slowly, the difference between my acceleration and the bulk of *Orisha-1's* makes me drift away in slow motion.

"Ah! Rotimi! What happened?!" Tinuke's words come after the long, lovely silence, throttled into a whine.

"I'm sorry Tinuke. For everything." I pause as she starts to sob. And then I add, "I love you very much." I owe her that much. She deserves that much.

I hit the comms button on my suit to shut out transmissions. Silence wraps itself around me like a blanket. I spin and drift lazily.

Something hits me.

Everything goes blurry for a few seconds or minutes or hours or even days, I can't tell.

When I manage to open my eyes again, there are stars. So many stars. Ineffable spheres of faraway light. Little jewels set into a tapestry of darkness. Coral beads embroidered into expensive black *aso-oke*. The million eyes of a lonely and fragile god. They shine and glint and gleam in every corner of my vision, and I see myself in every one of them. The tears fall.

I am alone, but I am no longer afraid.

I mattered to someone.

In the darkness and the cold, I finally let go of myself and cling to that knowledge.

Desperately.

COMMENTS ON YOUR PROVISIONAL PATENT APPLICATION FOR AN ETERNAL SPIRIT CORE

From: Emeka Nwobi

Sent: Thursday, November 24, 2034 4:29 PM
To: Chukwudi Nwobi <CNwobi@uh.edu >
Subject: Emeka Nwobi has shared the file "Provisional Patent Application For An Eternal Spirit Core Final Draft" with you.

Sender's Note: Please Review

The link below only works for direct recipients of this message.

PROVISIONAL PATENT APPLICATION FOR AN ETERNAL SPIRIT CORE

[Open File]

PATENT MEMORANDUM COVER SHEET

INVENTOR(S) INFORMATION

First Inventor's Name:
Engr. Emeka Nwobi, MNSE

Second Inventor's Name:
Prof. Chukwudi Nwobi

Commented [CNwobi]:
Why am I credited as co-inventor here? I don't know what this is exactly.

Home Address:
51 Akewi Road, Onitsha, Nigeria.

Home Address:
9324 Olivia Broek Lane, Katy, TX 91404, USA

Citizenship:
Nigerian

Citizenship:
Nigerian

INVENTION INFORMATION

Title of Invention:

Methodology and System for Generating, Installing and Running A Persistent Memrionic Emulator of Recorded Neural Patterns, Also Known As An "Eternal Spirit" Core (ESC) in A Human Personal Nanomachine Network Environment Node.

Commented [CNwobi]: *"Eternal spirit"? Is this a joke?*

Conception Date:

25 September 2032

Commented [CNwobi]: *You were really thinking about this during the funeral?*

First Disclosure to Whom/Where/When:

My brother, Prof. Chukwudi Nwobi and his wife, Dr. Mrs. Anwuli Nwobi, at their residence in Port Harcourt on 14 November 2032.

Commented [CNwobi]: *I had no idea you were taking this seriously. I thought we were just speculating about the possibilities to prepare for the meeting with LegbaTech.*

Is There a Sponsored Research Or Engineering Project Related To This Disclosure?

No

Commented [CNwobi]: *So you've been using the money they left us to develop this thing? How much has all this cost?*

To Your Knowledge, Has This Invention Been Used for Any Commercial Purpose?

No

To Your Knowledge, Has Any Specific Technical Information Relating to This Invention Been Disclosed to A Third Party?

No

Do You Plan To Publish/Disclose Information Relating to This Invention Within The Next Year?

Yes.

I will deliver a presentation on the fundamental theoretical framework I have developed, discuss the methodology with which this can be achieved, and illustrate the primary proposed application at the International Conference on Computing Frontiers (ICCF) in Denmark, between 14 and 17 December 2034.

Commented [CNwobi]: *Please withdraw the paper until we have a chance to talk properly. I can't believe the committee accepted an abstract based on this. They will laugh you out of the conference. Memrionic processing schemes cannot be downscaled to run on nanomachine units. The processes run at quantum level and still require large supercooled units just to emulate one human memrionic. Research into this is preliminary at best. Or did you find something new in the files I sent you last year before the LegbaTech meeting? Emeka, is this seriously what you've been doing for the last year? Why you didn't come to Anwuli's 35th? Why you haven't been answering my calls? I can see you're online, editing the document right now so answer the phone please.*

Prior Art

While the field of memory electronics (or "memrionics") has become well established and independent memrionic copies of high-value individuals have been generated and stored as part of established computing systems, no actual technologies and methods exist to embed such copies into a human personal nanomachine network environment with on-demand live responses.

Commented [CNwobi]: *There is a reason for that. It's impossible.*

Related Products/References:

- Google's Biocompatible Nanomachine Network Computing Environment—GLink© (commercially available)

- LegbaTech's Mem-One© Memrionic Neural Systems Scanner (commercially available)

- XiaXia Inc's Yige-Danao© Nanomachine Process Integration Software (commercially available)

- 3QPI Memrionic Mining Network Drivers (modified from opensource)

Commented [CNwobi]: *OK fine. How did you get 3QPI memrionic network drivers to run on GLink? How is the nanomachine node not overheating? Does any of this even work? We really need to discuss this. I have tried to call you five times already. I will finish putting my comments on this document and call you again at 10 am sharp today before I go to bed. Just pick up the phone this time. Please. Anwuli has been worried sick about you since the funeral.*

Summary of The Invention

A methodology and system for generating and installing a persistent memrionic emulator (the "eternal spirit" core) of any deceased individual whose neural patterns have been recorded (the "deceased") in the personal nanomachine network environment node of a living client (the "user") is described:

- The methodology allows quantum processes to be emulated on a nanomachine network by external modulation of the strong force between particles.

- The system can read in a full neural scan of the "deceased" as memrionic files and store this information optimally in a nanomachine network embedded in the "user" brain as modified 3QPI format files.

- The system can be configured to receive all neural information processed by the personal nanomachine network of the "user" and integrate them as direct streams of input.

- The system will generate a hypercubical memrionic matrix of response probabilities based on the recorded neural patterns of the "deceased." The system is configured to identify the response with the maximum confidence value based on feedforward simulation and relay this via auditory nerve stimulation to the "user." This sensation is expected to provide an optimal user experience that may be described as the "user" *hearing a voice* of the "deceased" in his or her head. The form of sensory stimulation can be modified to fit anticipated user preferences.

This invention will allow the generation of what may be described as an "eternal spirit" for those who are deceased or about to pass on. This "eternal spirit" has been designed to reside in the place it matters most: the minds of those who love them. It will also allow businesses to offer a unique and compelling solution to anyone who has lost loved ones and misses their counsel, their encouragement, and their love, by installing the live, context-optimized probabilistic memrionic models in their personal nanomachine networks. This will be particularly useful for those who wish to maintain a sense of constant contact with those who have passed on. Use cases include people who want to know what their parents would think of significant life choices, how they would have reacted to the sight of their grandchildren playing, what words of encouragement and advice they would give in moments of crisis, etc.

Commented [CNwobi]: *Ah. Emeka, Mama and Papa are gone. Even if you get this to work it won't bring them back. It won't be them. Not really. Memrionic scans aren't people. Just echoes. Please stop this Emeka. They're gone.*

If Field/Human Testing Is Planned for This Invention, When Is It Currently Scheduled To Begin?

An alpha version of the prototype system will be tested on 4 January 2035 using previously acquired memrionic scans of my mother, Mrs. Shiela Nwobi.

Commented [CNwobi]: *Oh No. No. No. Emeka. Seriously, I know you're reading this. Please, please, pick up my call.*

A DREAM OF ELECTRIC MOTHERS

Two hours into the third session of our fourth cabinet meeting on the border dispute with the co-operative Kingdom of Dahomey, my colleagues finally agree that we need to seek the dream-counsel of our electric mother.

The dream-counsel consultation ceremony was usually a somewhat elaborate half-day affair, with a Chief Babaláwo being called in from the Ile-Ifẹ̀ Technology Center of Excellence a day before to run diagnostics, read the Odù, dine with the Ọyọ Mesi, and remind us of our history and culture before we link our brains with that of our electric mother. Officially, the ceremony is performed to maintain transparency, to formally ensure that the public knows when this collective resource is being used. But everyone knows that the primary reason the ceremony was devised and is still performed is to maintain a sense of continuity of tradition because some of our people still believe that any contact with the ancestors should be mediated by a babaláwo. Even though they know that the electric mother isn't really the essence of our ancestors in the classical sense of the term, and that nothing more than an encrypted lifedock connection to the secure national memory data server and induced REM sleep are necessary to establish contact. Today though, we vote to forgo the ceremony and perform the consultation immediately due to the urgency of the situation. An efficient measure which I proposed, and which was thankfully agreed to by a majority vote without much objection. No need for all the bureaucratic *jagbajantis* that the government has developed a reputation for. We can make a full report after it is done. Besides, I have been waiting over a decade for an opportunity like this, and I don't want to wait another day if I can help it.

"Are you okay?" I ask my colleague, the Honorable Minister of Information and Culture, who is nervously fiddling with his bronze-framed spectacles as we exit the white-walled womb of the secure ministerial conference room. He was one of only two dissenting votes in the cabinet and the only cabinet member I have ever engaged with in more than a professional politeness since I was appointed minister of defense by the Alaafin three months ago, only the second woman in the history of the republic to hold the position. This is the first consultation I will be a part of, but the records show that he voted against the previous four as well. I have come to like him, but I find his apparent resistance to the consultation curious, especially since he is the one that will be responsible for the report and official broadcast once we are done.

Jibola Adegbite shakes his head, the sound of his shoes a metronome against the marble floor. "No. I'm not. And I maintain my objection. I really don't think this is necessary at all. At least not yet. It is a border dispute, not some brand new crisis. We can figure this out ourselves." He pauses. And then he says, "Besides, these consultations always leave me feeling somehow."

"How somehow?" I ask.

"Like it never really leaves my head, you know? Even after. The voice, or something. It is still there. Do you know what I mean?"

"No, I don't actually," I lie.

I have read classified reports of others who made similar claims, who thought they heard the voice in their heads or relived experiences from the consultation long after they were disengaged from the server. I don't say anything to Jibola about the others because I know it's not possible. Not really. Whatever they think they heard or perceived were probably just electric echoes in their brains. Like visual afterimages that persist in our vision after overexposure to the original image. An adaption of the brain to external neural overstimulation; at least that's the conclusion reached by the military intelligence experts who reviewed the reports, a conclusion which I completely agree with. Maybe he just hasn't come to terms with it yet. I don't have fond memories of my time at the Ogun School of Military Engineering, or with the Army Corps, but I have found that a background in engineering gives perspective on these types of things.

Jibola turns his head and looks at me like he is trying to scan my brain, and then he says, "Well I just hope it doesn't happen to you too," before turning away and walking a few steps ahead of me.

He is short, he'd stand shorter than I do if he didn't have his aṣọ òkè fabric cap on, with large sensitive eyes and an incipient pot belly that is starting to swell below his tailored white agbada. In a way, he reminds me of my father. At least the version of him that existed before the lunar spacelift accident. Not the broken, bloody version that spent his final seventy-five hours in and out of surgery as an army of babaláwos tried to save his life while my mother and I watched and prayed and cried to all the Òrìṣà to save him. That's what broke her in the end, I think. Not just the unexpectedness of the accident but the brief period of hope we held on to before they came out of the operating theater and told us he was dead. In some ways, the accident killed both my parents.

Jibola and I are the last ones to reach the elevator. Once we step in, a red light appears, and a door materializes from nothing as its constituent molecules are telecargoed into place. It almost makes me jump back with surprise, but I don't let it show. I don't think I will ever completely get used to building sections being beamed into or out of place on demand.

"I meant what I said," Jibola says, almost mumbling to himself, as we descend quietly under the carefully calibrated control of the building AI. "We can figure this out ourselves. We should. We have been navigating issues along that border with Dahomey off and on for centuries."

I lean in and whisper, "Maybe that's why we need help, so that we don't have to keep negotiating with them for centuries more."

"Funny." He snorts, waving his hand at me like he is swatting away invisible flies. "But I don't think you see the point I am making. We keep returning to the electric mother instead of fully considering and debating our points to consensus whenever there is a threat to the peace."

He seems a bit more agitated than usual. Perhaps the stress of the issue with Dahomey is getting to him, even though I am the one who will have to send troops into battle if the situation really deteriorates and we get to worse-case scenario. I'm the young, newly appointed minister of defense, and I may have to a manage a war already. Besides, I've never done this before. If anyone should be stressed, it's me. And yet, I am not. I have other things on my mind.

"That may be true, but does it really matter?" I ask. "We will get the best possible advice in the shortest amount of time this way. With the least amount of acrimony."

"Maybe you need a little bit of acrimony to be sure you are running a republic properly, especially when lives are at stake."

That comment, uttered a bit too loudly, draws looks from the other ministers of the Ọyọ Mesi. I cannot tell if he is serious or not, so I stay silent, straighten my back and stare ahead at the plain white door while we continue to descend two thousand meters below ground level towards the subterranean cavern protecting the data server that has hosted the collective digital memory of the Odua Republic since the 9878th year of the Kójódá.

We first began the mass archiving of memrionic copies of our citizens during the reign of Oba Abiodun III, when the great Iyaláwo Olusola Ajimobi first observed that if two digitized memrionic copies of human minds were synchronized and uploaded to the same operating environment, they would temporarily merge to form a new entity with its own unique, emergent identity. This entity could easily be deconstructed back to the individual memrionics using memory pulse stimulation with no apparent loss of fidelity. She called it a *digital emulsion.* Free of the artificial borders of tissue and silicon between minds, thought patterns of sentient individuals, when allowed to mix and interact, seemed to seamlessly flow into and merge with each other like rivers, completely miscible and yet still separable, with the right perturbation. It was she who first proposed the application of this observation to the creation of the National Memory Data Server (NMDS). A server that could be used to create a unique national computational consciousness based on the recorded thought patterns of every previous citizen of the republic whose neural scans could be obtained before they died. She referred to it as an artificial memrionic *supercitizen.* An entity made up of the minds of citizens past that could process billions of input parameters, thoughts, opinions, experiences and feelings in an instant and give advice on matters of national interest. An encoded and accessible electric voice of the ancestors. The Alaafin could not resist. Neither could the Qyọ Mesi. They approved her plans, gave her all the funding she needed, and she became the first director of the NMDS. In school, when they first taught me about the creation of our electric mother, I spent a lot of time wondering about Iya Ajimobi herself. I wondered why she had never taken a husband despite her reputation as a gentleman's woman. I wondered if she had intended for the new supercitizen to speak exclusively, with what sounds like a chorus of female voices, to everyone who makes a connection to their thoughtspace. Or if the supercitizen had chosen (I suppose that technically, it continuously chooses) that voice on its own because of the magnitude of Ajimobi's influence. I never met her, and yet her story has had such an influence on me and my life that I'd like to believe the latter. Perhaps our ancestral women are just more opinionated in liberated digital thoughtspace than their male counterparts, or perhaps she is still driving its identity from the inside. She is, after all, one of the ancestors now. But mostly, I wonder why hardly anyone in my family ever spoke about her, considering the fact that she was my great grand-aunt before she became a component of her own electric dream.

My ears are about to pop when the elevator finally slows to a stop and the door dematerializes. A blast of cold air hits us as we step out and into the expansive gray space of the NMDS center. An array of thick, black cables cut into and run across the high, hyperbolic ceiling. That's the first thing I notice—almost everything in the center is geometrically precise. Circles, rectangles, ellipses, parabolas, hyperbolas, triangles, and more. Shapes permute and combine in three dimensions all along the windowless, red walls which bear large abstract symbols drawn in harsh white, like academic graffiti.

In the middle of this expansive space sits the home of our electric mother. A large transparent cube housing an array of solid black cylindrical quantum processing nodes. Six programmable nanomaterial chairs sit on either side of it, facing away, with an assortment of cables and jacks and connection ports sticking into and out of them, some of which are connected to the cube, like an extended nervous system. Like lovely dark skin to a lover's touch, the nanoparticle surfaces of the chairs ripple and pulse, continuously adjusting to micro changes in the environment.

An array of holographic projections constantly streams information about the state of the server in bright orange ajami calligraphy. I recognize some of the projected readings from the technical description and reports: temperature, humidity, memrionic integration coefficients, air flow vector fields. But many of them I don't recognize. I don't think I'm supposed to anyway. I may have studied engineering, but I'm not a babaláwo.

"Welcome, ministers," says a man in a white shirt, embroidered with red at the collar and sleeves, as he steps into place beside us. He seems to be the on-duty babaláwo, but I hadn't even noticed him standing there until he spoke. His willowy body is stick-straight, crowned with a halo of perfectly combed salt-and-pepper hair. His eyes are bright and focused, set into a wrinkled face like jewels set in dark oak. "My name is Yemi Fasogbon. I believe all of you have participated in dream-counsel consultations before, is that correct?"

There is a chorus of discordant "yes," with only one exception—me.

"This is my first time," I say.

"Ah." Baba Yemi focuses on me. "You have read the standard briefing notes?"

"Yes," I respond. *Intimately. And I have read reports from previous consultations too. Even the classified ones.* But I don't tell him that.

"Very good. Then there is nothing to worry about. You already know everything you really need to know." He smiles, and kind lines crease his face. "Just relax. I will initiate the encrypted neural connection to your lifedock ports. Once the connection is made, a signal will be sent to your hypothalamus. You shouldn't feel anything unusual, it's just like falling asleep. I will monitor your brainwaves and once you are in REM sleep, I will connect your brain to the great memrionic supercitizen, allowing information exchange. Most of this will occur via auditory stimulation but some of it might be visual or tactile."

He pauses, looking right at me. I wonder if he has any suspicions about what I am thinking of doing once I am connected. What I have been thinking since the day I found out that my mother had starved herself to death in the home our family had owned for almost three hundred years. She'd retired from her teaching position a few weeks after my father's death, sold the house they had bought together, the house I grew up in, and left Ibadan. She spent her final months desiccating in the family redbrick villa in Ijebu-ode, ignoring most of my calls and sending the occasional cryptic message with apologies and encouragements and brief but false assurances that she was fine. I should have asked for compassionate leave from the battalion commander, but I was on the fast track to a promotion, and I felt I couldn't lose momentum. Not when she had always told me I had to be tough, to push through adversity and show them I could be every bit the soldier and military strategist as the men who made up most of my cohort. I thought the few messages and our quiet but constant love for each other would be enough to get us both through our grief, but in the end it wasn't. They found her sitting in my father's favorite leather chair, thin and depleted like all the life had been slowly leached out of her. The coroner told me that she hadn't eaten in fifty-three days. She didn't leave any final message. I never even got a chance to say goodbye. I want to change that. I need to change that.

Baba Yemi continues, "We are using the diminished external stimulation and increased brain activity of your minds in REM sleep to enable a direct connection to the complex digital system of the memrionic supercitizen. This is useful, but it also means that the connection can sometimes take on the inconsistent and unstructured qualities of a dream. Some of you may have experienced illusions before. It can seem unusual and perhaps even frightening sometimes, I know, but do not panic, no matter what happens. Just ask your questions and receive your answers. Open your mind to the ancestors and they will guide you. That's it."

I nod my understanding at him. I know all this. I just haven't experienced it yet.

"How long will this session take?" the energy minister asks. They are the oldest serving member of the Ọyọ Mesi and often concerned with time, so I am not surprised.

"You will all enter REM sleep at different rates depending on your unique brain chemistry and response to the direct neural sleep stimulation, but we hardly see any consultations taking longer than five minutes," Baba Yemi replies. "Once you are in REM sleep, the consultation itself should not take more than a few seconds. However, I will use a neuromodulation protocol to try to synchronize your emergence as a group."

"Thank you," they say.

Baba Yemi holds up his finger and flicks it once like it is a lever. "One final thing. Don't worry too much about the details of your consultation. All of you will receive the same answers regardless of how you ask the question, as long as it is indeed the same question. In fact, we count on it. It's a good control procedure, to see if there is any alternative or minority report of the consultation conclusion. I will manage the debriefing session once you are all done. Does anyone else have more queries?" he asks.

I look around and catch an earnest look in Jibola's eyes, like he is about to ask a question of his own, perhaps something that could delay or derail this consultation session, but then he changes his mind and looks away.

"Great. If there are no more questions, please follow me. I will make the connection." Baba Yemi bows gently.

Jibola takes what I imagine is a resigned step forward. I exhale with relief as we all march to the chairs surrounding the glass cube and take our places. Out of what I think is sympathy, I take the one beside him. I think it would be nice if he sees the face of a friend when he emerges from thoughtspace. Or maybe I'm lying to myself and I'm scared that I am the one who will need the comfort of a friendly face when I am done with what I plan to do. The moment is so close at hand, I am starting to feel nervous.

Baba Yemi makes the rounds: adjusting cables, pressing keys and checking displays while we sit there quietly, the hum of the servers constant and almost soothing, like waves on a beach.

When he comes to me, he smiles his open and kindly smile and asks, "Are you ready?" as he fiddles with the cables behind me, twisting and turning them without looking.

I think open the lifedock port embedded in the base of my neck and tell him, "I am." *I have been waiting for so long.*

"Good," he says, straightening up. "We will begin in a few minutes." And then he moves away.

I stare ahead at the symbols on the walls. I know that they represent something, something about the unclear nature of our connection to the ancestors, but I cannot place what it is exactly. I read about it when I was researching Iya Ajimobi's work on modern Ifá theory. I'm still trying to remember when something slides into the open lifedock port, sending what feels like a pulse of pure ice through my spine. My vision goes blurry, my body limp as the progmat chair adjusts to cradle me like a child falling asleep in its mother's arms. My consciousness starts to fade. The last signal I am sure my brain receives from realspace is Baba Yemi's voice repeatedly chanting in calm, confident Yoruba, "Relax and open your minds to the ancestors. Relax and open . . ."

Darkness.

Suddenly, I am somewhere. Thoughtspace. Stark and white. There are no corners or seams or edges or signs or horizons or anything to help me orient myself. I bring my hands up to my face to see what form I have taken but I see nothing. Am I just a mass of information floating around without a body? A disembodied consciousness? Or perhaps I am transparent, and I just see right through myself. I don't know. The sensation of being myself here is so different from realspace that I have no real frame of reference for comparison. It's a bit like floating in perfectly clear, colorless water. But also, not. I just feel . . . strange.

"Hello." I speak into the emptiness.

There is no response and so I try to clear my mind and repeat myself. "Hello."

"Our daughter, welcome," a voice choruses.

It sounds like it is coming from everywhere and nowhere at once. In it I hear millions of women speaking in unison—mothers, daughters, aunts, sisters, friends, lovers from generations gone by. But Iya Ajimobi's voice, which I heard so much of in the archives during my research, still stands out, like it is both the first and the last one to be added to this superposition of sounds entering my consciousness.

"Thank you," I respond.

"I am all. I am complete. What do you seek?"

The white of thoughtspace suddenly turns into a pale blue. Then cycles back to white. It keeps alternating, mesmerizing me. I don't know how long I have been silent when I finally remember both my duty and my real reason for coming here. I decide to start with duty by asking the question which every other member of the Ọyọ Mesi will also ask.

"As you must already know from the data feed, we are in dispute with Dahomey again. They have violated the Treaty of Allada by sending their representatives to the Ajashe region, claiming that the population voted to be part of their kingdom in the last referendum."

"This is true. We have validated the data."

I'd read it in some of the reports, but I am still surprised that the electric mother converses more like an AI than an actual person. I suppose I have been anthropomorphizing her for so long that I started to expect a more conversational human response. It's easy to trick your mind into things.

I continue, "They claim they want to renegotiate the treaty and so far, there has been no violence, but this is clearly a threat to us. We cannot allow them to just take away our control of the region, it is a part of the republic."

"This is true. Territorial integrity must be maintained."

"We need to take it back. But if we send in troops, we risk another war."

"This is also true. The probability of war exceeds current national security thresholds for conflict prevention."

A bit tired of the constant agreement, I ask finally, "We . . . I mean, I . . . have come to seek your guidance. What should we do?"

Thoughtspace adds a new color to its cycle, a deep, dark green, like moss. The cycle continues.

White. Blue. Green.

White. Blue. Green.

White. Blue. Green.

"Military confrontation with Dahomey is inevitable. Projections indicate that the probability of war increases with time. Projections also indicate that the probability of a successful invasion will also decrease with time. The best course of action is to invade now and take control while our chance of success is highest."

I am more shocked than I expected to be. The reports indicated that the electric mother typically highlights considerations that have been overlooked and points out trends in data that have not been cross-referenced and, as a result, does not usually provide simplistic answers.

This, a basic analysis with a simple conclusion, is not what I expected to hear. A straightforward push to war. I don't want to believe that this is the best advice we can receive. I wonder if the other ministers are hearing this and thinking the same thing I am.

"But to initiate a war would go against the Alaafin's policy of continental integration and cooperation. Besides, it will violate the will of the people in the territory and cost many of our people's lives."

"This is true."

More agreement. Another color joins the cycle. *Red.*

"Surely there must be better options?"

"This is not true. All considerations have been included in the evaluation of this situation. An extended negotiation will only delay war. Invasion is the best course of action. It will maximize the probability of the republic's life quality index remaining above eighty-three percent over the next one thousand years of the Kójódá. There are no better options for the overall good of the republic."

This feels wrong. I don't know why exactly; it just feels wrong. Like a badly constructed response based on fear, not logic, despite its scaffolding of data and numbers. But I don't know what else to say and I have done my duty, so I decide to finally attempt the thing that has been increasingly stepping out of the corners of my mind since my mother died, since I researched the archives, since I proposed this consultation.

"Iya Ajimobi, are you . . . in there?"

I have always wondered if she could distinguish herself from the supercitizen, even briefly, if she could float to the surface of this churning ocean of data and memories and instincts and thoughts and feelings. Her research notes indicated that she thought it was possible, that one or more memrionic records could sometimes "take over" the digital supercitizen for brief moments.

"I am all."

Apparently not.

I'm disappointed. If any mind could do it with any measure of control, surely it would be hers.

"Iya Ajimobi, can I talk to you? Just you?"

"I am all."

I have never been the type to give up easily and I am not about to start now. Not when I have been waiting for so long. Not when I am so close. Not when there is even a sliver of hope.

"Iya Ajimobi, please. If you can hear me. I need to talk to you," I say, not willing to lose this chance to get answers and say goodbye the way I should have. "It's your great grand-niece, Brigadier-General Dolapo Balogun. Please. I need your help." And then I break into rapid Yoruba, using her oríkì, her traditional praise greeting, which I have been practicing, to remind her of who she is and who I am.

Olusola Ajimobi, daughter of the great warrior clan
The one who gathered the threads of her people's minds
And wove a new Òrìṣà of them
Olusola Ajimobi, daughter of the moon and the sun
The one whose eyes deciphered the secrets of Ifá theory
And wrote the name of her family in the heavens

"Please, answer me," I plead.

There is a deep, overwhelming silence. Then, "I am . . ."

A pause.

The cycles of color seem to speed up.

White. Blue. Green. Red.

White. Blue. Green. Red.

White. Blue. Green. Red.

And then . . .

Red.

Red.

Red.

I can sense an abstract pressure on my consciousness like something is struggling to manifest itself in my mind but can't. The pressure grows and grows until it becomes something like pain. It is overwhelming, like I'm diving deep underwater without equalizing. I begin to see the symbols from the wall of the server room scroll past my vision like falling rain, but I still don't remember what they mean. A rattling sound like an opele being thrown accompanies the falling symbols, and the cycling colors seem to be coming closer, approaching me somehow. I am trying not to panic, but it's hard to keep my composure without my body, without being able to apply all the techniques they taught me in the Army Corps—closed eyes, steady breaths, stillness, mental focus. Here my mind is skinless and exposed, with all of these sensations and stimulations flowing in unrestrained. It all becomes too much, and I am about to let out something like a scream when finally, it stops. All of it. The cycling colors, the lights, the sound of the opele. All of it stops. Thoughtspace is white again and there is now a giant head in front of me, projected vividly like it has been sculpted from solid blue light. I recognize the wrinkled oval face: sharp-chinned, wide-nosed, and wise-eyed, with a crown of plaited gray hair.

"My daughter," the head says to me in a voice that is not a chorus but is hers. Just hers.

"Iya Ajimobi!" I cannot contain my excitement.

"Brigadier-General Dolapo Abimbola Titilope Balogun. I have heard you. You are one of my brother's great-grandchildren. I have tracked you in the datastream. Your Orí has guided you well. You have done the family proud."

I fill up with emotion, and I am still struggling for words to use in response when she continues, "Child. We must either be all or none. There is now a steep memrionic gradient. I cannot maintain this unstable state of the digital emulsion for long. How can I help you?"

It is strange not being able to exhale and relieve what I still sense as pressure in my chest. There are so many questions I want to ask, so many things I want to know, but I know I don't have much time, so I tell her the true reason I have come. "My mother, I need to talk to her. I just . . . I need to ask her why. And maybe say goodbye."

Her face seems to flicker, like the light it is being projected from just experienced a power surge. "My daughter, even if I can do what you assume I can, surely you must know that it is not truly your mother here with us? None of her essence, her Orí, is here, only her memories and her knowledge and a record of the neurochemical pathways that primarily drove her emotions."

It's even stranger, the sense that I am holding back tears when I am disembodied. "I know, ma, but you came to me. You came." I am pleading again. "If there is enough of you here to answer the call of your kin then I believe there is enough of her. I know she had her last memrionic scan appointment three weeks before she moved back to Ijebu-ode. Please. This is the only way I can speak to her now. I have to hope it is enough."

She flickers once more, this face that I have studied so much since I was a little girl, at first solely because I wanted to be like her: brilliant, full of life, independent, strong. And later, because I wanted to find something in her notes, something that maybe would lead me to this—my last chance to speak to my mother.

"I know you designed the architecture of thoughtspace. I know you can help me," I add.

Please help me.

The light flickers again and her face fades.

"I will attempt to retrieve her records and establish a direct connection only to you, but I don't know what form her isolated memrionic packet will take, or how long it will remain stable."

"Thank you!" I think I am shouting, but I am not sure.

"Thank you for thanking me," she says with a smile. And with that, she is gone. Thoughtspace suddenly seems to gain dimensions, directions, a sense of solidity. It's only when I notice that I am falling that I realize that I have also gained a body. What seems like a vast wall of nothingness sweeps past me. I am falling, falling. Falling into an endless void. I can see my legs tumbling around and I try stabilizing myself by spreading my arms and puffing out my chest, facing the oncoming emptiness. It is just starting to work when I see it appear—a square of green and red in the middle of the nothing ocean. I close my eyes and brace myself.

My landing is hard, but silent and painless even though it throws up a mass of compact red soil and displaced elephant grass. I stand up quickly, brushing the dust off my body, and see a small red brick hut with a thatch roof ahead of me. I can smell efirin-and-honey tea, her favorite, and I know where I am.

I am standing outside the hut that sits at the center of our village villa, the one that my great-great-great-grandfather, Oluseyi Balogun, had built with his own hands when he first migrated to Ijebu-ode at the end of the Second Akebu-lan War. The hut that had spawned what would become the family compound. The hut where I used to play games with my cousins every year during the Olojo Festival. The hut where she had finally gone to die.

I cannot linger. I don't have time.

I sprint to the thick wood door and knock, remembering that she hated it whenever my father or I came in without knocking. The door swings open on its rusty hinges before I finish knocking, and so I enter.

The hut is mustier than I remember, but everything is where I expect it to be. Except . . . the sight of her sitting in my father's favorite chair and staring at me with a steady smile. It stuns me to sessility.

"Mummy," is all I can manage to say. Her large brown mahogany eyes, lustrous hair and full cheeks are the same as they were when I saw her last: two weeks after my father's funeral, the day I went back to base.

She rises and I step forward to engulf her in an embrace. Her warmth suffuses me, and I allow myself to steep in it. The smell of her hair, the softness of her neck, the thinness of her arms.

"Dolly Dolapo. My darling. How are you?" she asks, when she finally pulls away.

She walks to a table made of iroko wood where a pot of efirin-and-honey tea is brewing, turns over an old mug, and starts to pour. It doesn't feel like this is thoughtspace or even a dream anymore. This feels . . . real.

"I'm fine," I say out of habit before catching myself. "Actually . . . I'm not fine."

She hands me the mug with a querying look, and I take a sip. Sweet and bitter dance on my tongue. I realize that my sense of urgency is gone. I've almost forgotten that this place is unstable, that Iya Ajimobi is giving me every precious second with my mother and I can't waste any of it.

"I . . . I need to know why. Why did you leave me?" I feel the tears that have escaped my eyes roll down my cheeks as the emotions start to overwhelm me. It feels good to be able to feel things in this place. "I know you were heartbroken when Daddy died but why didn't you stay . . . for me?"

"Leave you? I didn't . . . it is hard to explain, Dolly," she says mildly, picking up the mug. "Your father and I, we'd known each other since we were children, we went to the same school, the same university, we planned our lives together, and we planned for you, together. When we lost him, like that . . ." She pauses and looks up at me. "I knew what was the right thing to do. I knew that I should have focused on you, but I couldn't. I couldn't imagine a world without him because I never had. I was overwhelmed with grief. With a sense of hopelessness. That filled me with fear. It clouded everything."

I turn away from her and take a long sip of the tea. "It clouded your love for me?"

"No! I never stopped loving you, but I knew that you would be okay," she responds, setting down her mug and taking my hand. "We'd raised you to be self-sufficient. To be able to take on the world by yourself. You were our strong Dolly," she says, her voice soft. "I knew you were strong enough even if I wasn't."

"I was strong because I had you and Daddy! Without you I have been . . ."

My voice catches as a memory rushes to mind: my father walking me up to the neighbor's dog, a fearsome-looking Azawakh named Rover, when I was no older than six. My mother stood back, framed in the doorway of our Ibadan house. She kept calling out words of encouragement. *Don't be afraid. The dog won't bite. Not every animal that has sharp teeth is dangerous.*

"I wanted to be there for you, but I couldn't sleep. I couldn't eat. I didn't want to burden you. I know you would have thrown away your entire career just to come and try to care for me, and if that happened, I would have only hated myself."

I remember wondering why she wasn't coming with us to play with the neighbor's dog, why she was trembling, shaking visibly. I'd put my hand on the dog's neck and he barked. But my father held my hand in place, telling me to be gentle but firm. *Don't act out of fear. Not every animal that has sharp teeth is dangerous.* So, I held, and Rover eventually warmed to me. When I turned around to show my mother my new animal friend, she'd shut the door and continued to watch from the kitchen window. In my entire life I never saw my mother around any dogs or any animals, definitely none that had teeth.

"I just couldn't go on, Dolapo. But I knew you could. Please understand."

I think I am starting to understand. She'd raised me to be the woman she'd always wished she was. The image she idolized but never became. Strong, fearless, confident, independent. She was none of those things. Not like the great Olusola Ajimobi. On some level, I think I understand now, the depth and complexity of the emotions that drove her to do what she did. In the end she couldn't fight her own emotions.

"Mummy, I just miss you so much."

"I love you, Dolapo. I have since the moment I first felt you inside me. You are a better woman than I was. I hope you know that. Because it's all I ever wanted for you."

I let the tears fall as we fall into each other again and hold on tightly. I don't care about the border with Dahomey. I don't care about the cabinet meetings. I don't care if this is thoughtspace or a dream or an illusion or whatever. This is all I have left of my mother—imperfections, complexities, and all, and I want to hold on to her with every fiber of my being.

My head still nestled in her shoulder, I open my eyes and notice that the chair, the mug and the assorted items of furniture around us are starting to elevate, floating like we are entering a low-gravity environment.

The warmth of her body suddenly turns cold.

No.

I disengage and look into her eyes. She is perfectly still. There is an emotion frozen in place like sadness set in amber. Her lips start to move but it's Iya Ajimobi's voice that comes to me now. It's straining, stretching like it's being pulled.

"We have reached a critical memrionic gradient. I can no longer maintain this unstable state." I know this is the end. "I hope you heard what you needed to hear."

This is as much as I am going to get and for it, I am grateful. "Yes. Thank you. For everything."

"Thank you for thanking me." My mother's lips move with the voice of Iya Ajimobi and somehow it seems . . . right. "You know, that dog, Rover, it bit your mother when it was still a puppy."

I'm taken aback by the fact that she could sense my thoughts, but then I realize I should not be; my mind is completely porous and open to her here in thoughtspace. Still, I wonder, "But . . . then why did she lie?"

"She didn't want you to be afraid just because she was."

Of course. "I think I understand."

"Good. Don't hide from your fears or doubts. Embrace them. I hope you heard exactly what you needed to hear," she says again.

Before I can reply, the digital version of my family hut is gone, like it has been painted out of my vision in one broad brushstroke. I am plunged back into the absolute, directionless whiteness of empty thoughtspace. Disembodied and alone. The rattling sound like an opele returns and gets louder and louder until I feel something yank on my consciousness violently.

The last thing I hear in thoughtspace is her voice, once again accompanied by the chorus of memrionics, exploding into my consciousness like a bomb.

Exactly what you needed to hear.

I shoot out of thoughtspace like a mind missile, and my eyes fly open in realspace. I immediately collapse to the floor, vomiting all the moin-moin I ate for breakfast until I am so weak and empty that I feel separate from my body. I am not sure if the feeling is real, an illusion carried over from memory, or just an electronic echo. I can feel Baba Yemi's hands on my neck, trying to hold up my head, to get me some air, and close my lifedock, but I cannot see his face. I remember that nausea and dizziness are uncommon but documented side effects of the dream-counsel consultation, but I didn't expect to feel this way. The edges of my vision are dark and wooly, and I know I am probably going to pass out.

Darkness.

When I come to, I am sitting, staring up at the white ceiling of a conference room. I almost panic, thinking I have somehow been reconnected to thoughtspace, but then I see the corners, the edges, and I look down to see my fellow ministers seated around a long table with lightscreen voting panels in front of us, Baba Yemi at the head.

They are all staring at me, a few of them furrowing their brows, chattering to each other, or shaking their heads.

"Welcome back," Jibola says, when our eyes meet.

I smile. It *is* good to see a friendly face after all that.

"It seems Minister Balogun has recovered and is with us again," Baba Yemi says, staring at me. "How are you feeling?"

I tell him, "Great actually," because it's true.

"Good. You worried us for a bit, but all your neural scan readings are normal. Let's call it first-time thoughtspace-sickness." He smiles. "We can begin the debrief session now. It should not take long."

He rises and speaks to the group of us as a hologram of yellow light appears at the center of the table and begins to display information about the consultation. "Total consultation time was six minutes and three seconds. Stability of the digital memrionic emulsion was maintained throughout the session."

I start to raise my finger but hold it up to my lips instead, hesitant. Surely, there must be some kind of record of what I did. Some kind of anomaly in the readings?

"No local discontinuities or neural interface breakdowns were observed. Minister Balogun may have had a rough exit but nothing some of you haven't seen or experienced before." Baba Yemi waits for these facts to sink in as the information displays in front of us. "I believe you should all have received the same answers to your queries. Accordingly, I open the floor for a motion, after which you may vote."

I look around and that is when I notice it. They are all hesitant too. They must have all gotten the same advice—go to war. No one wants to disbelieve the advice of our electric mother, but given the consequences of such dire action, and the Alaafin's resistance which would be sure to follow, no one wants to admit what they must know we all know.

The silence grows sharp and piercing. I think of my mother, sitting in our ancient family hut—unchanged after hundreds of years—contemplating a life without my father, a life she couldn't even imagine. Can I imagine a world where we don't honor the dream-counsel of our electric mother?

Exactly what you needed to hear.

The voice in my head is clear as a talking drum. An electric echo? Or my own memories of that encounter just being replayed? What difference does it make? Perhaps Jibola was right all along. I look to him, and he meets my gaze.

As a flood of emotions begins to blanket my thoughts, I see my mother again, standing in the doorway of our Ibadan house. She told me Rover wouldn't bite even though he'd bit her in the past. I start to wonder what it means to help someone you love, to give them good advice, to help them become the best version of themselves that they could be, perhaps even better than you. Perhaps sometimes a useful lie is the best way to point someone in the direction they need to go.

My finger goes up, confidently this time.

"I propose that we put this consultation on hold and reconvene our original cabinet session. We can continue our deliberations until we reach a consensus."

I can almost feel the eyes of the ministers on me, focused like lasers, but I keep my focus on Jibola, whose face breaks out into a broad smile. I think he understands, just as I did, why the electric mother told us to go to war. I expect an uproar, objections, voices raised in protest for wasting our time, but there is nothing. The silence reestablishes itself.

I scan the room quickly and take in an assortment of expressions, but the only one I cannot read is Baba Yemi's. The only thing I am sure of is that he does not seem surprised at all even though I don't remember reading any other consultation reports which were frozen at the debrief stage. When he finally speaks and breaks the silence again, his words are clear and deliberate. "The motion is moved. I put it to you now, ministers of the Ọyọ Mesi, do you wish to put this consultation on hold? Your voting panels are before you. Yes or no."

I watch as the votes are entered, a lightstream of encrypted data beamed into the central hologram, and as I do, I start to wonder if I ever actually reached Iya Ajimobi and my mother at all, or if the digital supercitizen, our collective electric ancestor, simply showed me and told me exactly what I needed to hear.

The lights continue to weave themselves together. I enter my vote and when the weaving stops, the light in the center displays a unanimous *Yes* in bright yellow ajami calligraphy.

AUTHOR NOTES

DEBUT

In 2018, I was shortlisted for the Caine Prize for African Writing for "Wednesday's Story" (originally published in *Lightspeed Magazine* and reprinted in my first collection *Incomplete Solutions*). I attended the awards festivities in London which was a delightful experience—readings, meetings, school visits, interviews, dinners, all in the company of four other amazing authors.

One of the sponsors of the Prize was the Royal Overseas League (ROSL) who hosted us at their lovely accommodations at Park Place. That year, they also introduced a new ROSL Readers' Choice Award, which their members vote for in parallel to the Caine Prize Judging Panel's official selection. I did not win the official Caine Prize but I did win the Reader's Choice Award, which came with a nice £1,000 cash prize and an invitation to write a short original piece to be published in their *Overseas Magazine,* which is distributed to tens of thousands of members around the world. This story, "Debut," was written for their March-May 2019 issue, themed "Art behind the scenes." At the time, I'd already been thinking a lot about the fundamental nature of art a lot—what is art exactly? How do you define it? And what would it mean for an artificial intelligence to *truly* create original art, not just replicate what humans do? So their theme was a perfect fit for my headspace, and I drafted the story out fairly quickly. It's full of small references to the history of both human and computer-generated art. (See if you can spot all of them!)

Geoff Parkin, ROSL Director of Arts, and Mark Brierley, editor of Overseas Magazine, both loved this story and I am grateful to them for providing me the opportunity to write it and for publishing it.

In 2021, the story was optioned by a major US-based production studio for adaptation as part of a TV show. It remains to be seen if the show will eventually make it onto screens, but even if it doesn't, I've already been amazed by the reception this science-fictional meditation on the fundamental nature of art has received, which I never envisaged when I first wrote it.

In early 2023, I was commissioned to write another story about the future of art for MIT Press. And so I wrote a sequel to "Debut" called "Encore" which takes place three million years after the events of "Debut" and features a much evolved version of *BLOMBOS 7090 and 4020*. If you enjoyed this story, then perhaps you'll enjoy that one too.

AN ARC OF ELECTRIC SKIN

This story germinated from two seeds.

The first: I read an interesting paper[1] by Migliaccio et al (2019), in the journal *Frontiers in Chemistry*. This team of scientists in Italy described

---

1 Migliaccio L, Manini P, Altamura D, Giannini C, Tassini P, Maglione MG, Minarini C and Pezzella A (2019). Evidence of Unprecedented High Electronic Conductivity in Mammalian Pigment-Based Eumelanin Thin Films After Thermal Annealing in Vacuum. *Frontiers in Chemistry*. 7:162. doi: 10.3389/fchem.2019.00162

the successful use of heat treatment to increase the conductivity of melanin by several orders of magnitude. I found the paper fascinating. And I remember wondering (somewhat cheekily) if there would ever be a way to apply the process to the melanin in human skin (it's not quite the same) and how exactly that would work, assuming someone could even survive it.

The second: In October 2020, millions of young Nigerians took to the streets and the internet to protest the brutality of the Special Anti-Robbery Squad (SARS), a unit of the Nigerian Police notorious for abuses and extra-judicial killings. The #EndSARS movement quickly expanded to include demands for good governance, something that has been severely lacking in the country for decades and which had made the difficulties of the COVID-19 pandemic even worse than they needed to be. On the 20th of October, the Nigerian government responded by sending in the army to a major protest site at the Lekki tollgate in Lagos. They opened fire. At least 25 people were killed. Probably more. I observed the news online from afar, feeling sad and powerless and angry. Very angry.

It was when the two seeds met that this story was born.

I had already started trying to write a story based on the first seed, but it never really came together the way I wanted. It was missing a central character with a strong motivation but when the idea of a protagonist being willing to endure a terrible, painful process like thermal annealing to gain power to strike back against a government determined to crush its own people came to me fully, I knew I had a story that mattered to me. I had the final version of the story done a few weeks later.

The title, "An Arc of Electric Skin," has multiple meanings since "arc" can refer to a bright electrical discharge that burns and causes damage, but it can also refer to the change of a character through a story. Both apply to this story, I think. Especially considering how the main character gets his "electric skin," why, and what he does with it.

I sent the story to *Asimov's*, one of the great three legacy SF magazines that I really wanted to sell stories to when I first started writing professionally. It felt like an *Asimov's* kind of story because of the magazine's focus on "character oriented" science fiction stories. Thankfully, the editor, Sheila Williams, agreed and after giving a few notes, accepted the story for publication. The reception to it has been spectacular. It was a finalist for the Locus Award, the Nommo Award, reprinted in *Apex Magazine*, *Forever Magazine* and the *Year's Best African Speculative Fiction 2022* anthology.

Perhaps the strongest reaction I've had to the story was when I did a live reading of it for an online program called Story Hour, and it brought almost everyone to tears—myself included.

I dedicate this story to the memory of all the young Nigerians who lost their lives in the #EndSARS protests.

SATURDAY'S SONG

"Saturday's Song" is a sequel to "Wednesday's Story" (originally published in *Lightspeed Magazine* and later in my collection *Incomplete Solutions*), which itself was a sequel to another story called "Thursday," published in *The Kalahari Review* in 2014. I guess it's becoming a series now. I might keep returning to this world until I've exhausted all the days of the week.

It also features the eponymous protagonist from my novel *Shigidi and the Brass Head of Obalufon* as a supporting character.

The origins of this story are a bit unclear. I had many inspirations. First, I've always wanted to write a sequel to "Wednesday's Story," which ends with Wednesday, one of the personified Days of the week, having committed a crime. I wanted to follow up on the concept of that. But since the purpose of the Days is to tell stories, I knew I needed a story around which I could frame that story. I didn't want to return to my old trick of using another reimagined children's rhyme to frame the larger story, and so I went with an original story about love and grief and parenthood and magic which also serves in some way as one of the inciting incidents for my novel. Anyone who has read *Shigidi and the Brass Head of Obalufon* will probably find a deeper layer to Shigidi's personality after reading this. The story also borrows loosely from elements of both Yoruba mythology and traditional Bori practice, a spirituality and belief system from the people of Northern Nigeria.

Like "Wednesday's Story" and "Thursday" before it, "Saturday's Song" is a story about the nature and power of stories. Even stories that are also songs.

Lightspeed Magazine was the first and only place I submitted the story, and I was extremely pleased that editor John Joseph Adams, who originally first published "Wednesday's Story," immediately accepted this bigger, and more ambitious sequel. Publishing the story there felt right, like returning home.

LIGHTS IN THE SKY

From 2011 until 2016, I wrote and edited for a website that used to be called *The Toolsman's Blog*, later became an online magazine, *The Naked Convos*, and now is a full blown media company simply called *TNC Africa*. Back then, I ran a column called *The Alchemist's Corner* that was a regular part of the site and featured speculative, experimental and weird fiction. There were other columns for literary fiction, humor, general interest articles, and even news. One of the most fun things we did at TNC was the "12 Days of Christmas" special where we would publish twelve new stories by twelve authors, some of them regulars from the site and others guest authors invited to contribute. Each author would give a "gift" to the next author—something that they would feature in their story.

I wrote this story for the 2014 edition. It was originally titled *Open Your Eyes* when it appeared on the site and was shorter, basically SF action flash fiction with a Christmas theme and message. But I wasn't really happy with that initial version and fleshed it out a bit, then retitled it. I think this works.

If you're curious, the "gift" I got from the writer that preceded me was the bottle of Scotch.

BLOWOUT

Back in 2012, I started writing what I thought would be a novella about the children of inventors who die early and how their traumatized children, two siblings, deal with the aftermath of their deaths differently. But it never went anywhere. I wrote several thousand words before I finally trunked it. However, fragments of that story have woven their way in several other stories over the years, including, "Home Is Where My Mothers Heart is Buried," which appears in *Incomplete Solutions*; "Abeokuta52," which appears in this collection; and this story, "Blowout." You can see the fragments of that aborted novella in the relationship between Femi and Folake. For this story though, I also wanted to explore what the early days of exploration and settlement on Mars could be, and what unexpected problems might be encountered. The idea had been swirling around in my head for a while, but I never got around to writing it until 2022, when a friend told me that the Jim Baen Memorial Short Story Award Contest was open. This contest is specifically for realistic hard science fiction about what can be achieved in space exploration in the near future. It seemed like a perfect fit for the story I had been thinking about, but there were only a few days to the deadline. So I wrote fast and submitted the story. I was very pleasantly surprised when it was selected as one of the ten finalists. It didn't win in the end, but the judges really liked it and decided to award it an Honorable Mention, which they usually don't do. I guess it was just a very good crop of contest stories that year.

I ended up revising and sending it to *Analog* magazine, another place where I'd always wanted to be published, on the advice of the contest administrator, the wonderful Bill Ledbetter who also really liked the story. I'm very grateful to Trevor Quachri at *Analog* magazine for accepting and publishing it.

GAMMA (OR: LOVE IN THE AGE OF RADIATION POISONING)

Even though it was first published in 2014, I wrote this story earlier, and it's now been so long since I wrote it that I don't really remember all my inspirations for it. Except one: the song "Love You to Death" by American power metal band Kamelot. I am a huge fan and have listened to all of their albums (*The Black Halo* is one of my favorite albums of all time). "Love You to Death" is an incredibly moving song, and I remember this image of children falling in love in a postapocalyptic wasteland being imprinted on my mind when I listened to it one gray, rainy evening back when I lived in London. That image became one of the inspirations for this story which was first published in *The Kalahari Review*.

GANGER

My friend Bankole Oluwole gave me an interesting birthday gift in 2015. It was a story seed.

This is a condensed version of what he described:

An over-populated sci-fi world where there are no homes or personal spaces and everything is controlled by a central government, including daily regulated activities. Robots and drones do most of the labor so people are forced into social systems in order to have some kind of purpose. People are desperate for work, they want freedom and to be out in the open fields, so there is a healthy underground that trades in artificial doubles (hacked government robots with humanoid features called 'gangers') mapped with everything that is you. They fulfill your government obligations for you while you do something for a few hours.

The story?

Adelaide trades for a ganger but is unable to return to her life. So since she is out of the system she has nothing. She cannot eat or sleep. She is a featureless generic robot in appearance but is really a human with needs.

Things fall apart.

I thought it was a great birthday present and a great idea for a story which could be a springboard to explore the conflict between work for need and work for purpose. But as any author knows, there is always an overabundance of ideas, the tricky part is getting words down on the page. So I sat on the idea for a while, waiting for the right moment. And then one day I remembered an old Yoruba legend about an aged hunter who used magic to transform into a snake (a boa constrictor) every day until once day, he was unable to return to his previous form. I saw the overlaps with the seed from Bankole and returned to the story. I started writing what I thought would be a short story but once I started writing, I didn't stop. I couldn't stop. The story took on a life of its own, pulling in many of my ideas about capitalism, obsessive megalomaniac tech CEOs, climate change, individual identity, consciousness uploading, and so much more until it became this original novella, published here for the first time. I hope you enjoyed reading it as much as I enjoyed writing it. And thank you, Bankole.

ABEOKUTA52

Here's another story that contains fragments of the abandoned novella I mentioned earlier in the notes for "Blowout." I've been experimenting with story formats a lot recently, and for "Abeokuta52" I wanted to tell a story in the form of a blog post, with a significant part of the story taking place in the comments section. The idea of an African nation becoming a technological powerhouse at the unacknowledged expense of the lives of its citizens is one I have explored before in "Necessary and Sufficient Conditions" in *Incomplete Solutions*, but here the narrative is not only personal but also hints at the larger structures that enable nations to benefit from the suffering of people.

TENDS TO ZERO

Amos Tutuola's *The Palm-Wine Drinkard*, and Kojo Laing's *Woman of The Aeroplanes* have been a big influence on me ever since I read them. There is a wildness and freedom in their writing and descriptions. The unexpected and dark and bizarre occur seamlessly with the realistic, and the language used is almost a character in itself. Laing in particular would randomly reformat paragraphs as equations with words that make reading an intoxicating experience. It's pure weird fiction. So when Scott Gable at Broken Eye books invited me to submit a story for their weird fiction action anthology *Neverwhere: Weird Is Other People*, focused on the weirdness of urban settings and urban life and stories of the urban weird, I took inspiration from a line in that Tutuola book and some of the stylings of Kojo Laing. I used those as loose references to craft this story of depression set in Lagos City, where the city itself appears as a personification. It's perhaps the bleakest story I've ever written but also one I'm particularly proud of.

The opening line of the story is inspired by a similar opening line in the Carmen Maria Machado story, "My Body, Herself." Carmen's writing is lovely and every time I read her work I'm stunned anew by something in it.

The equations used to separate the three story sections are mathematical representations of the "title" for each section. I'll explain them here, just in case anyone is curious.

Section 1: Carnality—represented by Euler's identity which is considered to be "a physically beautiful equation" in mathematics because it describes an unlikely combination of five fundamental mathematical constants which, to me, makes it a surface-level aesthetic and representation of physical beauty.

Section 2: Divinity—represented by an equation whose solution is the divine proportion or the golden ratio, which Italian mathematician Luca Pacioli in 1509, praised as representing divinely inspired simplicity and orderliness. It is often associated with both nature and the supernatural and marks the part of the story where the true supernatural elements come to the fore.

Section 3: Infinity—represented by the mathematical notation for the limit of a generic function "u" (you) as time (t) tends to infinity, making "you" tend to zero (like everything else) with time.

NIGERIAN DREAMS

I was born and raised in Nigeria and I lived there until my twenties when I left after the deaths of my parents, and I haven't returned since except for brief visits. But being Nigerian is a huge part of my identity, as much as can be. Unfortunately it comes with a lot of complications. Nigeria is a country with huge potential but also huge problems, and these problems seem perpetual, repeated every generation. Because of that, many people choose to stop waiting for the country to fulfil its potential and leave in pursuit of a better quality of life overseas. I suppose I fall into this category. The economic downturn in the 1980s drove many citizens out of the country to survive and it's never really stopped although there have been major waves, one of which we seem to be living through. There are so many people leaving recently that there is a new slang term for it. "Japa" which in Yoruba means "to run, flee, or escape." Almost all my friends have left the country. Some remain, trying to improve things or taking advantage of the chaos. This story is my own extrapolation of this real issue of "brain drain," or "japa," that's always on my mind. It truly does seem that the main aspiration of young Nigerians is to leave the country for good.

SILENCE

Literary love stories and romance aren't stories I particularly enjoy reading or writing, and this is one of only two attempts I've ever made at it. The other is "A Certain Sort of Warm Magic" which appears in *Incomplete Solutions*. This story is shorter and allowed me to play a little bit with the scene transitions which is always fun. It first appeared in the lifestyle magazine *BellaNaija* and was later reprinted in the anthology *These Words Expose Us*, which I edited. I've never felt comfortable about that decision, but to be fair that was my first anthology as editor and I learned a lot from it, including not to include my own work. Here, however, in my own personal collection, I think it fits in just fine and is something a little bit different from my usual fare.

PERFORMANCE REVIEW

AI researchers and developments have made extraordinary leaps in generative AI tools. Tools that can generate "original" and coherent new material based on prompts. Essays, art, stories, computer code . . . these can all be generated. Something that seemed impossible just a few years ago. Now there is an ongoing debate about the ethics and legality of how these tools were created and "trained" and how they can and should be used.

The team at Google Research has been looking into this long before the debate spilled into the public. They built Wordcraft, an AI-powered text editor centered on story writing, to see how far they could push the limits of generative AI technology. Wordcraft is built atop the LaMDA language model (yes, the same AI that was in the news in 2022 because one of the engineers working on it thought it had become sentient). The team at Google Research wanted to see where these models can provide value, where they break down, and explore the future of writing by getting the perspective of actual writers. I liked that approach. Asking writers if the tool was actually valuable and useful to them, not recklessly releasing it out into the world without talking to the people that it's intended to serve (Wordcraft, as far as I know is still not on the market, yet).

I was one of thirteen professional writers from around the world whom they contacted to participate in a workshop where we used Wordcraft as an assistant to write stories and have an honest conversation about the rapidly evolving relationship between creativity and technology. This story was the outcome of that workshop.

The idea for the story itself has gestated for a long time. I made notes for it all the way back in 2013 after just completing my own first year of work at what was then my new job, and going through a performance review of my own. I just never got around to writing it until this workshop. Having the Wordcraft AI assist me in producing the story I already knew I wanted, was quite nice. I might have also asked it if it was sentient or not but even if I did, I won't tell you how it responded.

I have to give thanks to the wonderful S.B. Divya for recommending me to Andy Coenen at Google Research. My thanks to Daphne Ippolito, Ann Yuan and Sehmon Burnam for making it happen. It was an amazing experience working with you all, I admire your openness and honesty and willingness to listen to feedback we provided. I hope the outcomes from that workshop go on to help build tools to truly empower authors and I still think it's really cool that on some level, I got a chance to use AI to write a near future science fiction story, which is a bit like writing science fiction while living it.

But I must note my reservations about the use of AI in the creative industry more generally, given what we have seen with other generative AI tools and how they are being developed and applied.

I am an engineer, and I always will be, so making tools to achieve objectives is a fundamental part of my DNA. As it is for all of humanity.

My optimism in science and technology as boxes for tools to make a better world remains high. My dream for AI is one of enablement. As tools to do the things humans shouldn't do, or don't want to do or simply can't do. As a tool for external human cognition and the expansion of human potential. Not mimicry. Not theft. Not replacement. Not commodification of things that bring joy and meaning to our lives like creativity.

We need to ask important questions now and begin to frame answers that lay the foundations for what is to come. For better or worse. I think must. We have a responsibility to the future.

THE MILLION EYES OF A LONELY AND FRAGILE GOD
I wrote this story in 2014, the year I saw Alfonso Cuarón's awesome movie "Gravity," and the influence of that film on the story is obvious. It also contains fragments of one of my unpublished poems.

EMBERS
I work in the energy industry and have been thinking about its history and future for a long time. A long time ago, I wrote a version of this story for the lifestyle magazine *BellaNaija*, which published it in 2013. It was just over a thousand words long and while it contained all the elements of the story I wanted to tell, it was admittedly not great. I was still learning how to write well, and I didn't quite have all the tools to tell stories as effectively as I'd have liked. So for a long time I always wanted to return to that story and do it justice. This collection gave me a reason to do that. I finally returned to the story, took another look at it, and rewrote it. I fleshed out characters, filled out important background, clarified details of some of the core technologies and expanded it by turning it into this original dark science fiction novelette that appears in print for the first time in this collection. It explores the potential aftermath and impact of what I believe is an inevitable global energy transition on people in small towns and villages, in places like the Niger-delta, which has been exploited by both the Nigerian government and international oil and gas companies for decades. And for those people in such places who can't let go of dreams past.

COMMENTS ON YOUR PROVISIONAL PATENT APPLICATION FOR AN ETERNAL SPIRIT CORE

As mentioned in the notes for "Abeokuta52," I've been experimenting with story formats a lot recently. For this story I decided I wanted to tell a story in the form of a near-future patent application form (with real-time comments) for a device to record the minds of people and install such recorded minds in the minds of others. Why a patent application form? Well, because I hold two patents for things I have co-invented, and I have always found the process of patent registration to be very painful. I like turning painful things into something not-so-painful, like stories. I also personally really enjoy unexpected story formats and, in particular, I'd just read Namwali Serpell's "Account" in *Enkare Review*, which told a story in the form of purchase receipts. I thought it was brilliant and wanted to do something equally unexpected.

Originally, the idea behind "Comments on Your Provisional Patent Application for an Eternal Spirit Core" came to me when I saw the submissions call for the After+Life issue of *Jalada Magazine*. I sent an early version of it to them but it wasn't taken, I suppose there were still things to clean up. The late great Nick Wood gave me great feedback on that version and I revised it, made it stronger, and sold it to Neil Clarke at *Clarkesworld*, who thought it was quite clever. It received a lot of great reviews and, to my surprise, it was nominated for a Stabby Award, which is given by Reddit's r/Fantasy group (they have over 1.6 million members!). The story didn't win, which is a pity because the prize is an actual dagger which looks amazing. Ah, well.

I have explored the concept of digital consciousness in a lot of my previous work, and it's one I continue to return to. Specifically, the ideas of recording and recreating the consciousness, form the basis of "The Regression Test" and "Connectome Or, The Facts in the Case of Miss

Valerie DeMarco, (Ph.D)"—both of which appear in *Incomplete Solutions*. I return to it here for "Comments on Your Provisional Patent Application for An Eternal Spirit Core," as well as in the final story of this collection, "A Dream of Electric Mothers." Fun fact: all four of these stories are actually related, sharing characters and history, although "A Dream of Electric Mothers" takes place in a parallel timeline.

A DREAM OF ELECTRIC MOTHERS

One day back in July 2018, I woke up at 4:09 am and sent an email to myself with the subject, "Ancestral Computer." No other notes or details in the body of the email. Just that. Weird. Years later, it became this story.

I don't know what I was trying to tell myself in that email, but the more I read it, the more I became interested in imagining ways of consulting with the ancestors by merging traditional spiritual practices with modern computer technology. I also became very interested in an alternate history of Africa and the world, one in which European colonization had never happened. In my head I built up a very elaborate lore around it as background to this story. Essentially, I imagined what the world would be like today if, instead of forcibly subjugating and exploiting people they encountered, the European colonists had meaningfully engaged with the people and exchanged ideas and understanding of the world equitably; engaged with the natural philosophies and sciences and belief systems they encountered, merging them in unexpected ways and cooperating to move forward together. I imagined what that world would be today if that had been our history. Less conflict, less time spent fighting each other, and instead learning from each other while everyone maintains their historical lands, the fundamentals of their cultures, beliefs. I imagined this world, and I imagined that in it, we develop computing technologies far faster than we have in the real world. I then applied that framework of development to this story where, in an alternate Odua republic, traditional Ifa practice and knowledge has merged with quantum computer technology to create a different kind of artificial intelligence that is used to contact the ancestors. In a sense.

Once I had the background all built up in my head, I used it to tell this story of a society that has come to rely too much on the minds of ancestors, preserved by technology, to help them manage the nation, thereby depending too much on the past to help define the future, just like we do with modern AI and machine learning today. But African ancestors are tricky and they never give simplistic advice. Sometimes they tell you a riddle, or even a lie, and in unravelling it, you learn exactly what you needed to learn.

There is a very personal subplot about grief and learning, which I believe integrates with the larger narrative and brings thematic resonance to the entire story. I am absolutely thrilled that it found a home in the *Africa Risen* anthology edited by Oghenechovwe Donald Ekpeki, Sheree Renée Thomas, and Zelda Knight, and it has gone on to garner a lot of positive reviews, accolades, and award nominations including the Hugo, Nebula, and Locus Awards as well as the Sidewise Award for Alternate History, for which I am thankful. But most of all, I'm glad so many people have gotten to read this alternate history novelette which is deeply steeped in some lesser-known aspects of pre-colonial Yoruba culture. From the keeping of time and the calendar and the use of praise names, to the calligraphy; from the religion and science to the description of the political and military system. All of it is rooted in Yoruba history.

One final thing about culture.

No culture is static. They all change with time. Some aspects are lost, modified, improved. That is inevitable. What we hope for is the result of that change to be something better than what came before. Something that takes the best elements of the past, of what we learned from our parents and ancestors—which works for as many people as possible in the appropriate contexts—improves upon it with cleverness and creativity and then moves forward as we learn new things from each other and new things about our universe. There may be convergence problems along the way but as long as we communicate honestly and openly with each other in good faith, I believe we'll keep tending towards better, ad infinitum.

ABOUT THE AUTHOR

WOLE TALABI is an engineer, writer, and editor from Nigeria. He is the author of the novel SHIGIDI AND THE BRASS HEAD OF OBALU-FON (DAW Books/Gollancz, 2023). His short fiction has appeared in places like *Asimov's Science Fiction*, Lightspeed Magazine, and Tor.com, and is collected in CONVERGENCE PROBLEMS (DAW Books, 2024) and INCOMPLETE SOLUTIONS (Luna Press, 2019). He has been a finalist for the Hugo, Nebula, Locus, and Nommo awards, as well as the Caine Prize for African Writing and the Sidewise Award for Alternate History. He has edited five anthologies including a two-volume translation anthology in Bengali, AFRICANFUTURISM (Brittlepaper, 2020) and MOTHERSOUND: THE SAUÚTIVERSE ANTHOLOGY (Android Press, 2023). He likes scuba diving, elegant equations, and oddly shaped things. He currently lives and works in Malaysia. Find him at wtalabi.wordpress.com and at @wtalabi on Twitter, Instagram, Bluesky and TikTok.